# UNDER ATTACK

When the attack did come, it was silent and deadly. Crawford heard the click of a rifle being cocked and lifted his head to follow the sound. A second later an arrow slashed into his throat severing the jugular vein. He gushed blood, clutched his throat and, eyes bulging, died. Major Northey held back for a count of five and avoided the bullet that followed the arrow.

"Major, they is sneaking up that little dry wash to your right," Riley called out.

At three hundred yards an Apache, bare chest like a brown beer keg, wearing a cotton loincloth and knee-length deerskin moccasins, stood alone in a clearing. He brandished a rifle, one-handed, above his head, shouting insults.

"Out of range!" Northey yelled to his men, but a shot rang out anyway. The Indian stumbled, fell and then crawled spasmodically back into cover.

"No, he weren't. Not by a long shot! Not for old Meatmaster, here," said Charley Dirty Knife. The trapper patted the butt of his Hawkins rifle, then reloaded quickly.

# BOOK YOUR PLACE ON OUR WEBSITE AND MAKE THE READING CONNECTION!

We've created a customized website just for our very special readers, where you can get the inside scoop on everything that's going on with Zebra, Pinnacle and Kensington books.

When you come online, you'll have the exciting opportunity to:

- View covers of upcoming books
- Read sample chapters
- Learn about our future publishing schedule (listed by publication month *and author*)
- Find out when your favorite authors will be visiting a city near you
- Search for and order backlist books from our online catalog
- Check out author bios and background information
- Send e-mail to your favorite authors
- Meet the Kensington staff online
- Join us in weekly chats with authors, readers and other guests
- Get writing guidelines
- AND MUCH MORE!

**Visit our website at**
**http://www.pinnaclebooks.com**

# William W. Johnstone
## The *Mountain Man* Series

# APACHE AMBUSH

## *Austin Olsen*

Pinnacle Books
Kensington Publishing Corp.
http://www.pinnaclebooks.com

This novel is dedicated to all of the
Mexican Olsens, wherever they may be.

PINNACLE BOOKS are published by

Kensington Publishing Corp.
850 Third Avenue
New York, NY 10022

All Kensington Titles, Imprints, and Distributed Lines are
available at special quantity discounts for bulk purchases for
sales promotions, premiums, fund-raising, educational, or in-
stitutional use. Special book excerpts or customized printings
can also be created to fit specific needs. For details, write or
phone the office of the Kensington special sales manager:
Kensington Publishing Corp., 850 Third Avenue, New York,
NY 10022, attn: Special Sales Department, Phone: 1-800-221-
2647

Pinnacle and the P logo Reg. U.S. Pat. & TM Off.

First Printing: September, 2000
10 9 8 7 6 5 4 3 2 1

Printed in the United States of America

# One

Except for the one startling difference, the post was like many others located in the arid Southwest. It might have been Fort Wingate, but it was much too small. It was only a temporary post that still showed traces of its adobe ranch house and outbuildings. It would be generous, I thought, to call it a cantonment.

I paused, ostensibly to look around at my new home, and eased the weight and pain from my right leg. The trooper hauling my old green trunk on the company hand wagon dropped its tongue and looked pointedly across the square at the standard, the nearly square yard of blue with the embroidered eagle trembling ever so gently.

The bugler stood at attention, waiting at the flagstaff, for two men to tend the halyard. When one of them stepped forward to release the cord, the bugler brought his horn up with a flourish and the first comforting notes of retreat floated through the post, erasing all other sound and stilling movement. The muster had been taken, day was done.

Retreat is a magical time on any military base, but particularly so in the high, lonely desert country. The officers would have time for a whiskey before dinner and later perhaps, a game of chess or whist in the cool of the evening. I pivoted awkwardly on my right leg and saluted smartly.

One man ran the blue standard down quickly while the other caught it the instant it reached the level of his shoulders. They folded it deftly, never allowing the fringe to touch the dust lying like a blanket of dirty snow on the parade ground.

The last note seemed to linger in the air, even after the bugler had tucked the bright brass coil under his arm and marched off. He was followed by the two soldiers, one of them carrying the flag as carefully as if it were an altar cloth.

A sudden burst of musical laughter broke the silence. The troopers were standing here and there, in clusters of three or four, leaning against the adobe walls, now more pink than white in the glow of the setting sun. Now, of course, the difference was obvious. The soldiers were all Negroes, ranging in color from suntan brown to shiny black. Their pantaloons were of light blue flannel and their coats of dark blue, like my own. And although they moved with a certain feline grace, their bearing was as military as my own. They were likely as mean and as cowardly and as generous and heroic as the rest of us.

The trooper pulling my trunk, a heavy-shouldered man with the thin legs of a cavalryman, lifted the wagon tongue and looked straight into my eyes. Without saying a word, he managed to convey to me that while he was in no hurry, he too had his equivalent of a brandy and a cigar waiting for him and would like to proceed. I had begun my own career as a private in the Minnesota Volunteers and sympathized with him.

"Would you be wanting to see the colonel right away, suh?"

He had a deep gravelly voice that might have belonged to a white Confederate sergeant I had taken prisoner at Gettysburg.

"Yes. I am reporting for duty and must deliver my orders to the commanding officer immediately. I am Lieutenant William Northey. What is your name?"

"Serg— Private George Johnson, Lieutenant Northey, suh." He pronounced my name without the *r*. I put him down as deep South—Alabama, like that white sergeant.

While we walked, I kept a proprietary hand on my trunk. In reality I used it like a crutch and scarcely limped.

"How long have you been in the cavalry, Johnson?"

"Three years, suh, and two before that in the infantry."

"You served in the War then."

"Yes, suh."

His pantaloons did not have the yellow cavalry stripes of a noncommissioned officer, but I could discern an unweathered swatch of darker blue on each sleeve.

His eyes followed mine down to his sleeve. He smiled and then said, "I was a sergeant then."

"I was a major then," I said and smiled back.

His smile widened before he explained. "But, Major, I been a sergeant three times since the War."

"You win. I have been five years trying to make captain in the regular army."

"And you will, suh. You surely will. And major again, too. I can tell."

"How?" I asked. But I never found out, for there was an explosive pop of champagne being uncorked and a scratchy voice called out, "You there, Lieutenant!"

I turned and looked up slightly to a porch in front of what seemed to be the post trader's store. I tilted my head back to better see the face of the man who had called. He was tall for a cavalryman, but thin enough to weigh no more than a man a half a head shorter, like me. His hair was a shade darker than roan, but his mustache was frankly red and he had the kind of glassy blue eyes that some pinto ponies have. He might have been a year or so younger than I, about thirty. But that and the uniform were all that we had in common.

I am a bullet-headed Welshman with a battered nose. He had the delicate features of a Prussian aristocrat. There was even a thin scar placed so precisely across one cheek that it might have been the result of one of those safe, surgical duels so dear to the hearts of students at Heidelberg.

"Sir, I am looking for—"

I paused while a burly civilian caught most of the overflow from the cascade of champagne in a large tumbler.

"Continue," The uniformed officer said.

"I have been ordered here and am to report to Captain Horace Whigam. Could you direct me to him?"

"You have your orders with you?"

"Yes, sir," I answered, surprised. Why would I not have my orders with me? Then as he turned toward me, I saw the silver eagle on his shoulder board and I added, even more puzzled, "Colonel."

"Let me see them." His voice changed pitch and trembled like the greeting whinny of a favorite horse. I wondered what he would do should I whinny back.

"But, Colonel, I really should give them first to Captain Whigam."

"I am Colonel Horace Whigam. Unfortunately, I am also Captain Horace Whigam." He held out his hand impatiently.

I pulled my orders from the pocket inside my tunic and handed them to him.

" 'Northey. William Robert. First Lieutenant. Date of permanent commission, 21 November, 1866.' " He snorted, shook his head ruefully and then for the first time looked directly into my eyes.

"Welcome to Fort Leper."

"Fort what, sir?"

"Leper, Mr. North. Leper. Oh, it has another name. Rivas, I think. Named after the family that lived and died here. But I call it 'Leper' after its present inhabitants."

"Lepers are usually pale, are they not, sir?" I said.

"Of course," he said, smiling. "But the lepers here are white like you and me, not the Buffalo soldiers."

"Buffalo Soldiers?"

"The Negroes. The colored troopers. The Indians call them 'Buffalo Soldiers.' Likely they see a resemblance between the kinky black hair of the troopers and buffalo hair."

"Most informative, sir," I said. I had served under eccentric officers before. "I am grateful for the opportunity to serve under you at Fort Rivas and with the Ninth Colored Cavalry Regiment."

"What did you do to get sent here?" Whigam's smile became a smirk. "You get caught with a general's wife? Or did you get caught with your saber in a black scabbard. Eh?"

The civilian, much too large to have ever been in the cavalry or perhaps even on a horse, laughed nervously as if he might be embarrassed.

"Colonel Whigam, I know that some officers turned down a promotion if they were to serve with black troopers—Custer could have been regimental adjutant—but no one is assigned this duty. I volunteered."

"Come on, Mr. North. I'll find out sooner or later. You refused to lick some senator's boots or send your wife to sleep with a general."

"My name, sir, is Northey." I spelled it out. "And I am neither a sycophant nor married."

"Then do not send your wife to curry favor with me." He peered at Johnson, standing not quite at attention, impassive, eyes focused elsewhere. But when he spoke, it was to me.

"Why did you not come with the supply wagon?"

"There was no transportation waiting for me. I found a freighter in Las Cruces who was passing this way."

"That is the army," he said affably, holding his glass out for a refill. He drank deeply before he spoke again.

"You have been a lieutenant a very long time, sir. You will not make any quick advancement here trying to make soldiers out of illiterates who would rather sing than fight."

"The colored regiment that fought at The Crater was praised highly," I said.

"There are exceptions. Were you in the War?"

"Yes, sir," I answered, knowing that he knew it was all there in my folder, along with my orders. "I began as a private and was breveted a major at the Battle of—"

"I was breveted a colonel," he interrupted. "But now my commission is that of a captain. A captain, sir! My subordinates here address me as colonel, for they know that were it not for enemies in high places, I would hold that or higher rank today."

I stole a sideways look at Johnson. He was still ramrod straight, but relaxed in the way only an old soldier can manage.

"Would you allow me to proceed to my quarters, sir? It has been a long and dusty trip."

"I beg your pardon, Mr. Worth. Step right up here and have a glass of wine."

"Northey, sir. And if you do not mind—"

"But I do mind. Ascend, sir, ascend." Little lights danced in his eyes.

I walked carefully up the two steps onto the rough planking and leaned casually against a post. Whigam gave me his left hand so I shook his with my own left. We really barely touched fingers and then drew back as if the contact had been painful.

"George, give the lieutenant a glass of bubbly."

Whigam sat down onto a chair and I eased down onto a bench opposite him. He leaned forward to look deep into my eyes, perhaps, I thought, to discover whatever hidden vice had sent me to his command. He nodded affirmatively as if satisfied and said, "You will be second-in-command you know. Number-two leper in a company of black barbarians in blue uniforms."

"Allow me, Lieutenant Northey," the civilian said as he handed me a filled glass. "It is a pleasure to have you here, sir. I am George Sullivan, post sutler, that is, *trader,* now."

His hand engulfed mine. But for all his size and apparent strength, his grip was surprisingly gentle.

"Take a glass with us, George," Whigam said, then turning to me, in a stage whisper, added, "Drink champagne. It cannot be watered. Sealed, you know."

"Colonel Whigam!" George said indignantly.

"To your health, Colonel," I said quickly.

Whigam nodded and drained his glass in two swallows. I sipped mine and listened as they talked about the heat, the lack of rain and the high winds. Not a word about my duties or the Apaches.

I turned to Johnson and said, "At ease, Johnson. You may smoke if you like."

"Would you believe," Whigam said, eyeing Johnson curiously as if he had suddenly appeared, "that we do not have one enlisted man on this post with the wit to read and write?"

"What do you do for a clerk?"

"The junior officers, presently, that will be just you and Peter Barragan, take turns with the correspondence and the daily records. I put in a request six months ago for a literate Negro trooper. One would think that they might find an octoroon or even a mulatto with sense enough to write the daily report."

I was careful not to move my head, but I did swivel my eyes enough to see the face of Private Johnson. It was still impassive. He held an unlit pipe between his teeth. Otherwise, he might have been waiting for orders to fall in. Perhaps Whigam's words meant nothing to him. Might I be allowing him my own sensitivity? His features had not been softened by any infusion of white blood and I had a sudden vision of him standing, half naked in a jungle, a bloody spear in one hand.

"Worth! Wake up, man."

"Sorry, sir. I was daydreaming. I missed your comment."

"I made none. I am waiting for your comment."

"Yes, sir. If I might, may I send Johnson along to my quarters with my trunk?"

"First, Mr. Worthy, what about my company clerk?"

"Northey. My name is Northey. You have a lamentable situation here. Perhaps one of our junior officers might teach a few of our men to read and write and the quickest one would get the job and rating of company clerk."

"Sure and that's a grand idea," Sullivan said, in a voice that would have been more comfortable in a smaller body.

"Sure and that is a rotten idea," Whigam said. "Still, I always support my junior officers." He cocked his head at

Johnson, nodded, and said, "There you are." He smiled benignly. "There is your new company clerk. You shall have six months to ready him."

"But, Colonel, I do not even know Lieutenant Barragan. He may not be an able teacher."

"Right again. Barragan might not be the right instructor, but you must be. And if you want to be a captain, take your task seriously."

"You mean that I—"

"I do indeed, Professor Northey," he said, paused and then spelled out my last name.

I laughed loudly without malice. "I shall do my best, Colonel."

"It is indeed a task that, William." Sullivan paused for a heartbeat for me to nod approval of his use of my first name and then added, "But then you have a fine mind, a lovely mind and Johnson there was not the first sergeant for naught, now, was he?"

Whigam shook his head in consternation. "How do you do that, George?"

"Do what?"

"Tell them apart. That trooper has no stripes on his sleeve. He is an anonymous private."

"I see them all at the store. I sell them all their necessaries."

"Rum."

"That too," Sullivan said easily, "but not so much as I did with the white troopers."

"You should learn quickly," I said, speaking to Johnson. "A man who has been the company first sergeant must be quick and bright."

"Trying to teach me those signs would be a pure waste of your time, Lieutenant Northey," Johnson said sadly.

"I will decide that," Whigam said sharply. "Now then, Lieutenant South, are you all mouth?" He broke off to laugh at his poetical wit and then added, "Or will you act?"

I managed a weak smile.

"We should set a wager, say a bottle of bubbly that your student masters the alphabet?"

He had me boxed in nicely. If I refused, he could prevent my promotion and the army would boot me out for being too long in grade. If I lost, he would likely point out my shortcomings and I would be discharged. Heads I lose and tails he wins. Well, I thought, in for a penny, in for a pound.

"Shall we bet the whole case?" I suggested.

"Well put, sir. A case it is."

"And," I said, "George Sullivan shall pronounce the man literate or not."

"He might, if the commanding officer of Company E agrees."

"Yes, sir," I said uncertainly. "And if I might be off to my quarters now?"

"Yes, of course, but I must warn you. You have a problem. A conflict of interests."

"Sir?"

"You are, after me, the senior officer on the post, and entitled to the second choice of quarters, which at the present time is occupied by Peter Barragan."

"Peter is a lovely lad and comes from a very good family," Sullivan said. "His father owns the very land that our post sits on."

"And," Whigam added, "about half of the land you will be leading patrols through. He is a wealthy and influential man. Perhaps you would like the vacant room by the stable?"

"Rank has its privileges," I mouthed the military protocol. "I will look at the available rooms first."

"His father, *Don* Pedro Barragan, can do a lot of favors for a man, in or out of the army," Whigam said, grinning slyly.

"Likely I will move into the best quarters available to the senior lieutenant." My strong right arm and good left leg got me to my feet. "By your leave, Colonel?"

I saluted and held it until he nodded in dismissal. I stepped carefully down off the planks, slapped my scarred trunk, left my hand on it and said, "Move along, Johnson."

"Be sure to chat a bit with Peter before you decide," Sullivan said. "Will you do that now?"

"Yes, George. I will do that." He seemed to be an intelligent and compassionate man and I felt that he meant me well. Still, although I was neither angry nor resentful, I was tired and in pain and already wary of my new junior officer, Peter Barragan.

A massive hand-carved door that could never have belonged to an unsuccessful rancher named Rivas swung open and a squat, swarthy man, looking more Indian than Spanish, dressed in the loose white shirt and trousers of the Mexican peon, spoke.

*"Sí, señor?"*

*"Quiero hablar con el señor—?"*

A tall, good-looking man with too much black hair, a long wax-formed curled mustache and porcelain-white teeth shouldered his way past the servant and spoke. I took an instant dislike to him.

"Come in, Major Northey."

"I am First Lieutenant William Northey."

"And I am Second Lieutenant—"

"Peter Barragan," I interrupted rudely, for his complacency annoyed me. "I fear that I have bad news for you."

"Not for me," he said, smiling.

"You may be quite important outside the army, Lieutenant, but in the army you are a second lieutenant and my junior. I mean to have my prerogatives!"

In my anger I ignored my leg and stepped up onto the landing too quickly. The pain suddenly turned my leg into an impacted molar. I gasped, saw the door tilt and would have fallen had not strong hands lifted me and half carried me into a chair, soft, but firm enough to hold me pleasantly immobile.

"Are you all right?" It was the deeply timbered voice of

Peter Barragan, but I could not quite focus on his face. "Yes," I said. "It must have been the champagne."

"I heard that the colonel had welcomed you to the post," Barragan said.

"You will have to move, you know," I said.

"But I plan to move first thing in the morning, sir."

"No need to hurry," I said, mollified and vaguely ashamed of my behavior.

"I have to. Orders."

"Whose orders?" I said loudly. Whigam had gone too far.

"I think that it is I, Major, that you mean to throw out into the cold."

I opened my eyes and followed the new voice to its owner, a slight blond man wearing the blank golden epaulets of a second lieutenant. His eyes were an innocent blue, his face finely boned and thinly fleshed.

"I beg you for a one-night extension." He rolled his eyes up and his mouth down and mimed sorrow so naturally that I had to suppress a smile.

"I take it that you are the real Peter Barragan." I leaned forward to rise, but he moved up quickly and gave me his hand. He had strong fingers and a good grip. I wondered if he had the hands of a fine rider, as well. He was, I learned later, except for Johnson, the best all-around horseman in the company.

"It is because of the dinner party that I need the house tonight. My wife has worked very hard on the party." He shrugged helplessly. "You are not married."

No," I answered, as if he had asked a question. "I am a poor army officer who cannot afford a bride. Obviously you are married."

"Of course. That is why I have a wife."

"I likely would bump a second lieutenant out in a second," I said, smiling, in good humor now, "but I cannot evict his wife."

"I do not think," he said mournfully, "that she will stay without me."

The other second lieutenant and I broke out in loud laughter. Still chuckling, he offered me his hand and said, "I am Lieutenant Maxwell Bell and I am delighted that I was lucky enough to meet Major William Robert Northey. Medal of Honor! From private to major! From Shiloh to Vicksburg! Wounded three times!" He stepped back and saluted. Barragan joined him. I snapped off a quick salute. Bell's words warmed me, but I have never been comfortable with even sincere flattery.

"How is it that you know so much about me, Lieutenant Bell?"

"I saw your orders." He turned to Barragan. "They came in a couple of weeks ago, did they not?"

"Yes, with the supply wagon from Las Cruces."

"But that is impossible. Colonel Whigam—" I broke off in confusion and, unable to explain what I did not understand myself, said severely, "And what, Lieutenant Bell, was a junior officer doing with my file?"

"I just glimpsed a bit over the shoulder of Colonel Whigam. But then he read the commendations aloud."

"If you leave, we will be one officer short," I commented, deciding I had better not probe further into the strange workings of Colonel Whigam's mind.

"Yes, sir. But then I was only assigned temporarily to take Peter's place while he took your post."

"Then who will be in charge of the third platoon?"

"We do not have a third platoon, sir," Barragan answered.

My arm muscles have increased noticeably since my long stay in army hospitals. The only real advantage is I can mount a horse with little strain on my bad leg and I can also push up easily from a chair with only my arms. I was on my feet before Barragan could offer his hand again.

"I must go to my quarters now. That trooper outside has been waiting for me for over an hour now and I feel guilty."

Barragan laughed. "You were going to throw me and my wife out into the cold, but you hesitate to keep a trooper waiting."

"Give my respects to your wife, Lieutenant. I shall surely meet her soon."

"You certainly shall. At the party. Eight o'clock."

"No. On such short notice it would be an imposition," I said, wanting nothing more than a stiff drink and a bed.

"But, Major, she has known you are to be at the party for over a week. The party is in your honor."

I sighed. "Then I had better leave now, gentlemen." I returned their salutes, made my way down the steps, received a salute from Johnson, patted my old trunk affectionately and kept my right hand on it as we walked.

My quarters must have been a storehouse for grain, for it was high enough off the ground to have a wooden floor. Even in the dusk I could see the alterations. A glass window had been recently set into the adobe wall next to the door. And, although the rough planked door sagged from rawhide hinges, its new knob was brass.

Johnson took the three steps in one, opened the door and went inside. In seconds I saw a match flare and then the window let light out into the darkening night. I climbed the steps carefully and went inside to the most comfortable quarters I had ever been assigned.

A Mexican serape full of color and light hung on the far wall. Next to it was a back door. Alongside, two planks, doweled together for width, had been set into the corner so that the only other support needed was a thick leg of gnarled mesquite.

In its center sat a bottle of brandy. The cork had been pulled and then set back in just enough to keep the bugs out. A crystal goblet sparkled in the lamplight. And marvel of marvels, next to what would be my desk was a real chair. Not a box or a three-legged stool, but a real cushioned chair with armrests handcrafted from lustrous walnut. I sank into it and waved Johnson away.

"You are excused, Johnson. I am sorry I took so long. Go on about your business."

"Suh, you is my business."

"You are right. I guess we are both each other's business now. But we will talk about that tomorrow."

"I could help you with those boots, suh. That right one looks—"

"You may leave now, Johnson." The man was perceptive. I wondered if anyone else had noticed. Damn!

"Yes, suh." He saluted, waited for a second after I answered, then did a formal about-face and left, angrily, I thought. Well, I would have been angry too. I pulled my watch from its pocket and sat it on the desk. I would have time for a drink and a nap. I poured the squat glass half full, swirled the golden liquid, decided it was cognac and tasted it. My sip turned to swallow and I drained the glass. Even fine brandy burns when you gulp it down. The second drink was tasted and savored as I admired my room. To my right against the north wall was my bed. It was full length and wide enough to sleep two. It had a thick mattress with a soft gray Saltillo blanket as a cover and a plump pillow on top. A rug was soft under my feet.

Barragan, obviously a good officer, had planned for all eventualities and had furnished these rooms sumptuously, just in case he might be bumped. I was once bumped by an officer who was my senior by virtue of a commission signed one day earlier than mine. Of course I would not bump Barragan and his wife, but as lassitude overwhelmed me and just before I drifted into sleep, still in the chair, I decided that I would give back all of the Barragan accoutrements, but slowly.

# Two

There were two isolated shots and then a volley. One of the balls punched a hole in my right boot. I felt no pain until much later, after my boot had nearly filled with blood, warm as fresh urine—my first thought was that my bladder had given way.

The riflemen up ahead broke and ran as our cavalry neared the rail fence. I was just behind the first man to clear the fence, Sergeant Mulder, a magnificent rider, who could lift a horse higher than anyone else in the squadron. I leaned into the jump, but my leg failed and although my mount cleared the fence easily, I sailed off into oblivion. The dream should have ended there, but the shots began all over again and I did wake to an insistent rapping on my door.

"Come in. Enter!" I called out loudly in irritation.

"Yes, suh. Major." I recognized the deep voice of Johnson and replied testily.

"I am First Lieutenant Northey, former First Sergeant Johnson. Come in."

He opened the door and almost smiled. I made a motion to rise, but he shook his head slightly and said, "If you sit still, me and this recruit, Private Lee here, will pull off them boots and polish them up for the party, suh."

"My boot has a hole in it," I said and then wide awake, added, "what time is it?"

"You got almost a full hour to get ready, suh."

I leaned back in relief. "Thank you, Private Johnson." I pointed to the trunk. "My dress uniform is in the trunk. I think there is a brush in there somewhere as well."

Johnson had the large gentle hands of a born horseman and he used them to remove the boot from my right leg by supporting my right upper leg as he eased it off. Then he turned to the recruit, a skinny young man, more brown than black.

"Now, Lee, you saw me ease that boot off; you do the same."

"Yes, suh."

"No. You don't say 'suh' to nobody ain't at least a second lieutenant."

"Lee?" I looked askance at the boy.

"That's what the sergeant calls me. But that's my last name. I was just called Johnny before I came North."

"Private John Lee, suh!" Johnson corrected him.

"Yes, suh. Sergeant. That's right."

"No," Johnson said, in a tired voice. "You suhs a officer and I ain't even a sergeant no more." He spoke to me then. "He is a bright boy, suh, but they don't give them no training at them recruit depots at all. They all just have to learn by doing."

"Of course, Sergeant," I said. "Just like we did."

"But you ain't no sergeant or is you?" Lee asked, puzzled.

Johnson did grin then and when I laughed, young Lee joined in and then even Johnson permitted himself a deep chuckle before he answered.

"No, boy I ain't, but I likely will be again, just like the lieutenant will surely be a major again."

I nodded understandingly, but did not commit myself. Johnson pointed out my old coat with the new epaulets. The silver bars contrasted dully against the golden background. He held up my sword and belt, hesitated and then said, "I think the colonel will wear his sword tonight, suh."

"But you are not sure?"

"No, suh."

"Then, when in doubt, always assume that protocol rules."

"Yes, suh."

"Hang it on the wall, there." I pointed to a peg to one side of the door. "And Johnson, I will continue Private Lee's instruction. You may leave him safely in my hands."

Johnson looked at me dubiously, but then saluted and said, "Yes, suh." He nodded at Lee, who drew himself up as if at attention, and left quickly.

While Lee brushed and shined, I heated a tin cup of water over a candle and shaved. I used the soapy water to wash most of the grime from my neck and brushed my wiry hair until it lay in one direction. Then I slid into the old familiar blue wool trousers, shiny black boots, cotton shirt, dark blue coat made even heavier by brass epaulets and buttons gilded to resemble gold, a silk neck scarf under the collar and then, two turns of the crimson silk sash around my waist, and I was ready. I looked around for my hat, saw it and the sword belt at the same time. I pointed at the belt. Lee took it down and helped me buckle it over the sash. I set my hat squarely on my head, and said, "Private Lee, unpack my other clothes. Leave everything else in the trunk. You may go as soon as you finish. Good night."

I stepped outside. The heat of the day had already given way to the cool of a desert evening. I walked easily and felt little pain. Suddenly I was swept by a strong sense of nostalgia. I might have been a lost, frightened child who, on suddenly sighting his home, experiences blessed relief.

A rectangle of light led me to the open door. As I paused to adjust my sword, I heard Johnson speak, unseen, a deferential, friendly ghost.

"I could hold your sword for you, suh, if you want."

I almost laughed, but caught myself in time. He was a perceptive man and meant me no harm.

"I belted it on by habit," I said. "Would you take it back for me?"

"Yes, suh," he said. I had cocked my head at the sound of

his voice and I saw a flash of white teeth. I slipped off the belt and held it out. He took it, saluted, waited for me to return the salute, then did a smart about-face and in two strides disappeared into the night.

I stood in the entrance, hat under my arm, and looked across the room brightened by a large candelabra, right into the flashing, turquoise eyes of the beautiful wife of Peter Barragan.

She rose immediately, smiling at me, one hand extended in welcome. I could not move. I had had an ideal woman formed in my mind, I suppose since adolescence, but I had never expected to meet her. Young, perhaps ten years younger than I, she moved forward to meet me; her hair like a black wave ebbed and flowed over bare shoulders whiter than the sands of any sea.

"I am so happy that you arrived before the others, Lieutenant Northey."

She held her hand out to me. I took it, but did not understand what I was to do for I had heard her voice as if she were a musical instrument playing an unknown tune. Although her voice never failed to enchant me, it was, I learned later, the slight Spanish lilt that had first delighted my ear.

Then, as I struggled to break free from the spell, I caught the sense of her voice as well as the music as she added, "I am Mrs. Raquel María Genovés de Barragán, your hostess."

She glanced down at her hand, still clasped desperately in my own. I felt myself flush and withdrew my hand spasmodically.

"Lieutenant Robert Northey at your service," I stammered.

"Lieutenant Barragan!" She turned her head, but not her eyes and they transfixed my own as a cobra might a terrified rabbit's.

"Yes, Raquel?"

I wrenched my eyes away to look at Barragan. His uniform puzzled me. It was essentially the same dark blue that I wore, except of course his single gold bar would have been invisible, had one been imprinted on the gold shoulder board. As he moved toward me, blue eyes flashing, smiling widely, I realized that it was the same uniform, but one that had been cut out of far better cloth and by a far better tailor than my own. He was wearing his sword in a scabbard burnished so brightly that it reflected flashes of light from the candles.

He stopped short, saluted and when I tapped my forehead with my own hand, he held his hand out. As we shook hands he said, "Everyone is here—except for the colonel and Lieutenant Bell—people arrive early here, for entertainment is infrequent."

"I hope that I am dressed properly." I slapped my left hip to indicate my lack of what was once our basic weapon, the curved cavalry saber.

He frowned slightly. "I think that I had better lend you a sword until—"

He stopped short, turned away from me and saluted.

"Good evening, Colonel. So good of you to come."

I turned, saluted and said, "Good evening, sir."

He flicked his hand at us to acknowledge our salutes and turned to Raquel Barragan. She held a hand out to him, which he took and kissed. It angered me that he did what I most certainly should have done.

"Come along, Colonel," she said, taking his arm. "The champagne is this way."

"No sword." Barragan grinned at me. "We try to guess how formal to be. Most of the time we lose."

The colonel's voice floated back over the conversational hum. "Lieutenant Barragan, don't you know that the saber is an anachronism in this modern age of repeating firearms?"

Somehow Barragan managed a shrug that expressed every man's helpless frustration faced with the inexorable logic inherent in a pair of superior shoulder straps. He held the expression until I laughed and then smiled.

"Come along and meet our other guests." He led me to what appeared to be two married couples. I recognized the post trader, George Sullivan, and bowed to him.

"You have met Mr. Sullivan," Barragan said. "The lady in the chair is his wife, Mary." He waited until I nodded and took her hand. She was a square, buxom woman with dark auburn hair and a wide generous smile. I liked her immediately.

"And the other lady is Miss Adele O'Donahue, Mary's sister."

Adele, sitting beside her sister, little resembled her. She was thin and freckled and her hair was bright Irish red. When she looked up at me and extended her hand, I saw that her eyes were large and light blue. She stared frankly, almost sensuously at me. I quickly lowered my eyes and bent over her hand, extended palm down, obviously to be kissed. She leaned forward and her dress, cut even lower than that of Raquel Barragan's, revealed large round breasts so white that I could see the fine blue veins curving down to nipples the size of raspberries. I touched my lips to her hand—her skin was hot—and straightened up quickly, stepping back.

Barragan smiled conspiratorially at me and turned to the other man, who remained in his chair across from Adele O'Donahue.

"And now," Barragan said, "it is my pleasure to present you to a man I hope you do not have to see professionally, our post surgeon, on loan from Fort Stockton, Samuel Smith."

Perhaps the proximity of a surgeon was enough to set my leg to aching, for I suddenly felt that I must sit down. I smiled at the surgeon and, as I spoke, eased myself into a chair near Adele.

"My pleasure, Doctor. I know how difficult it is for you healers. I myself, was a year in and out of hospitals. The good surgeons were miraculous."

"I take you to mean that that to encounter a good surgeon is miraculous?"

The doctor reminded me of a tiny green frog with a kind of blower at his throat that gives him the volume of a full-grown bullfrog. The doctor was not green, but he was small, not over five feet tall.

"No, Dr. Smith." I smiled. "I admire your profession."

"No, Lieutenant Northey. I do not jest." He thrust his square-jawed face at me, nostrils distended as if in anger. "Your opinion is a common one. Even from a man whose leg was saved by a miraculous surgeon."

"But," I protested, "that is not my opinion—"

"Stick by your guns, sir! You may be right. In any case"—he leaned forward to tap my right leg—"I'll take that off for you. Should have been done by that miraculous surgeon."

"My leg is quite sound," I said, uncertainly.

He sniffed, said, "If it was the left leg, you could not haul yourself up on a horse."

I opened my mouth to retort, but he had turned to the trader.

"Vee Gee, you should order a case of Peruvian wine for your wife and her lovely sister." He turned his head from side to side like a parrot wanting to observe two different objects.

"Vee Gee?" I whispered to Barragan, who had moved to stand just behind me. "Peruvian wine?"

Although I turned my head to better hear Barragan, his whisper was too low.

"What?" I whispered again.

"He said that I have ears like a hound," the little doctor said smugly.

"They look normal enough to me," I said.

The surgeon swiveled his stiff neck to glare at me for a full minute and would have continued I was certain, had not both Sullivan and Barragan laughed.

I tried a smile, but his eyes were full of black anger.

"What Lieutenant Barragan meant is that I have an acuity of hearing equal if not superior to certain canines."

"Of course," I said. "I apologize for the bad joke."

"I call the sutler, Mr. Sullivan, Vee Gee instead of Victor George. I call Miss O'Donahue, Ideal, not Adele and I call—"

"And he calls the colonel an eccentric," Whigam interrupted, "a euphemism for crazy." He whinnied and tapped my shoulder.

"Our hostess would like to seat us at the table. Can you make it on your own, or should I call for a stretcher?"

There was a hint of laughter in his voice, but I saw none in his eyes. I took a deep breath and was on my feet. Whigam nodded and walked away. I noticed a look of concern on the face of both Sullivan and his wife. Barragan merely touched my arm and said, "This way."

I resisted the temptation to stride to the dinner table, bowed to the ladies and then walked slowly away. I could not see the tight, smug little smile on the doctor's face, but I knew that it was there.

Bell, the handsome second lieutenant that I had mistaken for Peter Barragan, was waiting to shake hands. His smile was dazzling and I wished I could have had his teeth, although on reflection, I would have preferred his good right leg. I chuckled at the thought.

"You are in a good mood, Major," he said.

"Lieutenant Northey is fine," I said and then, to take the edge off my words, smiled and added, "and so is ex-Brevet Major Northey."

He smiled, a bit nervously, I thought, and he did glance at Brevet Colonel Whigam as he shook hands.

"I hoped I might see you before I left. I must write out my own orders for the colonel to sign, and I am a most uncertain scribe."

"You will leave us tomorrow, then?"

"Yes, sir. With the wagon that brought you."

"Ladies and gentlemen," Barragan called out, "will you be seated? There are cards at the places."

Whigam, a glass of champagne in his hand, waited for the ladies to find their seats and then placed himself between Raquel Barragan and Adele O'Donahue. A look of dismay crossed the hostess's face, but she merely picked up the card in front of Whigam and switched it with the one opposite.

When I looked for my card, I found that it was my seat that he had usurped.

When I was seated, I looked up to meet her eyes and smiled. She gave the tiniest of shrugs that the Latins use to denote utter helplessness.

"Please," Barragan asked, tinkling a tiny silver serving bell. "I will say only a few words and then be quiet. We are here to honor our new companion and second-ranking officer, First Lieutenant Robert Northey, and to say good-bye to our temporary companion, Second Lieutenant Maxwell Bell. When he is gone, I shall be the third-ranking officer. To your health."

Bell and I raised our glasses to him, and then to each other, and then to the table in general, although I centered my general toast to the radiant Raquel Barragan.

When the Spanish-speaking Indian woman served iced oysters, I was surprised, but when a later course was spiny lobster, I was astonished. In return for Raquel's earlier small shrug, I lifted my shoulders along with my hands as I asked, "Is there a branch of the ocean nearby unknown to our geographers?"

"No, but the seafood is very fresh. The lobsters were transported alive by ship at Port Isabel, and then, in wagons, to the Barragan hacienda. When the wagons reached Las Cruces, a mule was despatched to Fort Rivas. My *suegro*, Don Pedro Barragan, hosts a special party twice a year in Santa Fe. We could not go there, so he sent the food here."

"And the ice?"

"There are many lakes high in the mountains of New Mexico that freeze early and deep," Barragan said. "We cut blocks of ice two feet thick and haul them down to the icehouse. My father has chilled wine with his meals and will not eat dried meat, so the icehouse is big enough to hang a couple of steers and an elk and maybe even a big mule deer as well."

"The hostiles do not impede your ice expeditions?" I asked.

"They move down from the high country in the winter. We do not pasture our animals now except on the little ranch."

"The little ranch is not even a million acres." Whigam

cocked his head quizzically at me. "Do you know how many acres the big one has?"

"No."

"Neither do I." Whigam went back to forking oysters from their shells, seemingly no longer interested in the big ranch.

"But," I asked, "you once did pasture stock on the big ranch as well?"

"Yes," Peter answered. His wife had opened her mouth. She shut it again and nodded.

"But why not now, then?"

"Apaches," he said, turning to the oysters in much the same manner as had Whigam.

"But were there not then hostile Apaches?"

"They paid them," Smith said maliciously. "Them and the Comanches too. Gave them cattle and horses and guns too."

The doctor had been waiting, empty fork in hand, to enter the conversation. "The savages even had their pick of the girls, as long as they weren't any of the household ladies. Yes, Lieutenant Northey, they paid them to leave them alone. That's the Mexican way. Us Americans, we say, sir, 'thousands for war, but not one penny for tribute!' "

"What a lovely sentiment, Dr. Smith," Adele said, her voice tremulous. "You make up the loveliest things."

"Now, now, my dear lady. Actually that was a quote from an American general fighting the Mexicans."

Whigam almost choked on his oyster and had to hold his napkin to his lips for several minutes. Barragan, ever the diplomat, smiled, but did not correct Smith's version of American history.

"Of course," Sullivan said, "I know that you should not trade with these heathen redskins until they give up their savagery and farm and trade like Christians. Why, if it was not for the Apaches, I would be a rich man right now."

Lieutenant Bell nodded assent and spoke with a smile in his voice. "Friend George has a silver and gold mine which the Apache fancy to be an abomination to Mother Earth. They believe, sir," Bell continued, looking at me, "that gold is the Earth Mother's blood and the extraction of it—indeed, the act of digging deep holes in her—is a sacrilegious act."

"Of course," Sullivan said quickly, "they are primitive peoples, but once they understand what Christianity is, they will be taking communion with the rest of us."

"Communion!" Smith sniffed, then with a side look at Adele, merely shook his head in disagreement.

"I meant, Dr. Smith," Sullivan said as if in apology, "that they would be good enough Christians if they knew how."

"How would that be, George?" I said. "Perhaps they might be as intractable as the Jews at Masada."

"Masada?" Sullivan looked at me blankly.

I opened my mouth to speak, but Whigam was quicker.

"Perhaps our temporary surgeon could enlighten us." Then, as Smith hesitated, added, "Come along, Smith, you do know?"

"It was one of those battles before God confounded the Jews and sent them a wandering through the world. They killed a bunch of Philistines."

"Close," I said quickly. The surgeon had already taken a dislike to me and I did not want him for an enemy. "The Jews died rather than surrender to Roman troops."

"Yes," Smith said smugly. He spoke to the table, but his eyes were on Adele. "The Roman Catholics would have made Christians out of them, but they would not heed God."

"Would you say that a Methodist missionary might have had more success, or maybe the Dutch Reformed Church?" Whigam asked.

"Religion is not a matter of the mind, Colonel," Mary Sullivan said sternly. "It is the heart."

"Right again," Peter Barragan said, held his glass up and added, "to our own lovely Mary Sullivan who corrects us when we err."

I lifted my glass, then glanced nervously at Whigam. But

the colonel was delighted. He drained his glass, then filled another and toasted Mary Sullivan again.

She buried her face in her hands and then peeked out, a timid smile breaking into a wide grin. Her sister frowned a warning at her, but she shook her head and said, "It's all right, Katie, baby. No one minds Mrs. Sullivan."

"Do not call me by that horrid name, Mary." Adele looked at me slyly, a smile forming and said. "Major Northey will think I am some old Irish washerwoman!"

I refused the rank of major and of course, denied any such thought, although I was not surprised to learn that she was in fact baptized Catherine one year before her sister, Mary.

"But then, George," I asked, "are the Apaches so fierce that you could not hire some old soldiers to protect your miners?"

"Sure, that I could if the colonel would loan me the squadron for a few months."

"How many shares for the squadron?" Whigam asked.

"You name the number, Colonel."

"If I said a thousand, would there be any left for you?"

"Of course," Sullivan said seriously, but with a slight smile. "I can always issue more. Besides the mine is mostly silver. Maybe the Apaches wouldn't care about silver," he added hopefully.

"Captain Northey." Adele spoke a bit louder than necessary, but then, as I discovered later, she did everything a bit more than necessary. "When were you last in the East?"

"I am a first lieutenant, Miss O'Donahue, and yes, I was in St. Louis a month ago and Washington a few weeks earlier."

"Well what were the ladies wearing? Do we look dowdy and frumpy in comparison to the ladies there?"

She took a deep breath before continuing and I thought her breasts might burst free from her bodice. "I just know you went to all kinds of formal balls and gala parties."

I opened and then closed my mouth. All that came to mind was an afternoon visit to a famous Washington brothel where the girls wore dresses designed to reveal and accentuate their charms.

"Well, cat got your tongue?" She laughed shrilly.

"No," I said, almost stuttering. "You would have fitted right in with the last ladies I saw in Washington."

"Why, Captain Northey," she said, pleased. "You are an old flatterer." She cocked her head inquiringly at Raquel Barragan. "Isn't he an old flatterer?"

"Not so old," Raquel said. I smiled foolishly and mumbled that I was indeed thirty-three years old.

"That's not old at all," Adele gushed. "You're only seven years older than me."

"I am a few years older than he is," Smith said testily to Adele. "And I am in the prime of life."

"So am I," Whigam said, "but I have eaten oysters and spiny lobster, venison and quail, beans and rice, and something sweet made from cactus and if I do not have brandy and a cigar soon, I may get no older."

Barragan stood up and held his wife's chair. I arose easily, but there was no one for me to attend, so I followed Whigam into a chamber furnished with rude but comfortable cushioned chairs. We arranged ourselves in a semicircle around Whigam while the dark servant glided in to place a bottle and humidor on a low table.

Barragan poured generous portions of brandy in each glass and then added even more to the last one and presented that to Whigam.

We each took a cigar from the humidor and took turns with a lighter candle. Soon the air was redolent with cigars rolled with Cuban tobacco by Mexicans in New Orleans.

"How do you like duty on the wild frontier?" Whigam asked softly.

"I have seen worse."

"Food good?"

"Excellent."

"Brandy and cigar?"

"The best," I answered, puzzled.

"Good!" He laughed scratchily and slapped me on my leg. "Drink up and take your cigar with you to smoke while you prepare for bed, for you must be in the saddle at dawn tomorrow."

"Patrol, sir? A patrol?" I repeated stupidly, wondering if he might be playing with me.

"You call it anything you like except"—another burst of laughter before he continued—"the lost patrol. You will have acting Sergeant Green and a scout and you will regain a horse herd that the Apaches have taken from a local rancher."

"Sawyer again?" Barragan asked.

Whigam nodded.

"But Colonel," Sullivan said, "that man is daft. No one has ever even seen the raiders."

"Well then," Whigam said softly, "who will you send out on the patrol, Colonel Sullivan?"

"I beg your pardon, Colonel Whigam. I will attend to my store and leave the soldiering to you."

"Colonel," Barragan said, "might I accompany Lieutenant Northey on his patrol? I do know the area—"

"Yes, you do. And you have turned up nothing. Northey can hardly do worse, now can he?"

"Then, a mount, sir. He has no horse."

"Lieutenant Bell." Whigam cocked his head at Bell. "Would you tell me why you have not procured a suitable mount for our new officer?"

"We had begun to train a fine well-formed gelding for Major Northey, but—"

"Othello!" Whigam interrupted. "A magnificent mount. Peter, you worry too much." He turned to me. "Is there anything else that I can do for you?"

"Yes," I said nodding as the idea struck me. "Might I name my own sergeant?"

"Of course," he said magnanimously. "As soon as you get to know your men—"

"I would like to name Private George Johnson as sergeant of the first platoon," I interrupted him, flinching inside at my temerity, but Whigam was not angry. He even smiled as he talked.

"Of course. He will have to be acting first sergeant, but no matter. You can teach him to read and write on patrol. Nothing much happens anyway. Of course you can have Johnson. You find him and tell him to have Custer saddled for you."

I opened my mouth to ask for clarification, but he waved me away. I saluted Whigam. When he brushed a salute back at me, I did an about-face and left. Bell walked along with me. When I stopped and looked about for the ladies, Bell told me that they were likely to be in the card room which was a sewing room most of the time.

I asked him to say good night for me and started out, but he shook his head and said, "I am still officially on duty and will be until I am relieved tomorrow morning. Come along. We will leave a wake-up call for you, for Johnson and for the colonel's horse."

"Custer is a horse?"

Bell nodded and said, "Colonel Whigam's personal mount."

"Did the colonel name his own horse?"

"He did. The colonel is not a great admirer of General Custer."

"And he named my horse Othello?"

"Yes, he did. Our horses are mostly black and the colonel is a literary man."

"But," I said stupidly. "I am not to ride my horse, but that of the colonel?"

"Yes, sir. And as far as I know you will be the only other rider, outside of an occasional exerciser, that has ever ridden Custer."

"Tell me, now that we will not likely see each other for some time, is the colonel always so . . . rare?"

"No," he said, "some days he is even rarer."

He laughed loudly and was still chuckling when I left him at his post. I could hear his laughter until I reached my quarters and closed the door behind me.

# Three

Riding was not easier than walking, for I could bear little direct weight on my right leg without hampering the performance of my excellent borrowed mount. Custer was a lively black gelding larger than most cavalry mounts; at least fifteen hands high, he must have weighed twelve hundred pounds.

The first sergeant, his chevrons neatly sewed back on his sleeves, had the special hands of a born rider and used them to lengthen the stride of his horse a bit further than the rest of us so that when he led at a walk, someone always had, sooner or later, to break momentarily into a trot or be left behind. When my turn came, inevitably, Johnson relinquished the lead, and shaking his head sadly, said, loudly enough for the rest of the platoon to hear, "That Custer, he been too long without a good rider exercising him, suh."

I touched the maligned Custer with a spur and lifted up in the saddle to post, even for the brief trot, to regain my original position to the right of the platoon guidon, which, had we had one, would have hung limp from its staff. The wound smarted, nothing more. The other, deeper pain had disappeared.

All of the horses, mostly solid blacks, were geldings and named Sam, Joe or Bill. The army decided that they be gelded. The regimental commander chose the color and the men who trained them, often their riders under the tutelage of a master horseman such as Johnson, named them.

Our patrol was to take us over territory unknown to any of

us including the mixed Seminole-Negro scout who was on loan to us from regiment. I had been told that he was an excellent tracker.

We had no pack animals and were prepared to fight and if necessary to outrun a larger, but not as well-mounted force. We carried no swords. Each trooper carried, slung across his chest a .56-50 caliber Spencer carbine, barrel down, the muzzle anchored in a socket fastened to the saddle. The carbine held seven metal rim-fire metal cartridges in a tube that loaded through the butt. Each also had a Blakeslee box on a strap under the carbine sling that could hold seven loaded tubes. My troopers had been issued five tubes, which made each one of them responsible for thirty-six cartridges, with the one extra cartridge provided to insert into the chamber so that the initially loaded weapon held eight rounds. If we met no resistance, that same number of rounds would be returned to supply or remain debited to its rifle number.

Each man carried his own three-day supply of hard bread, cold bacon and a quart canteen of water. Every fourth man carried a small frying pan and coffeepot. Also each man must carry a picket rope, currycomb and one blanket. However if the nights were cold, the men might double up and even add a horse blanket for extra warmth.

I had the identical rations and solitary blanket, but I carried a .44-caliber Colt revolver that had been converted from cap and ball to take the Henry rim-fire rifle cartridge. Although I carried no saber, the pistol was belted to my left side, butt forward, leaving my right hand free to draw either the nonexistent saber or, after unsnapping the flap, the revolver.

We had all been allowed two pounds of personal items. Included in my own saddlebags were a pint flask of brandy, a two-ounce vial of laudanum, several bandages and a pound of hard candy.

We had made one camp near water, breakfasted there and were keeping a watch for a clump of trees that might mean water. If we did not find water before dark, we would have to go back to the previous water or endanger our horses.

We paused at the crest of a gentle rise, the gray surface relieved only by the green of cactus I was not yet familiar with, except that they all had fishhook spines. Far away and rising in the east I saw a high column of dust. Our flankers were well out in front, moving southeast.

"Let's see what is making all that dust, Sergeant," I said, bringing up my binoculars.

"That dust is smoke, sir," Johnson said.

I could not focus on that long thin gray line swirling against slate-colored mountains. I tilted the glasses higher to the bright blue. My horse moved a step and I lost the column of dust or smoke.

"Damn!" I said, swung my leg up stiffly over the high McClellan cantle, and called out, "Horse holder!"

Our holder was there, on foot, to take my reins. If necessary, he'd tie my reins to the bridle ring of his horse and then relinquish his reins to a third man, who would in turn pass his reins over to a fourth, who would be responsible for holding all four mounts—out of harm's way, if possible—while the other three fought.

Standing, I focused again on the thin gray spiral and followed it down until it touched the base of some sort of a structure. A wooden building, of course, either smoldering or on fire.

"You have good eyes, Sergeant," I said. "Bring in the flankers."

The bugle flashed in the sun, but before I could speak, Johnson spoke sharply. "No! Crawford, ain't you got no sense at all? Get that horn away from your mouth! Now ride out in front and make circles like I showed you."

"Yes, Sergeant." Crawford nodded eagerly as if forcing an affirmative. "I will. But can I blow the charge when we runs into them hostiles?"

"Only if I tell you and not before."

He nodded and, a wide white grin on his thin young black face, rode out in front of the platoon.

Johnson shook his head ruefully. "He got a call for that bugle, but he sure ain't no trooper yet."

I nodded my sympathy, although I said nothing. He knew what he was doing. Some of the men, including the bugler, had just graduated from marching drill and had not yet finished riding school.

"He'll be a good soldier," Johnson said. "He just needs some seasoning."

"How many old soldiers do we have?"

"You mean ones as has done some fighting? Well, suh"—he grinned widely for the first time—"they is you and me."

I mounted and saw that the flankers were returning at a trot. Johnson stood up in his stirrups and, shading his eyes, peered to the south of the smoke.

"Put your glasses, suh, to south by southeast. I think the Seminole is coming back at a run."

I swept to the right of the smoke and saw the scout, dust now billowing up after him. I lifted the glasses slightly and could distinguish at least eight riders in hot pursuit.

"He has at least eight hostiles after him," I said. "Take a file out to meet him. I will follow with the rest of the platoon."

He called out, "Brown, first file, ride with me."

They left at a gallop. I called out for a trot and winced as I posted. I would have much preferred the gentler gait of a gallop, but we would need our horses fresh when we met the hostiles. There must be more of them to dare to harass our scout so close to our platoon, even if they knew that we were short nine men.

The terrain, flat, with no more cover than a clump of prickly pear cactus or a bit of brush, precluded an ambush. At a hundred yards from the scout, the hostiles veered away. Johnson waited for the scout to reach him, then turned toward us at a walk. Exactly as I would have done. Save the horses and be ready for an attack, even if it appeared unlikely.

I also held to a walk, which of course was the proper thing to do, but I felt uneasy. A divided command should be reunited as soon as possible. Still, as I scanned the horizon, I could see nothing within five hundred yards except the dust from the Indian ponies swirling toward the smoke.

We rode along from a sandy soil onto white alkali which crusted, dried and became a fine dust that the smallest movement sent billowing into the air, stinging eyes and nose. The feeling of dread, of extreme danger swept over me again and trusting to instinct alone, I raised my left hand and halted the riders.

I looked up ahead, waiting for Johnson and his men to reach us, and saw what looked like a wind line separating the alkali from a darker substance. And suddenly I heard and almost saw the description of an officer who had been, while with the California volunteers, ambushed by Apaches. The circumstances had been most similar. I hesitated, then thought, if I am wrong, I shall be embarrassed. But, if not, then likely I shall be dead.

I twisted my revolver out of its holster, called out for horse holders, and dismounted. I aimed at the black line and fired.

As if by magic, the desert seemed to unfold and forms emerged from the earth, cradling rifles and shrugging off ghostly white serapes. I had disrupted their timing. Not only were we not in a cloud of thick blinding dust, but we managed to get off one ragged volley before they could fire. But as often happened with hurried shooting we missed. But, then, so did they.

"Take your time. Pick a target!" I yelled, but by then the dust had risen and I could not see more than a couple of yards in any direction. A ghost suddenly appeared out of the dusty fog, a rifle pointed at me. The sound of our shots were as one. Mine was an explosion of dust between his legs. His must have been a near miss. And then there was one of those eternities when all details are clear, each motion easily seen and time is almost stopped. He lifted his other hand to point a cocked Dragoon Colt at me. Although we again fired simultaneously, I had taken a fraction of a second longer, I believe, to extend my arm. The barrel could have been no more than two feet from his chest when I fired.

My shot was more deliberate or perhaps just luckier. In any case my ball took him in the belly, while his merely took away my holster and a pinch of flesh. He dropped both pistol and rifle and sat down to watch bright red blood well through the ghostly white dust on his stomach and paint his fingers red.

I switched targets as the dust cleared, but the Apaches were running like goats, twisting to shoot, and then darting in another direction and then away and out of range. I looked back for the man I had shot, but he had disappeared. Up ahead some fifty yards I saw two men trotting through the brush, dragging a man between them. I aimed at one, but my heart's pounding made my sights dance and the range was much too great in any case. I lowered the hammer and looked about.

My troopers looked almost as ghostly as had the Apaches. They milled around aimlessly, pointing their rifles now one way and then another.

"Mount up!" I called.

As I hoisted myself up into the saddle the bugler played "Boots and Saddles!"

First there was nervous laughter and then guffaws so loud that we could clearly hear the deep basso of Sergeant Johnson who must have been almost a hundred yards away. That bugle call is reserved for parades and other formal occasions.

"Casualties?" I asked automatically, even as I saw that each man was mounted.

"Only you, sir." Corporal Carter nodded nervously at the blood seeping through my pant leg. I holstered my pistol, twisted it away from the blood, opened my saddlebag, pulled out a bandage, and stuffed it down inside my pants.

"You wounded, suh?" Johnson rode up alongside me.

"Just creased. I have the bleeding stopped now. What about your file?"

"One hurt real bad."

I nodded and scanned the horizon. Two dust trails were rising in the air. There were enough sharp intakes of breath to be audible. We all wondered, I supposed, whether they were leaving or arriving.

I called for the scout. He pointed back to where he had been chased to trick us into the ambush.

"Many Apaches. Many," he said. He was a small man with a deep voice and a way of pronouncing one word as if it were a sentence. He opened and closed his hands to show at least thirty fingers.

"But there were no more than eight or nine or five after you."

"Many," he corrected me. He flashed his fingers again. "Before they chase, I see many tracks."

I nodded. I turned to Johnson. "Is that dust trail getting closer?"

He nodded. So did the scout.

"Can your wounded man ride?"

Johnson pointed to a man in the saddle but holding the pommel with both hands while another man held the reins. I rode to him. His eyes were luminous with pain.

"The ball took him in the chest, Lieutenant." Johnson was at my side. "But they ain't no bubbles in the blood. I think the bleeding is stopped."

"Can you stay in the saddle?" I asked.

"I reckon I can if we don't go trotting, sir."

"You thinks you can, Jimmy?" Green, who was one of the file corporals, asked anxiously.

"If you can stay in that saddle, Jimmy—"

I looked a question at Green and he spoke up quickly, "Private James Brown, sir."

"Well then, Corporal Brown." I spoke loudly so that all could hear. "If you can stick in that saddle at a walk, then we will walk our horses together back to the post. We will never leave a wounded man behind. We will all go back together or die fighting together."

I called the scout over and asked him if he could ride directly to the post with a message. He nodded, but when I offered to send a couple of soldiers with him, he shook his head emphatically. He gave me to understand that he could take care of himself, but not anyone else.

I wrote quickly to Barragan, asking that an ambulance meet us to attend the wounded man. I gave our position as fifty miles south by southwest from the post and added that we were proceeding at a walk.

The scout pointed toward the dust trails, and said, "Better quick." He tapped his fingers against one palm, miming a horse trotting.

I shook my head and pointed to the wounded man, hanging on to the pommel with both hands, head down, chin resting on his breast.

He shook his head, then, pointing to a slight rise half a mile or so away, said, "Die there. Better."

When I said nothing, he nodded as if I agreed with him completely and rode at a gallop toward the post.

"He does not have a high opinion of our fighting ability," I said to Johnson after the Seminole had ridden off.

"Them Seminole niggers is more Injun than Nigger, Lieutenant. They even speak Injun to each other, not English like folks. Trouble is," he added, "they don't think like the Apaches neither."

"We should have an Apache scout," I said, surprising both of us.

"If he was on the guard, I wouldn't sleep much," Johnson said.

"Nor would I," I said and gave the order to walk the horses back to the post. I sent flankers wide on both sides with instructions to fire a warning shot at any sign of hostiles and then return to the platoon.

While we kept glancing apprehensively at the two dust trails following us, I reflected on the Apaches. All I knew I had read from military writings or from scraps of conversations with others almost as ignorant as I. The first step it seemed to me would be to learn the language.

"Sergeant," I called to Johnson, who was riding at the right of the platoon while I kept to the center, "where did we get our Seminole?"

"Regiment sends them over. Seminoles or Navajos."

"Why Navajos?"

"I don't know except they is all Injun, knows the country some and hates Apaches."

"Regiment sends us Seminoles or Navajos," I said reflectively, thinking that the Seminoles were even more isolated than our troopers or myself. The Navajos would know the country better and maybe think like an Apache.

"Sergeant," I said decisively, "send a request to Regiment for a Navajo scout."

"That will need writing, suh."

"Tell the company clerk," I said automatically.

"We got no clerk, suh."

"Right. But then, who does the communications?"

"It was Lieutenant Bell or Lieutenant Barragan, suh."

I laughed and said, "So now it will be Second Lieutenant Barragan or First Lieutenant Northey."

"Yes, suh," he said. Then shading his eyes as he peered at the dust trails he added, "I think those hostiles has joined up, suh."

I did not bother to lift the binoculars. I could see that there was indeed only one dust trail.

While we talked, I had kept in constant view the rise the scout had pointed out, calculating its distance. We were now no more than two hundred yards away.

"Take the second file up to that rise, Sergeant. If it is good ground, set up a perimeter. Now!"

He saluted, called out the second file and galloped up the rise. Once on top, he turned his horse in a circle and waved his hat. We turned slightly and still at a walk, moved along, glancing occasionally back over our shoulders. The bugler called in the flankers and within five minutes we rode inside the thin line of riflemen protecting the mound that the survivors would one day call Brown's Hill.

The hill did have a slight depression on one side and I had the horses staked there. We could fire over their heads and keep them safe, unless there were too many hostiles. But in that case, it would matter little whether or not we had horses.

Once we had settled in, each man scraped up whatever he could as a breastwork. I called Johnson to my place at the center of the ragged circle.

"We have most of our ammunition left, as well as the high ground," I said cheerfully. "They will not chance an attack against us. They will most likely try to run off or kill our horses and then attempt to pick us off one by one."

"Yes, suh," he said in exactly the same doubting tone of agreement that sergeants always use when they disagree with an officer.

"Well?"

"Lieutenant, every man as wasn't holding horses fired more than just too much."

"Fired until the tube was empty," I said. "But that is understandable. They are battle green and that was the worst ambuscade I have ever been in. Why, I emptied my pistol. Did you keep a round in your carbine?"

"I emptied a tube, but I reloaded. Some of them boys, they went through three tubes before I could get them stopped."

"My God! What were they shooting at?"

"Nothing. Just to hear the noise. Maybe they think it scares the Apaches away."

"Find out how many cartridges we have left. Take the loading tubes away from those who fired the most and give them a handful to load one at a time. Give full cylinders only to the steadier ones."

"I put the cut-off order on everyone except Green."

"Good, Sergeant," I said, as if I had known that the Spencer, new to me, could be set for single fire.

I dug the brown bottle of laudanum from my saddlebag, took my extra canteen and walked quickly to the blanket where the wounded trooper lay. A horse blanket, pinned to yucca on one side and weighted with a stone on the other, kept the sun from his upper body. I knelt, stiffly, on one knee. Brown looked up at me with such relief and gratitude that I felt hollow with nothing useful inside.

"Are you in much pain?"

"Not real bad, sir, now that I ain't on that jolting old horse."

"He hurts bad, sir, even if he don't say so," his friend, Corporal Green, looking anxious, said.

"I want to look at your wound, front and back," I said, pulling the cork on the laudanum. "So take a good swallow and after a few minutes I'll take off the bandage."

Green held out his tin cup and I put about half an inch of the opiate in the cup. I gave the corporal the glass vial and told him to save it for Brown.

A shadow cooled my back. I looked up to see Johnson. He held an extra rifle and a loading box.

"Who is the extra rifle for, Sergeant?" I asked.

"You asked me to give the loading tubes to the steady men, Major." I decided that I might as well be a major while I was out on the patrol and did not correct him. "But you only got the pistol, so I figure maybe you might take Brown's Spencer."

"You trying to make Sergeant-Major on this patrol?" I asked. The look of utter dismay was so apparent that I could not continue my banter.

"I thank you for the compliment and I will be proud to take my place with the other steady men." He looked down on me, his face impassive, but there was a hint of laughter in his eyes. I held my hand up to him. He hesitated and then took mine and helped me to my feet.

I disengaged the tube. It was full. I checked the rifle chamber. It held an unfired round. I inserted the tube, let the hammer back down to safe and then slipped rifle over one shoulder and the ammunition box over the other. I caught Johnson nodding approval, embarrassing him.

To cover his confusion, he handed me the binoculars and pointed. "There ain't but two hostiles riding out there and they ain't doing nothing but making a lot of dust pulling some brush along behind them."

Two riders. Then where were the others?

"Sergeant. Have all troopers ready to fire. A round in the chamber, but hammer down. Do not cock the rifle unless they see the enemy."

"Sergeant," a young voice fraught with tension called out, "I got cotton in my mouth. Can we have a drink?"

"Let them all have a long drink," I told Johnson. Why go into the fight thirsty? If we won, there would be plenty of water when the relief arrived. If not, then it would not matter a great deal to any of us.

# Four

I knew that reinforcements could not come before night fell, but I had been told that Indians avoided night fights, that they believed that if they were slain at night they would wander blindly, wailing forever through eternity. The thought made me shiver. I too dislike night fighting. It is too much of a gamble, although it is a better gamble to be the man lying silently, rifle loaded, waiting for the assailant to betray his position by movement or sound.

There was not much written about the Apaches. However I did read a report in a journal by an army officer attached to the American surveying group charged with establishing the new border imposed upon Mexico by the victorious Americans. I have forgotten the author's name, but he felt that the Apache, with some justification, considered himself a far superior warrior than any other race and as such it was unthinkable for an Apache warrior to be killed by some vastly inferior red, white or, in our case, black fighter. Because of this, they avoid encounters in which luck might play a part. We should have generals so astute.

I held my left arm out straight, palm at ninety degrees, and measured two hand widths between the bottom rim of the sun and the still light gray horizon. We could count on half an hour of light.

Johnson was down among the horses checking picket ropes,

moving carefully between horses, never exposing himself to a possible shot from the silent but menacing desert around us.

"Sergeant," I called, "if we have enough fuel to boil coffee, each man might have a cup before the sun goes down. Only take water from those who want the coffee."

"We got plenty dry yucca. Burns quick but hot."

"Two fires then," I said, "and two men to watch the pots."

As I turned away, I saw a trooper squatting out in the open, kindling a fire from yellow shreds of cactus, whistling cheerfully as he fed the fire.

"You, at the fire, get down!"

Intent on his fire, he ignored me.

He did not ignore Johnson. The parade voice might have startled the Apaches even if they were miles away.

"Lee, you dumb shithead, get your ass and head the same tall!"

The trooper's body convulsed and seemed to snap into a flat blue line, one hand still holding a piece of cactus burning like a candle.

"You recruits look at that trooper there tending that fire." Johnson moved carefully out from the tethered horses and hunkered down partially shaded and hidden by a large cactus. "I wants another man over at the other end to do the same and then you all pass the pots around and collect the water. The corporals will see to the coffee. And make it strong."

Just before the sun flamed into the dark purple edge of the ragged Sacramento mountains, the fires were extinguished and the coffee, piping hot, passed around. The cool, protective darkness was welcomed with sighs of relief. We stretched our legs and massaged aching muscles and knew that we would live at least until dawn.

"Sergeant, bring your coffee and a cup for me over here."

"Yes, suh." The darkness was sudden and so complete that I could smell the coffee before I could make out Johnson, walking erectly without hesitation. Was it only three nights ago that he told me he could see in the night?

"If you hold out your hand, Major?"

I did and he turned the mug handle to my hand. I took it quickly, knowing the tin cup would be as hot as the coffee itself.

"The bread is on top," he said. I grasped it with my left hand and when he squatted down beside me, we both dunked the rock-hard squares of bread into the sweetened coffee. Even Johnson's magnificent teeth were no match for that aged army bread.

"How is the morale?" I asked, waiting for the coffee to sink into the bread.

"Good. They all want to shoot Apaches."

"Excellent. If they rush us at dawn, we will stay put and shoot them like targets on a rifle range.

"Like targets, suh?"

"Yes. You *have* been on a firing range."

"Me, yes. Maybe Corporal Green. But the rest of them— even the steady ones—they point that carbine like it was a spear and just jerk away on the trigger."

I should have known better. Why would the colored troopers get any more training with a rifle than the white ones? There was never any free ammunition for practice.

"Sorry, suh, but them boys is some green."

"No need to be sorry. We will rearrange our perimeter from a circle to a rough triangle. Three equal sides. I will take the point overlooking the horses, you the one to my back and Corporal Green will be on the other. The steady men will fill in along the lines."

"Yes, suh. I hopes they comes after us. Mostly they just ambushes us and runs the horses off."

"They will not run our horses off," I said. "I want all the horses saddled well before dawn. I want three of your best riders and their horses up here along with my horse. If they attack at dawn, we will fight defensively. If they do not, I will lead a charge through the brush to stir them up so that you and Green can pick them off. If they bring up horsemen in force, we will ride back in. If the number is no larger than ours, our reserve will mount and join us."

"Could I ride out with you, Major?"

"No. I need competent riflemen. You and Green. The others are not to shoot unless an Apache is about to bite them. I do not want to be shot by one of our own men."

"Yes, suh. I'll put Henry Carter in charge of the detail. He is some steady and a good rider."

"Separate the horses into three groups and check the pickets. I want every other man in the line to stay alert while the others sleep. They will alternate as you and I will."

While Johnson carried out my orders, I reviewed my tactics. I set up a chessboard. The black pawns wore blue coats and pants with yellow stripes. The red pawns wore breechclouts and headbands. I obviously was playing the blacks and would have to wait for the reds to move first. When Johnson came back to report, I had found no flaw in my strategy and was so smug that I almost hoped that the relief would not arrive until we had a chance to strike back at the savages.

"When the dipper is spilling out the water, Corporal Green, you wake me up." Johnson's deep voice was not loud, but I could hear him clearly as he spoke.

"Sergeant," I said, "I would prefer you to be nearby. I will wake you at midnight."

"Yes, suh."

I leaned against a rock, squirmed, and told myself stories until the Big Dipper, the soldiers' clock, had turned across the sky and was beginning to empty. I pulled out my watch, clicked the face open and tilted it to catch the moonlight. It was just after midnight.

When I touched Johnson's shoulder, he responded so quickly that I wondered if he had been asleep at all.

I rolled up in my blanket, not to sleep, for I knew that I could not, but because the heat had gone out of the ground and it was cold. And then a hand was shaking my shoulder and I wondered why I was sleeping on the ground.

"Major Northey!"

"Major? I thought the War was over."

"Suh?"

"Oh," I said, fully awake. "Are we ready?"

And then, as Johnson still knelt by my side, the first horse was hit by one of the arrows that rained down upon us. The horse screamed and broke free to run off into the night.

"Double up your blankets and cover your heads," Johnson yelled.

"And move the horses farther apart," I said, covering my head with my blanket. "As soon as the arrows stop."

But they did not stop. The arrows came down as if they had been shot from mortars. I called out to be vigilant. They might attack while we were literally pinned down by the Apache mortars. But there was not much to be done. Although the barrage lasted only a few minutes, it seemed like hours before the last arrow thudded into my blanket and sliced through the two folds to cut through the brim of my hat. We never knew how many arrows they fired, but later, some of the men found flint-tipped arrows, which meant that they had fired all of their arrows, for they only tipped an arrow with flint when they found an old one. It was much easier to make a point from an old barrel hoop or any other piece of scrap iron.

After a long ten minutes of calm, I called out for a head count. There were three men wounded, one badly and several horses hit, three of which had broken loose and run off into the night.

When it seemed certain that the barrage of arrows was over, I slipped the blanket from my head, lifted up to lean on an elbow and said, "I am certainly happy, Sergeant, that the Apaches do not fight at night."

"Me too, Major. If I was to unhunch my back I be scared they is arrows in it."

"I think they have run out of arrows," I said, grinning in the dark as I unhunched my own back.

"Carter," Johnson called out. "You ready?"

"We is but I'm borrowing Will Henry's horse. Mine run off."

"Good. I'll bring the major to his mount. Suh?"

I could not see his face, but I was sure that his forehead was wrinkled wondering how he could help me to my feet without offending me.

"I am stiff with this desert cold, Sergeant. Would you give me a hand up?"

"Yes, suh," he said, took my extended hand and pulled me to my feet. "If you want to hold on to my sleeve, Major, I know the trail through all these cactus bushes and rocks."

"Yes, of course." I took his sleeve and we walked slowly through the camp until Custer neighed. I put out one hand and touched his velvety soft lips probing for a bit of dried fruit. I ran my hand along his back until my fingers found the pommel. I felt my foot guided into a stirrup and then Johnson lifted me up and I swung my right leg over the saddle.

Light filtered through the dark, melting the black away, and lighted the far mountains. I drew my Colt, thumb-cocked the hammer and held the heavy revolver, barrel up, at the ready. There was a glow on the eastern horizon and I could make out individual clumps of cactus.

They will attack now, I thought, and when they did not, I yelled *"Charge!"* and spurred Custer out into the dark. I glimpsed one fearsome warrior, hand raised to hurl a hatchet at me, but I held my fire until I recognized the pointed headdress of a large yucca cactus and rode on. By the time we had made a fast circuit of the high ground, it was light enough to see clearly.

It was then that the Indian suddenly appeared, standing erect, his carbine barrel tilted down. He yelled angrily, defiantly and then there was one shot followed by a ragged fusillade. All misses. I kneed Custer toward the hostile, my revolver held steadily, waiting for the range to shorten. At twenty yards, I flipped the pistol barrel skyward. The Indian wore a regulation black Kossuth hat with crossed sabers pinned to its front.

"Do not shoot!" I yelled as loudly as I could and pulled the big gelding back on its haunches.

At that moment everything slowed down and I could see Carter, one of the steady men, galloping over the rough ground pointing his Spencer carbine, one-handed, as if it were a walking stick. I screamed *"No!"* or thought I did, but Carter who surely should never have been able to hit a barn from a galloping horse, shot and the Indian dropped the way a man does who is killed instantly.

Carter yelled triumphantly and waved his rifle exultantly. I waved the troopers on and we made another three circuits of our perimeter. No other Apaches appeared.

I rode back to the dead man and dismounted. He was crumpled on one side, one arm flung awkwardly over his face, the other still clutching the Spencer carbine. His black hat was still firmly on his head. The unpolished brass sabers were green, but the numbers of the regiment and platoon, 9 and E were clear.

Carter, his voice and movement animated by his first brush with death, rode up, talking even before he saluted.

"I got him, sir, yes, sir, I did. I just rode right at him and fired that Spencer like it was a great big pistol. Yes, sir, I did."

"It was not your fault, Carter. Anyone might have done it."

"But nobody else did. They all missed. I'm the one got him."

"Carter," I said quietly, "this is our own scout."

"No! No, sir. That is a Apache. He was out here waiting to shoot us just like he did poor Jim a-dying up there." Then his voice lost its intensity. He turned to the other riders looking down from their mounts at the dead Indian.

"You all know that ain't our scout? You know that?" Carter pleaded with the other riders.

One of the men slung his carbine over his shoulder and looked a question at me. Before he could speak, I said, "Dismount, trooper, and look."

He nodded and floated off his horse to land softly alongside me and the dead man. He looked at him for a long second and then said, "Yes, sir. That is—was our scout. We never knowed his real name, but we called him Sundown on account he wouldn't do anything outside after dark."

"Well," I said, thinking out loud, "at least he died in the light."

Carter flung his reins over his horse's head and, the carbine still clutched in one hand, slid off his horse and stared in horror at the dead Indian. He swallowed twice before he could speak and when he did, his voice had tears in it.

"I never went to kill no scout. Never did."

"Of course you did not. But it happens too often in battle. He should never have tried to come into camp with the Apaches about."

"I expect," Carter said hollowly, "he was just waiting, scared to death himself, for them Apaches to leave so's he could go back with his own troops. He didn't study me shooting him."

"Listen to me, all of you," I said loudly, knowing my voice would carry now or later to all of the men. "Several of us shot at Sundown. It was a bad thing, but an accident. As far as I am concerned, the Apaches killed Sundown just as surely as if they had put an arrow into his heart. He died in action against the enemy and I intend to see that he gets a full military funeral."

"But, Major, I shot him and I near run my horse right over him after." Carter spoke calmly, but with a note of despair in his voice.

"In actions like this one, accidents happen. I was in a melee in the war, a recruit, like you, and I fired wildly. I killed a man in my own platoon—my own friend. But just as I am telling you, my lieutenant told me, he was killed fighting the rebels."

"What did you do, sir?" There was a note of hope in Carter's voice now.

"I never again fired without being sure of my target and I

fought the rest of the War twice as hard as before. We got a medal from congress for my friend," I added, lying shamelessly, "and sent it to his mother.

"Now, I have just told you a secret and I want you to swear to keep that secret, just as we all will, about what happened here today. Yes?"

"Yes, sir. I will." He saluted and remounted, but he rode no more than a hundred yards before he dropped his reins and slipped from the saddle. His horse stopped immediately. Carter kept his back to us, but I could see his shoulders move as he retched.

In spite of my superficial wound, or perhaps because of it, my leg was limber and I remounted easily and rode to the center of the perimeter. Johnson stood there, his carbine held at the ready, awaiting orders. I held out my hand for his weapon.

"Load in the chamber, suh," he said, as he held his rifle out for me to inspect. I took it up from him, sniffed the breech and smiled as I handed it back. It had not been fired.

"Did anyone fire from here?"

"Yes, suh. Two rounds, suh."

"Would you ask them not to repeat that error, Sergeant?"

"I have already done that, suh, but we ain't finished talking about the details."

"Good enough. There will be no loose talk?"

"No, Major, not from any trooper listening to me." He swiveled his head to take in the twenty-odd men and then asked, "Should I reconnoiter, suh?"

Later I discovered that Johnson had mastered all of the technical words of his trade and when speaking to officers, pronounced them slowly and carefully in what seemed to him to be Yankee English. However he usually translated them into language sometimes brutally vivid when relaying those same orders to the men.

"Approved. Take along the bugler. If you meet hostiles,

sound retreat and rejoin us. Do not proceed beyond the point where we first met the Apaches."

He took out the first file at a trot, he in the center and the rest fanned out so that the dust would not obscure their vision and they would not present a compact target. I caught myself nodding approbation. Except for the obvious racial differences, Johnson reminded me of an Irish sergeant who had made my life miserable as an enlisted man.

When I was commissioned I had chuckled, anticipating the many small revenges I would take, but within a month he was my platoon sergeant and I missed him sorely when he was killed by our own pickets one dark night returning from a long reconnaissance patrol.

There would be wounded horses whose riders could not care for them. I called out, "Any man who cannot care for his own mount will need someone in his place. You," I pointed at a man whose name I did not yet know, and added, "See to it."

I handed my reins to Carter and said, "Follow me, I may need to mount suddenly."

James Brown, the first man hit, was lying on his back, head resting on a rolled blanket, watching the sun slowly rise. He turned his head to look up. I dropped to my right knee.

"Corporal Brown, how are you?" My heavy parade-ground voice embarrassed me. Lowering my voice, I added, "We are going to get you back to the surgeon today."

He nodded and then as if in apology, said, "I guess I can make it if it don't dark up on me."

He seemed so much like a man who was drifting off into another gentler world. I had seen many die under similar circumstances, almost grateful for the surcease of pain and fear.

"We will get you back, Corporal Brown and, unless you give up, alive."

He did not open his eyes, but he smiled slightly, and said, "Yes, sir. I sure don't want Sergeant Johnson pestering me if I don't."

I found the three men who had been hit by arrows. One was lying on his stomach, the shaft quivering as he groaned, the head imbedded in his buttocks. A gangly young trooper nearby, grinning broadly with relief, held up a bandaged wrist. "I can ride back, yes, suh, I can." He saluted left-handed.

I returned his salute, looked inquiringly at him and said, "What is your name, soldier?"

"Private Tom Jefferson."

"Where is the third wounded man?"

"That him. He just sitting there not talking. He ain't hurt bad. Old Pappy Berry there"—he pointed to another man, who looked older than the rest, perhaps thirty years old, his forehead wrinkled, probably with anxiety, wondering if he had done the right thing—"he doctored the both of us. He done pushed that arrow right through the fat part of his leg and it just bled a little bit, like he did me too. But then Johnny Lee there, he got sick and made a mess—he couldn't help hisself, suh. And then he drank all his water and just crawled back under that spiny bush and curled up."

I followed his finger and saw the curled-up form. It was the same young recruit who had been assigned to be my striker by Johnson. "Private John Lee," I said, "are you going to be able to ride back?"

The form twitched and turned and as soon as I saw his face, I knew that his was not a simple wound.

"Is that you Uncle Willy?" He made a convulsive movement and turned to face me, not quite sitting erect. "Wasn't me took that salt pork. No, it must of been that new nigger from up north."

"Carter," I said, "Help me bring him out."

Between the two of us, we pulled and coaxed him out into the open. I touched his head and knew he had a bad fever.

"It ain't bad," Jefferson said uncertainly. "Look here, suh."

He pulled a bloody corner of torn cloth back to reveal a bandaged upper leg. "The head just went in one side and Pappy—I means Private Daniel Berry—he didn't need but to slice a little skin to get it out." He stopped and then added proudly, "Mine was in deep and Lordy, how he had to push!"

"Begging your pardon, suh," Berry agreed. "I did just like the boy here said and I sure meant to help him."

"And you did," I said positively. "All that you could, out here in the field. But we are going to have to make some litters to carry the badly wounded men."

Berry looked blankly at Carter, who turned to look just as blankly at me.

"We don't have any poles," I said, "but a coat stretched over a pair of carbines will make do for a litter."

"Sure enough. I seen one used back at the recruit depot," Jefferson said. "I could put together one, Major Northey, if my hand was working."

"You can show someone with two good hands how to rig a couple of stretchers for Brown and Lee there."

"Yes, suh!" Jefferson said proudly.

"Major," a deep voice boomed up from the prone man. "You going to have me toted all the way back on one of them stretcher litters, facedown?"

I fought the laughter and choked. Berry giggled like a girl. But there was not a smile in Carter.

"We could try to cut it out here," I said. "But all I have to deaden the pain is half a vial of laudanum. The surgeon will likely have morphine."

"Yes, suh. We sure hopes so."

"Good. We will wait for the surgeon then. Private Jefferson, you are in charge of transporting the wounded. Try to find a way to carry this man that will not aggravate his pain."

"We is Private William Benson, suh," the prone man said. "I think if you gives me some of that laudanum, I might stand to have someone quick, like the sergeant, cut that shaft off."

"Here comes the sergeant now," Jefferson said.

Johnson gave the order to dismount and then hurried over to report.

"No hostiles near us, Major. But we counted near thirty

tracks. They left their horses near where we had the first fight and just trotted over here afoot to bedevil us and then trotted back again."

He eyed the arrow shaft protruding from Benson, then, still talking, grasped it between thumb and finger of each hand and snapped it.

Benson howled with rage and pain, and then his basso voice trembling with indignation called out, "Who did that to me? Is he Apache or Comanche or what?"

Jefferson answered, obviously afraid of Johnson, yet too tickled not to say, "That Apache is the Sarge!"

A large seemingly disembodied hand crept up behind Benson's buttocks, felt the splintered arrow shaft and then, gingerly, traced the stump to his buttock. "My head thanks you, Sarge, but my ass is sore."

I laughed along with the men. Only the boy with the high fever and Carter did not join in.

"No horses recovered?" I asked Johnson.

He shook his head, threw the snapped shaft away and answered, "We found two dead, steaks cut out of one. Saw tracks of the other two mixed up with the Apache horses."

"We had better inspect the horses," I said.

There were two horses, blood running from arrows sticking up like flags from their flanks and one from a shoulder. I ordered them thrown and using my clasp knife, as sharp as many a razor, sliced the skin on each side of the arrowhead while Johnson plucked them out like feathers from a chicken. The two horses lay still until their riders urged them to their feet.

The more sorely wounded horse trembled in his skin and his anguished master looked imploringly at me as he held a hand over the new wound, trying to staunch the bright red blood.

My first impulse was to tell him that it was only his horse and not himself that might bleed to death. But then an image flashed in my mind of a young man who had lost his first horse in a battle and had no one to turn to. I had cried, shot my faithful mount, Star, and gone on to fight on foot.

"Trooper," I asked, "will your horse allow you to mount?"

He turned from his horse to look at me. "Yes, suh. But he's bad hurt."

I emptied the contents of my cotton bag onto a blanket and folded the bag once.

"Do you need help to mount, Private—?"

"Private Benjamin Bagley, suh, and I don't need no help. Old Buck here, he's the best horse in the platoon. Maybe the whole company."

"Good horse," I said as Bagley eased himself into the saddle.

I held the cotton sack over the wound and said, "Now press your knee over the bandage and keep it there while we ride back to the post."

"Yes, suh, Major." He was grinning now, unconsciously patting Buck on the neck with his left hand, even as he saluted.

I turned to call Johnson and found him just behind me nodding approval. His approbation warmed me.

"We need the company ambulance to meet us as soon as possible on the way back," I said. "I need a volunteer, one man riding a horse fast enough to outrun any of the Indian ponies."

"Me, suh," Johnson said. And, as I learned later, he was right, for he was the best rider I had ever known and knew horses like no one else.

"No. I need you here. Pick a volunteer."

"I can go, Major Northey," Carter said. "And I exercise Custer whenever the colonel don't ride him enough."

"No," Johnson said. "I'll send Dewey. He's a feather in the saddle and—"

"Major," Carter appealed. "You said that after you killed your best friend and all, you fought twice as hard after to make up. I can ride twice as fast as anybody. I surely can."

"How would you make the ride back?" I asked.

"How, suh?"

"Yes. Tell me what you will take, how you will pace your horse."

"That Custer can run fast and gallop from breakfast to supper. And if the hostiles don't chase me, I'll keep him a loping along until I hit the post." He looked to me, eyebrows raised, waiting for approval.

"Sergeant," I said, "how would you make that ride?"

"Light, suh. Maybe you would lend me that cartridge revolver and then I wouldn't take nothing else. Except a handful of oats and maybe a canteen of water. I'd ride my horse, Abe, and walk him until you can't see me no more and then I gallop that horse and run him if I got to, to get away from the Apaches. But once I outruns them, I stands up in the stirrups and helps that horse trot to the Big Rock water hole. After we rests a bit and drinks some, and walks and drinks some more, then we gallops to the post."

"I gets there in four hours, Major," Carter said. "Custer and me don't need no water and no guns neither."

"Sergeant, your reasoning is excellent."

Carter's eyes misted and he choked back a sob. I unbuckled my damaged but serviceable gun belt and handed it to Carter. "It has six loads," I said.

"Listen carefully to Sergeant Johnson and do exactly as he says." I turned to Johnson and asked, "Should he take your horse or Custer?"

Johnson bit out the words. "Take Abe."

"I can get there quicker with Custer," Carter said to me, looking at Johnson out of the corner of his eye.

"No! Abe, it is. Carter, when you ride out, we will start back at a slow walk, carrying the wounded on litters. I will want the ambulance and if the surgeon is at the post, he should come along with the medicines that we will need. You can tell him that we have men badly wounded by arrows and bullets."

"I will give you a note to Captain— Colonel Whigam," I said. "If he is not there, give it to Lieutenant Barragan."

While Carter switched saddles with Johnson, I wrote a brief communique describing our situation, folded it and watched Carter place it carefully inside his jacket. He looped my gun belt over his shoulder and mounted the large raw-boned gelding that Johnson had named Abe.

When we were assembled for the march back, flankers out and outriders in front, Carter rode at a fast walk until he was with the lead rider. There was a high mesa a few miles ahead. As soon as we reached it, Carter was to gallop Abe through its shadow. Then, once in the clear open country beyond, trot the strong black gelding to the water hole some twenty miles north, water and rest the horse, and then gallop the three or four miles to the post.

It was a good plan and would have worked if Carter had not, an hour before we reached the mountain's shadow, suddenly shouted defiantly and spurred his mount into a dead run.

The last we saw of that poor demon-driven young man alive, he was leaning low over the pommel of his saddle, a shadow of a windblown dark cloud flying over a pale desert. A few minutes later a flanker trotted back to hand me my gun belt with the flap snapped over my revolver. He had found it dangling from a cactus arm.

# Five

The lightly wounded, myself included, rode. The others, excepting young Bagley, who kept the bandage compressed against his horse's right shoulder with his own right knee, and the flankers, walked. The stretcher bearers for the three seriously wounded rotated every half hour. The flankers changed horses at the same time.

I consulted my watch and waited until the minute hand reached the bottom. As it did, I heard Johnson call out, "Stretcher bearers change! Relieve the flankers!"

I reined in, still amazed at the clock inside Johnson's head, then walked Custer over by Bagley and asked him to lift his leg. The bandage was crusted with dried blood. He looked at me anxiously until I said, "It seems that old Buck has stopped bleeding. You can join the walkers now, Private Bagley."

"Yes, suh, Major suh!"

He fairly flew from the saddle to inspect the wound.

"Let it alone," I warned. "When we get back, you can soak away the bandage with warm water."

I left him stroking his horse, smiling, to inspect the men in the makeshift stretchers.

Daniel Berry, our unofficial surgeon, was inspecting Lee, who, in his delirium, had fought off the troopers until he had collapsed. They had then tied him into a stretcher.

Berry seemed puzzled, then placed his ear to Lee's chest. When the new men slipped into place, Berry looked up at me and shook his head. He looked down at Brown and said, "Jimmy, you is doing just fine."

"Pappy!" Benson, lying on his side, was trying to rise, but the men changing place were pushing him back. "Tell these cotton pickers that I ain't going to ride no more carbine. It ain't long enough. I would rather walk. I would!"

Johnson strode over, glanced down at Benson and bent over him.

"No, Sergeant. I ain't complaining. You leave that arrow alone. Hear?"

"Come lend a hand, Pappy," Johnson said.

Benson shrieked, "No!"

Johnson grasped his right leg and lifted while Berry took the other. Benson wrapped an arm around each man's neck and sighed loudly, musically, in relief.

"Oh that do feel better, Sergeant. Let me off at the infirmary."

"Riley," Johnson called out, "get over here and take my place. Long Straw, you takes Pappy's place. Now!"

The switch was quick and elicited only one groan from Benson. The flankers were relieved and dismounted to lead their horses in close to the column. I looked at my watch again. Carter had left just after dawn. Perhaps Carter had flung the heavy revolver away, not just in a gesture of despair, but to give Johnson's horse a better chance to stay ahead of the Apaches. He had left just after dawn. Maybe Johnson's horse had outrun the Apaches and he might very well have reached the post two hours ago. If Whigam reacted swiftly and sent riders on ahead of the ambulance, we should be seeing their dust trail anytime now.

"Sergeant, take one of the fresher horses and ride on up a way with me."

He saluted and called for Bottom, which signaled general laughter and ribald comments, for that mount just happened to belong to the man with the arrowhead in his buttocks, Private William Benson. His new name, once his recovery was assured, would be Bottom Benson.

Once we had moved up ahead of the column, I took out my journal and checked the map I had sketched on our ride out. The water hole should have been about eight miles at a bearing of north by northwest.

I reined in Custer. Johnson pulled up alongside. I held the paper up for him to see.

"I calculate that we are no more than two hours from the water. There." I pointed a finger at the map.

"I don't read no maps, Major, but the water hole is about two hours all right, horse walking, but them men carrying the litters, ain't going to be there in no two hours."

I nodded agreement, pulled out my compass and took cross sights from distant blue peaks. I moved my position up three miles closer to the water and then, replacing compass and journal in the pommel saddlebag, lifted my right arm high and then swung it left to point out the slightly altered course to the water hole.

A cheer erupted from the men. Bewildered, I looked back at them and then, when I saw that they were looking past me, swung around in the saddle to see a swirl of dust that just might have been made by the rugged curtained wagon that was our ambulance. I lifted my glasses and focused on the dust trail. But when I followed the thin line down, I lost it in the heavy green thorn and bush of the ground cover.

Corporal Green caught up with us, trotting on foot.

"Suh," he said quickly, "the men wants to be drinking the last of their water."

Johnson turned to look back at the men, some of them with canteens already tipped up high.

"Anybody got any water left, pass it on to Pappy Berry for them that can't carry extra water in their canteens!"

"Major?" Green looked up at me for confirmation.

I handed down my canteen. "I suppose there might be a couple of swallows in that." The wounded would need more

water. I turned away and motioned for Johnson to ride alongside me.

"That dust is moving away, up into the foothills. That ain't
no ambulance, Major," Johnson said.

He was right. But then, we would not have to fight for water
and that had preoccupied me. I used the glasses, but could see
that Johnson's prediction was correct. Unless they were using
a decoy to throw us off guard, we would have water in another
hour.

"Do you think they might damage the water? Poison it?"

"No, suh. They got to have that water just like we do. But
they might ambush us. Except it's open there and they know
about the Spencers shooting fast."

"Fast, yes. Maybe if we could get some ammunition money
for practice on the range, the Apaches might learn we can
shoot straight, too."

He nodded, but he was a realist and knew the chances of
firing practice ammunition was as likely as a pay raise.

"I wonder if the men might chip in to buy ammunition for
target practice?"

No answer.

"Of course you will receive sergeant's pay from the day we
went on patrol," I said.

"Yes, suh."

"Well," I said defensively, "it is six dollars more than Private Johnson earned."

"Yes, suh. I wonder how many cartridges I could buy with
that six dollars. Enough for a platoon or a file."

I was wondering how we might use the company money to
finance target practice when Corporal Green reported.

"Suh. Private John Lee convulsed and Private Berry says
he is dead."

This time Johnson waited for me to answer.

"Blindfold a horse and lay the body across the saddle. When
the horse quiets down, take off the blindfold and lead him

along behind the rest. Tell the men that we will be at the water hole soon."

"Yes, suh." Green saluted, but when I returned his salute, he stood there, obviously not through yet.

"What is it?"

"The ambulance, suh? That wasn't our wagon?"

"No. I suppose that it will be along soon. Probably while we rest at the water hole."

He nodded bleakly, saluted again, and trotted back to the column.

We were still together, Johnson and I, slightly ahead of the column, when we first saw the buzzards, mostly still circling, but as we rode up, a few were dropping down to feed.

The buzzards hopped awkwardly away and then beat their black wings to gain air space before they settled down nearby, waiting.

We could not expect the ambulance for our messenger, Private Henry Carter, lay spread-eagled across the trail that we had made on our ride out. He had been stripped and mutilated. I thought it curious that they had left his red undershirt intact while ripping away his other clothes until I realized that he had been flayed from shoulder to waist. I gagged and turned away. I never think of that day without seeing that piece of butchered flesh, black and red, against the gray desert floor.

The meaning was clear. A sign had been posted for us to read. *Beware! If you invade Apache land, this is what happens to you.*

My platoon lurched up to the dead man. Even the stretcher bearers crowded in. There were men who retched and others who cried. Some cursed and some trembled.

"Form a perimeter!" I shouted. "Be ready to fire. Expect an attack!"

There was no reaction to my order. I drew my revolver and fired a shot into the air.

"Sergeant Johnson," I said angrily, "is this a gang of slaves pretending to be troopers in the Ninth cavalry?"

"You Goddamn recruits," Johnson roared. "You hear the major? Move your asses, now!"

He walked his horse around the rapidly deploying men, looking each one in the face. When they were all in their places, he moved the stretcher bearers up near the front of the line and then called to Corporal Green.

"Bring me a blanket to wrap this trooper in and a horse to tie him on."

Green hurried up with a blanket, followed by Benjamin Bagley and Daniel Berry. "Buck will pack anything I ask him to, Major," Bagley said, "wounded or not."

Johnson dismounted and turned the body over to roll it onto the blanket. I was pleased to see two broken shafted arrows sticking into his back.

"You men," I said. "You see these arrows? Carter was dead when they mutilated his body. They do that to scare the green recruits, but that trick will not work with the men of the Ninth, will it?"

"No, sir," Green and Bagley answered simultaneously. Berry nodded, but whether in assent, or mere recognition of my observation, I could not tell.

"Good," I said. "Bring up the horse. And tell the others about the arrows."

They said they would, saluted and trotted back for old Buck.

"I won't let on to anyone, Major," Johnson said softly. "I mean about Carter being dead while they was cutting him up."

"What?" I asked.

"Oh," he said hastily, taking my surprise for censure. "I surely does agree. It won't do to let the recruits know. It is too big a dose of medicine now. They needs some seasoning."

"What makes you so sure he was not dead?"

"Why, Major, them buzzards just settled down as we rode up. Them arrows was used to prop him up so as he could see us ride up. Them arrows was not in deep enough to kill."

I spurred the colonel's big black horse so hard that he jumped and then ran far ahead before I could bring horse and rider under control and rejoin the slowly moving troopers, mounted and walking, wounded and dead.

# Six

"Amputate. Of course. Cut it off. No good to you. I have ample chloroform and ether. An excellent mix. You will not feel the steel on your skin, let alone the teeth of the saw on the bone."

"You are persuasive and poetic, Dr. Smith. What a beautiful phrase, 'teeth of the saw on the bone.' But," I added hastily as he began to nod in agreement, "I shall keep the leg for a while yet."

"I tell you, sir, that you will limp and you will be in pain and the vital internal fluids will surely be drawn into that diseased leg generating even worse pain and—"

"Yes. And how is the other wound, the new one?"

"Oh that." He sniffed. "As well as can be expected on *that* leg."

"Well"—I shrugged—"I have only the two legs and if I must be shot in one of them, it might as well be the bad one."

I smiled broadly to invite him to share the joke, but the man had no humor in him.

"Sheer folly to keep it."

I wriggled back and up against the adobe wall to a sitting position and then swung my legs off the rough workbench that was now both the surgeon's examination and operating table. He held my pantaloon's legs for me. I slid into them, eased down onto the floor and stood up. The floor was pleasantly cool to my bare feet. Strangely enough the new wound smarted, but my old battle-weary leg felt just fine.

"Doctor," Sullivan called out, "might me and the ladies come in and visit?"

Smith called out a nasal affirmative. I shouted negatively, but they did not hear—or ignored me. I barely had time to slip the braces over my shoulders as the three ladies, followed by George Sullivan, swept into the room.

Adele wrinkled her nose at the strong odor of turpentine and arnica. Her sister, Mary, shook her head at the cluttered and dirty room. Raquel looked up at me and smiled to see me struggling into my coat and then down at my bare feet and said, "If we have a formal inspection, Major, you should have your feet blacked."

"William"—Sullivan suppressed a smile—"let me help you." He bent down and as I leaned against him, held my right boot out straight from my leg and then slid the boot on much like running a sheath up onto a sword. My left leg was no problem.

"Thank you, George," I said.

"Think nothing of it. It is not every day that we have a wounded hero in our midst."

"I would not say that."

"Neither would I," Smith said. "And I put it to you, sir, neither did the colonel. Four dead and half a dozen wounded."

"Three dead, Doctor," Raquel said. "You will surely save that poor boy."

No one could have said no to that aura of loveliness with the voice of an angel. Except that insensitive surgeon.

"If anyone can, I will," Smith said, but he still shook his head.

"And unless you count the horses," Mary Sullivan said, looking straight at the surgeon, "there are three slightly wounded and only the one badly."

"But not one casualty among the savages." Smith shrugged off the discrepancy.

"We shot one mortally and wounded another," I said.

"But you brought back no proof. Not even a scalp." Smith turned up the corner of his mouth and looked sideways at Adele.

"No opportunity," I said, beginning to lose control. "And we certainly did wound at least one."

"You wounded savages? What wounded? Where?"

The man had an impenetrable skin. It would have taken an Apache arrow to get his attention. Very well, I thought. An arrow it shall be.

"They took their wounded back to a medicine man," I said. "He does not amputate, but then he has no degree from Boston. Of course, he has no need of a saw, for he cures the whole man."

I stopped abruptly, embarrassed and determined not to let the little man arouse me further.

"If the doctor had any experience with Apaches," Raquel said, "he would know that the Apaches never leave a warrior to the enemy, dead or alive."

"Nor do we, Mrs. Barragan," I said.

"And that poor man, the courier," Adele asked, cocking her head at me as if to facilitate my answer, "was he badly tortured?"

"No!" I answered quickly before the surgeon could open his mouth and I looked straight at him as I spoke. "He was killed instantly by the two arrows that struck him in the back. Correct, Dr. Smith?"

"Why, yes, but none of the arrows did penetrate the—"

"Thank you, Doctor," I said.

"The poor lad," Mary Sullivan sniffed. "Still it was a merciful death. Worse could happen to you, George Sullivan, if you go traipsing off into their country a looking for a mine of gold."

"Silver," Smith corrected her. "A lost silver mine."

"Now, Dr. Smith, my dear man," George said, burlesquing his own rich brogue, "if I know where it is, then it sure ain't lost, now is it?"

"Well I remember years ago," Adele said, "I was just a child and George was already talking about lost mines, silver or gold."

"Silver!" Smith said.

"A stockholder?" I asked and Smith muttered what I took to be an affirmative.

"I would be honored to have you join us," Sullivan said seriously.

"I have no money," I said.

"You are a fighting man, sir. And I am afraid that we shall have to fight for our mine if we want to be rich in this life."

"Do not encourage him, Major. Please." Mary Sullivan looked up at me fearfully.

"I can refuse you nothing," I said to her and then turned to her husband. "However, George, I too have a mine, gold and silver, I believe, somewhere west in Arizona. I could trade, but I would have to have something to boot. For the gold."

"Sure and that's fair. But what could I offer?" He glanced slyly at his wife and sister-in-law and then nodding as if he had resolved a weighty problem, said, "I could give you Adele, I suppose. Or that mule I traded for yesterday. Although to be honest with you, neither one is broken."

"George!" Adele shrieked, but she was giggling, obviously enjoying the attention.

"I would certainly prefer the lady," I said, "even if the mule were trained."

"Major Northey!" Adele exclaimed, in mock modesty for her eyes were wide with expectation.

"Now, William," Sullivan said. "Suppose the mule is trained to the pack and the saddle."

"Well," I said musingly. "A good riding mule is very hard to find."

"I do not care for a mule," Smith said. "Stiff-legged, hard riding and stubborn."

"Adele," Sullivan said, "would not be hard—"

"George!" Mary spoke sharply. Although Sullivan did shut

his mouth, I could see he wanted to let the other word pop out.

His wife took his arm firmly and said good-bye. George shrugged helplessly, but did manage to say, "If you're serious about the mine in the west, we might exchange stock," before Mary marched him off.

"Have you thought of a walk round the shady side of the post, Ideal?" Smith asked.

"Yes, I have," Adele said and moved to take my arm. "Would you like to walk me around the post, Major?"

I glanced at Raquel Barragan and lost myself in the turquoise depths of her eyes. I wondered why she could not have been the single one and Adele the married. But it was Adele who tugged at my arm. I turned to her, managed a smile and took a tentative step.

I made no sound, but I must have winced, for Raquel lifted a hand and said, "I think the major is not quite ready yet for a promenade, Adele, even with a beautiful young lady."

"Of course, dear," Adele simpered. "I guess, Major, I will just have to wait until your wounds are healed."

"It will be my pleasure," I said and then added, "in any case, I have to give a class here in just a few minutes."

"A class. What kind of a class?" Smith turned his head like a parrot to better view me.

"Just simple reading and writing."

"Oh," Raquel said. "Then you will teach Sergeant Johnson to read and write?"

"I fervently hope so. And a corporal and a few privates as well. The dean of this college has decided that the dull-witted professor can manage no more."

"And who is the dean that calls the professor dull-witted?"

When Raquel spoke, the rich timbre of her voice with just a trace of an accent seemed to give even common words an exotic sound.

"Unfortunately, I am president, dean and dull-witted professor."

"Don't pay to be too hard on yourself," Smith said. "You are likely smart enough to teach the colored.

"Let us go, Ideal." Smith offered her his arm, but she came to me again and held out her hand to me. I bent over and kissed it. She let it lie in my hand for a long count. When she withdrew it suddenly, it felt like the escape of a lightly held bird.

Ideal Adele stood up on her toes, kissed my cheek and turned to hurry out with the doctor, who turned his head halfway around to glare at me as they left.

"Would you permit a get-well kiss from an old married woman?" Raquel Barragan, ten years my junior, said. There was a fluttering as of butterfly wings on my cheek and a scent of lilac. Then she was gone in a swirl of blue cloth with a tinge of scarlet at her neck. I limped to the door to watch her walk away, back to the house that she shared with Lieutenant Peter Barragan.

I listened to retreat, then lit the coal-oil lamp that hung above the operating table which had just become my lectern.

Private Leroy Dewey was the first by five minutes. He was always the first man to arrive for muster, for mess and even for extra duty. Small, even for a cavalryman, he was the rider chosen to represent the company in the unofficial regimental races. He usually arrived first in these competitions too. As I was to learn, his company name was Too Soon Dewey. He was darker than most, but his high cheekbones and thin nose gave his face an Oriental cast.

After the military formalities, I sat him down at the table I had recently vacated. On the table were five plate-sized fragments of slate and a cigar box filled with shards of plaster which I had decided to call chalk.

"Suh?" Dewey squirmed in his seat, and drew fine lines with his chalk.

"Yes?"

"Is you all right, Major, suh?"

"Yes, I am. You remember I was just touched by a bullet."

"I knows. I was the one what had the bandage ready."

"I don't remember that," I said, puzzled.

"Well, I did, but then we all got too busy and you bandaged yourself so I stuck it back inside my jacket."

"Thank you. You kept your head."

I took up a slate and a stub of chalk, but he obviously wanted to say something else, but seemed too embarrassed to continue.

"Do you want to tell me something else?"

He looked down and said, "I only wants to tell you that all of us are glad that you is our platoon officer. We specially likes not leaving no wounded, not even dead, troopers behind."

"You can tell the men that I am also pleased with them."

A trooper appeared at the door. He saluted smartly and then asked, "Lieutenant, suh, is this reading just for the first platoon?"

Dewey, eyes blazing turned to face the trooper. "This here is Major Northey, you dumb nigger."

"Sorry, suh." He looked at the silver bar on my shoulder board and added, "I thought you was a first lieutenant."

"Corporal Tadpole Logan, you is—" Dewey raged. I quickly cut him off in midsentence.

"You are right, Corporal Logan. I am a first lieutenant in the United States Army. During the War, I was a brevet major. When I am called major, it is merely a courtesy, an honorary title."

Logan smiled maliciously at Dewey. "Dumb nigger, your own self. You heard the lieutenant."

"Tadpole," Dewey said, eyes glittering, "I is going to separate your head from your tail."

Logan, a third again as heavy and taller than Dewey held his hands up protectively and took a step back.

"Enough!" I turned on my parade-ground voice and both men jumped to attention.

"Major Northey, suh." Johnson stood in the doorway. "I have a couple of saddles that might fit these mules, suh. I could fill the saddlebags with horseshoes and trot them around the parade ground until taps."

His voice had a note of supplication that worried me.

"We shall see after we finish our class. Sit down, Sergeant, and help yourself to a slate and chalk."

He sat down, but looked puzzled when Dewey handed him a triangular slate and a thumb-sized piece of plaster.

I held a slate in my left hand so that they could see it clearly. "I am going to write three letters on this slate to make a word that you all know and one that you say to an officer every day." As I wrote, I pronounced each letter. *"S. I. R.* same as Sir. When you write them in this same order, they mean sir."

"Them marks mean suh?" Dewey asked, frowning.

"Yes." I sounded them out. *"S. I. R."*

Dewey muttered to himself, then he grinned. "It means suh, when you say it, Major."

"Right, Dewey. If you say it the way I do, it means sir. Each letter has a sound that spells out a word we know. The way you write the letters to make a word, that is, to make the sounds for a word is to spell them."

"Sir," Dewey said, his eyes shining with knowledge. *"S. I. R.,* sir. Yes, suh!"

"Dewey?"

"Yes, suh." His voice rang with confidence. "I draws them pictures and it means you."

He grinned widely. He was enlightened and ached to enlighten the uninformed world, but he caught my warning glance and with a great effort, shut his mouth.

"Johnson?"

"Ain't no use, Major. My head don't hold writing."

"It will. Now hold your chalk the way I hold mine. See?"

When he had a reasonable grip on the odd piece of "chalk" I drew an *s* and called it a snake. Then the *i,* a bayonet and last, the *r,* a horse's ass and tail.

I thought it would prove to be difficult and it was. Dewey managed a fair copy after three tries, and Lee after half a dozen, but Johnson could not. He stared down at the slate with unseeing eyes, shaking his head slowly, breathing shallowly with wrinkles of pain in his forehead, much like my own when my leg sent white-hot pangs into my brain.

"Are you well, Sergeant?" I asked.

"It's the writing, Major. It hurts me."

"Hurts? That snake bit you, Sarge?" Logan frowned, an exaggerated woeful countenance, but a laugh was already twitching at his lips.

Dewey opened his mouth into a long oval to match his long face and waited, as did I, for Johnson to act.

"I suppose it did. Yes. I don't figure them marks and I just a-wasting time."

It was my turn to be left open-mouthed and speechless.

Logan grinned then and laughed tentatively, inviting me and Dewey to join in. My mouth snapped shut and before I could open it again to speak, Johnson stood up at attention.

"Major Northey, sir." The *r* was as crisp as my own. He might not write an *r,* but he could certainly pronounce one. "Permission to return to duty. Sir."

"Duty? This school is on your free time."

"I teaches the newest recruits horse handling, sir."

"Teaches. You is a teacher?" Logan said.

"Major?" Johnson ignored the corporal.

"You can change the hours of your other class, Johnson. Sit down."

Johnson sat down.

"This class is of course voluntary. No one has to attend. However, the noncommissioned officers in this company will one day be literate or privates."

Logan, now the self-appointed classroom wit, grinned and opened his mouth to speak. And open it stayed, for I put a bite on my words and stared directly at him,

"Corporal Logan, we are not going to worry much about army protocol here in the classroom, but I will not tolerate disparaging remarks either. However, when we find someone with knowledge or experience that he wishes to share with us, we will be overjoyed. Proceed."

Logan shrunk in his seat, suddenly preoccupied with his shoes. I wondered if one of them might fit in his mouth. Dewey blinked at me and said nothing. Johnson might have been one of the postwar statues had he been a white colonel mounted on a rearing horse instead of a black sergeant seated on a chair, a broken plate in one hand and a shred of plaster in the other.

At the end of the hour, I checked their slates. Dewey, smiling slightly was handling the chalk familiarly, fashioning small letters. Logan, obviously bored, wrote large clumsy letters. The one three-letter word filled his entire slate. Johnson moved the chalk up and down as a blind man might, his slate filled with vertical lines.

"Class dismissed," I said.

Johnson jumped to his feet at attention and saluted. "Yes, sir."

Logan stood up and saluted. I returned their salutes and they left quickly, Johnson first.

Dewey cleaned his slate. He stood up, saluted. "Could I come in later to practice?"

"Of course you can, Dewey."

"Thank you, sir." When I did not return his salute, he looked puzzled, then asked, "I done something dumb again, sir?"

"Not that it cannot be remedied. Here in the school you may write with your left hand, but when school is over, you are back in the army and while the army graciously allows you to write and eat and even brush your hair left-handed, it insists that you shoot—and salute—right-handed."

And so the first day of my school ended. Young Dewey already knew and strongly desired to learn and literacy would be a step on a long journey with him. One man, Logan knew, or thought he did, that the road to rank and power, was to appear to be what his officers wanted and that seemed to be literate. The third, the enigmatic Sergeant Johnson, obviously equal and likely superior in intellect to the other two, could not even begin to learn. Had I known more then or had I the intuition of that strange beautiful lady, Raquel Barragan, what course might all of our lives have taken rather than that tangled trail which led us all to such glory and tragedy?

# Seven

"Now these horses ain't recruits like you all, but they ain't cavalry yet neither."

Johnson felt my presence, but as he turned, I called out, "Carry on, Sergeant."

He nodded and swung around to face seven men dressed for stable duty.

"The strategy is that you and the horses are going to go through this school together. You will train your own mount and break him from bad habits and he likely will kick a few bad ones out of you."

Dewey led a horse from outside the corral and handed the lead rope to Johnson. He led it easily around the corral. Johnson nodded his head in approval. Dewey retrieved the horse, trotted out, led the horse away and then came back pulling the lead of a snorting, neck-arched gelding, black, but with a touch of white on both front feet.

Johnson took the lead rope from Dewey, who stepped nimbly aside. Johnson held the rope gently, but firmly. He tapped the horse in the chest with his crop and tugged gently. When the horse yanked its head away and backed up a step, he followed quietly, rapping the crop sharply against the gelding's neck. The horse planted all four feet, but did not move back. Johnson spoke softly, slowly as he increased the pressure on the guide rope. The horse took a step forward to ease the pressure on his halter.

"That's my boy. You are a good horse. A fine mount. Yes, suh. Sam will be a fine mount for the United States Cavalry." Johnson did not quite sing the words, but it was as much a lullaby as a speech.

As he led the horse around the ring, it occurred to me that he was following the official cavalry manual written by General Saint George-Cooke just before the War. I wondered if the sergeant had read the manual and immediately dismissed the vagrant thought. Was I not trying to teach the man to read?

"Good work, Sergeant," I said. "Who taught you horse handling?"

Johnson turned the horse over to Dewey and turned to answer me.

"The colonel, sir."

"What colonel would that be?"

"Why, our colonel, Whigam, sir."

"Colonel Whigam!"

"No need to shout, Major. What is it?"

I turned and saluted. Whigam had magically appeared behind me. "Nothing, sir. I just found out that you taught Johnson his superb equestrian skills."

"Yes, I suppose I did." He waved a casual salute at me. "Did you bet me a case of champagne that I could not?"

"No, sir," I said, puzzled. "I didn't know you then."

"You did not?" He seemed surprised. He turned to Johnson. "What year was that, Sergeant?"

"The year I transferred from the infantry. I got to keep my stripes. I was a corporal then."

"Three years ago?" I asked.

"Three years, four months and fourteen days."

"Remarkable memory," I said. "Do you know arithmetic?"

"No, sir. I knows the numbers but I can't write them."

"No," Whigam said ruefully. "He cannot write them. Can he, Major?" he added sharply, looking at me.

"No, not yet, sir."

"Then what is it that you wanted?"

"Nothing, Colonel. I thought that you might have wanted to speak to me."

"I did," he said thoughtfully and then added casually, "you are the commanding officer here."

"What?"

"Yes, but do not get too used to it. I will be back from Santa Fe soon."

"Will you be gone long?"

"A week likely. I shall be bringing back Mrs. Whigam for an indefinite stay."

"That will be good news for the other ladies."

"Perhaps." He waved a hand at Johnson, saying, "Proceed, Sergeant" and led me away from the corral. "My wife is a most sensitive lady, who finds it difficult to exist even in the relatively civilized city of Santa Fe."

"I am sure that the ladies will do their best to make her stay here an agreeable one. Mrs. Sullivan is such a pleasant lady and Mrs. Barragan is, I believe, quite well educated and reads avidly in both English and Spanish."

He shook his head in negation. "It is the Latin heritage of immorality that upsets her the most and then of course the religious thing. They are mostly Papist, you know."

"A great number of Catholics fought with us in the War and then the Sullivans are also Catholic."

"And," he said, smiling as he made a point, "so are the Barragans!"

I saw no need to comment further and stood still, waiting.

"I will take a small escort and the ambulance with me. I have scheduled no daily patrols, but you should see that our presence is not unnoticed. Do not send out patrols on a routine schedule and vary the routes."

"Yes, sir."

"My trip is not an official one, so do not make any reports in which my absence is noted."

"But Colonel Whigam!" I was astonished. "I can't report you as present."

"No," he agreed, "but you do not have to report me as absent, either."

I cocked my head as I tried to formulate an answer, but by the time I had decided to ask for written confirmation of my status as the temporary commanding officer, he had strode off. His escort moved out from the stable area, along with the ambulance.

His horse, Custer, was held by a trooper. I called out after Whigam, wanting to clarify, at least orally, my orders, but he broke into a trot, swung up on Custer and, contrary to usual procedure, left the post at a gallop. The ambulance swayed and bounced as the driver whipped the team into a run to keep up with his escort.

The colonel's office was a model of neatness and order. Not a single paper cluttered his desktop. Even the ink bottle was tightly corked and the pen nib showed not even a dried spot of ink. I found out why when, looking for the daily order, I opened a desk drawer.

It was jammed shut. I wriggled it back and forth and pulled slowly, an inch at a time, until it opened a couple of inches and I was able to remove, a sheet at a time, the documents that had been jammed inside. I knew immediately that I would never get all the paper back in and called for the orderly to bring me whatever containers he could find so that I could sort the papers into what must be kept at hand and the rest which might be stored or destroyed.

Beginning with the latest, a two-week-old requisition for supplies, I was struck by the penmanship, easily the most legible hand that I had read in my career in the army. It was not a long list. One barrel of desiccated potatoes, two fifty-pound sacks of beans, a barrel of salt pork, twenty pounds of coffee beans, a fifty-pound sack of sugar and four cases of hard bread. The last would probably have entered the army about the same time as I.

An addition had been made in another hand—likely that of Whigam—for a hundred-and-twenty-five-pound sack of dried apples. I added four slates and a box of chalk, signed the form and called the orderly.

Peter Barragan came in right after the orderly, waited politely, then saluted and said, "Good morning, Major."

I replied and then held the paper up for him to see and said, "You write beautifully, Peter. Is there a copy somewhere in this paper mountain?"

"Yes, there should be and I will pass on your comments to my clerk."

"You have a clerk?"

"Raquel. My wife. It is her hand that forms such beautiful letters, not mine."

"What a beautiful hand," I blurted out and then felt the blood heat my cheeks as she entered the office, smiling.

"Thank you, Major Northey. If I can help, please call on me. I have too much spare time."

"That is gracious of you," I said and looked straight into her eyes and again for an instant lost myself in those deep pools of shifting shades of turquoise. I wrenched my eyes away, ashamed. I had been too long without female society, I thought, and turned resolutely to Peter.

"As a result of my temporary change of duty, you will have to be the acting officer of the day until the colonel returns."

"But, Major, I am ready now to take out the patrol. The men are assembled and—" He broke off, comprehension brightening his pale blue eyes. "The colonel did not tell you."

"He gave you the order just before he left?"

"Yes, sir."

"I shall not countermand the colonel's order. I will assume the duties of the officer of the day until your return."

"I might take Peter's place." Raquel smiled. "I know the routine as well as he does."

"I am sure that you do. However, I think that even the rawest recruit will note the difference."

She laughed merrily, but Peter became most military. I assumed then that it was because of the patrol and its obvious danger.

"I have your permission to depart, sir?"

"Of course, once you acquaint me with your route and calendar."

He drew a paper from inside his short cavalry jacket, unfolded it, pushed one of the piles of paper aside and placed it on my desk. It was a rough map with compass directions, distances and times. It was basically the same route that I had followed when we were ambushed, except that Barragan would follow it in reverse. It seemed a reasonable tactic if the Apaches did not learn the patrol location as soon as it passed the first water hole.

"Excellent. Perhaps you might make the first leg a short one and then travel at night."

"Yes. They do not stir about much at night." His voice rose. "If only we could punish one band. Just hit one group hard enough so that they would take us seriously!"

"And they do not now?" I asked, smiling.

"Sorry, sir. I did not mean to imply—"

"Nonsense!" I cut him off. "They do not take us any more seriously than our battle-oriented officers do the Apaches. But I think that we here can change both opinions."

"You are right. We do need a new approach. If we could only find them as easily as they locate us."

"I wrote the request for a Navajo scout," Raquel said, looking at her husband.

"And I delivered it and the copy to the colonel," Peter said.

"I did not find any papers predating the requisition for supplies," I said, somewhat querulously.

"The colonel probably took them along with him to deliver personally."

"But he is going to Santa Fe unofficially."

"Still," Peter said, "I suspect that he will—officially or otherwise—send the request on its way."

"Let us hope that the request is granted."

"Yes, sir. Am I at liberty to proceed?"

"Yes and good luck."

He saluted and then, taking Raquel by the arm, escorted her from the office. I waited a few minutes and then stepped out onto the porch to watch the patrol leave. Peter swung up into the saddle of his mount, Diablo, the fastest horse in the company now that Sergeant Johnson's horse had been killed.

He motioned to Raquel. Then as she stood closely, he leaned low to grasp her by a shoulder and speak. She twisted free and turned toward me, almost running, then the grimace as if of pain changed to a too-wide smile like the one painted on those fragile china dolls that wealthy parents give their daughters.

Peter stood straight in the stirrups, his rigid body an exclamation mark at the end of an angry sentence. When she did not look back, he lifted an arm in signal and the patrol moved out. But not in a fast walk. I saw Peter lift his right arm high and crack his whip across Diablo's flank. He left the post at a run, much like Whigam had done earlier. Some of the horses bolted and others changed gaits from walk to trot. In any case, a huge cloud of dust rose and I thought that we might as well have sent the Apaches a telegram advising them of our intentions. But then, I thought, that is just what we had done. That dust cloud was quicker and more graphic than any telegram.

# Eight

Late in the afternoon of the first Friday of my temporary command, Sergeant Johnson came into my office with a peculiar request.

"Some of the men from our platoon would like passes, suh."

"Passes? Where on earth would they go?"

"They has heard of what we calls a frolic farm?" When I did not comment, he added, "It is a Mexican place. They call it a cantina and they don't mind if us colored drinks and dances with the girls."

"And I suppose that a sergeant will have to accompany them to keep order." I smiled, but when he replied, he was deadly serious.

"I certainly should go with them, Major. But then that leaves you without no help at all."

"Right. I do need you here. Do you think it proper for the men to go to that farm—that is the cantina?"

"Yes, suh, I surely do, for they ain't had no time off post since we been here."

I looked at the duty roster. Whigam had taken Sergeant Blaine of the second platoon with him. The other acting sergeant, my clownish pupil, "Tadpole" Logan, was out on patrol with Peter Barragan.

"How far is this cantina?"

"Two hours, suh. South and east. Some calls it the Water Hole Cantina."

"All right. Corporal Green will be in charge. He will not drink and will be responsible for getting the men back for reveille. They may leave right after the roll call at retreat."

"Yes, suh! I will tell them right after I check the guard."

Just after retreat, at sundown, seven men, led by Corporal Green, rode out of the post. I listened for the change of pace and heard the horses break into a trot. Most of the men had been with me on the patrol and I could imagine their wide anticipatory grins and high-spirited braggings.

Back in my office, I lit a lamp and wrote the entry for the roll call at sunset and entered the names of the men who had been granted passes for recreation outside the post.

I blotted the sheet just as Private Dewey entered. He started to salute with his left hand, then jerked his hand down and saluted with his right hand. I returned his salute and asked him to state his business.

"School, sir. You said every day except Saturday and Sunday and today is Friday."

"Correct, Dewey, However it seems that I am both commanding officer and officer of the day, which means no schoolteacher."

"Well, Sergeant Johnson could be the officer of the day and the commanding one too for a bit while you teaches the school."

I laughed and shook my head. "Johnson is a noncommissioned officer, a sergeant. The officer of the day must be a commissioned officer."

"Couldn't you commission him then?"

I started to say no automatically, but then thought better. Why not name Johnson as my officer of the day until one of the other officers returned?

"Bring Sergeant Johnson here, Private Dewey. On the double. Run!"

He threw a quick left-handed salute and sprinted out of the door.

They were back within seconds. Johnson must have been at the guardhouse just across the square.

I returned the salutes and answered the question posed by Johnson's quizzical "Sir?"

"I need your help. Sit down."

"Suh?"

Johnson, rattled by my unorthodox invitation, lost the crisp *r* that he had cultivated. Leroy snickered and then promptly sat down in the only other chair, aside from the one in back of the desk.

"Get your black ass off that chair, *Dewey,* and fetch another chair. Run!"

Dewey shot from the chair and ran backward out of the office.

"Sorry about my bad words, sir," Johnson apologized. "Sometimes I has to get their attention."

"When I was a sergeant, I called them dumb sons of bitches. After a while it became almost a term of affection."

"Yes, sir." The crisp *r* was back. "That's it. A term of affection."

"Are you familiar with the duties of the officer of the day?"

"Yes, sir."

"Good. You have the job."

"You want me to help out, sir?"

"No, I want you to be the officer of the day while I pretend to be the company commander."

"But you is the company commander."

"Acting."

"But acting or not, you is still the company commander."

"And you will be the acting officer of the day."

"But what if I has to report to some officer?"

"Let's try it. Sergeant Johnson, acting officer of the day, what is the state of the post?"

"The guard is posted. There are no prisoners. The second platoon is in the field. Colonel Whigam and his escort, six men from the second file, first platoon. The first file of the first platoon, except for Private Dewey are off the post. There are no prisoners. Corporal Brown and Private Bagley are in the infirmary."

"Excellent. State your name, rank and present position."

"Sergeant George Johnson, sir, acting officer of the day for E company, Ninth Cavalry, Colored Regiment."

"Well done, Sergeant."

Dewey hurried in, carrying a three-legged stool in his left hand.

I had visions of a falling milkmaid and chuckled at the thought. Both men looked at me but said nothing. Fearful that Dewey might salute with his left hand and knock himself silly, I said quickly, "Now sit down both of you and we will talk."

Dewey flipped the stool over and sat down. Johnson moved the chair to the edge of the desk and looked at me expectantly. I sat down. He sat immediately. If he had been standing, he would have been at attention.

"Why is it, Dewey," I asked, "that you did not go with the others to the cantina?"

"Tonight was supposed to be school," he said, looking at me reproachfully.

"The major and me ain't got time for teaching you. Ain't that right, sir?" Johnson looked to me for confirmation.

"We might," I said, "work on another word while we keep an eye on the office."

As if by magic a bit of slate appeared in Dewey's right hand and in his left the bit of plaster that I called chalk.

"Yes, suh," Dewey said, then grinning widely, wrote the word *sir* easily. He had been practicing.

"You can write it, Dewey. Now listen to Johnson pronounce all the letters."

"Yes, *sir*," Johnson said.

"Now, you."

"Yes, suh," Dewey said.

"Say *all* the letters, Dewey."

He did, grasped the idea and added the *r.* He looked at me

anxiously. I turned to Johnson and asked, "What do you think, Sergeant?"

"I heard the *r* all right, sir."

"Good. Now we are going to change the last letter, the *r* to an *n* and change the meaning completely. Dewey, lend me your slate and chalk." I rubbed out the last letter and wrote a large *n* in its place. "Sound out the letters now."

Johnson echoed Dewey as he sounded out the word, but he never even glanced at the slate.

"Esseen. What that mean, Major?" Dewey cocked his head at me, but Johnson answered.

*"Sin* is what you should be doing at that Water Hole Cantina instead of pestering Major Northey."

There was a sudden burst of laughter that came through the open door and caressed me like sunlight on a cold day.

Ignoring the pain, I stood up quickly and called out, "Please come in."

Raquel Barragan stepped into the room, tucked a sheaf of papers under her arm and threw me a mock salute. "Private Barragan reporting for duty, sir." She rolled the *r* theatrically and added, "And begs the major's pardon for eavesdropping."

"You are pardoned," I said, likely blushing and then said lamely, "We are just learning the alphabet and simple words. Like *sir*. Words that a soldier uses."

She laid the papers on the desk. I looked at the top one and saw that it was a request for a Navajo scout.

"Why, Mrs. Barragan, you should be the acting company commander."

"I help when I can for I have little to do. I thought I might help with your school, but then we would have as many teachers as students."

"We will have many more when the men are back. And I would be delighted."

"And where are the missing students?" she asked innocently, but I thought I saw a smile worrying at the corner of her mouth.

"Most of my platoon are off the post on free time."

"What are they doing? It is dark outside now."

"They went to a kind of a cafe," I said.

"Imagine that. Way out here. Would it be a sidewalk cafe?"

Of course I knew that she was teasing me, but I could not bring myself to tell her where the men were, much less what they might be doing. And while she waited, smiling up at me with those lovely turquoise eyes, I heard Dewey volunteer, "Mrs. Barragan, they is all at a cantina doing esseen."

"Well, I know what a cantina is, but I do not know what 'esseen' means. Major?" She looked at me again and the smile broke through.

"*Sin* is when a lovely young lady bedevils a poor old soldier."

"Touché." Still smiling, she saluted, nodded at the men, and floated out of my office.

"Nobody told me they was young good-looking girls at that Water Hole Cantina," Dewey said thoughtfully.

"There ain't," Johnson said.

"Then what—"

"The word," I interrupted, "pronounced correctly is sin. The Bible lists ten commandments. And to break any one of them is a sin."

"Like what, sir?" Dewey asked, pronouncing the *r*.

"Acting officer of the day," I said, "escort Private Leroy Dewey outside and explain sin and the commandments."

As they walked away, I heard Johnson say, "A sin is when you don't take care of your horse before you go to bed or when you don't clean your carbine."

The only commandments that came to my mind were the charges not to covet thy neighbor's wife nor commit adultery.

# Nine

I was somehow on my feet in the dark fumbling for my matches aware only that the bugler, Crawford, who had been with us at Brown's Hill, was blowing his version of "To Horse." Then I heard three sharp raps on my door and Johnson called out, "Major Northey! They be killing our troopers."

"Come in," I answered. "Apaches? Do they have Barragan ambushed?"

Johnson, swinging a lantern, came in, followed by Corporal Green.

"No, sir. It's the troopers at the cantina."

"Cantina?" I sat on a table, the better to draw on my trousers and boots. "There are Apaches at the cantina?"

"No, sir." Green, the slim steady man who had been with me on that brutal first patrol, spoke urgently. "Some drunken white folks is shooting at my troopers. Nobody was killed yet when I snuck away and run old Noah half to death to get here."

"I have eight men ready," Johnson said. "I could be there in an hour, riding hard."

"These are white men shooting at United States soldiers?"

"Yes, sir."

"Then I guess we had better have a white man talk to them. Sergeant Johnson, you are in charge of this post until relieved by an officer."

"Yes, sir." He cleared his throat and then, his voice no more than a husky whisper, asked, "Do I issue ammunition?"

"Yes, but tell the men not to chamber a round until I give the order. And find a fresh horse for Corporal Green."

"I have one saddled for him, sir. Will you be riding Othello?"

"I don't know. Will I?"

"I think so, Major. He is better at school than I am."

I buckled on my revolver and moved out to the group of troopers ready to mount, waiting for me. I gave the order and we trotted out into the dark, waiting for our eyes to adjust to the bright moonlight. Othello leaned his long black head into the reins. He wanted to run. I eased up slightly and he shifted into a smooth fast gallop. I reined him back to a trot and called out to Corporal Green, riding ahead to my left to change gait whenever he felt ready. Although I could not yet see him clearly, I am sure that he lifted a hand automatically as he called out for the change and then we were all galloping along in the moonlight.


We heard the scattered shots minutes before we crested a rise and could see the flashes of gunfire like so many lightning bugs ringing a small building, gray in the moonlight. Two trees hovered over a second larger building. A light shone faintly from a window. There were no flashes emanating from either building. Evidently the besiegers were the only ones firing.

"Bugler," I called out. "Blow a call and repeat it until we are recognized."

"Yes, suh. What call, Major?"

"Something that will not cause our men to abandon their position and expose themselves to fire."

"I knows tattoo."

"No, I want something lively enough to catch the attention of those white civilians down there and let them know that the cavalry is here."

"He knows reveille pretty good," Green suggested.

I nodded and the bugler, Corporal Crawford, much improved since our first patrol, blew reveille enthusiastically. All firing ceased.

"Major," Crawford said, as if taking credit for awakening the sun, "it's lightening up."

The desert dawn with nothing to block out the sun is quick and bright. I could already make out the individual horsemen mounting up to ride toward us.

"Unsling your carbines and wait here, in line," I ordered and walked my mount down the rise to meet the riders.

Two men rode out to meet me. The rest waited in a group, silent. The two men, both white, wore the large black hats called planter's hats in the South. As they drew nearer, I could see that they both wore converted Colt pistols, like mine, but without the protective flap on the holster I used to keep the dust out.

Both men had skin darkened and roughed by the sun. One might have been a lightly colored Indian with eyes as gray as the buildings in back of him. The other man raised a hand in greeting and reined up. His eyes were soft brown, his mustache nearer red than brown. Before he spoke, he smiled widely.

"We are sure glad to see a white man. Them niggers is running wild. They is all, every man jack of them, under arrest, but some of them will not surrender.

"The bad ones is holed up in the bedding rooms, yonder." He pointed out the smaller of the buildings, now recognizably white adobe. "I figure that with another ten rifles, we can smoke them out pronto. You just take your men and give them a hot fire on the north side there and we'll go in the back and enfilade them good. I don't mind telling you that I was a captain with the Texas volunteers in the late War, but that's over and done and I don't hold it against you. After all, us white men, we got to stick together, right?"

He smiled again, so completely assured, so complacent in his superiority, that I lost my temper. I knew that I would regret it and if I had but known to what degree, I certainly would have acted differently. But what I said, in anger and loudly enough so that all the men, black and white could hear, was: "No, you are not. Not only are you wrong, but you are an ass. If you actually were an officer in the Confederate Army, then Texas must have been more pressed for men than were the gallant officers from Virginia and Georgia that I encountered in battles during that necessary but lamentable War."

His face whitened, his mouth opened and eyes bulged. He slapped his hand on the butt of his pistol.

"No, Pace." The other man spoke quietly, almost thoughtfully. "He is right. You are an ass. Can't you see that all his soldiers are niggers?"

"Niggers?" He looked up the slope and smiled again, but there was no laughter in his eyes. "I did make a mistake. I thought you had real soldiers with you. Well, no matter. You just ride on out of here and"—he opened his coat so that I could see the silver badge—"Sheriff John Pace will take care of these lawbreakers."

Remembering that often a good defense is a quick offense, I said, quickly, "What laws have they broken and how is it that you dare to arrest soldiers of the Unites States of America?"

"Charges! Why they are niggers and they was fucking white women!"

"They were copulating with prostitutes?" I asked.

"They was fucking whores. And they was not nigger whores."

"I will want to talk with the girls who are charging the soldiers with a criminal act."

"Oh, hell," Pace said, smiling again now, his voice as friendly as before. "The girls likely don't care, but white men come to this place too, and they don't want the niggers giving the girls the clap."

"But what is the charge?" I insisted.

"Resisting arrest!" Pace shouted.

"My men were arrested for resisting arrest?"

"Disturbing the peace," the other man said. "The initial charge was disturbing the peace."

"How then did a trooper disturb the peace?"

"He got into a fight with a white man," Pace said triumphantly.

"They did, John," the other man said. "Why don't you shut up and let me do the talking?"

"Goddamn it anyway, Rex. You are just the deputy and that's all. I am the goddamn elected sheriff!"

"That is certainly correct, John. Now shut up."

Pace turned his lips down and seemed to squint against the sun. Tears appeared in his eyes. He turned his horse away and walked it back down toward the group of riders.

"We happened to be riding by," Rex said, "and we heard a racket. So we looked in. Two big niggers was fighting a rancher from nearby, Harold Sawyer. We arrested the two niggers, but then an uppity soldier, said he was a corporal, said he would take them back to the post so as his colonel could deal with them. Now that would not do, so we took them outside the saloon, as the Mexicans say, *pistol in hand.* Somebody fired a shot, so we took the prisoners away and then yelled at the others to surrender, but they forted up where they are now."

"You just happened to be riding by. And the posse of white men down there, they were just riding by on their way to church?"

"All right," Rex said easily. "It was this way. We were at Sawyer's ranch. Nine of us. Some playing poker and others just drinking. When the trouble started here, Sawyer rode back and got us, including me, Deputy Rex Miles."

He saw my objection before I could verbalize it and added, "Pace deputized everybody—Sawyer's hired hands too."

"Wounded?"

"Two of Sawyer's hands and, of course, the girl that got beat up."

"Girl?"

"Yes. The one your trooper roughed up."

"If that is the case, then the soldier responsible will be court-martialed and turned over to a federal court."

"No." His gray eyes stared into mine. I felt a chill. "We will jail that man for assault and all of them for disturbing the peace. And those in the girl's bedroom for resisting arrest. We have over a dozen white men here who have smelled gunpowder before."

He had a point. I had only eight men with me. However, they were disciplined soldiers who could fight and fight well. But would they fight against white men?

"We will take all of the troopers back to the post," I said, trying to appear confident. "We will want all of the witnesses, including the girl and the peace officers at the court-martial. Now, keep those armed civilians out of my way."

"They ain't about to move for eight nigger soldiers and a white man with a flap over his pistol handle."

"They are battle-tested soldiers and the flap on my holster keeps dust from caking inside the hammer spring on my revolver. I suspect yours will not even cock."

When he glanced down at his pistol, I unsnapped the flap of my holster and, knowing that he would never think me capable of such an act, drew the revolver, thumb-cocking the hammer as I did. The barrel was pointing up away from Miles, but ready to fire.

"I find that by thinking ahead," I said, "I am able to plan my actions so that when it is necessary to have a pistol in my hand, I will know that it is ready to fire and I will be close enough to make sure of a killing shot."

Our eyes locked as I remembered the first time I had shot a man at close range with a pistol. I remembered how his shirt had ignited when the ball pierced it, along with burning bits of red-hot powder. This time, Miles looked away, turned and called down to the group waiting with Pace.

"The Yankee officer says he will take the niggers back to the army post and try them there."

I heard yells and angry epithets, but only one man, a bloody bandage wrapped around his bare head, rode up.

"Carbines ready," I called out. There was a series of loud clicks as the troopers levered loads into the chambers of the carbines.

"You nigger-loving son of a bitch!" the rider yelled, but he reined in his horse.

I holstered my pistol and looked at the deputy.

"I could draw right now and shoot you three times before you might wiggle that pistol out of its case," Miles spoke without passion.

"If you are very fast, you might put two balls into me before my men riddle your carcass," I said.

"You do not scare easily," Miles said. "I do not want to fight the Yankee Army, but the other men here might. They are angry and scared and Sawyer is egging them on."

I nodded as if to thank him for his explanation and stood up in the stirrups. I took a deep breath and spoke as loudly as if on a parade-ground exercise.

"Private Berry. Do you hear me?"

"Yes, suh, Major Northey." I was thankful that he answered me in a loud and firm voice.

"We are about to escort you back to the post. If you hear shots, come out quickly and take the riders in the rear. Fight with whatever you have." I turned around to see the line behind me, each trooper with his carbine at the ready.

I nodded pleasantly at Miles and he moved aside and turned his mount away to position himself apart from the action. I walked the big bony horse that Johnson had trained, but Whigam had named Othello, down the slope. Pace trotted his horse away from the group to position himself by his deputy. Four more riders followed.

A thin-faced bearded man with blond hair flowing from under his wide-brimmed hat placed himself in the center of a ragged line, wider by three horses than ours. They moved out uncertainly to meet us. One horse shied and reared so high that the rider dropped his pistol and grasped the horse's mane with both hands. Their line formed about thirty yards from my besieged troopers.

"At the trot!" I called out and touched Othello with the spurs.

Our sudden move gave them just an instant to decide to fight or move. They moved, all except the man in the center. Screaming defiance, he spurred his mount forward, aiming his pistol directly at me. I spurred Othello, meaning to smash into his lighter mount, but his reared. He lost his balance and had to lower his pistol. As we passed, I leaned over and, using my pistol as a saber, slashed at his hand. The sound of steel against steel was followed an instant later by an explosion as his cocked pistol hit the dirt.

One of the men who had been sitting his horse to one side cried out, "Boys, they have shot me. Help me for God's sake." He clutched his stomach and slowly slipped out of the saddle.

Two men dismounted instantly and caught him just before he hit the ground.

I rode back, took a handful of long hair and jerked the furious rider, now disarmed, from the saddle. I held him as I rode forward, his feet skipping along like a boy hanging on to the tailgate of a wagon. The door of the room where my men were swung open and I rode the man right up to it and released him to plunge headlong inside with my besieged troopers.

"Hold that man. He is charged with attempted murder!" I called out, then slipped from my horse as I saw troopers emerging, carbines held at the ready. I dropped the reins and Othello stood still, waiting.

Rex Miles was at the wounded man's side, on one knee.

"I have some experience with gunshot wounds," I said, wondering if I could kneel gracefully.

"I have seen a few myself," Miles said, saving me the trouble. He spoke to the wounded man. "Sandy, you have to move your hands. I cannot see the wound unless you move your hands."

Sandy looked up suddenly. He was as young as my youngest trooper. His eyes and voice were full of fear. He wrenched his bloody hands away, but then held them almost together as if in uncertain prayer, ready to clap them back on the wound.

His shirt was soaked with blood. I could not see the source of the bleeding nor could Miles, for he ripped the shirt away and then used a white remnant to wipe the abdomen. I was relieved to see that the entry hole was to the left far enough to have missed the intestines.

"What do you think, Lieutenant?" Miles looked up at me, his face impassive.

"Stop the hemorrhage," I said. I pulled my medical sack from a saddlebag, pulled out the largest bandage and gave it to Rex.

He pressed it over the wound and then said, "Hold it down tight as you can for a bit, Sandy."

"Yes, sir, Mr. Miles. Is it . . . fatal?"

"Likely not, but we got to get you to a doctor right soon, boy. Nearest one is El Paso. Maybe a two-day ride in a wagon."

"Well, do something! Can't you see he's hurt real bad?" A cowboy who might have been sixteen looked at Miles as he spoke, but then he turned toward the blond man who had done the shooting, and appealed to him.

"Mr. Sawyer, Sandy is bad shot." The boy turned to me and yelled, "Why didn't you shoot him in the head instead of the belly? Then it wouldn't hurt him no more!"

I turned to see Sawyer, face contorted with rage, held between two of my men.

"Answer the boy, you nigger-loving, belly-shooting, Yankee son of a bitch."

The man blamed me for his cocked revolver blowing a hole in the cowboy's belly. I thought him mad, but when I turned back to face the boy, his blazing eyes met mine and I knew that his hatred was directed at me, not Sawyer. I wondered if they were all insane.

"You Goddamn Yankees and your niggers can't run this country like you used to when Sheridan was here. No more," Pace said, both hands folded over his saddle horn. No one had reached for a gun since the shot was fired. "I got friends," Pace added truculently, "in high places."

I had resolved to control my anger, but I decided to use it instead, use it to ridicule the bombastic sheriff.

"Are those friends Goddamn Yankees, or just Goddamn sycophants of Goddamn Yankees?" I pointed a finger at his face in emphasis. He flung both hands up in front of his face and cried out in alarm.

"No. For God's sake, don't shoot!"

"What?" I said, puzzled. He lost color so quickly that the stubble on his bloated face was black against his skin. I suddenly realized that the hand pointing at him still held a Colt revolver. I quickly holstered it.

"We could bring a surgeon from the post," I said quietly. "Once we get our men out and on their way."

"A surgeon ain't going to help the kid," Sawyer said. "He's gut shot."

For a long minute no one spoke and then Sandy, his voice even higher than before, asked, "I ain't? Is I, Mr. Miles?"

"No, you ain't," Miles said, then turned to me. "You reckon the surgeon will ride over here real quick to tend to a civilian?"

"I believe he would," I said, but Miles sensed my uncertainty.

"He would come right away with an ambulance if they were wounded soldiers?" he asked.

"Of course, but we have no wounded."

"There are two. One is just busted up a bit, but the other one got his belly slit open."

"Where?"

He pointed to the small outbuilding. I took two steps and

then, my leg on the verge of collapse, called out, "Corporal Green, see to our wounded inside that adobe hut."

"Major," Green's voice came from behind me. "They ain't inside. They is tied outside a window round the corner. They had a sharpshooter inside shooting at us from that window."

Anger overcame pain. I nodded and walked ahead into the shadow formed by the hut and saw the men sagging against the wall, kept from falling by ropes leading inside.

"If there is anyone in there, come out now, for I will fire through the window in ten seconds."

"Nobody in there." I recognized the sheriff's voice.

I nodded, then without exposing myself, I pointed my pistol inside and emptied it into the room. When the smoke cleared, I looked in. The room was empty.

"I knowed you would come, Major. I told Josh here you would come and sew up his stomach. Didn't I, Josh?"

I looked down then and saw the two men. The one who spoke smiled at me and I remembered him from the ambush. Berry had been one of those who had emptied his rifle at nothing. But he had also doctored our wounded as best he could. The other, Josh Clay, held his eyes shut so tightly that I knew he was conscious. Both his hands, clasped over his stomach, were covered with coagulated blood.

"Corporal Green," I called out loudly, "send our fastest rider to the post and bring back the surgeon and the ambulance."

"Trooper Dewey." Green picked out one of our best young riders still mounted. "You run that bony hoss till he near drops. And, then, Leroy, you ride along back in the ambulance to show them the way."

Dewey nodded, uncocked his carbine, slipped it over his shoulder, snapped the barrel into the saddle ring and galloped over the rise.

I holstered my pistol and pulled my belt knife out. "I'll cut you loose first, Berry," I said, working the blade in between cloth and cord, "and then we can both ease Josh down."

"Yes, suh," he said doubtfully.

I understood his doubt when I cut his bonds and he slid down the wall and cried out in pain as the blood began to circulate freely again in his wrists. "If Josh has a special friend, come here and help me, now! The rest stay at the ready."

Tom Jefferson, the man who looked like a skinny Apache, was at my side in seconds. He held Josh in his arms while I cut him free and then sat down with the now unconscious man still cradled in his arms.

I wanted to move Josh's hands to check the wound, but I was sure that the gray-eyed man called Rex would have described the knife wound accurately.

"How bad is it?" I asked Berry.

"It's just like that white man told you, Major, except that it ain't just his belly. If it hadn't been for the sheriff, they would have busted both his legs."

"The same man that told me about Josh. He stopped them?"

"No, suh. The fat one that talks like a sheriff. That one."

"The sheriff stopped men from beating Josh?"

"Yes. And they was slamming me too. They was using a pick handle and the sheriff says they wasn't to hit us no more in the kidneys. Said they wasn't to kill us. Not with that old pick handle, anyway."

"Pappy," Jefferson spoke, "is you all right?"

"Sure. I be fine in a day or two." Pappy, at about thirty-five-years old, was the old man of the platoon.

I nodded and turned back to Josh. I found the break just below his left knee. But when I moved it slightly, he cried out and opened his eyes. When he saw me, he smiled.

"Major Northey. Pappy said you would come and get us. I was scared you wouldn't. I ain't dying, is I, Major?"

"No, Clay. The surgeon will be here in a few hours and he will take care of the stomach wound. Berry and I will splint that leg—it's a simple fracture—and once you get out of the hospital, you will be fit as a fiddle."

"Hospital. I guess I can learn me the alphabet while I'm getting better?"

"You can do just that."

He nodded, smiling, pleased at the thought. An engaging young man who might have been a messmate of mine from Michigan, had his skin been two shades lighter or had that long-dead young man from Michigan had a darker skin.

There is a horror that comes with fresh red blood always, but when it suddenly gushes from a man's mouth like red water over a spillway it is horrifying. Josh looked up at me. I could see no fear in his eyes, but rather a complete wonder. Surprise. Then he turned his head and shut his eyes tightly as if to hold out harsh reality.

"Take care of him, Jefferson," I said. "Take a blanket from the house."

I tried to rise from one knee and could not. Then I saw the hand extended to me. It was black and belonged to Berry. I took it gladly and got to my feet.

"Find your carbine, Berry," I said.

He nodded, raised his hand almost waist high in what would have been a salute. I saluted smartly. He dropped his hand again and went to search for his Spencer.

I reloaded my own sidearm as Green and I walked back to the two groups quietly facing each other.

The young red-haired cowboy was lying hunched up with a hand on his bandaged stomach. Someone had rolled a coat under his head. His hat was tipped over his eyes.

"See if you can rig up a blanket to shade the wounded men while we wait for the ambulance." I spoke to Corporal Green, but I looked at the other men, the civilians, all armed, but half of them on foot now. I called for horse holders and then gave the order to dismount and uncock the carbines.

When my men safetyed their Spencers, I heard clicks from the group facing us as they eased the hammers back on their own weapons. I felt certain that there would be no more shooting.

"These wounded men could use some shade," I called out.

"Anybody have a spare blanket we could rig up to keep that hot sun off them?"

"Sure, soldier." A stooped-over man with grizzled hair and smoky eyes that seemed to be looking past me at a far horizon spoke while he bent over and lifted a roll from a small pile of what must have been his personal gear. "You can use my ground sheet." He unrolled a length of Indian rubber and held it out to Green.

"Never used to need nothing 'twixt my bones and the ground but buckskin britches, but the bones and the buckskin got old and the cold got colder. Comes night I want my rubber sheet back. Hear?"

"I hear and I thank you. I had my fill of sleeping in wet blankets in the War."

"Which war was that?"

The easy feeling left me and I felt anger again, but when I looked at his weathered face, old but as guileless as that of a child, I knew that he meant no harm.

"Were it Apaches or Comanches or maybe them Sioux niggers up North?"

"No," I said solemnly. "It was white niggers down South. We called it the 'War of the Rebellion,' or just plain *the War.*"

"Oh, I heard of that, but we didn't have no time for that, what with fighting the red niggers out here."

"How can you have a red nigger when nigger means black?"

"Why no, son. They is all kinds of niggers. Red and yellow and brown, you said white ones, and you got some black ones here with you."

"You mean people. There are all kinds of different colors of people."

"That's what I said." He sounded as if he thought I was not very bright. "My white name is Charley, but if you like long Injun ones you can call me Long Man with a Dirty Knife."

"I'll call you Charley," I said hastily. "You willing to tell me what happened here?"

"All I saw was them two that you cut down. They was trying to get away from some fellers that had a pick handle and a sickle."

"A sickle?"

"A bloody one it was. That's when they cracked the one across the leg and he went down. The sheriff stopped them so I went over and pissed off all the dirt from the cut one's gut that was hanging out and pushed it back in."

"You cleaned the intestine with urine?" I asked, incredulous.

"No," he said testily. "I pissed on it and then I stuffed—"

"Yes," I agreed. "And you saw the man with the sickle cut him. Which man was it?"

"I don't know. They said it was a whore did it."

"I want you to come in to the post and tell the officers of the court-martial what you saw."

"No. I been hunting wolves around here, but with the bad fur and cheap bounty, I aim to move on. Maybe dig for gold or such."

"If you don't, maybe they will shoot that boy you tried to save."

"The one that I pissed—"

"That very one."

"That ain't right. You leave word here at the cantina. When I ain't out setting traps, I stay here. I'll tell what I saw."

"I don't figure you will, Charley," Rex Miles said, moving to my left where my cross-draw would be even more awkward. "You been getting bounty on those wolves from the Sawyer ranch, ain't you?"

Charley turned from me to eye the gray-eyed gunman as if he were a wolf that had his foot in a trap with a broken chain.

"You want to see what kind of medicine I can make, Rex?"

"No, Charley. Just want you to remember your friends."

"You sure as shit ain't one."

Miles's eyes turned icy with an intensity that I had never seen before. He took a quick step back and touched the butt of his pistol with his right hand.

Charley followed him, a Bowie knife magically in his left hand, waist high, thumb lined up with the sharp edge of the blade, ready to rip up or slash either way.

"How many times you figure you can shoot me 'fore I cut your liver out?" Charley grinned, an old gray wolf inviting Miles to draw.

"No cutting and no shooting," I called out loudly. "This cantina is now under martial law and I, representing the United States of America, will not allow any more violence."

"Martial law?" Charley asked querulously. He cocked his head to see Pace while keeping Miles in view. "Is they such a thing, Sheriff?"

"Oh, yes. Yes indeed. Maybe even more so. My God, yes! Put that cutlass away, Charley." Pace opened both hands as if in supplication.

Charley turned to me and said, "Then the major here is the law?"

"He is and you might just put that blade away, Charley."

Charley flicked the fighting knife in the air, caught the blade, somehow without slicing off a finger and then it disappeared somewhere inside his greasy deerskin jacket.

" 'Course I will if that's what the major wants. He ain't going to beat a poor nigger to death nor cut his belly open." He glared at Pace before he added, "And he knows enough to piss on a man's gut before he stuffs it back in his belly."

Miles moved back one more step and then withdrew his hand from his revolver. "Charley there is half grizzly. He just might have sliced a piece off me before I put out his lights."

Before Charley could reply, using my parade-ground voice, I called out, "I want all weapons surrendered to Corporal Green, who will give a written receipt for them."

"Major!"

Sheriff Pace was puffed up, shaking a finger at me. Before he could speak, I said quickly, "Forgive me, Sheriff. I did not refer to the officers of the law."

The sheriff nodded and looked around at his posse. "You

see, boys," he said, "we ain't powerless against the army. The War is over." He paused it seemed for applause, but did not quite bow, and then spoke to Miles.

"Rex, you can collect the firearms of them as we did not deputize regularly."

"Sure, Sheriff, if the major would separate Charley from that oversized knife."

"It would not be necessary, Deputy," I said, trying to match the emotionless voice of Miles, "if you would deputize Charley the regular way."

There was a two-second silence and then one of the white men laughed. Others followed and if some of my troopers did not laugh, they all grinned. The fighting was over.

# Ten

Although the cantina was known to its customers as the Water Hole, the owner a busty woman called The Guera because she was a shade lighter than most of her girls, had optimistically named it *El Porvenir*. If, however, it had a future as the Spanish name stated, it was the location of the artesian well that brought the customers for her strong mescal, weak beer and weekend whores. She was busy in the kitchen, supervising two small girls who were patting out tortillas, stirring beans and grinding up chiles on a porous stone slab called a *molcajete* when I introduced myself. I soon learned that she was from the territory of New Mexico, and spoke a mixture of Spanish and English. She was as complete a cynic as anyone I had ever met.

"It pains me, Señorita," I started to say in Spanish, but she smiled broadly, blinked large luminous eyes at me, and interrupted.

"Please, my general. You call me Guera and I will talk to you in the English. Okay?"

"Okay, Blondie."

"Blondie. That is the English for The Guera?"

I nodded as she reached out to give my shoulder a mischievous pinch.

"Good. I like."

"Now"—I shrugged in apology—"I must tell you that your cantina is closed temporarily."

"I don't like. Closed, no. Plenty of men cut up here, killed too, but I don't stop serving mescal."

"Sorry, but the bar will be closed."

"I'll stop the beer," she said eagerly. "No profit in it anyway."

She nodded and then pointed to a table near the door.

"Please sit, General."

"I am a first lieutenant."

"I bet my life you are," she said, leaving me puzzled. Then she called out in a voice that would have won her a sergeant's stripes in the army. "Bring a charola number one."

One of the girls dropped a spoon and scampered out. Before I could ask about the charola, she was back with a tray, a bottle, salt in a small bowl, quartered limes and two miniature clay cups.

She filled one of the cups and then, ignoring my protest, filled the other.

"No!" I said sternly. "The cantina is closed."

"Okay. Okay. You get two cents for beer and five for mescal!"

"No. The bar is closed."

"Okay. I give five cents cash for the charola number one and seven cents for every *olla* of mescal we sell to soldiers."

"No," I said, but before I could say another word she grimaced, and said, "Okay. You too tough for me. Okay. I give you a silver peso for every soldier who buys something in my cantina. Okay?" She tried a smile. "I don't sell beer and I don't sell mescal. How about girls? Nobody gets drunk on girls."

"No. But they do fight over them. No?"

"Only when they are drunk."

"The white ones said they could not stand our black soldiers dancing with white girls."

"My girls is not light like me, but the men was drunk," she conceded. Then she added, "They just wanted to watch. When the black boy with the big *chile* said no, the *loco*, that Sawyer, he took off his clothes and jumped onto the bed with them."

She paused, wrinkled her forehead in obvious thought, eyed me and then said, "He don't care what he sticks his *chile* into."

"Corporal Green!"

Green stepped inside, saluted and waited at attention.

"At ease, Corporal. I want you to listen to this witness—"

"Witness? What's that? like a *testigo?*" she said harshly.

"Yes. Exactly. You just tell the corporal what you saw."

"No witness," she said.

"And then you can open the bar again," I said. "Just as soon as we ride out."

"I don't go to the *juzgado* and tell the judge nothing," she said, head back and nostrils flaring.

"Just tell us what you saw," I said, thinking that we could talk about the court proceedings later.

"Okay. But no court."

When I nodded, she smiled and continued, a natural story-teller, pausing for effect and emphasizing the high points with both voice and facial expressions.

"That boy, Josh, they call him, he took Rosario to the bed and the *loco* wanted to watch, but Josh didn't want to take his clothes off so that *ranchero* tried to peel them off with a machete."

"Sawyer!" I said. "It was Sawyer that cut him."

"No. I never said that. Josh took that machete away from him and threw it out back. That's what I saw."

She looked at me sullenly until I spoke.

"Thank you, Blondie. Please continue."

"Well," she said grudgingly, "that was when the *loco* started to cuss out the niggers and told me to throw them out. Throw out them boys, all with pockets full of *dinero!* Now them boys, they don't drink as much as the *gringos,* but they do everything else and that brings in more gold than even mescal." She winked at me to make sure that I got the point and added, "And *that* don't get spilled or broken when it drops on the floor."

"You refused?"

*"Sí, mí* General."

I was a general again. I smiled encouragement and she continued, happy again.

"I say no and the *loco,* he pulls out his *pistola* but the *soldados,* they got guns too so the *gringos* take Sawyer and his *pistola* and ride away. Everything is *quieto* and then they come riding back with a bunch more and that is when the bad trouble started."

"And that is when the *gringos* cut Josh?"

"No. That is when the *gringa* cut him."

*"Gringa?"*

"Yes. I got one that comes up from El Paso some times."

*"¿Como se llama?"* I asked. But the answer I asked came back to me in an English, if accented at all, much like my own.

"My name is Beth Anderson."

I twisted in my chair and saw a blue-eyed blond version of The Guera. She was dressed for work, wearing a skirt slit up to a creamy thigh. Her breasts were pushed up and half exposed by some kind of a special corset. One nipple, the size and color of a raspberry, peeked over black lace.

"You cut my trooper?"

"Yes, I did. But it wasn't no manslaughter. I mean I did it in self-defense justified by . . . self-defense. It was justified and I ain't going to no jail."

"I see," I said. "Where is the sheriff?"

"Just outside. I mean I just saw him outside, there."

"Sheriff Pace told you that you would not be tried for attempted murder?"

"It was justified," she said.

"Ask the sheriff to step in here," I said to Green.

"Blondie, bring in the girl that was with Josh. Rosario, you called her."

"That's her. The *gringa.* Betty we call her."

"You called her Rosario."

"I forgot. I got six girls this week. I get mixed up."

Pace walked into the room, removed his wide-brimmed planter's hat and fanned himself with it. He grinned at me. A stout man with a white band of skin where his hat fit to his forehead just above bright blue eyes that exuded friendship. I felt that he might ask me to vote for him, but all he said was, "You wanted to see me, suh?"

"This Miss Beth Anderson says that she was the one who has grievously wounded a soldier of the Army of the United States of America."

"She surely did in the course of defending her honor."

"Honor?"

"She may be a whore," Pace admitted, "but she is a white whore."

"You told me, Sheriff, that I wouldn't have to go to no court." The girl's eyes teared and she looked frightened and years younger.

"That's right, honey. Ain't no judge in Texas going to charge a white woman who cuts a nigger rape-fiend."

"Trooper Joshua Clay was not even with this woman. There are witnesses," I said, with what I thought was a great deal of conviction.

"White ones?"

"Black soldiers. Honorable men. And, in court, maybe Blondie and this girl will tell the truth."

"Blondie?" He looked at me quizzically and then grinned. "You mean The Guera."

When The Guera spoke in a torrent of Spanish that I could only partially follow, Pace listened intently, shook a finger at her once in reprimand, I thought, and then exploded in laughter.

When he could talk, he told me that Blondie—he liked the English translation—would go back to working the streets of El Paso before she would testify against Sawyer.

"What about Sawyer?" I asked. "He threatened Private Clay with a sickle. He wanted him to perform for him with one of the girls. Couple with her right in front of him!"

"Look, Lieutenant. We are both men of the world and I got to tell you that Sawyer is peculiar, but he owns a big part of this country and he does a lot of business in livestock along the border."

"The girl will not be charged for attempted homicide?"

"Come on, Lieutenant. Sure, your soldier got cut bad, but we figure as long as the girl is all right we can forget the rape charge and you just take your soldiers along with that ambulance when it gets here and go on back to the post. My men ain't fighting any more, but there are a couple that would like to see you charged with manslaughter."

"That would be you and Sawyer?"

"You will have to turn Sawyer over to my custody," he said, ignoring my question. "Besides that cowboy that got shot, Sandy, ain't about to testify against his boss."

"I intend to see that Sawyer is charged in a federal court."

"He is a civilian," Pace said. "I get custody."

He was right. I left Green to keep an eye on Blondie and took Pace to the room where I had posted a guard to keep Sawyer away from the others.

The guard saluted and stood aside.

Sawyer looked up at me. He was sitting on an unmade cot. A woman's clothes hung from a wooden peg set into the adobe wall. A crude shelf extended from one corner. A cross made of brass and wood leaned from it against the wall and there were several lit candles standing in puddles of wax on the shelf. There was no window, but high up, well above eye level, every other brick had been left out, I supposed for both ventilation and privacy.

"First Lieutenant Northey," Sawyer said, his voice trembling with emotion. "I would like to tender to you my most abject apology for my drunken, abominable actions. I beg you to forgive me. I have sworn never to touch another drop of spirits."

I was prepared for anger, arrogance and even physical violence, but not for what seemed to be genuine repentance. I looked into his eyes and did not see a glimmer of that crazed rage which had distorted his face before.

In spite of his bloodshot eyes and dirty linen, he was a handsome, impressive man who spoke the soft easy English of the Southern aristocracy. He was dark with black curly hair and gray eyes. He would likely have been my age or a few years older.

I nodded my understanding of his apology and said, "Mr. Sawyer, I will release you to the custody of the sheriff, but there will be an official inquiry."

"I remember very little of the tragic events leading up to the shooting of my loyal employee, Sandy."

"If you do not remember, then who has related the happening to you?"

His eyes changed color or his passion was so intensely mirrored that instinctively I unsnapped the flap of my pistol holster.

"I told him," Pace said quickly. "Through the window. I mean them air slits up there."

I nodded and then said softly, "Then, sir, you do not remember slitting the stomach of Trooper Clay open with a sickle?"

"No, Lieutenant. I did not do that. There was a girl. A white girl. Beth something. She did that."

"Then you do remember some of the things that happened while you were . . . intoxicated?"

"Vaguely. As if they had happened to another person."

"Lieutenant Northey," Pace said earnestly. "What I want is for you to release Mr. Sawyer in my custody. Then you can take your men and ride on out. Maybe that white whore won't press charges and we can just forget about the whole mess."

"What about the cowboy, Sandy? If he should die?"

"I saw that," the sheriff said easily. "And I will testify that it was an unfortunate accident."

I felt that I had led a charge across an open field enfiladed by rifle and cannon, only to find that the stone fence we had meant to jump was seven feet high.

"All right. I will release Sawyer to you. Do you want me to take your wounded man to the hospital at the post?"

"Of course," Pace said, but Sawyer, looking disturbed, shook his head, but evidently not in negation. "Is your surgeon a white man?"

"Yes, he is."

"Good. I will pay him a hundred dollars to keep my man alive and well. Tell him that."

"I need no instruction from you, Mr. Sawyer," I said and saw the wild light again in his eyes. The man was dangerous and given an opportunity, I would have jailed him myself. I looked inquisitively at Pace.

"You understand, Lieutenant. Mr. Sawyer here sticks by his men and when he says he will pay, he will do that. Yes, sir, he surely will."

I heard a flurry of soft Southern speech outside, black and white. To my ear the accents sounded the same. The guard at the door called out, "The ambulance is coming over the rise, Major."

"I believe we have a stalemate," I said. "I will agree to your terms subject to my own commanding officer's approval."

Sawyer stood up. He smiled and said, "When I played chess, Major, a stalemate was considered a victory for the blacks, what with the white's advantage of first move."

"We might just leave the pieces the way they are until we see how things turn out," I said, then looked directly at Pace, who shrugged.

"I say it's a Mexican standoff," Pace said, "which means nobody wins. Go on, Lieutenant Northey. Get them wounded men to the hospital."

Outside, I saw an ambulance, not ours, but an almost-new Studebaker. Which meant that Whigam must not have returned. Smith sat alongside the driver. I hurried over and offered to help the little man down, but he waved me away and said, "I need no help to climb down from a wagon. Besides you might injure that leg."

Touché, I thought. The feisty little man was right. I knew

what it was like to have well-intentioned people offer unwanted assistance.

"What is the status of the wounded?" he asked.

I pointed to the men lying in the shade of the old mountain man's ground sheet. "Two troopers, one with a stomach sliced open. Another with what might be fractured legs and a civilian with a gunshot wound in the abdomen."

He stomped over to the men as I talked and exclaimed, "One is a white man!" He knelt down to examine him.

I counted up to a minute and said, "You will now examine the trooper with the stomach wound, Dr. Smith."

He said over his shoulder. "In good time. We have to get this boy into the ambulance."

Pain suddenly and agonizingly struck my leg. I felt close to losing consciousness. I held on and when my vision cleared, I pulled out my revolver, wondering if I might be doomed to have it surgically attached to my hand. I put the barrel to the back of Smith's neck and cocked it. The click sounded as loud as a blacksmith's hammer.

"The trooper first! Then the white boy and then the other trooper."

"Yes, sir. Stretchers!" he croaked, head immobile, but frog eyes bulging and peering out the sides. Two white troopers came from the ambulance, glancing fearfully at both the black soldiers and the armed white men and then helped the now-solicitous surgeon place the men in the ambulance. He hopped up inside and I gave the order to ride out.

Once we were over the rise, I called a halt, dismounted by the ambulance, tied my horse to the tailgate, said, "Make room for one more," and crawled up over the tailgate into the back. I found a space in one corner and let myself fall into the deep painless black.

# Eleven

When I awoke from what had been more of a coma than a deep sleep the following day after the incident at the Water Hole Cantina, I was so miraculously free of pain that I frantically slapped my leg, fearful that it was no longer there, that a vindictive surgeon had taken advantage of my condition to amputate.

Now, a week later and still free of pain, I whistled as I walked to the hospital, which on this Sunday afternoon would also be a school. I even trotted up the steps. I'd had remissions of pain before, but I was certain that this time the vagrant piece of metal in my leg had found a safe and permanent lodging and would torture me no more.

My students that could stood at attention. The three that could not—the white cowboy, Sandy Morey, Private Joshua Clay and Corporal James Brown—were propped up in hospital cots. Morey and Clay were almost touching. Brown was alongside Clay, but an arm's length away.

Thomas Jefferson, always quietly competent, had found two old crates that furnished him with a chair and desk. He shared the desk with the sad-eyed young man who had brought his wounded mount back from what we now called the Fight for Brown's Hill, Benjamin Bagley.

Sergeant Johnson, who had called the room to attention, stood near the window, looking even more muscular alongside the diminutive Leroy Dewey.

"At ease. Sit down." I smiled. "If you can find room." I turned to the men on the cots. "You look a whole lot better than the last time I saw you."

"I shore do, Major," Sandy said, grinning wide enough to make his freckles jump. "I thought both me and Josh here was goners."

Josh shook his head and rolled his eyes and mimed that he was in total agreement. We all laughed.

"Corporal Brown?"

"Dr. Smith said that when he comes back, he studying to put me back on duty, maybe."

When I laughed, everyone joined me. Although their laughter might have been an act of courtesy, it did not matter. My spirit soared.

"We have eight real slates and a full box of real chalk so everyone has one. Right?"

"Suh," Clay said, nervously, "I think we gonna be one short."

"Here, sir!" Johnson stepped forward. "Take mine."

"No, Sergeant. I want you to sleep with that slate. Who needs a slate?"

"I do, suh." The white cowboy and the black soldier lying alongside spoke simultaneously.

"One at a time. Private Clay, you first."

"Yes, suh. I guess I gave mine to Mister Sandy there."

"Gave? That slate is government property." I tried my best to scowl.

"Suh," Sandy said earnestly, "Josh just loaned me that slate. He was teaching me to write. I would like to write and read too. I'd likely be the only cowboy in the New Mexico territory and maybe in West Texas too that could might read and write."

I sighed and delivered my slate to Joshua and then took my place behind the operating table. I fished out a piece of tile that had been our original equipment.

"Private Clay, I wish you a speedy recovery so that you can take over this class and release me for my other minor duties."

There was a terrible and long silence until Thomas Jefferson released a series of muffled guffaws and then the others, excepting Johnson, joined in, for Jefferson was known for his good judgment.

"Have we come up with any new words by adding a letter to *s-i?*"

As was my custom I looked first to Johnson, but what I called the school glaze had already settled over his eyes. Even Jefferson shook his head.

"Well, I am surprised. You could add a *t* and get the word *sit* or an *x* and have the word *six.*" I held up six fingers.

Jefferson frowned, then held up his hand.

"Yes, Jefferson."

"Where did you find that *t* and that *x?*"

"From the alphabet," I said impatiently.

"What's a 'alphabet'?"

What indeed? I was floundering about seeking an explanation when Johnson straightened up and called out, "Attention!"

I turned toward the door, saluting automatically for Whigam was due back at any time. But it was not Whigam I saluted, but Raquel Barragan. "Colonel—" I began.

"I have been promoted again. Very well. At ease. Please excuse me. I forgot to deliver these with the slates and chalk."

She handed me a sheath of paper.

"Sorry, Mrs. Barragan. I thought that the colonel was back."

"Is there such a strong resemblance?"

I could not utter a word but she took pity on me and, hand still on the door, said, "Also I wanted to remind you that the doctor will be here for dinner with us—you included, Major—and will likely look in on his patients."

"The doctor will be here?" I said blankly.

"Yes. He said he must report to Fort Stockton, but would be back soon. When he is here, he always dines with us."

She looked pointedly at the blanket that had been rolled up and tied to a rafter just above the cowboy's cot. "Any minute now. Good-bye, Major."

I stood quietly, savoring the vision of loveliness and her scent until Johnson spoke.

"Do you want me to roll that segregator down now, sir, or wait until the doctor gets here?"

"Segregator. What's a segregator?"

"It's that blanket, sir," Johnson explained. "When it's rolled down, it segregates Mr. Sandy there from Josh."

"Sandy," I asked, "you want that blanket rolled down?"

"No, suh. How is Josh gonna learn me to read with that durn blanket hanging there?"

"Good point," I said. "Now, about that alphabet. Well, an alphabet is all of the letters that make up a language. . . ." I looked down at the top paper and saw the written alphabet printed beautifully, upper and lower case, by my lovely assistant, Raquel Barragan. I held up the paper. "This is an alphabet. It has all of the letters that make the sounds of the English language. These were done for you by Mrs. Barragan. Try to copy them as closely as you can, for they are perfect."

There were twelve sheets. On the back of seven of them I printed each man's name and then wrote it in script. I told them as I handed out the sheets that books and newspapers and magazines were printed, but that required type and ink and machinery so that clerks usually wrote in a clear hand the communications for the army in script. I pointed out that when they learned to write, they could also write their names using the script letters that I had used to write their names.

"Sir?" Jefferson had picked up Johnson's pronunciation. When I nodded, he continued. "Why do the letters go from *a* to *z?*"

"It is a way to remember all of them. There are twenty-six. You can all count to twenty-six?" Sandy grinned and flashed his hand open and closed five times counting by five. He called out, "Twenty-five and one is twenty-six!"

"Hooray for Sandy!" Joshua said.

I borrowed Sandy's slate and wrote the number twenty-six

and told them what it stood for and that after they learned the alphabet, I would teach them numbers as well.

We were all smiling and laughing when I turned to see Johnson standing at the window, looking bleakly out toward the empty parade ground.

I quickly crossed the room in three steps and took his arm.

"Sergeant, wouldn't you like to learn to write all of the numbers and the names of the men in our company?"

"There is nothing I would like more, Major Northey, sir. Nothing at all. But," he added, agony in his voice, "I cannot read and I will never read. No, sir."

"You are as intelligent as any man on this post, Johnson. Of course, you can learn to read."

He turned to me and said in his normal voice, "I can hear the ambulance. The doctor will be here soon."

I opened the door and listened and heard nothing. But just as I was about to close the door, I heard the faint sound of horses' hooves against the packed dirt of the road. And then I could see the ambulance, a small green block on the horizon slowly growing in size.

"It's the new ambulance," I said.

"Yes," Johnson said. "But I don't see Dr. Smith. I do believe that the man riding alongside the driver is our new scout, the Navajo."

"How can a man who can see like an eagle not learn to write?"

"Yes, sir." He continued in a monotone. "He's wearing braids and he shore looks like a Apache."

"An Apache," I corrected him. "So the *a* sound does not run into the *a* sound of Apache."

He looked directly at me, the glaze gone and said, "A Navajo and *an* Apache."

"Right, Sergeant Johnson. Absolutely right."

I just might not have to pay Whigam that case of champagne after all, I thought.

I turned back to the class. "You shall have to learn the names of the letters in order and by sound so you can find each letter when you begin to read."

"The first letter is *a.* Say it and then move on to the next." By the time I had run through the alphabet with them twice, the ambulance had reached the edge of the parade ground. When I shut the door behind me, they were chanting the letters in unison.

The ambulance rolled to a stop in front of the headquarters building. I saw a flash of red as Peter came out, covering his hair with his hat. He waved a salute at me and I returned it just as carelessly. Dr. Smith waited until one of his two assistants left the wagon, let down the tailgate and held a hand up to help him down. He shook hands with Peter and looked startled as I walked briskly, still smiling, up to him with my hand extended.

"A pleasure to see you Dr. Smith. I have been anxious to tell you how much I admire your surgery," I said, honestly.

"Well, sir, thank you." He permitted himself a small cat-smile. "I have been complimented by a general officer for my skill with the bistoury."

"I was never much with the bistoury," Peter said, looking at me, "but I was quite good with the saber."

"Peter," Smith said without a glimmer of humor, "the bistoury is a small surgical knife."

"Like a scalpel?" I asked.

"Yes, but smaller and is used for more delicate work." He went on to tell us in detail about the time that he had removed a wooden splinter from the upper thigh of a general who had almost received the command of an army during the War. Peter excused himself and went back into the office. I walked the doctor and his assistant back to the hospital, hearing his voice in the background, but really listening to the musical sound of the voices singing out the alphabet to a tune that I recognized but could not name.

"Lieutenant Northey, sir!"

"Yes, Dr. Smith," I said, back from my reverie.

"I asked you what is going on in my hospital? What is that caterwauling disturbing my patients?"

"Sorry, Doctor. The infirmary is also a school Sunday afternoons and they are singing the alphabet to some pleasant air."

"I shall hold you responsible for the well-being of that young cowboy. I took a bullet from inside that boy's—"

"He is fine, Doctor. A tribute to your skill. You also took a bullet from Corporal Brown and he is waiting to be discharged from the hospital if you so allow, and I must mention how skillfully you sewed up the ripped stomach of Private Clay!"

I opened the door for him. He nodded curtly and stepped inside. The singing stopped as the door opened. The doctor taking two steps to my one trotted to the far end of the room, checked the blanket hanging from the ceiling and actually turned to me to nod approval. I glanced at Johnson, who had called for attention when we entered.

"At ease, men," I said. "Sergeant, would you see that our new scout and his mount are fed and quartered?"

Johnson saluted and left.

"A remarkable recovery, young man," Smith said, examining Sandy. "No sign of fever. We might send you back to the ranch in another week."

"A week!" Sandy was outraged.

"Now, young man. You are still not ready to go back. I will tell Mr. Sawyer so. Yes, I will, Mr. . . . uh."

"Sandy," I said. "His name is Sandy."

"Of course," Smith said, implying by his tone that only an idiot would think that he did not know the boy's name.

"Sandy, I am sorry to confine you in a room with colored men, but you do have the curtain and it will be only for another week."

"No, Doc. It ain't that. I don't want to go back now. I'd ruther wait two or even three more weeks so's I can learn that durn alphabet and then get to writing."

"You do not want to go back to the Sawyer Ranch?" Smith was openmouthed in disbelief. "You want to learn to read and write? What for? Why would a ranch hand want to read? What would you read?"

"Doc," Sandy said, "I plain don't know. I'd have to learn to read so as to know, wouldn't I?"

"Preposterous," Smith said. He was so taken aback that he threw back the blanket that Johnson called the segregator, over Sandy's bed so that the light would be better to see Clay's wound.

He nodded to Clay, removed the bandage, nodded again, talking to himself as he removed stitches and cleansed the wound before calling for a bandage that his assistant had ready.

"Yes. Healed nicely. No fever. Yes. Another week, maybe two, then light duty. Yes."

He checked Brown and released him to regular duty. He asked about Berry and when he learned that he had been back on duty since the beating at the water hole, merely nodded and muttered that you could not kill some of these people with a club.

When he finished, he straightened up to his full height. I quickly bent over to examine a boot heel so that our heads were at the same level when he spoke.

"My patients are all right, Lieutenant Northey. And although it seems a waste of time to teach one ignorant black man to write so as to be a clerk for the colonel, I think it a waste of time to teach everyone, willy-nilly, to read. To read what? To write what?"

The question seemed to me rhetorical. So did his nurse's question. He glanced at the surgeon and then, in a stage whisper, asked, "Do I eat with the Injun or—"

"Sergeant Johnson will have asked the cook to see that you get a hot meal. We try to treat our visitors here," I said tongue in cheek, "as they would treat us if we were their guests."

The soldier who might have been taller than the surgeon, had he not have been so bowlegged, nodded, saluted me and getting a consenting nod from Smith, waddled out, taking the medical bag with him.

As I escorted Smith from the building, he stopped at the door, looked back to Sandy's cot, trotted back and pulled the segregator into place.

Outside the door, I waited for the doctor to precede me. When he started across the parade ground on his way to report officially to the officer of the day, Peter Barragan, I tarried by the steps, listening. I heard whispers from inside and then Sandy said loudly, "I don't care. Pin that old horse blanket up out of the way."

And then Josh said something softly that I could not hear and the two of them were giggling like teenagers. Which, of course, is what they were.

I walked happily toward my quarters to ready myself for a dinner in which I would likely have to endure the idiocies of the overbearing, pompous Dr. Smith, but then I would also be able to feast my eyes on the beautiful Raquel Barragan.

# Twelve

The dinner was not the sumptuous affair that had been prepared in my honor when I first arrived at the post, but at least I would be able to stay for brandy and cigars. Although Peter Barragan was officially on duty, Sergeant Johnson was his physical presence at the company headquarters.

When I arrived, I paused to speak Spanish to the attendant at the door. Raquel heard me and came right out, her gown rustling, sending a faint and sweet message to my nostrils.

"Where did you learn Spanish?"

"My father spoke to me when I was young. I remember basic children's words and when I was in the hospital after the War, an officer from Santa Fe, my roommate, talked to me in Spanish. It helped us both to endure."

I stopped, embarrassed. I had not meant to seek sympathy.

"It must be a terrible thing to be young, alone and badly hurt."

I was engulfed by the earth goddess that we men all seek and admitted to myself then that I had wanted love, but sympathy was a substitute.

"Yes. There were women who would visit us and at times even work as nurses with the wounded."

"I asked to assist the surgeon, but Colonel Whigam would not hear of it."

"I find myself agreeing with the colonel. However, when the surgeon has finished and—"

"When the blood has been mopped up and the limbs put out of sight, the ladies can come in and press damp cloths to the temples of the wounded heroes?"

"I would not say that," I said stiffly, realizing as I spoke, that I had said just that.

"Come in," she said, taking my arm. "We shall get the surgeon's opinion. And you must ask Peter about Spanish. Maybe," she said mischievously, "he will allow me to teach you. I could hold my classes in the infirmary when it is no longer a hospital."

"Nor a simple school," I said solemnly, "but a college where foreign languages are taught."

Peter came forward, leaving the cluster of guests seated in a semicircle. He held a glass in one hand, which he presented to me. "A glass of madeira, compliments of George Sullivan."

I took it from him with my left and shook hands. He looked thinner, and his blue eyes still seemed charged with energy, but I sensed a weariness.

"I believe we have met some time ago," I said, smiling. "I think that it was back when we had twice our present staff. No word from Whigam?"

"Not unless he sent a message with Dr. Smith," Peter said. "Which he did not."

He turned to lead me to the guests when Raquel spoke to him in a Spanish that I could scarcely follow, although I had understood most of what the man at the entrance had said. Peter stopped then and spoke to me in a Spanish that I followed easily.

*"¿La señora me dice que habla español?"*

I answered him in halting Spanish, searching for the right words, answering that I did but poorly. He waited politely until I was finished and then lit the room with his smile as he said, "You will learn quickly and we will teach you, Raquel and I. Maybe we can win a case of champagne from the colonel?"

We three, arm in arm, entered the drawing room. George Sullivan stood up quickly, beaming with pleasure at our laughter. Dr. Smith popped up, said, "Good evening, Northey," and popped back down, his knee almost touching that of Adele O'Donahue. The lady must have had a store of low-cut dresses, for had not the yellow top of her bodice had a fringe of lace, the nipples of her large breasts would have been visible at eye level instead of only from above as was I when I kissed her hand.

"Major. You are naughty. Why you have been here weeks and I have seen you hardly at all."

"Perhaps all of you ladies could help me prepare a small dinner to show my appreciation to all of you, once the colonel is back and we have a free day."

"I would love to," Adele gushed. "Do come by one evening and we will plan something."

She giggled and I blushed. It is an affliction caused by almost any woman who is kind to me. And, as I knew it would, it set off gales of laughter followed by witticisms that I suffered as I had many times before. I smiled foolishly until Mary Sullivan took pity on me and, pulling me to a seat by her, called out loudly, "Just you all stop. Or I shall tell some tales that I know, beginning with how my own true love, George Sullivan, lost his trousers at a meeting of the Ladies for Temperance at the Travelers Hotel ballroom in Independence."

Although I felt like a Judas Goat, I was so relieved that I joined in, not only in the laughter, but the banter that followed while George blushed and squirmed.

At dinner, I found myself across from Adele and to the right of Peter, who was at the head of the table, while Raquel sat at the other end. Mary was at my left next to George. Smith sat alongside Adele.

"Have you given more thought to the silver mine, William?" George spoke around his wife.

"Call me Bill," I said. "No. Except to think of how little I know about mining. And I must confess that my mine in Arizona consists of a map I won in a poker game in lieu of ten dollars."

"But, lad, you don't have to mine this kind of silver. It is a natural silver it is. Grows inside a shaft in clusters like grapes and to harvest, you just pick them and throw them into a furnace." He stuck his large round face out past his wife's blue puffed shoulder pads, nodded owlishly and added triumphantly, "It is self-fluxing you see!"

I nodded, accepting that it was "self-fluxing," whatever that might be.

"You see, Ideal, you flux the silver right there in the mine so that you just transport the pure silver to the nearest mint." Smith had a habit of nodding when making a point. Invariably, when finished, he would lean back and smile with satisfaction as if he had tasted something that he liked.

"There you have it," George said. "Am I to take it that you are ready to invest in the Sullivan Silver and Smelting Company?"

Smith smiled shrewdly and replied, "I might, George Sullivan, when and if you show me a sample and give me its location!"

"Not the location. I can give you my word that it is not on private property, and our company can claim it, once the Apaches become peaceful."

"Ha!" The doctor returned to his broiled antelope.

"Major," Raquel asked, "does this conversation seem familiar to you?"

"Déjà vu," I said.

"That's French," Adele said.

"Sounds like one of those Indian fakirs," Mary said. "We saw one lie right down on a bed of sharp nails."

"Peter," George appealed. "Do I know where that silver is or not?"

"You do, George," Peter said.

"Where then?" Smith lifted his face from his plate.

Peter made a sad clown face, pointed to the south and west and said, "Out there. But do not ask me where. I am sworn to secrecy. I am a stockholder, but I will not go there yet, not even with Major Northey and a company of the Ninth Cavalry!"

"I would go there," Smith said, "with General Custer and a platoon of the Seventh Cavalry."

"Then, Doctor," Peter said in Spanish, looking at me to see if I understood, "you would be buried with Custer."

I choked on my wine. Raquel laughed and then pretended she was laughing at me. George Sullivan looked as if he might have understood, but said nothing.

"I, of course, speak classical Latin," Smith said, "but I understand little of the modern bastardized language."

Raquel then said something that I thought referred to languages, but we all stopped to look expectantly at her for an explanation. However it was Peter who spoke.

"Raquel has just reminded me that our ancestors spoke an ancient language when they lived in Spain. We still are able to speak a bit, as it is similar to Spanish. It is called Ladino."

"The Mexicans speak it too," Smith said.

"I speak a little Spanish," Sullivan said, "and I can get by with the Mexicans just like I can with Spaniards."

"But I bet they talk bad Spanish, George," Adele said. "Just like them immigrants from Sweden or Germany can't hardly talk English."

"Our people have been Christians for a long time," Peter said, "but when they were Jews, they spoke Ladino. And as my father has told me—"

"Jews." Smith stopped eating. "All Jews speak some kind of German and they wrote the old Testament in it."

"Yes," Peter said patiently. "The German Jews speak Yiddish, which is a kind of archaic German. When the Jews were expelled from Spain and Portugal just before Columbus discovered America, the Jews that did not convert to Catholicism, spoke what was basically archaic Spanish that included words in Aramic, Greek and Hebrew."

"Then you are of the Hebrew race."

Peter Barragan treated the doctor's statement as a question and answered it.

"Our people converted early, but when they settled in northern Mexico and prospered, they were also envied. Thus it was that the Inquisition decided that the Barragans, being wealthy and recent converts to the church were suspect. They carted them off to the capital and interrogated them until they either died or donated their money to the good inquisitors."

"Oh and they were horrible times," Mary said, tears in her voice.

"You are then a Jew," Smith stated.

"I suppose so," Peter said, "and I suppose then that you are a Roman Catholic."

"Me. A Papist! Not likely." Smith puffed his cheeks like the little frog that he had reminded me of when we first met.

"Were not your forefathers English Catholics?" Peter asked.

"But, sir, what has that to do with me? I am an American, born-again, Christian Baptist."

"And I, sir, am a Christian Catholic." Peter let his irritation surface.

"I was speaking of race."

"Oh," Peter said softly. "And I had thought we were discussing religion."

When Smith narrowed his eyes and again puffed his cheeks, I entered the lists, not to do battle, but to change the direction of the lances.

"They do mix, do they not," I said. "Race and religion. I, for example, grew up calling everyone not a member of my religious group, gentiles."

I caught everyone's attention, particularly that of the Barragans.

"You are Jewish?" Peter was astonished.

"No, although some hold that one of the lost tribes of Israel populated this continent before Columbus and some claim that there is an Indian tribe lost in the great American desert, that speaks Welsh. I do not speak the language, but I have been assured that my grandparents came from Wales."

"Your regiment *was* from Missouri?" Sullivan asked.

"Minnesota," I said, "but I lived in Missouri a while."

"What kind of a religion is Welsh?" Adele asked the room.

"It is a language," I said. "My father spoke English, Ute, Welsh and a bit of Spanish. He said that Welsh was by far the most poetic of the languages."

"You don't look Welsh," Smith said.

"Neither do you," I said.

Smith opened his mouth to speak, thought better about it and drank some wine. I lifted my glass to the company and we all sipped wine.

"If you don't worship Welsh, then what?" Adele asked.

"The Truth," I said, wondering how I was going to work my way out of the situation. I did not want to take Peter's place as scapegoat, I meant only to distract the Philistines.

"I never heard of that one," Mary said doubtfully. "Maybe he's a Mohammedan with a bundle of wives back in Missouri." I am sure that Mary was trying to help me as I had Peter, but she had touched a chord of Smith's memory harp and he responded immediately.

"The Mormons. That's it. You, sir, are a Mormon!"

"With a bunch of wives?" Adele licked her upper lip and nodded as if to encourage me to reveal the Mormons' arcane sexual rites.

"Bigamy?" Raquel Barragan looked at me, her turquoise eyes even wider. "Plural marriages?"

"George," I asked, "have you no comment?"

"I have run into Mormons before. They are honest enough and all right if you don't discuss religion."

"Hear! Hear!" Peter said.

"But, Bill, my lad, you might have been a member of that church—what do they call it?"

"The Church of the Latter Day Saints," I said drily.

"The very one. Yes. You might have been baptized but you are not a churchgoer now, are you?"

"You have me, George. My father came from Wales, and as the Book of Mormon says, begat me and took me to Nauvoo. Then, while he went off to fight with the Mormon Battalion in the Mexican War, my mother and I walked almost all of the way to Salt Lake, pushing a cart full of what little we had."

"How many wives does your father have?" Smith asked.

"He had the one," I said. "One day in the mountain, singing 'Put Your Shoulder to the Wheel Push Along,' she stepped back from the cart, looked down over the wild snow-covered crags, smiled and said, 'Look, Billy. It's a lovely valley.' And then she just crumpled down onto the trail.

"She was buried there, somewhere in the wild Wasatch Mountains of Utah. My father never believed in plural marriages, nor was it a part of the church when he joined. He was with General Doniphan when they took Chihuahua. Somehow he got the better part of his pay away from the Mormon paymaster and as soon as he could, he took me back to Missouri. He joined the old church there, led by Joseph Smith's son."

I lifted a hand to fend off Smith's next question and turned to Sullivan. "But, to answer your question, George, no, I do not belong to any organized religion."

"Your father learned enough Spanish," Raquel asked, "fighting in Chihuahua, to teach you?" Her tone was doubtful.

"He was a bookish man and liked esoteric beliefs and he had a good ear. We were only in Utah two years and he was said to be fluent in Ute."

"Are we to have dessert, Mrs. Barragan?" Smith peered at the sideboard.

"Yes, we are. Maria has brought us tunas from the cactus, the red ones as big as prunes, and we have candied them. They are good, Doctor," she added hastily as his face fell, "you will see."

And he did. Smith probed his with his dessert fork, stuck

a tiny bit of the glazed fruit on a tine and touched his tongue to it. His eyes brightened and he took a tentative bite and then said nothing until he had finished.

"At our last dinner," Peter said, "when our Colonel Whigam and Lieutenant Bell were here with us, our acting commandant, Major Northey, barely had time to finish his cigar and brandy before he had to leave to prepare his first patrol against the Apaches. Tonight will be different. If the ladies will pardon us?"

Before the ladies could answer, there was a rap on the door. The maid's husband appeared from the dimly lit entrance hall and opened the door.

Sergeant Johnson saluted and said, "Colonel Whigam sends his compliments and would like to speak to the Officer of the Day."

"Yes, Sergeant," I answered for Peter. "Both Lieutenant Barragan and I will be right there. I did not hear the ambulance."

"He came on ahead, sir. Sergeant Blaine and the escort will be in soon."

"Yes, Sergeant. Tell the colonel that we are on our way."

Johnson saluted, about-faced and walked briskly out into the night. Peter excused himself quickly, as I did, and then we left. I suppose that we must have made the hundred-yard walk in less than a minute, but Whigam was not there.

"The colonel asks that you carry on. He will see Lieutenant Barragan at the morning muster and Lieutenant Northey after his patrol through the Sawyer Ranch."

"Patrol! Sawyer?"

"Yes, sir. The colonel crossed trails with a cowboy riding north from the Sawyer Ranch. He was to take a message to the Indian agent. It was a claim for a horse herd run off from the ranch."

"When?"

"Today. This morning early, I guess."

"Hallelujah!" I said joyfully.

"Why so happy?" Peter said, smiling.

"We shall leave as soon as Johnson can get the platoon provisioned. It is providential. We should be there with a fresh trail and with a Navajo scout that likely knows the area."

"You wouldn't want me to take the trail, sir?" Peter asked.

"Not this one. I promise you the next, Colonel Whigam willing. But please ask your sergeant to help Johnson prepare our patrol to leave by moonrise."

"Done! I hope you catch them. All of them. No matter what kind of Apaches they are."

"What do you mean," I said, "what kind of Apache?"

"Like Mescalaro, or White Mountain, or just plain White Apaches. Good hunting," Peter said and trotted off.

I walked quickly to my quarters for I had little time. But what had Peter meant by White Apaches?

# Thirteen

We rode silently past the Water Hole Cantina, its squat buildings black in the shadows of the cottonwood trees. Once well out of sight, as the sky lightened in the east, I would have stopped for a dry breakfast, but the Navajo, whose name was written as Red Woods on the pay voucher, made signs that we should ride on. I agreed, and by the time the eastern rim of the mountains was being washed from black to purple, we followed him up from sparse creosote brush into a formation of weathered rock and scrub cedar. We then dipped down into a basin just large enough to hide the fourteen mounts that comprised the available file of the first platoon.

It was also small enough to defend against a larger group and I marked it on my personal map. Water trickled slowly from beneath a huge boulder at one end into what seemed to be a natural rock basin. It would not be enough to replace water lost from evaporation and I supposed that it would be a seasonal source of water. Perhaps good for a month or two after one of the rare heavy rains. The horses were walked around the inner rim to cool off while we filled canteens and coffeepots. I picked up a small green stone and laid it at the water's edge. After the horses had been watered, my green marker was a foot higher than the water level.

The horses breakfasted first, munching oats from feed bags that had been stuffed into the ends of bedrolls tied behind each rider's saddle cantle. The men messed in fours, cooking for themselves. On a long stay in camp we had two cooks, chosen by lottery, called Long and Short Straw. Long Straw boiled coffee and dropped chunks of hard bread onto a slab of bacon for me as the others not on duty gathered around small cooking fires doing the same.

My coffee was hot and sweet, the bacon tasty and the bread almost as hard as it must have been when the War began. I ate the outside of it and left the rest for some poor unsuspecting coyote. I saw that Johnson and the Navajo had both finished their meal and motioned to Johnson to bring the scout to me.

The two walked over to where I sat comfortably on a slab of sandstone. I motioned for them to sit. Johnson sat near me on a small rounded boulder and the Indian sat on air. Later, when I saw Apaches leave horses to run up rock cliffs as if they were goats, I would remember the powerful thighs of our new scout as he squatted so easily that morning of our first conversation.

"Red Woods?" I said.

He looked behind him, then at me again and, as realization set in, grinned and pointed at his own chest.

"Yes," I said. "You are Red Woods. I am Lieutenant Northey. He is"—I pointed—"Sergeant Johnson."

"Okay," Red Woods said.

"Good. Now some Apaches have run off a band of horses from a rancher not far from here. Where would they take them?"

"Apaches." He drew a finger across his throat, cutting it with his finger. "Okay."

He obviously knew the country. And Apaches. What he did not know was English.

I had a go at sign language. Johnson did better, but all we got from the Navajo was a vague idea about something to the north that was several sleeps away. Then he knelt down, smoothed out the sand and with twigs and pebbles fashioned a kind of rustic painting of mountains and trees. He pointed to the north again, then tapped his chest and said, "Bosque Redondo."

He looked up at me and then repeated the phrase and drew a circle around the trees.

Lightning flashed. He was speaking Spanish. *Bosque* meant forest and *redondo* was round. A circle of woodland. Bosque Redondo. "You were with the Navajos at Bosque Redondo."

His face fell and he shrugged helplessly as he said the only English word he seemed to know, "Okay."

"I have it," I said to Johnson. "They call him Red as short for Redondo and woods because that is where he used to live. They were ordered to live there by the Indian Department."

"Bosque Redondo," Johnson repeated giving the words the English pronunciation. "They was on a reservation there."

"Right." I turned to the Navajo and in my halting imperfect Spanish we communicated. His Spanish, though rough by Peter Barragan's standards, was fluent, but he took pains to explain himself, sometimes with signs, occasionally using a Navajo word for some familiar object that I would readily recognize.

I was jubilant. A fresh trail, a scout familiar with the country and I was healthy. We drank sweet coffee, ate the bacon, gnawed at the bread hungrily and were ready to move on. I huddled with Johnson and the scout, speaking Spanish and interpreting in English for Johnson. I ordered them to ride far enough ahead to protect the column from ambush while we sent out flankers to cut the trail of the raiders. I called little Leroy Dewey over and introduced him to the scout.

"Private Dewey," I said ceremoniously, "this is our new scout, Red Woods."

"How," Dewey said with a grin. "Redwood. Welcome to our platoon."

The Navajo frowned. "Redwood," he repeated distastefully.

"It is a good name," I said in Spanish. "In our language it is the name of the biggest tree in the world." I raised both hands as high as I could. "Redwood!"

He grinned back at Dewey then, put a hand out and touched fingers, barely, and repeated, "Redwood."

Redwood was short, but with a tremendous chest and heavily muscled arms. He was the only man in the company as strong as Johnson. He wore a regulation sky-blue jacket and black hat, but preferred a breechclout and deerskin pants. He carried a blanket made by his people that was as watertight as the ones from Saltillo. He had been issued a .50-caliber Sharps breechloader. A good weapon, but old. It used a paper cartridge, with a lead ball attached and after loading, a percussion cap must be placed on the nipple where the hammer would strike it and ignite the powder inside.

His hull—army slang for a saddle—was a standard issue McClellan. His saddle blanket, folded as we did ours, once the long way and then twice more to make a thick pad, was Navajo, made from something he called bayeta cloth. My own saddle blanket was covered by an old, faded-blue shadrack to keep the sweat from my horse off my legs.

He had evidently trained his own horse, for he mounted— sprang would be a better word—onto the saddle from the right side. He had fastened a crescent cut from a silver peso to the head strap of the cavalry bridle and it dangled, points down, flashing in the sun. He told me that it was a *naja* and was good medicine against witchcraft.

When we were ready to ride again, I checked the level of the water. I could see no discernible difference. It would fill very slowly.

After the scouts moved out, we followed until we were in open country again and then I sent a squad out, on both flanks to ride out at a forty-five-degree angle and then back to cut the trail of the raiders.

The sun was halfway to overhead as we walked the horses, while the flankers trotted in and out and then were replaced by the files who had been walking their mounts.

Bagley, riding his own horse, Buck, now completely recovered from an Apache arrow, galloped back. He called out to me as he slid his mount to a stop.

"Major! We done cut the trail. They is too many tracks. All going dead south."

"Well done!" I looked at the line of riders. "Who has a fresh horse?"

"I do." Tom Jefferson spoke just before the chorus of volunteers.

"Ride quickly and fetch the scouts."

He saluted and was gone.

I stood up in the stirrups, waved the right-hand flankers back in, and then led the remaining men to the left, against the sun, at a walk, for we would have to wait for Johnson and Redwood to ride back from the south. We had found the trail, not yet, I thought with satisfaction, two days old.

The three riders were back within minutes, Johnson leading, riding his new horse, Baldy, a deep-chested gelding with just enough white above one ear not to disqualify him as a "black mount for Whigam's company." The Indian had brought his own horse which, unfortunately for our color choice, was a solid buckskin with a black mane and tail. However, Redwood would not be riding in many parades, so I figured we would let him keep the horse, at least, until the colonel saw him. Whigam, always unpredictable, when he did see the horse for the first time, liked its color. He said it matched the color of the Indian's trousers. We never knew the horse's Navajo name, but the men all called the horse "Okay."

Johnson and Redwood left their mounts with a horse holder and walked alongside the trail. They separated, one to each side, but they prowled back and forth like hounds on a trail. Occasionally they paused to study individual tracks, sometimes dropping to a knee to poke through the crust of a plop of manure.

Basically they both told the same story, which was reassuring as they could not talk to each other without my help as an interpreter. There were twenty-four horses being driven, mostly shod. But there were three startling conclusions: One, they were being driven by only six riders. Two, they were all riding shod horses. Three, the tracks were no more than six hours old.

"How far are we from the Sawyer ranch?" I asked Johnson.

"About four hours from his horse pasture."

"But Colonel Whigam met the rider yesterday."

We three huddled together. Johnson said, reluctantly, that the tracks might be a day old. Redwood shook his head and said nothing more.

"If you were an Apache and had a day's start, where would you drive the *caballada?"*

He turned away angrily and it was not until I apologized for my poor Spanish and assured him that I never meant to say he was Apache that he spoke.

"This *caballada* is being driven slow. From here in half a day, even faster, at a trot, south, there is only one place for the enemies to water."

"Enemies?"

"That is how you say Apache in Spanish. *Enemigo."*

"Apache means enemy, Why?"

"I don't know," Redwood said. "Ask the Zunis."

I understood then. Apache was obviously a Zuni word that had been adopted into several other languages.

"When you speak Navajo, what do you call Apaches?"

"Apaches. But we are speaking Spanish."

"And what do you call the Navajo?"

"The People, of course."

"Of course," I agreed, but wondered if the world might be divided between the People and the Enemies. "Might we catch up to the Enemies if we ride at the gallop?"

"Maybe. Maybe they will leave the *caballada* and run when they see us."

"I want the Apaches," I said.

"There is a long way to ride there, but a good rider like the sergeant and that boy soldier and me, we could circle around so as they would not see our dust and get there first. Maybe," he added fatalistically as he sensed my doubt.

"Even if you get there first," I said, explaining to Johnson Redwood's suggestion, "could you hold off six Apaches?"

I never met a better fighting man with a great instinct for tactics than Johnson so it was a tribute to the Apaches when he said, "Maybe we should take Corporal Green and Jefferson."

"They are both well mounted," I said, thinking aloud, "and Jefferson is as steady as Green. Can he ride?"

"He will be near as good as Dewey, sir, in another month."

I turned to the scout again. "Do you know the rifle that the sergeant is carrying?"

Although we were dismounted, every trooper carried his carbine on a sling over his breast, barrel down. When mounted, carbine still strapped to him, the trooper would immobilize his carbine by snapping the muzzle down into a tube fastened to the saddle.

"Sure. I left mine with my compadre when I joined the army."

"How do you load and fire?" I asked, while Johnson, listening intently, tried to follow the Spanish.

"You load him with a tube full of cartridges and then you lever in a cartridge and you pull back the hammer, shoot an enemy and then you lever in another one and you—"

"Good." I cut him off before he went through half a dozen tubes.

"Sergeant, bring me a Spencer and tubes from one of the troopers. The trooper can use the Indian's single shot."

Redwood was delighted. I did not look forward to an exchange later. I smiled and wondered if he might call me an Indian giver. But then, I could issue him our dead scout's carbine.

The unlucky trooper, Thaddeus Stevens, a light-skinned man from New Orleans, who was said to speak French, merely shrugged, and handed his carbine to the Navajo. I smiled at him with what I meant to be sympathy, but his eyes, set like coals deep in the face of an oriental snowman, seemed to take fire. I had better talk with that man, I thought.

Had I done so then, just taken a few minutes to listen to that tormented man, how many sad hours might I have saved myself later?

The four men gathered around me. I told them that if they reached the water before the Apaches, they were to hold it and not allow the hostiles entry. If that meant shooting horses, they must shoot them. The rest of the platoon would alternately trot and gallop until we reached the water hole at least one hour before sunset. If we were to hear gunfire, Crawford would sound the charge and we would come in immediately. If not, he would blow any other call and we would wait for a rider to come out.

"All right, Sergeant. If you should run into any hostiles except the raiders, return to this command immediately."

"Yes, sir." Johnson saluted.

"Leave everything here except your carbines, ammunition, canteens and a ration of oats. We will bring what you leave to you. Good luck."

The troopers left their saddlebags and bedrolls in one pile. Redwood mounted, watched. When I finally asked him why he did not leave any unnecessary weight behind, he shrugged and threw his blanket down to settle gently over the small pile that contained the necessities and one or two niceties of a trooper's equipment. Johnson mounted, smiled at the Navajo, saluted me, and then motioned to Redwood to lead. Redwood nodded and gave Okay his head. The buckskin settled into an easy lope and in minutes all I could see of the four riders was a faint plume of dust moving east, almost ninety degrees from the trail which we would follow.

Acting Corporal Jededia Robeson, who had taken the place of Corporal Brown, out of the hospital, but on light duty, had sent out one rider to scout ahead. He would race back if he sighted the Apaches or sighted the water hole. Robeson had also posted flankers riding about a hundred yards on either side.

Every half an hour or so I rode around the column, taking care not to ride near the forward observer. It kept the men alert and helped break the terrible monotony of riding toward a horizon that never changed, under a burning sun that squeezed the moisture from already dry skin and through a malignant growth armored with a variety of spines to puncture that mummified skin.

As I made my rounds, I asked myself questions and attempted answers. All the horses were shod. Strange? Yes, but Apaches often traveled long distances by foot and then stole horses which, unlike their own, were shod. The trail was at the most a day old, but the Sawyer cowboy had seen the Indian raiders approaching and ridden like the wind to cross the colonel's path. But with a letter? Only Sawyer could sign a letter with a claim for stolen stock. And just six warriors? More than enough to drive twenty-four horses. But to fight as many as twenty Sawyer employees? Or to raid for more horses? More questions than answers.

"Major!" Bagley, showing off, cantered up beside me, then slowed to a walk, our stirrups a foot apart. He had a melodious laugh, a ready smile, but also, Johnson had said, a quick temper.

He pointed up toward a slight rise. Our designated scout had halted, waiting for us to catch up. I lifted the reins slightly and touched Othello with spurs.

The scout, William Wilson—called Blue by the men, not only to differentiate him from the other "Bills," but because of his peculiar eyes that although gray seemed to have a touch of blue in them—was looking at a cliff some distance away.

"I think maybe there are some men climbing those cliffs," he said.

I looked but could see nothing, nor could Bagley. I twisted in the saddle and pulled my binoculars from the top of my round valise bag. By sighting along his arm, I got the general area and then picked out a large boulder and adjusted the lenses.

Two men, upper bodies dark brown against the white rocks, were climbing the cliff to what appeared to be one of those flat-topped hills called mesas by the Spanish. I handed the glasses to Bagley.

"Tell me what you see," I ordered.

He looked, waited, and then said, embarrassed, "I can't see nothing, Major."

"Put your finger on this knob"—I took his right forefinger and placed it—"and turn it slowly, easily until everything is sharp."

His breath hissed in. "Major, I can see all there is."

His forehead wrinkled with concentration, but he said nothing until I called out sharply, "Private Bagley. Do you see anything at all?"

"Those same two hostile Apache Indians is a-climbing away. A blue jay is a-yammering at them and an old rattlesnake just slid out of the way. And one Apache has got a blanket and the other one is carrying a bow and a quiver of arrows and they are on top picking up sticks and such." He stopped and looked at me puzzled. "I think that they mean to build a fire."

He held the glasses to me and I took them. He was right, for one of the men was squatting down, running a fire drill from a small bow. I rode to a nearby rock about as high as my belt buckle and dismounted.

"Wilson," I said urgently, "you ride ahead, at the gallop. We will catch up with you shortly. I am going to try to keep the fire makers from their job so you will hear my shots. Do not be alarmed, just ride on."

He saluted and wheeled his horse around to return to the column.

"Dismount, Bagley, and loan me your carbine."

I looked through the glasses again, marked a pine, just to the right of the fire maker and exchanged the reins of my horse and the binoculars for his carbine. I estimated the dis-

tance at seven hundred yards, knelt behind the rock, placed
the barrel in a natural crease in the rock and tilted it upward
until the sights touched halfway up the pine and squeezed the
trigger. The roar seemed deafening. Smoke floated slowly up
from the muzzle and then just as slowly drifted away with a
current of air that I did not feel.

"What do you see?" I called out.

"Nothing, suh." I turned to see him, the reins of the horses
in one hand and the binoculars in the other, peering up at the
mesa.

"Wrap the reins around your arm and use both hands to
look through the glasses with the other," I said.

He looked from one hand to the other helplessly. Time was
critical and I was about to lose my temper. I took a deep breath
and closed my eyes. The boy was nervous. Likely frightened
and confused.

"Just lift the glasses up and look through them the way you
did before," I said softly.

He looked at me as if I had spoken to him in Apache. I let
the butt of the Spencer slide down to the sand and making
circles with thumb and finger of both hands placed them over
my eyes and looked at him, then up at the mesa.

"Yes, suh, Major."

He mimicked me exactly and then, just as my storm was
about to break, quickly tucked the reins under his left arm,
lifted the binoculars to his eyes and said, "The two of them
are looking down here. I think they see us."

"All right. Take a turn around your left wrist with those
reins and then watch closely. Try to see where my shot hits."

He kept the glasses steady and said, "Yes, suh. I will."

I raised my sights to the tip of the pine and touched off the
second shot.

"That one hit something close, 'cause the one with the little
bow jumped behind the tree."

I kept the sight right where it was. "Tell me when he comes
back to light the fire."

"Yes, suh."

After a long pause—perhaps three minutes—Bagley said, "He's squatting down again."

My third shot rang out and Bagley shouted, "He gone. They both gone."

After a long wait, I checked my watch. It was almost six o'clock. When ten minutes had passed, I relaxed and let the carbine slide back down against the rock.

"Major! He got hisself a torch. He done threw it on that wood pile."

"What wood pile?"

"The one behind the tree. Look at the smoke."

A straight column of white smoke fueled, I thought, by pine and creosote brush, rose higher and higher. It could be seen for miles. Still, I thought, they might not be able to use the blanket to send signals. In those innocent days I thought they used a blanket to send puffs of timed smoke like the dots and dashes of Morse code. I put the sights at the top of the pine and emptied the chamber to give them something to think about while we moved on.

"What effect?" I asked.

"Suh?"

"Did you see any hits?"

"No, suh. But you effected them Apaches, 'cause they is coming down that hill a whole lot faster than they went up."

"Good! Well done, Bagley. We will rejoin the platoon quickly before the hostiles can set up an ambush."

We remounted and galloped, following easily the now well-marked trail, glancing back occasionally, apprehensively, at the large column of smoke rising higher and higher into the cloud-less sky.

# Fourteen

Corporal Robeson would alternate the pace between a trot and a gallop until the front rider sighted either a dust trail or the horse herd. They would have about a fifteen-minute advantage on us, so I kept Othello at a gallop. Finally as we reached a rise, we saw a dust trail and then the group and finally the blue-clad troopers themselves. Another mile, perhaps two, a thin line of dust marked the stolen herd and it was heading straight for a clump of trees that could only be the water.

I reined up and quieted Othello while I retrieved my binoculars. Although I could now see the group of horses, I could not make out individual riders nor, of course, see what kind of arms they possessed. The thought of leading a troop of thirsty horses and men against six well-armed Apaches fighting from cover was as dismal a prospect as it would be to walk the troop back to the closest water, leaving the Apaches unscathed, with their stolen property.

Then I heard the shots and the horse herd twisted and turned like a large snake in its death throes. *Hallelujah!* Johnson must be in possession of the water hole. I heard more shots and turned to Robeson.

"Did you count the shots?"

"More than ten, Major."

The mess call blown less discordantly now than a month

ago, drifted sweetly to my ears. "Can we charge them, suh?"
Bagley asked anxiously.

Wilson and his group were riding into the trees lining the
water hole. The horse herd had turned and was heading for
the nearest pile of rocks and boulders leading up into the
mountains. I made a quick calculation and decided that Robeson, Bagley, and I, by cutting to our right, riding almost dead
into the sun, could reach them before they could reach the
foothills.

"Yes," I said. "Maybe we can beat them to the hills."

And we did, almost. The herd, unfed and unwatered, faltered
and, left alone, trotted back toward the water. Four riders shot
out from the herd, like stars from a meteorite to race us to the
edge of the rocky slope. I pulled up about a hundred yards
short and yelled, "Dismount! Fight on foot!"

As I hit the ground, reins in my hand, so did my entire
command, Private Benjamin Bagley.

"Give me your reins," I ordered, not bothering to draw my
revolver, useless at this range. "Sit down, rest your rifle the
way you do on the practice range." A rifle range without ammunition! "Sight in at a hundred yards and squeeze the trigger."

He nodded, acting like a cool veteran, sat down, cocked an
elbow on a knee and, with the strap holding his arm firm,
fired. Outside of the smoke and an explosion almost in my
ear, I saw no result. I glanced at his sight and saw that it was
where I had left it—at maximum range.

I reached over and slid the range marker down and said,
"Try it again. Whenever a man stops to look back, squeeze
off a shot."

He was in deep concentration now, I knew, but he heard
me, for he nodded. The first three men left their horses and
ran up into the rocks out of sight. Bagley fired and missed
the third man, who was exposed for a few seconds, as he
scrambled up the hillside. The fourth man, ten yards behind
the others, sprang from his mount just as Robeson fired his

second shot. The hostile made the fatal mistake of pausing for an instant to look back, like a hunted deer will often do, toward his pursuers.

Bagley fired again. The Apache dropped his unaimed weapon and toppled over.

Bagley stood up, exultant. "I got me a Apache!"

Not lifting from where I knelt, I shoved the flat of my right hand against his leg as hard as I could and he fell heavily. There were two shots that followed immediately. His, when he fell, and inadvertently yanked the trigger. That one went harmlessly into the air. The other came from the rocky slope and exploded sand and prickly pear cactus directly behind where Bagley had stood.

We stayed down until Redwood and Johnson rode up and rose only when they dismounted. Johnson fired a warning shot at smoke drifting from the hillside and then kept a wary eye on the hillside. I called out loudly in Spanish to Redwood, telling him to come on foot, carefully, to our position. He was with us before I could scan the hillside with the binoculars. I sensed his presence and spoke.

"Only four came this way. Where are others?"

"They are back not far from the water hole. Only one rode in. He came in like a deer to drink," Redwood said. "The Enemies had seen the smoke signal from the hill. That made them wary."

Johnson slipped in beside me, and knelt, his carbine pointing toward the hillside where the Apaches had taken refuge.

"But they did not know that you were there?" I asked Redwood.

"No, else they would not have come in at all. I shot that one," Redwood said proudly. "And then the big black medicine man, the one you call Sergeant, he stood up and he shot the second one. That one had waited with the others, away from the trees. When he heard my shot, he left so quick. He was riding away so quick. But that sergeant, he shot that Apache right off his horse. He never even touched the horse. He makes big medicine with that rifle."

After interpreting Redwood's praise to Johnson as best I could, I asked the Navajo, "Didn't that smoke signal warn them about you at the water hole?"

"No. Those Enemies up in the hills just saw you. They did not see us. So they sent up a warning to any of their own people. It meant, 'Danger. Be alert.' "

A sudden thought struck me and I asked, in dismay, "Did you scalp those Enemies—I mean Apaches."

"Of course not," he said, offended. "Do you think I am a barbarian?"

Redwood puzzled me, but I apologized all the same.

"If we wait here long enough, they will have to come down for water," I said.

"They will know where to get water. And if you wait here much longer, there will be more warriors with good guns here. To answer the smoke."

"I believe that we have had a *Hallelujah* patrol. We have recovered an entire horse herd and we have killed three Apache warriors with not one casualty!"

"These boy warriors had old guns. Two muzzle loaders and a breechloader like that Sharps I had. The grown fighters take the good guns." Redwood looked up at the hillside, nodded to himself and walked over to the dead Apache sprawled face-down on the sand.

He was careful not to touch the body. He picked up the gun and brandished it. He yelled what must have been an insult at the hills and then brought the gun to me. It was old, all right. I saw that it was a clean but extremely worn flintlock. I took it from Redwood. It was uncocked. I cocked it and pointed it toward the hills. It fired.

"He might have killed us," Bagley said resentfully.

"Grown fighters?" I asked. "Then these three were all boys."

"They were warriors," Redwood said. "Young, but warriors. Maybe the leader was older."

"The other two, back there," Johnson said, "they too young to get into our army, Major."

I walked over to the dead Apache and turned over a boy, an expression of surprise on his dark brown face, his eyes wide open, staring at eternity.

"We can bury these men while the horses water," I said. "Set up a perimeter and be ready to pull out as soon as we can." I had no strong desire to wait there until the grown warriors with their good guns arrived.

"Yes, sir," Johnson said.

When the three bodies were laid one alongside the other, and the men began to dig a common grave, Redwood shook his head and spoke to me.

"I would not put them in the ground. Besides, after we leave, they will come and take them away."

"We will give them a decent burial," I said.

"They will dig them up again," Redwood said and then looking up toward the menacing hills added, "The horses are all watered."

I knew that the Apaches seldom left their dead and would likely be back soon. I said, "All right. Bring the Apache weapons along. We will make camp back at Redwood's water."

We moved out with the sun behind us and just before sunset, Redwood and Johnson rode ahead of us to light a fire on the ridge above the water that we could use as a beacon to guide us in. It would not have been needed, for the loose horses smelled the water and trotted ahead before we ever saw the welcome red light in the lonely darkness.

As soon as we had set up the pickets, cooled, watered all the horses, fed our own mounts, and enclosed the loose horses in a rope corral, we ate. I had ordered our sometime cooks to double up the rations and hauled a bag of hard candy from my valise for dessert. After bacon and bread crushed into a pot of beans, we had a last cup of coffee and a handful of candy to suck on.

One of the men, I could no longer see who, sang softly, a song I had not heard before. It was sad and plaintive. Most of the men sang along. I found myself humming, thinking of my parents and the long ago. When the last note trailed off into a complete silence, Johnson asked if he should put out the fire.

"Not quite yet," I said. "Let's have one more song. Something livelier like 'When Johnny Comes Marching Home' or 'The Battle Hymn of the Republic.' "

They sang both and then finished off with Private Benjamin Bagley singing the tenor questions of a shy young maiden, while the deep bass chorus, including Sergeant Johnson and Corporal Green, sang the answers.

I found six feet of rock-free sand, scooped out a fit for my hips and shoulders and squirmed into my blankets, chuckling at the lively repartee. The last thing I remembered was the clear tenor of Bagley asking plaintively, "But then, is my true love in the swamp or on the hill?"

Before the bassos could reply, a coyote howled and then half a dozen others and the platoon was laughing. Just before I drifted off, I thought I heard Redwood laugh.

# Fifteen

There was no attack at dawn. But had there been, we would
have been ready. Shadows no longer turned into hidden
Apaches nor did yucca cactus take the shape of a warrior aiming his rifle. Now that we had fought the Apache, had seen
what the old-timers used to call "The Elephant," we were no
longer so fearful. Not that we were less wary. If anything, we
were more careful but our fear had been replaced by an angry
respect.

We breakfasted, set up the line of march and detailed four
troopers as horse herders. Although they were jeered at and
called "cowboys," the other troopers were envious. Any break
in military routine is almost as welcome a diversion as a complete escape from the stringent military discipline that a soldier
feels when he is off duty and away from his post.

Redwood and Johnson came back from their scout at the
trot.

"The Water Hole Cantina is an hour ahead," Johnson reported.

I nodded.

Johnson looked at Redwood, who lifted a hand with the two
outer fingers projected and said, "Okay."

"Sir," Johnson continued. "Redwood saw some antelope.
He figures we could ride ahead, get one and maybe have fresh
meat for dinner?"

"Is it open country?"

"Yes, sir."

"How do you plan to approach these antelope? Are they not as wary as deer?"

"They are scarier, Major. I ain't been able to get close enough for a shot, but Redwood here, he says he knows how and he been right about things so far."

"Is it true, Redwood," I said, "that you can kill one of those two-horned deer and still meet us at the Water Hole Cantina early enough to cook the meat?"

He nodded and shrugged as if he would drop by a local meat market and pick up a roast for dinner.

"And there will be no Apaches nearby to hunt you?"

"Not with the black man's medicine gun. I shoot deer while he watch out for both of us. Besides, no Enemies will come. Not for a while. No."

"All right," I agreed. "We will have fires ready."

Johnson listened anxiously, almost understanding. He had picked up some Spanish on the frontier and would soon know more. I repeated, briefly, in English what the Navajo had told me and gave Johnson permission to go on the hunt.

Johnson grinned, said, "Thank you, Major," then extended his right arm as if sighting a pistol. "The line of march should be a bit to the right of that crag sticking up out of the shadow of the big mountain there, like a boar's tooth."

Johnson saluted and the two of them rode off about ten degrees to the north of our line of march. I waved Green over and told him that we would noon at the Water Hole.

"Maybe the squadron money box could buy us some of them corn pancakes they makes there?"

"Tortillas? I don't know," I said. There might be money in the cash box, but that was back at the squadron. I had very little cash, maybe some silver in my coin purse.

"Major, maybe we could trade all that hard bread we got left."

"The Guera will never trade for that. She has good teeth, but not that good."

"Major Northey, sir," Green said innocently, "I never meant to break the lady's teeth. I figured they might use the bread instead of that soft adobe to build themselves a waterproof outhouse."

"No," I said, my brain lagging behind my mouth, "they will never—" I broke off, staring at Green with amazement. He had never made even a small attempt at humor with me nor even joked with the others when I was near.

He turned his head slightly, eyeing me warily, but when my laughter erupted, he smiled and laughed. An hour later, when we looked down at the adobe buildings now lit by the sun, our eyes met and we laughed again.

There were no horses tied in front of the cantina and only two geldings and a mare in the horse corral under the charge of a boy, who was trailing the butt of an old musket behind him. I did not think that he would have been able to raise it unaided. However, I realized that it was his symbol of authority and gravely reported to him.

"I am Lieutenant Northey, commanding the first platoon of Company E of the Ninth Cavalry Regiment."

"I am called Juan Jose Valtierra Sanchez, at your service, and I am in charge of the stock."

I saluted. His eyes grew large and he leaned his musket against a rail of the corral and tried a salute.

"Would you grant me permission to water our horses and fill our canteens?"

"Yes, sir." He tried another tentative salute and when I responded, his grin grew until his thin brown face was split by a half-inch line of perfect white teeth.

We did not need water for beasts or men, but it was protocol to ask and I was relieved not to hear a price for the water. I dismounted, let Dewey lead my horse away, and walked around the scattered buildings, recalling vividly the events that had taken place just a few weeks ago.

Juan Jose followed me. When I stopped to examine the sagging corral gate, he stopped too and ran his fingers as I had done over the faulty rawhide hinge. The cooks were eyeing a large woodpile not far from the kitchen.

"Do not use The Guera's wood without permission," I said. "You must ask first."

"You better not, *teniente.*" The boy spoke English fluently with a slight Mexican accent almost lost in the West Texas twang. "She shot the other boy who had this job when he woke her up before noon."

"Shot him?"

"Yes, sir. Right through the heart."

"How do you know that?"

"She told me," he said without a flicker of doubt in voice or expression.

"Well then, if she would shoot a boy, I suppose she might shoot a *teniente*—a lieutenant—as well," I said, deciding to keep the conversation in one language.

"Besides, I bring in the wood. I get you all you want. Mesquite, over yonder."

I nodded at the cook. Following procedures laid down thousands of years earlier, the cook sent his helper, who, I am sure, allowed the boy to volunteer his services.

Green pleased me by placing pickets around the camp, safe as it was. The occasional camp cook's helper rode back, his lariat dragging an interlocking tangle of mesquite so dry it resembled a huge black and gray tarantula. The boy trotted upwind to avoid the dust and then waved his arm to detain the rider.

"There"—he pointed—"that is where we do the *barbacoa.*"

"Barbacoa?"

"Sure. The pit it is dug. You just lay the logs crisscrossed and then you put the rocks on the wood and light it. When the rocks sink down to the bottom, they get hot, hot. You shovel on a little dirt, then you split some mescal leaves, the longest ones, and you cover everything before you put the meat on. More leaves on top and then fill it up with dirt and wait. In a while, we dig up the meat, juicy and tender. Of course," he added seriously, "you must have some onion and tomato and chile for the salsa."

"Of course," I agreed.

"And maybe some of them tortillas," the cook's helper said anxiously. His name was William Long, but he was called Long Straw just as the cook whose name was Samuel Short, was called Short Straw. Short was a moon-faced man who could sleep in the saddle, sitting upright or, even, Dewey alleged, while he cooked. Long had an anxious quality about him as if he was worried that there would be a meal or a party and no one would invite him.

The timing could not have been better. The rocks were indeed white and at the bottom of the five-foot pit when one of the pickets rode in and sang out, "They is coming in yonder and they got two of them big goats tied back of their hulls."

The men crowded around the riders, mixing friendly insults with congratulations. I went to the back door of the outbuilding that housed the kitchen cantina. I meant to barter. Green had a sack of hard bread and I had found a silver dollar in my purse. I hesitated at the door, but my shadow, Juan Jose called out, "Maria," and then lost me with a burst of staccato Spanish.

The door opened and I recognized the cook, a woman in her forties with braided hair touched with gray. Her face was barely wrinkled, but she must have had bad luck with her teeth, for when she smiled, I could see few opposing teeth.

"We would like a supply of tortillas. Enough for fourteen"—I put my hand on the boy's shoulder—"fifteen men."

He looked up at me, eyebrows lifted like question marks. I nodded and he grinned.

My Spanish amused the cook, but she understood me. She pretended to swat Juan Jose with her apron when he said impudently, "I can eat four tacos made with that wild goat. Ay, Maria." He added as the thought struck him, "You will surely trade tortillas for *barbacoa?* And The Guera! She would be in a good mood if she had *barbacoa* tacos for breakfast."

Maria nodded and called to her helpers, two girls not much

older than Juan Jose. As I walked away, I could hear the sweet sound of tortillas being patted out.

Johnson, in some mysterious way conferring with Redwood, supervised the dismembering of the antelopes by the cooks. They first removed the skin, cinnamon stripes on white, carefully stripping away all of the flesh from the skin, then reducing the meat to a pile of easily handled cuts. The pit had been lined with intertwining fingers of long, limp agave leaves, the ones the Apaches eat and gives the Mescaleros their name. They laid the cuts of meat carefully in a layer covering the leaves and then Maria and Juan Jose covered the meat with more leaves until it looked like a thatched roof and finally, Long Straw shoveled dirt in until the hole was filled.

The cook looked from Johnson to Redwood and then to the boy, Juan Jose, who nodded approval.

"When the sun is there," the boy announced, pointing some two hours past the clock, "they will be cooked."

I checked my watch. It was just past ten o'clock.

"Sergeant Johnson," I said, "I think we might deliver these horses to the Sawyer ranch."

"Yes, sir. Shall we change the herders?"

"Why not? I will want you here in command. I will take Corporal Green with me. You pick three troopers who deserve to play cowboy."

"Yes, sir. The ranch house is three miles south of the horse pasture. You will see the first windmill as you ride south. Another four miles and you will see another. The ranch house is just beyond it under a couple of big cottonwoods. Green knows the way. We was there together once, with Lieutenant Barragan."

While we readied for the short drive to the Sawyer Ranch, I wrote a brief description of each horse along with its brand, a simple *S* with an *R* up tight against the *S*. I folded the document and placed it inside my tunic. The horses were all between four and five years old, well built and would have been acceptable to the most exacting officer buying for our cavalry.

We reached the pasture, large enough to furnish grazing for several hundred horses, but drove our small herd on toward the ranch. I wanted a receipt from Sawyer, or in his stead, the ranch foreman.

When we came up over a rise and could see the line of cottonwood trees, two riders appeared and galloped out to meet us.

"Hello, Major." The young cowboy who had almost but not quite called me a murderer, rode straight up to me. "I heard that you all took real good care of Sandy."

"As we would have of any wounded man, including you."

He nodded thoughtfully. "I don't figure on getting myself shot. I thank you for Sandy."

I touched my hat in a kind of salute. Embarrassed, he turned to the horse herd. "You got the horses back."

"That we did. Twenty-six head. Fourteen geldings and twelve mares."

"Would you look at that, Tommy?" The other rider pulled up. "I would have thought the Apaches had run them down to Mexico by now."

"In two days?" I asked.

"No. They run that bunch off maybe four, five days ago."

"No, Tommy," The rider said. "It was two days ago. We was playing penny ante in the bunkhouse when Charley come in to tell us."

"Jake, it was four days."

"I guess it don't matter, now the army got 'em back." Jake leaned over to squirt tobacco juice, and then asked, "Did you see the Injuns?"

"We did," I said. "Is Mr. Sawyer in? I want a receipt for these horses."

"He is," Jake said, wiping tobacco juice from week-old whiskers. "I guess maybe he'll come out."

Before I could speak, he spurred his horse into a gallop and was gone. I turned to Tommy and said, "Maybe you should ride ahead and tell Mr. Sawyer that if I do not get a signed receipt for these horses, I will be forced to confiscate the herd."

"Yes, sir." Tommy trotted away.

There was a breaking corral and a barn some fifty yards from what appeared to be the bunkhouse and a hundred yards farther one of those ubiquitous ranch houses Texans build to catch the prevailing wind and cool off an open area they call a dogtrot, roofed over and joined on both sides by a couple of rooms. The whole structure was built with logs and lined with roughly split shingles, weathered silver.

A cowboy, neither Jake nor Tommy, opened the corral gate and the horses trotted right in. As I rode up to the house, I saw someone bring a wagon over to the rail and begin to fork hay into the corral.

Just as I dismounted, the front door of the unit to my left flew open and Sawyer, unshaven, but dressed in clean linen and wearing a black coat stepped out onto the open porch. He frowned at me as if trying to remember my name.

I slid from the saddle easily and stepped up onto the porch. He did not offer his hand.

"I am Lieutenant Northey," I said. "We have met."

"Lieutenant?" He looked at me, puzzled, then smiled and said, "Major Northey. Of course. What brings you here?"

"The stolen horses," I said, now more puzzled than he. I looked to one side and saw the tobacco chewer, Jake, watching.

"Of course. They were taken from the north pasture about four days ago. If you get right on those tracks you might catch them before they cross the river."

"Mr. Sawyer. We found the tracks three days ago, and—"

"Well, don't waste any more time," Sawyer interrupted. "After them, man. Speed is of the essence. Fifty-two of my best horses are being ridden to death right now by a band of thieving Apaches."

"Please. I would like to start all over. We have recovered your horses. What I want—what I asked for—was, *is* a receipt for twenty-four horses." I took the paper and pencil from inside my jacket. "I have a description of the horses and brands."

"You recovered twenty-four—"

"Mr. Sawyer," Jake cut in, "I told you. The nigger troopers, they brought them in. Look in the corral."

Sawyer reacted to that. He looked at the corral, saw the horses, and turned to me, and said in disbelief, "You caught up with the Apaches and recovered my horses?"

"Yes, we did."

"The Apaches ran away." It was not a question, but I treated it as such.

"There were six. Three got away. Three were killed."

"You killed three Apaches. How many troopers did you lose?"

"Not one casualty. Not one wounded man," I said with some pride.

He looked at me then as if wondering why I was standing on his veranda at this particular time and then started as if awakening suddenly and said sharply, "You let them get away with the rest of my herd. They took the best of the horses. Of course! They saw you dogging along the trail and left the culls for you while they ran off with twenty-eight head. Stallions and brood mares!"

"There were no other horses. We followed the tracks of twenty-four horses from your pasture. And we brought twenty-four back."

"You killed three adult Apaches in a fight! Where are their scalps? Your black troops killed real Apache warriors? I think not!"

"We killed three Apache warriors. They were not well armed, but armed, and came close to killing one of my men."

"I have a claim for fifty-four horses and I want my money."

His voice had been rising in pitch, little by little. A half dozen men, not including ourselves, were standing within earshot, listening. Jake and Tommy looked apprehensively at him. Seemingly, at Tommy's urging, Jake spoke.

"Mr. Sawyer, the major ain't got nothing to do with the payment. He just brought back the horses. Just sign for the horses he brought back and he will go along. Won't you, Major?" he added, nodding as if he could influence my answer.

"Yes. I will. I will also make a complete report of the number of animals, their tracks and when we first found them."

"And just what do you mean by that? I have twenty armed men here—white men!'"

"Is that a threat, Mr. Sawyer?"

Sawyer opened his mouth to speak. Then, with a crafty smile on his face as if he had caught me in some sort of ruse, he said, "No. Not at all. That was a fact. In case you need to be rescued from some real Apaches. All right, Jake. You may sign the receipt."

He turned on his heel and went back into his house.

Jake held out his hand, took the paper uncertainly and turned it all the way around.

"The date is on top," I said.

"Which is the top?"

I took the paper from him, turned it right-side up, read the text aloud, then using a porch post to write on, penciled in the present date and marked a space below it with an $X$.

"Sign there," I said, holding the paper for him.

He did, but so slowly and laboriously that he almost bit his tongue off. It was obvious that even if he could sign his own name, he was illiterate.

I checked the signature and said, "Jake Guyman?"

"Yes, sir."

"Thank you, Jake. You might tell Mr. Sawyer that I shall give my superior officer, Colonel Whigam, a detailed report of this incident including Mr. Sawyer's comments."

As we rode out past the horse pasture on our way back, a shaggy figure mounted on a horse just as shaggy and perhaps as bony, hailed me.

"How, Major. Been making medicine with Sawyer?"

"Hello, Charley," I said recognizing the wild old mountain

man. "Not much compared with you. The boy whose intestines you cleaned is all right."

"The one I pissed on his guts and stuffed them back in. That one?"

I resisted the temptation to ask how many intestines he had handled that month and said, "Yes."

"Good. I liked that nigger. Never made no fuss. He'll do to trap with. You tell him," he said, animated now, "that Charley Dirty Knife will learn him to trap wolves as soon as he gets to walking."

"I will pass the offer on to him," I said. I had no desire whatsoever to try to explain the terms of enlistment in the Army of the United States to a man who was as free as the wind with the temperament of a grizzly bear, and a knife almost as big as a saber.

# Sixteen

Before I could even see the Water Hole Cantina, Charley could smell it. To be precise he could smell *berrendo* tacos. Or said he could. Charley was not a man to worry much about truth. Later, as I got to know him better, I realized that he never lied maliciously. It was just that his world was filled with spirits and omens and strange beings never seen or even imagined by more worldly people.

"What is a *berrendo* taco?" I asked.

"Well you take a good corn or even wheat tortilla and you put the *berrendo* in it and wrap it in the tortilla—"

"I know what a taco is," I said, realizing that my short temper was, in part, due to hunger. "What is a *berrendo?*"

"It's one of them striped goats about the size of a small whitetail deer."

"Antelope!" I said. "That is what Redwood brought in and what you claim you can smell."

"No." He sniffed again and shook his head. "What I smell is *berrendo.* Maybe you can smell antelope."

"No. I cannot smell anything except maybe wolf fur." He had at least one fresh pelt rolled up and tied back of his saddle.

"You want a pelt, Major? One of them half-Injun girls could make that into a good coat for you. Warmer than deer hide."

"Is *berrendo* an Indian word?"

"I might know and then again I might not." He closed his eyes and then, after several minutes, turned in the saddle to look straight at me. "Major, I got that pelt promised to that cute little girl that cooks for me. You'll just have to trap your own wolf. Maybe that black nigger boy can learn you how."

"Charley, I do not want a wolf pelt."

"Of course you do. Who wouldn't want a prime wolf skin?"

Johnson, mounted on his new horse, Baldy, waited for us, by the picket at the top of the gentle rise above the Water Hole Cantina. I touched my hat to the crusty old mountain man and trotted forward.

Johnson saluted and said, "The horses have been cleaned and curried and our dinner is almost ready to be served."

I nodded and sniffed the air.

"Do you smell it, Major?"

"Yes, I guess." I sniffed again and could smell nothing. Maybe I was losing what little sense of smell I had once had.

Jefferson was waiting for my horse. I dismounted, untied my valise and walked over to the men waiting around the cooking area. Johnson called them to attention and I put them at ease and sniffed again. I could smell coffee and the smell edged my hunger. I pulled my oversize tin cup from the valise.

Dewey took my cup from me, showed me a chair that had been borrowed, he said, from the cantina, and sat me down in the shade of a large cottonwood. He was back in a minute with a half a pint of steaming coffee.

"Sure smells good, don't it, Major?" Dewey sniffed appreciatively.

"Yes," I said, testing the rim of the cup with a finger. I hazarded a sip and burnt my lips on the rim. I wondered how many times I had repeated that exact act. The coffee was sweet and strong, but it did not taste as good as it had smelled. Jefferson came back with my old dented mess kit.

"That meat makes my teeth itch," he said. "It smells too good."

Juan Jose marched up, his musket trailing him, and saluted. I returned his salute and before he could speak, said, "Good work, Private. That meat certainly smells good."

"It does?" he said doubtfully. And then, with a glance at the sun, he turned to call out, "It is time."

"Time!" the cook, Short Straw yelled, and the men cheered.

Long Straw held a shovel at port arms and then with a flourish began to dig away the dirt, carefully. When his shovel scraped up a shred of green skin from a leaf, there were hisses of apprehension followed by sighs of relief as the cooks, aided by the boy and the two young girls who worked in the kitchen, got down on their knees and took off layer after layer of the long leaves almost woven into green mats. They snatched the last ones off and threw them back over their shoulders. Up came the steam and the pungent almost sweet odor of the meat cooked to perfection in its natural oven, tasting even better than it had smelled.

But the crowning moment was, after everyone present, not all soldiers, tasted the meat, when the two young girls brought out freshly cooked tortillas the size of plates and as thick as my little finger. They laid strips of steaming meat on the tortillas, ladled out a green sauce made from chiles and a small kind of wild tomato they called *tomatillos,* rolled meat and sauce into the tortillas and dealt them out so quickly that within a few minutes, everyone, including the cooks and even the pickets, still on duty, was eating tacos.

There was little conversation and the only sound at all had to do with the preparation or eating of the succulent tacos. So it was that when Blondie spoke, all heads turned and all eyes were upon her.

She had dressed with a great deal of care. Her dress was long and ample, the points of her shoes peeping out from the hem were white satin. Her hair was brushed back and held in place by a large tortoiseshell comb. She carried a white parasol. "I thank the Ninth Cavalry for inviting me to breakfast." She dipped her parasol to me as if it were a flag.

I rose quickly and escorted her to my chair. She nodded graciously and both girls ran to bring her coffee and a taco. Her eyes widened when she tasted the meat.

"Ooh." She sighed with pleasure. "It is a long time since I eat *berrendo* tacos. Too long."

She pointed to the Navajo and spoke to him mostly in Spanish, with a few words in English, which he did not understand and a few in what I presumed was Navajo, that I did not understand.

"Tell me, *hombre* from Bosque Redondo, how do you catch these *berrendos?*"

"We shoot them. Me and that big-shouldered man. But you can't sneak up on one of those goats. They don't smell the hunters so good, but they see better than the major with his medicine glasses."

Juan Jose was giving the soldiers a rapid-fire interpretation, but as Redwood begin to act out the hunt, miming both hunters and hunted, oral language was secondary.

Redwood held his rifle in his left hand and then tied a scarlet rag to his moccasin. He lowered himself to the ground and then lifted both feet high, upside down, resting on his shoulders.

"This animal has one big weakness. He is too curious. I wave my foot with the red cloth and he wonders."

He waved the foot back and forth and then, laying his rifle carefully down, he stood up, held a finger to each temple and cocking his head back and forth, craning his neck to see better, became a curious antelope, slowly edging closer to the hunter.

Back and forth he moved between the roles of hunter and hunted until finally the hunter lifted the rifle and one-armed, shot the antelope. Quickly he became the dead animal and then a live one just beginning to run when he pointed over to Johnson, who mimed a shot with an imaginary rifle and the second antelope tumbled to the ground.

The audience, including one First Lieutenant William Northey cheered. He was at least as good an actor as a scout. Charley Dirty Knife, a joint of meat in one hand—he said he never ate bread, had got out of the habit—was vociferous in his praise.

"That red nigger knows *berrendos*. Why they got no nose at all, like he says. But they can see the fleas on that rabbit in the moon."

"You mean the man in the moon," I corrected.

"Folks around here and them *berrendos* see a rabbit in the moon. I go along with them," he said testily, thrusting his gray-whiskered face at me. "Now if you want to wait for the moon to come up, I'll point out the rabbit to you."

"Sorry, Charley," I said hastily. "I'll take your word for it. You ever shoot a *berrendo?*"

"I never shot a single *berrendo* in my life, but I sure have shot a lot of *berrendos*."

I sighed. Charley had me, but I had no idea how. "If you have not shot a single antelope, then how is it that you have shot a lot?"

We had an audience by then and Charley was enjoying himself. "Why, Major, I got myself a Hawkins rifle. It will shoot about as far as a *berrendo* can see. When I hunts *berrendos,* I wait until at least two are lined up and then I shoots me *two berrendos!*"

Everyone who heard the story laughed and cheered. Charley glowed. "Why I have killed so many of them antelopes that I lost count. It was me that told Redwood about that herd up past that red rock sink."

"And," I said, understanding at last, "that is also how you have that remarkable facility for smelling *berrendo* tacos?"

"Why, Major," he said, shaking his head at my ignorance, "ain't no kind of nigger can smell something cooking under four feet of dirt."

"Charley, you said—"

But Charley was gone and although I was to hear more of his stories, I never heard more about antelope. He did not have the vice of some old men of repeating stories ad nauseam.

We split the meat that was left, almost fifty pounds, between the cantina and the army. We would have enough to feed those at the post who had missed the big meal. Later on, after the big battle with the Apaches, there was not one trooper at Fort Rivas who would admit that he had not been there. Even troopers from other companies, once the story was out, claimed to have not only eaten the antelope tacos, but had seen Charley Dirty Knife shoot two antelopes with one shot. That is how legends are made and we now had a small one all our own.

Reluctantly, I gave the order to move out. I had a private word with Blondie inside the cantina while I waited for Johnson to ready the platoon.

"Your boys can come back anytime, General. If you send me word first, I'll tell you when the others will not be here. No need to even let the *loco* Sawyer know. I give your buffalo soldiers sweet things. Girls and maybe candy. I give you some too, General. You got time now? No charge."

"I am sorely tempted," I said truthfully, "but if an officer has privileges, he also has duties, and the first one is to take care of his men first."

"General!" She was shocked. "Counting yourself, you have fourteen men. And I don't have even one working girl here to help me."

I must have been shocked too, because before I could phrase an answer, she wrinkled her brow, moved lips and fingers as if toting up a bill and asked, "How much time you got?"

I laughed then. No, I exploded. When I stopped laughing, she pretended to be serious, but she had to smile even as she spoke.

"No good? Well, what the hell! *Mañana,* maybe?"

The bugle called the troop to saddle. I held out my hand, but she stepped in close, pressed me mightily and kissed me. When I stepped outside into the bright sun in front of my assembled troopers, Dewey was waiting, holding my horse, Othello, who neighed loudly. I wondered if it was in approbation or disapproval.

"A rider is coming in, Major," Johnson called.

I waited, holding the reins of Othello until I could see the rider clearly. It was the young cowboy called Tommy. He trotted up to me, touched his hat, and swung down from his mount. "Major, I got a letter to deliver to Fort Rivas."

Our temporary camp had become a fort at least to the Whigam company and the civilians who lived in the area. I held my hand out, but he shook his head.

"Mr. Sawyer done told me I got to put this in the hand of the colonel there at the fort."

"Of course. I suppose it is a complaint?"

"I suppose too, Major. Mr. Sawyer said I should get there as soonest I could, but I ain't riding a Sawyer horse. This here mustang is my own horse. I don't reckon to ruin him riding at a dead run to that fort, do I?"

I nodded and then, as the scent of the blond madam reached me, turned to see her at my elbow.

*"Hola,* Tommy. *Como estás?* You want a cold beer and a hot mamá?"

Tommy blushed redder than had I at my recent encounter with Blondie.

"No, ma'am. I mean I'd like to, but I'm broke and I got to deliver a letter for the boss."

"Blondie," I asked, "is my credit good here?"

"Hey, change your mind, eh? You may be a *militar,* but you are a *hombre* with *cojones,* no?"

She had a knack for asking unanswerable questions so I did not venture an answer.

"I, too, am broke, like Tommy here. But I would like to treat him to a beer and, ah . . . something hot."

"You pay for little Tommy Morrison. *Está bien.* He is okay and you too, General."

"Thank you—" I stopped myself from saying "madam," and said instead, "do you want me to sign a chit?" She frowned. I explained. "A paper that states how much I owe you."

She understood that and laughed. "No. I toll you when you soldiers have a payday and then you got to *montar* your *caballo* and ride over to see The Guera, me, Blondie. Then, General, I tell you how much—or what—you owe me!"

I said nothing, but did flick her a salute. I mounted and then said, "If you would like to rest here for a bit, Tommy, I will tell the colonel that you are on your way."

Tommy looked as dazed as a small boy who on Christmas Day has found a shiny new Barlow folding knife in his stocking. Juan Jose came up to wave a salute at me and to take the reins from the unresisting hand of the cowboy. When we rode out and I looked back over my shoulder, Blondie was leading Tommy in one direction toward her bedroom, while Juan Jose lead the cowboy's horse in another toward the corral.

# Seventeen

Whigam was back. The old ambulance was in its place between the hospital and the granary. I groaned silently and then told myself that it might have been worse. True, I would not have time to write a full report, but at least I could prepare the colonel for Sawyer's letter.

I dismounted, removed my valise from the saddle, gave the reins to Dewey and walked up the steps to report. The door was open. Whigam stood with his back to me, shoulders slumped, arms listlessly at his sides.

"Colonel Whigam," I said, saluting. "Glad to have you back."

"You are?" he said, as if surprised, turned, returned my salute with a tired flick of his hand and then surprised me with a sad smile and his extended hand.

"I am glad to be back," he said, surprising me even more.

"You are?" I smiled then, realizing that we seemed to be repeating each other. "I mean you never seemed to be fond of this post."

"I have been two weeks in Albuquerque trying to convince my wife to leave that godforsaken jumble of pretentious gringos, supercilious Spaniards and bitter brown people, all living in angry disharmony."

"I hope you have been successful," I said, wondering if he had taken over the Barragans' quarters.

"Oh, yes." He laughed, but it was a sad whinny. "She has

left by stage for the East. But we will of course be as close as ever. We shall write."

"I am sorry," I said.

"Why?"

It did not do to speak lightly nor in banalities with Whigam. "I suppose that if I were married, I would hate to be separated from my wife and it makes me sad."

"All right," Whigam said, dismissing the matter. "I have read your reports. I talked to the men in the hospital, including the cowboy who can now write his own name. They all support you and your report. I am convinced that the report is factual. However you know that Sheriff Pace is a lawman devoted to upholding the law and himself. Sawyer backs his political aspirations with good hard cash." He paused, cocking his head and raising his eyebrows, waiting for me to respond.

"Yes, sir. All that is true. It is also likely that Sawyer, personally, attempted to murder a soldier of the United States Army."

"Yes, I believe he did. Do you think Sawyer will let the matter rest?"

"I do not know." I sighed audibly and continued. "I would like to report the events of our last patrol. Based on the information you sent to us, we were able to make contact with the Apache."

I recounted the events of our patrol as tersely as I could without omitting any relevant detail. He was jubilant when I spoke of the encounter with the oddly fresh trail and even more so as he learned of our victory and the recovery of the herd. He was as puzzled as I over Sawyer's reaction and the impending delivery of a threatening letter.

Whigam pulled out a bottle from his desk, along with two heavy glass tumblers. He motioned me to sit and poured each glass nearly full, about four times as much brandy as an eastern bartender might serve in a shot glass or a larger snifter.

"Well done, Major Northey."

We clicked glasses.

"Thank you," I said. "We have men who will fight and win against the Apache."

We drank to that.

"Do you think that they would have fired on white men?" he asked, referring to the incident at the Water Hole Cantina.

"I don't know. I am certainly glad we did not have to find out."

"So am I," Whigam said fervently. "Although I do not think Sheridan would have hesitated a second to send a black squadron against some of the white rascals we have to contend with."

"I agree. That redheaded Irishman would not have been intimidated."

"Yes," Whigam agreed. "But it did cost him the job. The two-faced politicians, both North and South, maneuvered a more malleable man into his place."

Whigam filled my glass again.

"Sir," I protested, "I must write my report as well as a copy for you to send along with Sawyer's letter."

"Of course you must. We must all write reports. That, sir, is what makes the army run. Reports, sir. And who must write them? Not brevet majors, nor the wives of brevet majors."

"I have no wife to write my reports, sir," I said.

"Nor do I. Only Lieutenant Barragan has a wife. However, First Lieutenant Northey, what has that to do with your written report?"

"Nothing, sir." He was off again. I braced myself mentally.

"And why do you not have a wife?"

"I do not know."

"You are correct. Exactly right! You lack the opportunity. You are in the wrong place. I put it to you, sir, if you were an army officer stationed near New York or Boston or New Orleans or even that gem of the West, El Paso, you would certainly be happily married."

"Yes, sir. Might I write the report?"

"We will need an extra copy," Whigam said, nodding as if

answering my question affirmatively. "Have Johnson make two true copies."

"Who, sir?"

"That man you taught to write. You made him a sergeant."

"Sergeant Johnson? Yes, sir. But he cannot yet write. I have held but six classes."

"In the three months since you claimed to be able to teach your new first sergeant to read and write, you have held only six classes?"

"Yes, sir. The incident at the cantina and the patrols left me little time."

"All right. I am a fair man. I shall allow you classes six days a week for the next month. I want a sergeant who can read and a corporal for a clerk who can make true copies. Understood?"

"Yes, sir."

"Carry on."

I nodded, saluted, and in a soldier's petty revenge, did a perfect about-face and marched away, Whigam's words echoing in my mind. What he meant, of course, was to go about my business, which meant that, in addition to my other duties, I would be teaching school every evening between retreat and taps.

Peter Barragan was waiting for me. He, being officer of the day, was at the post headquarters. We exchanged salutes rapidly and he spoke excitedly, his words running together in his impatience.

"Tell me about the battle. You defeated an enormous Apache war party. You recovered a huge horse herd. Did you also capture an Apache princess?"

"Yes," I said. "The Apache princess is in my room. And that is the only true part of the story."

"You did not personally shoot a dozen antelope?"

"No. That was Redwood and Johnson."

"Redwood?"

"Our new guide, the Navajo. Johnson thinks he is the best tracker he has ever seen."

"If Johnson says he is good, then the man must be excellent. And, of course, he speaks Apache."

"How do you know that?" I asked.

"They may hate each other, but they share a common language. When my ancestors came to this country, they called them the Navajo Apaches."

"This Navajo also speaks Spanish. A lot better than mine, but at least we can communicate."

"In this territory one should speak Spanish, Navajo and a little English. Navajo is a barbaric guttural language and I never cared to learn it. I concentrated on English."

"Unfortunately," I said, "I have to write a long report and every word of it in English."

"Very long?"

"Several pages and the colonel wants two true copies to send on."

"Do it in here, I will help you with the copies and you can tell me what you will not put in writing, no?"

So we drank coffee and Peter copied each page as I wrote it. Then Raquel arrived and she decided that she would copy a page from Peter as soon as he finished a copy. The report, which I managed to condense into two pages, and copies, was finished an hour before "Taps."

I told Peter that he would likely get most of the patrols while I taught school. He was ecstatic with joy. Raquel looked worried, but only asked if she might help with the school. Peter, distracted by a horseman entering the parade ground, nodded, although I suspected that he had not even heard the question.

The rider was Tommy Morrison. I waved him down and walked along beside him to the colonel's residence. Whigam was waiting for us at the door. Tommy dismounted by slipping his right leg over the saddle horn and then dropping lightly to his feet. He let both reins fall and the well-trained horse stood still.

"Colonel," I said, saluting smartly, "this young man was chosen by the owner of the Sawyer Ranch to deliver a message to you."

"Colonel Whigam, sir," Tommy said, "I have a letter here for you. It has got your name written on the envelope and Mr. Sawyer sealed it hisself and he told me to put it in your hand only."

It was a speech that he must have memorized on the long ride from the ranch to the post via the cantina.

"Just a minute, Mr. Morrison." Whigam turned to me. "Do you have a report for me?"

"Yes, sir." I handed him the three copies. He nodded and then took the report from Tommy.

"See to it that the messenger is made comfortable. He will not ride back at night."

"Yes, sir." I saluted and then took Tommy by the arm.

"I will take you to the mess hall. Maybe you could bunk in the hospital alongside Sandy Morey."

"Hey, Major, can I see old Sandy?"

"Old" Sandy was sitting up in his bunk, leaning over toward Joshua Clay, comparing his slate with that of Clay. They were so intent that neither one heard us trot up the steps.

"But Josh, that ain't right. A cat has got a *k* in front of it. Just you sound it out and you'll soon see."

"I know it sounds right, Sandy, but look at the words that Mrs. Barragan sent over. That there is a *c.*"

"Hey! Sandy. You getting well, ain't you now?"

Both boys looked up. Sandy grinned and said loudly, "Why if it ain't the kid. How you doing Tommy?"

"I brung a letter here from the boss. Took it right up and handed it to the colonel."

"No, you didn't?"

"Sure did," Tommy said proudly. Then eyeing Josh he asked, "You gonna come back to the bunkhouse pretty soon?"

"Yeah." Sandy frowned. Then smiled again as he added, "I been learning to write. Me and Josh here, we are bed patients here in the infirmary"—he pronounced the word carefully, enjoying his use of a technical military word—"but we have school here too. The major teaches us when he ain't out shooting Apaches."

"You sleep here?" Tommy spoke to Sandy, but he looked directly at Josh. Of course what he meant to say was, *You sleep here with the nigger?*

"Oh, Tommy, it don't matter. I got a curtain to segregate me when I want, but it's a bother. Ain't it, Josh?"

"Sure is, Mr. Sandy."

Tommy shook his head. The "Mr." had helped and the blanket segregator was a plus, but he was still nervous. He reminded me of a skittish horse that hears a rattle but cannot see the snake.

"Corporal Brown is on active duty, is he not?" I asked.

"He is about half active, sir," Private Joshua Clay sat up straight and reported. "He comes in here to make sure we been fed and such, but he sleeps in his own bunk now."

I looked over in the corner at the bare slats of the bed that Brown had vacated.

"Tommy," I said, "you can put that cot alongside Sandy and sleep in here tonight, or sleep by yourself in the day room."

He pondered the idea for several minutes and then said, "I guess I'll just bunk in here with Sandy."

"Good. Come along and we'll get you a blanket. Would you rather eat here or in the mess hall?"

"Here, Major. If it ain't too much trouble."

"No trouble. Not for a messenger that had to ride all day to get here." I winked at him and then immediately felt guilty for he turned absolutely crimson.

"Thank you, Mr. Morrison," I said quickly. "The army appreciates the support of civilians like you."

Tommy grinned self-consciously, sneaking looks out of the corner of his eye at both Sandy and Clay. When I saluted him, he beamed, removed his hat and said, "You are welcome, Major Northey."

As I closed the door, I glanced back and saw that he had sat down on the foot of Sandy's cot and both Sandy and Clay were listening to Tommy, who was gesturing with his hands.

While Peter stood muster for reveille, I sat inside the office with Raquel and bragged about our platoon and our squadron and even our commanding officer. I might just as well have walked on my hands or done somersaults for I wanted nothing more than to impress that sensual lovely woman with my uniqueness.

"You have fallen in love with the army," she said, when I paused for breath.

"I suppose that I have. I cannot think of another pursuit that I would follow with such passion."

"Not even the rich silver mine of George Sullivan. Or the affections of his sister-in-law, Adele."

"No! Never," I added indignantly. Perhaps, even then, I meant to expiate my guilt at the sexual appetite Adele had aroused.

"It is better to marry than to burn," she teased.

"It would take an exceptional woman to turn me from the army," I said unthinkingly, not realizing that I had spoken so wistfully until she colored and turned away.

I stood up immediately, aching with embarrassment, wishing fervently that I could remove that last stupid remark as I might wrench out a rotten tooth. I said, "Please excuse me, Mrs. Barragan, I must see to my duties."

"Major Northey," she said softly, "it must be very difficult for a single man to live such a lonely life. Somewhat like one of the ancient ascetic warriors."

"Yes. I plead guilty to the ancient, and the warrior, but the asceticism is accidental."

Peter hurried in to the headquarters office and said, "Major, would you walk Raquel home?" His eyes danced. "I am to take out a full patrol tomorrow and I must see to my men and mounts and draw supplies and I must talk to Redwood—he speaks Spanish, Raquel—and would you show the major my maps? He might fill in the mysterious water source that the Navajo showed him."

"He will likely show you," I said, "if we did not deplete it."

"Still, look at the maps. Colonel Whigam was enthusiastic when I began them last year."

"But not now," Raquel said dubiously. "He has switched to a new project: pedagogics."

"What?" Both Peter and I spoke as if one.

Raquel's tinkling laugh was always a delight to my ear.

"I looked it up. It is from the Greek, *paidagõgos,* and means the art of teaching. The colonel has assigned that post to our very own Major Northey and I am his second-in-command."

"Colonel Whigam asked you?" Peter said doubtfully.

"No," she said. "He asked me to ask you. But then, I did, and you said yes."

"I did?"

"Yes, you did. Right, Major?"

"You did that," I said, reminding him of the brief conversation. However I did think it strange for even an eccentric like Whigam to ask a married lady to associate, even as a teacher, with a group of men, however respectful they might be.

But Raquel had not told the whole truth. Indeed, it was she who had asked a reluctant Whigam to give her the opportunity.

# Eighteen

"No, Sergeant. You have got the right letters, but in the wrong order. *S-r-i* does not mean anything."

Johnson looked up at me, but his bright searching eyes had muddied over. "I reckon that my head is too thick for these little letters, sir."

"Nonsense. If a private soldier, almost a recruit, like Jefferson or an old soldier like Stevens can learn, First Sergeant George Johnson certainly can too."

"Yes, suh."

"Suh," I mimicked. "Sergeant, the word ends in an *r*. Does it not?"

He corrected himself instantly and repeated, "Yes, sir," crisply, his eyes as bright as black obsidian.

"Now, then, if you will just sound out the letters *s, i,* and *r,* you will know the correct order."

His eyes clouded over immediately.

"Major Northey." Raquel Barragan was at my elbow, her sketch pad in one hand. "Might I try a few sketches?"

"Of course, Mrs. Barragan. Proceed."

She held the sketchbook with her right hand and drew with quick deft strokes as she talked.

"The letters of 'sir' are very proper and are all most military."

The letters became soldiers. The *s* and the *i* both peered apprehensively at the *r*, which was not only a white officer, but a wickedly accurate caricature of myself.

Corporal Green grinned widely and laughed, I was sure, but silently. Dewey guffawed. Jefferson waited until he saw my smile and then laughed. Benson grinned widely. Stevens remained impassive.

"Mrs. Barragan," Johnson exclaimed. "You are surely the first sergeant of all the drawers."

"Thank you, Sergeant. I was only a private when I came in here today."

"You will likely be a general by quitting time," I said and then explained to Johnson, "Those little drawings would be called caricatures or sketches and you see why the *s* and the *i* sounds come before the *r.*"

She tore the paper from the pad and gave it to Johnson. Then she wrote "sin" and illustrated that word. The *s,* a serpent, smiled with sensuous lips, its eyes brazen with invitation. Its tail barely covered a shapely bosom. Next to it stood Trader Sullivan dispensing rum while the last letter, *n,* turned into me once again, a dance-hall girl, who might have been Adele O'Donahue, perched on my knees, sipping from a champagne glass.

"I guess," Jefferson said, "that the word with the *r* is when the soldier is on duty and the *n* is when he ain't."

"I believe that will be all for tonight," I said quickly, "Class dismissed!"

It would never do to let the men know that their officers were like themselves. They might not follow orders promptly and unthinkingly if they suspected that the men who led them were often uncertain and confused. In short, human.

"Attention," Johnson called out.

Except for Joshua Clay, who, still in bed, sat at attention, those who had been standing snapped into statues of soldiers. The three who had brought rude stools, Wilson, Jefferson and Dewey, jumped to their feet.

Two men were missing. The cowboy, Sandy, had decided to return to the Sawyer Ranch, riding double behind his young friend, Tommy Morrison. Corporal Brown, just recently discharged from the hospital, was on light duty as an orderly. There were men waiting to join the school, but there was simply not enough room.

"At ease and good night," I said.

Stevens waited just outside the door and, as they left, said, "George, you can learn. I know you can."

*George.* No one in my presence had ever called Johnson by his first name.

Raquel gathered up her sketchbook, refusing to take back the first sketch from Johnson, but, to my relief, she did retrieve the sheet on which sin had been depicted.

Outside, she took my arm as we walked across the parade ground, past the headquarters, toward the old ranch house where the Barragans were housed. Her firm breast burned into my upper arm when she leaned against me to avoid loose footing and her scent filled my nostrils. I could not resist looking down into her eyes, as luminous in the dusk as if they carried their own light.

"You are not only attractive, Mrs. Barragan, but a most talented lady." I thought her to be the loveliest, most enchanting woman I had ever known, but I could not, of course, say that.

Even so, she was as perceptive as her drawings had indicated, for I had allowed too much emotion into my words for she colored slightly before she replied.

"Thank you, Major Northey. I have enjoyed helping you. You deal so well with the men. I suspect that they are as fond of you as I am."

When to my consternation I could not utter a single word, so utterly joyous was I, she added quickly, "Of course, I think it possible for a woman to have a male friend. No?"

"It would be a great honor and, if not unseemly, I would be happy for you to use my Christian name."

"Of course," she said happily. "William. And when we are not among the soldiers you must call me Raquel."

"Raquel," I said. "It is a melodious name."

"It sounds like a seagull's squawk," she said, giggling.

"No! Nothing like that," I protested and then saw the sly smile and smiled back before I spoke. "And where did Raquel hear a seagull squawk?"

"When she took a boat when very young from Vera Cruz to New Orleans. They squawk the same in Spanish as English—and, I suppose, French."

"Why did you leave Mexico?"

"To hear the seagulls squawk in English."

I suppressed a smile and asked, "And what did they squawk?"

"Ra-quel, Ra-quel!"

She was as good a mimic with her voice as she was a caricaturist with charcoal.

"You win," I said, "friend seagull. When I come calling, I shall not bring roses, but herring."

"Pickled or fresh?"

"Pickled, of course. I do not have an icehouse nor a wagon to send to the ocean."

We stopped in front of her quarters. She took a step up and turned, to look at me. We were almost at eye level.

"Then I suppose that I will have the roses pickled."

"Pickled roses!" I burst out laughing. "No. You shall have fresh ones."

"And where will you get these roses?"

"I shall pick them." I pointed out toward the desert where the different forms of cactus were in bloom. One, located not more than a hundred yards from where we stood, was now covered with fist-sized flowers that looked as if they had been carved from red wax.

"Roses?"

"Yes." I paused and brought to memory one of the books in Spanish that my father had in his library. I quoted the lines in halting Spanish. " 'There are many roses in New Spain. They are of many different colors and forms, both with and without thorns.' "

She shook her head, puzzled.

"I am trying to remember," I explained, "the writings of a Spanish soldier who, not knowing the names of the multitude of exotic Mexican flowers, solved the problem by simply calling them all roses."

She laughed delightedly. "Good. Be sure and wear gloves when you pick them."

I nodded assent, but, unfortunately, later forgot her advice.

"Will you be at the school tomorrow?" I asked, delaying her departure.

"Of course. Am I not Private Barragan, a trooper in the Ninth Cavalry Regiment, assigned to the Whigam Squadron on duty with E Company in the first file of the first platoon, Major William Northey commanding?"

"You are indeed." I saluted. She returned my salute and then, as if the maid had been waiting for her, the door swung open. She skipped up the remaining steps to disappear inside.

Whistling "When Johnny Comes Marching Home," I marched briskly in time to my own music to the mess hall, an extension of the barracks, which had as the Rivas barn housed livestock, now sheltered our company. The officers' mess, a table at the far end of the enlisted men's mess hall, frequented mostly by me, was lit by a coal oil lantern. Before I could move into its circle of light, the second cook, Long Straw, materialized with a china cup and I could smell the aroma of sweetened coffee.

I sat down gratefully and drank the best coffee I had ever tasted while the cook brought me the best food I had ever eaten, which I think might have been hash stew, beans and pan-fried bread.

On my way to my cot at headquarters, I passed one of the sentinels, Private Benson. He saluted me with his rifle, reported that he was at his post, everything was under control, the password was "Custer," and then repeated the first thirteen letters of the alphabet. I commended his memory and commiserated with him over his reluctance to place his buttocks, still tender from the arrow wound, into a saddle. He much preferred duty on foot.

I said that I would speak to the commanding officer and try to place him, like Corporal Brown, on limited duty. Whigam, of course, was the official officer of the day, but I would be the one sleeping on a cot at headquarters, and could dispose of Benson's case myself. Which, I would do after giving the matter some thought. By the time I had reached the office, I had decided that if Benson, who, for a cavalryman, was heavy, could be the first to sit at dinner and the last to leave, he could also sit a saddle with the rest of us.

The next morning, after Johnson had mustered men for guard duty and made work assignments, I ran them through a bit of the manual of arms and then made every man repeat the first thirteen letters of the alphabet. After the new guard had been posted—the new password was "pedagogue"—and the men sent to their duty stations, Corporal Brown, still assigned the easy task of headquarters orderly, arrived with a message from Colonel Whigam. I was to report to him on the double!

Whigam was sitting at the desk, writing with a steel-pointed pen. He did not stop writing to return my salute, but motioned me with a flick of his head to sit. While I waited on Whigam, I closed my eyes and lost myself in memory, listening again to the voice of Raquel speaking my name. She had likened her lovely name to that of seagull. Indeed! I chuckled, then laughed again, I suppose loudly, for the sharp querulous voice of my commanding officer punctured my dream.

"Sir?" I sat up straight.

"I said, 'sir, what is the joke?' "

"Sorry, sir," I said, "I was laughing at something that happened earlier."

He said nothing, but cocked his head to one side, eyeing me, as if he were an entomologist trying to decide my phylum.

"Just a small, joke, sir," I said, but still the man waited.

"It was The Guera," I added, desperately trying to remember something—anything to avoid mentioning Raquel—"the blond owner of the cantina. I wrote about her in the report. She offered me a sexual service, but when I explained that an officer must see to the comfort of his men first, she said, 'I am all by myself and you have thirteen men.' "

I laughed loudly and, was about to repeat the last line when I realized that I was laughing by myself.

"Have you lost your sense of humor completely?"

"Sorry, sir, not very funny. But at the time . . ." I let the words trail off, but he merely waited a long, long time, staring at me with those wild blue eyes. I kept my eyes on his until they became unfocused.

Finally, he said, "I have received two communications today, both concerning you. One: Sawyer has written again, charging the United States Army with the theft of twenty-eight Morgan stallions and mares, the mares all pregnant, of course. The charge was sent by regiment to squadron, and from squadron to platoon, which brings us to the platoon officer, one Lieutenant William Northey. Did you steal twenty-eight horses, sir?"

"No, sir!"

"Then, sir, how many did you steal?"

"How many?" Whigam must have slipped into total insanity. But then there was usually some method to his madness. "How many? Why none, sir. Not one single horse!"

"I did not think so, but it is always good procedure to clear these things up." He smiled at me. I wondered if he might pat me on the head and call me Billy.

"Yes, sir. Would not regiment wonder how a platoon of cavalry would have disposed of twenty-eight horses?"

"You did have fourteen men, counting yourself?"

"Yes, sir. My platoon is far from complete. There are still troopers unfit for duty and the replacements have not arrived."

He shrugged. "The next communication is from a Mr. Oliver R. Ballard. He is a friend of yours?"

"No, sir. I have never heard of the man."

"Strange. He has heard of you. Says something about wanting to meet the renowned Indian fighter, Major William R. Northey."

"What?" I was astounded. How had he heard of me and how did I get to be a renowned Indian fighter?

"What does the *R* in your name stand for?"

"Randolph."

"So you claim that you have never heard of Oliver Randolph Ballard?"

"I have never heard of this man."

"He is not a relative?"

"Not to my knowledge, sir."

"Interesting," Whigam mused. "Why would a famous journalist and painter of the Western habitat, want to interview you?"

"My God!" I said. *"That* Ballard. The one who painted *Death of a Rocky Mountain Trapper!"*

"Then you have not been entirely candid with me, have you, Northey?"

"Yes, sir. I mean no, sir. No. I mean that had I realized that Ballard was in the West, I would have known the name. Or had you told me he was a journalist or a painter."

"And you are kin?"

"No."

"You have the same name."

"No," I said, puzzled, wondering what he was after, for I knew that the fox inside him was at work.

"You said that the *R* stood for Randolph?"

"Yes, it does."

"Then Oliver *Randolph* Ballard is not related," Whigam challenged me, "in any way, to William *Randolph* Northey?"

I shook my head, not only in negation, but trying to clear it.

"Good. I detest nepotism in any of its forms." Whigam nodded. I had answered correctly.

"Yes, sir." I was still bewildered, but quite ready to let the matter drop.

"In any case, I have granted his request. His party will be here next week. At that time you will take them on a patrol. Show him some Apaches. Let those military politicians in the East see how life is in the field."

"A moment, Colonel." I held up my hand. "We lost two men in a pitched battle with Apache warriors. Our under-strength platoon of sixteen troopers surprised a group of Apaches and killed three boys scarcely into their teens. Does that make me a renowned Indian fighter?"

"Well," Whigam said gleefully, "it does make you renowned."

"But, sir, I respectfully ask that I be released from this assignment. Why would he not prefer that you, who has much more experience than I, conduct the tour?"

"But, my dear Northey, although my colonel beats your major, I have not killed one single Apache warrior and you have!"

"I do not see the relevancy," I said.

"It is this way, Northey. A brevet general, who is now a major at regiment, has suggested that I, once a breveted full colonel in charge of a regiment, now a captain of a squadron, assign a former brevet major, now First Lieutenant William *Randolph* Northey, a platoon leader, to conduct a famous journalist and painter around and about the Apache Land."

Whigam stopped, beamed at me in a fatherly way and added, "Now do you understand?"

"Yes, sir. Is that all?"

"Yes, Major. You may go."

I saluted, spun about and was at the door when his voice caught me. I stopped and turned.

"Major Northey."

"Yes, Colonel?"

"That story you told me about the blonde. It would really go a lot better if, after you tell her that there are thirteen men with you and she says she is all alone . . ." He paused, then, hard-pressed to keep his laughter confined, said, "She might ask you, 'How much time you soldier boys got?' "

His high-pitched whinny must have been heard throughout the post. He was still laughing as I, even more confused, left him pounding on the desk with one hand.

How did he know that part of the story? Had someone overheard Blondie and I talking? Had she told Tommy and Tommy the colonel? No, never! The boy would not have dared. But if not Tommy, who? Surely not one of my men. On the other hand, did it really matter?

# Nineteen

School was interrupted before it had quite begun. That afternoon Dr. Smith had arrived, ostensibly to attend sick call at the infirmary and then examine Private Clay in the hospital, which, after his departure, would metamorphose into our school. He had arrived early in a newly painted buggy, which turned out to be his private property.

Private Dewey, who had a mortal fear of being late, was at the infirmary waiting for school to start when I arrived to meet Dr. Smith, who was usually late. I sent Dewey to tell the other students to wait outside until they saw the doctor leave.

The door was open to catch whatever breeze might drift through and out the rear window. It had no glass, but was screened, at the doctor's request, for he could not abide flies. We had made a summer door out of sacking. It did keep out the flies, but unfortunately, the light breezes as well.

It was through this new door that I saw a dark shape and wondered who might be there before me, for I had seen the doctor at the trader's minutes before.

However there was a trooper inside, busily making up Clay's bed. An orderly was assigned daily to work at the infirmary, but unofficially, Private Daniel Berry, once known as "Pappy" and now called "Doc" by the company, cared for most of Clay's needs. To both their relief, Clay had been able to use the outhouse for several days and was anxious to return to duty.

"You, soldier," I called out.

The soldier turned awkwardly, and saluted.

"Clay!" I exclaimed. "Private Joshua Clay."

"Yes, sir. I is ready for duty. I is, Major."

I returned his salute.

"You know the doctor is here to decide whether you should be released from the hospital?"

"Yes, sir. Doc Berry told me. Doc, he thinks I can go home, Major Northey. Ask him, sir." He swallowed hard and appealed to me with his face, gestures and voice. "I surely wants to be back with the Whigams."

I knew how he felt. Home was the squadron, the company. Home was your bunk and your few stored possessions and the army accoutrements including a horse that you missed and hoped missed you. Home was Company E, or, if the men liked the commanding officer, the Whigam Squadron or simply, the Whigams.

I was touched by his concern. If it were in my power, I would have allowed him to convalesce in the company bunkhouse. But then that would be the surgeon's decision.

"We will talk to Dr. Smith," I said.

Tears formed in his eyes and he, embarrassed, turned away. He was disappointed. He had expected his platoon leader to rescue him and that officer had not.

I heard Whigam first, saying something about the penury of the War Department and then Smith's bass in counterpoint to Whigam's falsetto, repeating, "Rascals, sir. Rascals!" And then they were inside.

"Hello, Northey," Smith said. "Where is the patient?"

"And a good morning to you, too, Dr. Smith. Welcome to my school, Colonel."

"Orderly," Smith said, "has the wounded man gone to the latrine?"

"Yes, sir," Clay answered. "Early this morning."

"Well, see to him, man. Quickly. He may have had a relapse."

"Slow down, Doctor," I said, taking Smith's arm as he tried to leave the room. "This trooper is Joshua Clay, your patient."

Smith, who with bared teeth might have bitten me, let the teeth recede and the mouth open. He peered at Clay and finally spoke. "It is you? You are the man whose stomach was ripped open?"

"Yes, sir."

"But you are walking, in uniform." He turned to me and said accusingly, "How long has this been going on?"

Before I could reply, Whigam gently but firmly took Smith by the shoulders and moved him to one side.

"Private Clay, you went to the latrine early this morning?"

"Yes, sir."

"You were in pain?"

"No, sir."

"Remarkable." He turned to me. "Do you not find that remarkable?"

"I do, indeed, Colonel."

"How about you, Smith?" Before Smith could answer, Whigam said, "It always causes me a great deal of discomfort, particularly early on in the morning when the seat is still icy."

Smith gulped air, reinforcing my image of him as a small plump frog, and declared, "If you please, Colonel Whigam, I must examine this man at once. Sir, not two months ago his stomach was ripped open and his intestines stuffed back into—"

"Yes?" Whigam blinked at the surgeon, a corner of his mouth twitching. Almost certain that his caustic wit would not be turned on me, I relaxed, and smiling inside, resolved to keep my mouth shut.

"Well, sir. The man was not only disemboweled, but some filthy drunk stuffed them back in, like, like—"

"Sausages," Whigam suggested.

"Yes, sir. Like sausages."

"What kind? Link I suppose."

"What difference does it make?" Smith was irritated, and

had it been me who had asked, he would have corrected me quickly and angrily.

"Big difference, Smith. Mexicans make them mixed with pork and chili peppers and they might damage the intestine. Although, perhaps taken that way, they might be easier on the taste buds, still—"

"Colonel Whigam." Smith would endure no more. "This is a serious matter."

"Then why are you talking about sausages?"

While Smith sputtered and fumed, I told Clay to remove his jacket and shirt—he would not have been wearing the flannel shirt under the wool jacket, had he not been expecting the inspection.

"Colonel Whigam." Smith found his voice. It was loud and indignant. "I would like to call your attention to the fact that some drunken trapper also pissed all over this man's intestines."

"And he was the one that did the stuffing?" Whigam spoke quietly which worried me. "What would you have done, Smith, surgeon and doctor of medicine?"

"With clean hands and delicately, I would have washed the intestines carefully in a saline solution, replaced them and then sutured the wound, as I did."

"Saline solution. Hmm." Whigam looked at me. "Would you say, Major, that urine might be called a saline solution?"

"Not I, sir," I said, shaking my head, meaning that I would not become involved. "I know little about medicine, but," I added enthusiastically, "I have seen a lot of terrible scars from simple wounds. But Colonel, just look at that."

I pointed at the half-moon scar, more blue than crimson now, running from Clay's left side to curve up on the right, with as much pride in my voice as if I had done it myself.

"Beautiful. First-class work," I said and meant it.

"Indeed it was," Smith, mollified, said. He motioned for Clay to lie down and after several minutes of prodding and poking, decided to release him after one last treatment.

I stepped outside quickly to outwit the flies, and called to the sentinel to send the headquarters orderly, still Corporal Brown, to fetch the doctor's medical case.

Smith eyed me curiously as I slipped back into the room through the sacking door, as agile as a young girl skipping rope.

"Your leg does not bother you today. No excruciating pain along the sciatic nerve?"

"No, doctor. Sorry, but if I have to have an operation, I would like you to wield the knife." I was serious, but Smith would never believe that I was not, in some mysterious way, conspiring against him.

"It will have to come off some day." Smith might have been reading one of the ten commandments. "Might as well do it while you are in good health. An amputation can be debilitating."

"Yes," Whigam said. "Especially for the patient."

Before Smith could take umbrage, Whigam added, "Here comes Brown with the doctor's tools. Major Northey, Clay will be orderly for a while. Assign Brown regular duty. See you at supper, Doctor?"

I was relieved. Not a chuckle from Whigam. I had bitten my lip so hard that I could taste salt and that connection cost me all my efforts, for I laughed.

Unfortunately, as Brown came in, from afar I heard a whinny, and knew, as did Smith, that the whinny was not that of a horse, but our own commanding officer, Colonel Whigam.

Smith glared at me, did not answer my good-bye and strode out, banging the loose door behind him. I relieved Brown as orderly and assigned Clay in his place. Both were happy, although Clay was reluctant to miss class.

"Yesterday," he said sadly, "Mrs. Barragan said we was about to put words together into a sentence."

"If that is what *we* said, that is what *we* will do. However, you, Private Clay, will be at headquarters. I might add," I said sternly, "that while you two have been lying abed, loafing and sleeping half the day while your comrades did your duty, you got more schooling than anyone else."

Corporal Brown, with almost two years in the army had become an old soldier, and simply nodded and said, "Yes, sir."

Clay, however, with not three months in the cavalry, was still not much more than a recruit.

"Sir," he said indignantly, "we was both wounded!" When I did not respond, he added hopefully, "Bad, Major. Pretty bad." He turned to Brown, who shook his head, but said nothing.

"Yes, sir," Clay said finally, saluted, and almost tripped doing an about-face and stepped outside carefully.

I resisted an impulse to help him, saw Brown with the same worry and said, "Corporal Brown, you had better see that Clay understands what his duties will be." I made a show of looking at my watch. "Class will start in five minutes."

"Yes, sir." He saluted and was gone.

I pushed the cot alongside a wall. It would seat at least two of my students. I heard the door open and called out, "This is now a school. No saluting. Find a seat."

"The assistant pedagogue will sit?"

I turned smiling and took her hand. I forced myself to hold it briefly and not to linger, but to brush my lips briefly over the smooth scented skin.

"I have been told that we are to write sentences today."

"Oh, dear. Corporal Brown brought me a message today and I said something about putting words together on paper so that they described a thought and . . ." She stopped to smile ruefully and twist my heart, then added, "And I suppose that I said that it was called a sentence."

"So be it. I think that the Fort Rivas Academy is ready to undertake the construction of a sentence."

"Yes, sir." She saluted.

"No, soldier. No saluting in the classroom."

We were laughing when the students entered, Dewey first, with Jefferson, carrying in crates to sit on, calling them desks.

Jefferson, who now that he could write his name, had discarded Tom in favor of Thomas, and as a reward for his pretentiousness was now called Tomato.

Johnson was next, his face already settled into the mask of a man bewildered and suffering, but in spite of everything, doing his duty.

Corporal Green followed Johnson, his idol, in. He too was learning slowly; perhaps he was reluctant to surpass Johnson.

Next came Benson, almost but not quite stout, always ready with a comment, followed by Stevens, lean and taciturn, who spoke only when asked a question.

When Brown came in, I motioned him to a seat on the cot. He removed his hat, greeted Raquel and then addressed the cot.

"Hello, Mr. Sack. Long time, no see."

There was another wave of laughter, which was cut by the parade voice of Johnson.

"Attention!"

"Sergeant—" I started to object and then came to attention myself. Whigam, for the first time since our school had started, had entered while a class was in session.

"As you were." Whigam strode up to the table and took Raquel's hand to kiss, then shrugging at me, said, "Do not pay any attention to me, Major. I will just observe from a corner. Quiet as a mouse."

He put a finger to his lips to seal them which would, had he succeeded, been as miraculous as my horse, Othello, quoting from Shakespeare.

"Thank you, Colonel Whigam. We are about to study the way words are connected to make sentences to express an idea, such as"—I turned to speak to the men, still standing at attention—"Sit down."

"Those that can," I added hastily. "The others stand at ease.

"We all know the word *sit* and how to write it. How many can write the four-letter word *down?*" I asked. Jefferson and Brown both raised their hands. I asked them to write the words on their slates. They did, and compared slates. Brown erased a letter and rewrote the word.

They held up their slates for me to see. I nodded approval and the other men copied the word.

"Good. Now write *sit* in front of the word *down*."

I picked up Green's slate.

"You see we now have one word that seems to say, *sitdown*. But we want two words not one all run together like a horse and buggy. So we just separate them." I paused and held my hand out to Dewey. He passed his slate to me and I showed the class.

"Our jockey, Private Dewey here, has separated the words and they are no longer a horse and buggy, but the horse is not even in the same corral." Dewey had put the words on opposite sides of his slate.

"What we need," I said, walking about the room, peering at the slates, "is to put a singletree on the buggy and harness the horse the space of the tongue." I looked out of the corner of my eye at the one held by Johnson. It was blank.

Whigam moved casually to the other end of the room and peered over the shoulder of Stevens. He picked up Stevens's slate and called out, "Look at this!"

Not only were the words printed correctly and spaced as a master sign painter might have done, but the printing was almost as artistic as that of Raquel Barragan's.

"That is excellent, Stevens," I said.

He looked first at Johnson, then at me and I was sure that he meant to speak, but he shook his head and lowered his eyes again. At the time, I did not know that Stevens was just as protective of Johnson as was Corporal Green.

We proceeded with a class quieter than usual, but not as subdued as I had feared it might be under the watchful eye of the commanding officer. After a few minutes, Whigam straightened up out of his slouch and said quietly, "You must excuse me. Please carry on as soon as I leave. However, I have a small present for the Fort Leper Academy."

He had tucked into his jacket a small book. He gave it to me, held up a hand in warning to Johnson, who was about to call the room to attention. "No, Sergeant. The rules are"—he smiled wickedly at me—"no saluting in the schoolroom. Ergo, no standing at attention."

He walked to the door, turned to look at Johnson, took his slate from his hand, nodded and handed it back. Hand on the door, he spoke to me. "Next week, when you take the journalist, Oliver R. Ballard, with you on patrol, your sergeant should be a man who can write a legible sentence."

"But, Colonel," I protested, "there are other factors to be considered. Literacy is desirable, but so is knowledge, experience and the ability to command."

Whigam cocked an eyebrow at me and pursed his lips as if in thought before he answered.

"You have a point, Major. Several, as a matter of fact. When you designate a man who can write a simple sentence as your sergeant, I suggest you keep the other virtues in mind."

I responded with a frustrated, "Yes, sir," but Whigam was already out the door, on his way to supper at the trader's, I supposed.

"Sergeant," I said, "I will want a word with you. The rest of you are dismissed. Just file out. It is still a school. Good night."

There was a chorus of "good nights" and they left talking like schoolboys, except for the introspective Thaddeus Stevens. He glanced at Johnson with what I took to be a look of commiseration and then, a small smile breaking the severity of his thin face, set his slate up against the wall as if it were a sign in a law office, and left quickly, alone.

Johnson waited, not quite at attention, expectantly.

I turned to Raquel. "You had better be on your way, Private Barragan or you will miss your supper."

"My supper will wait for me."

"You are not dining with the Sullivans? The doctor is staying over."

"I will have a headache in just a few minutes."

"You will? I am sorry."

She shook her hair, a curling black wave breaking on a white strand of neck and laughed. "It will not last. Besides, you will shortly receive your invitation and then my headache will go away and we will both dine at the Sullivans'."

"What?"

"I will see you later," she said enigmatically and held out her hand for me to kiss and was gone. I suspected that the doctor and Adele were about to announce a formal engagement and he did not want me present at that event. I shrugged mentally and motioned for Johnson to sit down. I picked up Stevens's slate and handed it to him. He took it and turned it upside down.

"You know that I will teach you to write if it kills the both of us."

"Major Northey, if it was in my power to read, I would read. I would rather read than be sergeant major of the regiment. But I am a field hand. Not even a house nigger."

"A what?" I asked, amazed.

His eyes widened and he began to breathe deeply. Tiny beads of sweat appeared on his forehead. He shook his head. "No, sir!" he cried out. "I was never a house slave. Only once." He looked puzzled and added, "I worked in the field until I run away and followed the army. I followed the army until I stopped being a slave and I was a recruit and I fought and I killed. I ain't— I am not a slave no more. And I was never a house nigger."

"Was it a hard life, Johnson, being a slave?"

"Not in the house. Out in the field it was fierce. Not that they didn't take good care of us. Only the best horses got as good care as a prime hand. But then the house niggers was treated good. They ate what the white folks ate and they wore clothes like the white folks did. But they could not . . ." He swallowed hard and his lips moved spasmodically.

"Could not what?" I said anxiously, strangely afraid that if he could not find the word he sought, he might stop breathing.

"Read!" The word was wrenched out, vomited from his soul and it meant triumph and defeat, euphoria and pain, laughter and terror, reward and punishment.

I looked into his eyes then and almost saw the boy who had been a slave.

"Was your master harsh?"

"Master David? No, he was good to me. So was his daddy. He let me ride the blood horses."

"But he put you to work in the fields?"

"Yes, sir. But it was my fault."

"He beat you?"

"No, sir," he said too quickly.

"He never had you whipped?"

"No, suh." His eyes clouded the way his eyes did when he had a slate in his hand.

"Sergeant Johnson. There is no law against a black man who was a slave to learn to read and to write. You will not be whipped for trying to read."

"No, suh."

"Listen to me. You are George Johnson, a free man, a sergeant in the Army of the United States and you can learn to read. You must learn!"

I so desperately wanted to reach into his mind and drag out whatever evil thing it was that was entrenched there that my intensity touched something inside Johnson. He looked at me clearly, eyes unclouded, as bright as when he commanded in the field and said crisply, "Yes, sir, Major Northey. I will certainly try."

# Twenty

The big carved door that Peter Barragan had ordered from Mexico City swung open silently and Raquel appeared, lighted by the house lamps. An ivory comb held her black hair folded like an obsidian wave high on her head. She wore a string of pearls that almost touched a blue velvet bodice. Her skirt was light blue silk that clung to her hips when she curtsied in answer to my bow.

When she extended her hand, instead of kissing it as I longed to do, I turned her hand over and placed a red cactus flower in her palm.

She held it there, immobile, carefully, and called, *"Maria, ven."*

Maria came quickly and lifted the flower by thumb and forefinger, shook her head disapprovingly and was gone.

"Is Maria angry with me?" I asked.

"No. Do your fingers itch or burn?"

I shook my head.

"Well then, no matter. Maria will put it into a vase. It is a beautiful rose."

I held out my hand again to guide her down the steps, but I did not relinquish it, nor did she withdraw her hand until we neared the first sentinel.

"Will you dine with us?" she asked, after the sentinel had repeated his litany to the officer of the day.

"The colonel has allowed me to attend the supper. The messenger will be just outside and Sergeant Johnson will be at headquarters. Are you pleased?" I asked as anxiously as if I were her suitor and not an escort to see her safely to a dinner party while her husband was away.

She did not answer, but squeezed my arm. My heart filled and I felt a grin fix itself on my face and hoped that I might remove it before we met the guests at the Sullivans'.

Johnson met me at the steps that led up to the trader's bar, store and living quarters. He saluted and then produced my sword and sash.

"No," I said. "The colonel is not wearing his sword?"

He nodded yes and helped me unbuckle my holstered Colt revolver and then wind the sash and attach the saber to it. Clay appeared behind Johnson, saluted and reported. Johnson looped the pistol belt around Clay's shoulder. We three exchanged salutes again. I followed Raquel up the stairs, through the bar, lit by a coal oil lantern hanging motionless from the roof, through an open door, past a room that was by day a store and then farther to a door which I had never entered.

It was a thin door made from odd lengths of hand-sawn lumber patched together like a homemade quilt. Both light and sound passed through its cracks. I paused at the door, reluctant to enter and be just one of the many surrounding Raquel. She must have read my mind, for she smiled—I thought compassionately—and said, "You will walk me home again, will you not, William?"

"Yes, Raquel. I will. Always."

She placed her hand on the wooden latch, but I placed my hand over hers before she could open the door. She left her hand on the latch for a heartbeat before she withdrew it from mine to allow me to open the door.

George Sullivan crossed the room quickly to greet us. His wife, Mary, followed in his wake, like a pilot boat overhauling a clipper ship.

The ladies kissed. George and I shook hands and I kissed

the hand of his wife, who I thought exceedingly pretty in her bright new gown of blue cotton and told her so. She blushed and smiled. Adele was seated between the colonel and Dr. Smith.

They were absorbed in their conversation, which seemed to be centered upon the surgeon. I saw Adele look up, frown, and then avert her gaze quickly, her eyes on Smith. The four of us walked over to the seated group.

Whigam stood up quickly, but before I could salute, said, "As you were, Northey. And get rid of that sword. How can a man walk around inspecting a post with a saber rattling against his leg at every step?"

"Yes, sir." I refrained from pointing out that he was wearing a sword, albeit a light ceremonial one that would not rattle against his long skinny legs.

His lips lingered overlong against Raquel's hand, but she merely smiled until he finally released her hand and turned to me, talking while I disentangled my sword.

"We have been talking about morality and the single man. And, although I am alone, I am evidently not single, so you are the only officer stationed on this post who is alone and single, so you must educate us."

I nodded, but did not reply. Sullivan took my saber from me and found a convenient nail by the door to hang it on. I waited while Adele, who had risen with an explanation of surprise as if meeting Raquel for the first time in months. She and Raquel kissed and appraised each other. Adele was wearing a dress new to me, that I learned later from her candid sister, Mary, was her very best. Both sisters had sewn it using a pattern sent from Philadelphia and a bolt of white silk George Sullivan had found in Chicago.

After each lady had exclaimed over the dowdiness of her own costume and the brilliance of the dress of the other, conversation lagged. I presented myself to Adele, kissed her hand and said both she and her dress were handsome. She smiled perfunctorily, eyed me stonily and sat down again by the doctor, placing a hand on his knee, startling him, as she spoke animatedly.

Seven chairs, only two of which were alike, were arranged in a circle. Raquel was placed across from Adele. Whigam sat himself to Raquel's left, but when I placed my hand on the chair to her right, George shook his head, smiling, and waved me to the chair next to Adele. Mary sat between Whigam and Raquel. Although Sullivan would have been seated between Raquel and me, he was not often in his chair, but at the table, mixing toddies or opening wine. I eyed the vacant chair longingly, but in consolation decided that it would be easier to watch Raquel, discreetly, seated as I was, almost in front of her.

"Dr. Smith." Whigam took charge of the conversation. "You, an educated medical man, a physician, think it harmful for a man to live wifeless as I am, or, womanless, as is Northey. Now, you, sir, are also in Northey's position. What do you do to alleviate this, ah . . ." He paused, grimaced, and then, as he found the exact word, beamed. "This malady!"

"Why, marry, sir. Marry. It is better to burn—no. It is better to marry than burn."

"How well you put things," Adele said.

"Marriage is not so bad, but I do wish the Lord would bless us with children," Mary said and then, smiling shyly, would say no more.

"I take it that you mean to say that a man alone here on the frontier should marry before the Apaches burn him?" Whigam said, staring intently at Smith.

"Yes. No. That is . . . a man is created with certain desires and weaknesses that can cause extreme physical problems if not attended to. However, a man is also a mortal being created in the image of his God and he cannot just go sashaying around using any kind of a remedy, even if it be close to hand."

"Aha!" Whigam said. "If I understand you correctly, you refer to dance halls and cantinas."

"I do, sir. They are a source of disease and dissension."

"Dissension?" I asked, then regretted the question immediately.

Whigam was delighted. He had drawn me into his web.

"Yes," Smith answered. "I do not wish to offend the ladies, but I must mention the incident at the Water Hole Cantina."

The ladies might have been offended, but they were also listening intently.

"There was dissension aplenty." He turned to glare at me. "You would not dispute that there was dissension?"

"No," I said, not allowing my voice to rise. "Indeed there was."

"And drink was the cause?" Whigam said, raising his glass and flashing his wolfish smile at the doctor.

"No, sir. The cause was misgeneration. The mongolization of the white race."

"Imagine that," Whigam said, looking at me. "Your platoon, Major Northey, was trying to mongolize Rosa Maria's girls."

"Rosa Maria?" I said blankly.

"La Guera."

"Oh," I said. "That lady. I might point out that the dissension was caused by a crazy white man who was responsible for the near death of two men whom you all know: the white cowboy called Sandy and his friend, the young black trooper, Joshua Clay, standing outside this door." I paused for a second to scratch the fingers of my right hand with those of my left and to make sure I was speaking softly.

Raquel giggled suddenly, then covered her hand with her mouth, and said, "Sorry, Major, please continue."

I looked at her mystified, then turned back to Smith. "I might add that Rosa Maria is called La Guera, literally, the Light One, because she is the color of light chocolate and therefore has the lightest color skin of all her girls."

"Except," Whigam said, "for the blond girl called Beth Anderson."

"Yes," I said, wondering why Whigam mentioned the white girl, "the perjured witness."

"Perjured?" Smith challenged.

"She claimed to have slashed the boy with a knife to protect her honor. She lied. I know Sawyer cut the trooper with a sickle."

"The incident, as you call it, was racial. She refused the attentions of a Negro. You have the word of a black man against that of a white woman. And you call it penury."

"No," I said, losing the battle with my temper. "You call it penury which describes your spirit. The word is *perjury* and it means, Dr. Smith, to lie under oath, and if she does so in a court of law, she will then be a perjured witness." I would have stopped there, but Smith sniffed and thrust his chin out at me so I added, "And one of my troopers could only mongolize one of Blondie's girls if he were a Chinaman."

"Dr. Smith meant mongrelize," said Sullivan, helpfully, and received a glare that would have killed him had Smith been God.

"What Texas judge will not take her word against that of a Negro!" Smith said, his eyes as angry as ever. He placed a hand inside a pocket. I wondered if he might be merely aping Napoleon, bound to be one of his heroes, or if he carried one of the popular pocket derringers. I caught myself hoping that he did and would attempt to use it. I counted five deep breaths before I answered him and regained control of my voice.

"A colored trooper of my command," I said, "a member of the Army of the United States of America, will plead not guilty and he will be supported by other witnesses, whose names I will not, at this time, reveal."

"His word against that of a white woman?" Smith repeated smugly.

"The word of a white prostitute," I said.

"Gentlemen," Sullivan said. "I think we had better find a more fitting subject until we men retire for cigars."

"I am sorry," I said. But when I glanced apologetically at the ladies, if there was resentment, it would have been caused by them being excluded from further discussion of the incident at the Water Hole Cantina.

"You place too much faith in your soldiers," Smith said. firing a parting shot. "Even the white ones are, for the most part, the dregs of our society."

I opened my mouth and closed it. The only sound from me was the clicking of my teeth.

"Might I inquire," Whigam said softly, "if these dregs include the officers?"

Thick-skinned as he was, Smith still understood that he had blundered and spoke hastily. "Of course not. You white officers are all gentlemen, sir."

"Do the dregs include white people who work for the army?" Whigam inclined his head toward Sullivan, who was at his improvised bar renewing drinks.

"Good heavens, no!"

"How would you place people who work for us under contract, packers and scouts and so on?"

"The white ones might be honorable if ignorant men."

Smith was of a type that I had met many times before, both in civil and military life. The man was incapable of admitting an error. Whigam led him cleverly and relentlessly into a trap the man simply could not avoid.

"I believe you, Surgeon Smith, are paid one hundred and twenty-five dollars a month for your services." Whigam paused long enough to swallow brandy and then added, "Are you a dreg of society?"

"Colonel Whigam, sir, you have gone too far!"

"From what?" he asked as if perplexed, but I knew better.

"What, sir? You call me a dreg?"

"No," Whigam said. "I would guess that your grandfather was an Englishman, likely a Yorkshireman."

Whigam never failed to amaze me. There was a moment of silence before I broke into uncontrollable laughter, with perhaps a touch of hysteria. Even so, my wild laugh broke the tension. Everyone laughed with me. Even Smith, who had no choice but to retreat any way that he could to save face, joined in. The surgeon brought his hand, empty, from his pocket. The crisis was over.

We arranged the chairs around the table that had been used for the bar, now cleared off and resplendent with an embroidered tablecloth topped by two silver candlesticks, one at each end, with candles lit, and glazed glass plates. The silverware was not silver, and the coffee cups were enameled tin and the food was plain, but plentiful and tasty. The stew, Sullivan told us was Irish, but the meat in it was Texas jackrabbit, the onions from New Mexico and the potatoes were a gift of Colonel Whigam. Our salad, a long green plant appropriately named *verdolaga* in Spanish, had been gathered the day before, high in the nearby hills and raw, tasted much like watercress. We had homemade bread with our dinner and were to be served a special dessert. However the fates had decreed that there would be no dessert for me that night.

I had been seated next to Adele, across from Mary Sullivan, and although the surgeon was to Adele's right, she chose to infuriate Smith even more by ignoring him and flirting with me.

Not that Adele was not attractive. The woman exuded sex. She would turn to talk to me, her leg pressing against mine, while her eyes bored into mine, unblinking, almost brazen. She reminded me of the woman that Whigam had called Rosa Maria, the one I called Blondie and the one known by her customers as La Guera, the proprietor of the Water Hole Cantina. I scratched the palm of my hand and thought of the offer Blondie had made me. I wondered how an officer might visit her discreetly and safely.

"You army officers lead such adventurous lives," Adele said. "But I suppose it must be lonely, too. But then you have a girl back home, Major."

"No," I said. "Not one that would have a broken-down old cavalryman like me."

"But that is silly." She pressed her thigh urgently against

mine. "There must be a lot of nice girls who would like to catch you, Major. Isn't that right, Mrs. Barragan?"

Adele turned to look at Raquel, but not only did she keep the pressure against my leg, but she lifted her left hand and touched my face playfully.

"Of course." Raquel smiled at me. "If I were not married, I would certainly be happy to find myself seated between two handsome bachelors."

"Yes," Adele said. "You are so sweet, dear Mrs. Barragan." She accented the *Mrs.* and smiled as sweetly as a crocodile might at a washerwoman on the riverbank. I edged away, but Adele, sensing an advantage, moved even closer.

She insisted that I try special bits of the stew, that crust of bread was tastier and my wineglass needed to be refilled. I wondered if the doctor was fingering his derringer.

Mary announced that dessert would be served by her little sister, Adele, who had prepared a sweet made from the fruit of the strawberry cactus, all by herself.

Raquel rose at the same time and one hand to her head, said, "I have the most terrible headache. I am so sorry. I have felt it coming on all day, but I did so want to come to the party. But I must go. Please excuse me."

I stood up immediately, as did Whigam and George Sullivan.

"I have some quinine," he offered, looking at Smith, who stood up, reluctantly, I thought.

Smith said, "I think laudanum would be better."

"No, please, continue. I have these headaches at times and if I lie down with a wet cloth on my forehead, they always go away. Please, everyone."

I looked at Whigam and asked, "I should make my rounds about now. Might I see Mrs. Barragan home?"

"Of course. You are excused, Major."

Raquel walked quickly, and then, once outside the first door, almost ran. I trotted after her and meant to take her arm at the stairs, but she shrugged my hand off. Her voice sent an icy dagger into my heart.

"Why do you not go back to your redheaded sweetheart, Major Northey?"

"Raquel!" I was aghast. What had I done?

"You call me Raquel and yet you love Adele!"

"Me? Love Adele? No. Never. Only you."

She took my arm and said, "It is so good of you, Major, to see me home."

A soldier, Clay, approached. "Private Joshua Clay, sir. I am the headquarters orderly. The password is 'railroad' and I have your sidearm, sir." He handed me my gun belt and holstered revolver and saluted.

"How are you, Private Clay?" Raquel asked.

"Just fine, ma'am," Clay said.

The Big Dipper had turned. It was after midnight. The moon, a yellow crescent high in the sky gave little light and the only lamp lit was the one just inside the Barragans' door. We strolled slowly toward it. She paused and still holding my arm said, "That Adele is a hateful bitch."

My jaw dropped. I had never heard a lady use such a word. I was embarrassed. Of course, she was right. It was a fit description for Adele. Fumbling for words I began to scratch my fingers again.

Raquel took my hand and ran her fingers along my palm. "You picked the cactus rose without gloves."

"What?"

She smiled and my heart soared.

We stood in an island of light just in front of her house. She lifted my hand at an angle to the light. "They are too tiny to see. Come inside into the light, William, and I will rub alcohol onto your poor hand."

I opened the door for her, stepped inside after her, still holding the door open. She shut it firmly behind us, looked up at me strangely, and said, "Do you love Adele?"

"Adele is nothing to me. I love you."

"Is that true, William?"

I could only nod. I wanted to melt into the turquoise depths of her eyes and bent my head until I felt her breath and her scent flood my nostrils. I moved my left arm tentatively toward her and she stepped into my arms. We held each other tightly, then kissed. Her breasts and thighs melted my control. My instant erection was painfully hard and so obvious that she broke off the kiss, gasping. But when I tried to speak, to apologize, she put a finger to my lips, and whispered huskily, "The servants are asleep in the *chosa* behind the house."

She slipped out of my arms, turned the wick down and then moved the lamp to a table at the far end of the room. There was a rustle of cloth and she was in front of me again, barely visible now, but as lovely as she had ever been in my erotic dreams.

"I think, William," she said huskily, "that you had better remove that pistol, and you might help me with the buttons."

I could not speak and, gasping for breath, tore at the buckles of my revolver belt, fumbled at buttons and we fell to the floor together, removing clothes from each other, whimpering in frustration, moaning in ecstasy and finally, like two panthers that had sought each other out in some exotic jungle, we mated there on the floor of the house of my friend and junior officer, Peter Barragan.

# Twenty-one

A ghastly Peter Barragan, riding his ghost horse, Diablo, once jet black, but now gray, led the bloody remnants of his platoon, just one file of phantom troopers, back into the post. Peter rode straight to me and looked down. His burning red eyes drilled into mine. He knew. One bony, taloned hand reached for my throat. I awoke, stifling a scream.

Johnson took his hand from my shoulder.

"Sir," he said. "The bugler is about to blow reveille."

"Where is Lieutenant Barragan?"

"I suppose, sir, that he will be north toward the Tularosa."

"He is not back?" I said, shivering.

"No, sir. It's a cold morning. Could I get you a cup of coffee?"

"Yes, please."

The nightmare faded and a sense of immense relief flooded my being. I had not seen Peter and I had not taken his wife on the floor of his home. I felt like singing, then pursed my lips to whistle instead.

"Clay brought your saber back here, sir. He guessed you didn't stop in your quarters."

The whistle died in a hiss. The memory was instantly clear, both gratifying and mortifying. Desire surged but so did shame. How could I have so forgotten myself?

The coffee burned my lips but I did not cry out. The moral pain had outreached the physical. By the light of the lantern over my shoulder, I shaved quickly, replaced razor, mug and brush, and was outside as the first light touched bugler and flag and the lively notes woke the people of the post.

Whigam strode up. We exchanged salutes and although he had technically been officer of the day, he relieved me. But, as I left, he asked one of the guards, Stevens, to give him a new password and he had said, "Venus."

Why would he have said that? Why Venus? The love goddess. Did he know? My God! Did the whole camp know? I thought of Raquel and again that deadly mixture of desire and shame set fire to my brain. Ordinarily I would have breakfasted at the table called the officers' mess and then retired to my own bed for a few hours' sleep, but I had no appetite. None.

I hurried across the parade ground, cutting away from the men forming work parties or drilling and limped up the steps to my quarters, so nicely furnished for me by the Barragans, and brought out a half bottle of what was left of the brandy, also furnished by Peter Barragan. As I drank it out of the bottle, I thought with savage humor, had Peter suspected that he would also furnish his wife to his interloping superior officer?

I awoke, half drugged and thick tongued from the brandy and my heart was beating spikes of pain into my head. I willed myself not to remember, but did. In short, I had two terrible hangovers, and the moral one was far too painful to contemplate.

When I swung my legs off the bed and put my feet on the floor, the sounds of my heartbeat were even louder. I sat very still, then, and realized that what had awakened me was likely not my heart at all, but the sound of someone rapping loudly on my door.

"Yes," I called out. "What is it?"

"Colonel Whigam wants you to come to the trader's right away, Major."

*Judas Priest,* the childhood curse, erupted into my mind.

The colonel and Sullivan both knew. "Thank you, Dewey," I said, recognizing the voice. "I will be there in ten minutes."

Actually when the worst really happens, it has always been a relief. I felt better. I had often envied the Catholic confession and as I sometimes did, when musing about religious philosophy, picking over the odds and ends of the ubiquitous beliefs of those righteous ubiquitous believers, secure in their knowledge that they were unique. Like a child in a candy store, I would choose odds and ends that pleased me and I always included the rite of the confessional when I formed my own godless church.

I arrived five minutes before the ten I had promised Whigam, but he was already there, a wineglass in his hand. An open bottle of champagne had already melted most of the ice in a tin bucket sitting on the weathered plank that was Sullivan's daytime bar. Sullivan, grinning widely, called out to me while I was still twenty paces from the steps.

"Come along, Bill. Hurry up, lad."

His voice was jovial, not that of a man about to castigate another. Whigam, engaged in conversation with a large, florid man, and another slim youngster who wore his hair long in the Custer style, waved me in and said, "Come along, Major, you are late."

Late, indeed! However, I did not stand accused as yet and that lightened my spirits, enough so that I replied, "Sorry, Colonel. I came on foot."

Up the steps quickly, I saluted Whigam, who, as was his custom waved a kind of a salute back and introduced me to his guests.

"This is Oliver Ballard and his photographer, Jean Lajeunesse."

We shook hands. Ballard was large, with browning hair thinning and marked with gray, and large brown friendly eyes that invited you to tell him your troubles. He might have been in his early fifties. The photographer, who looked more Indian than French was half the size of Ballard and young enough to have been his son, waved long-fingered graceful hands when he talked. Eyes like smoke-colored almonds shone through what seemed like an oriental mask, carved from the wood of a walnut tree.

"I have seen several of your paintings, Mr. Ballard," I said. "In the Washington Gallery."

*"Death of a Trapper.* Yes. Did it from sketches. Trying out photography, now. Once you get the picture, you have all the details. Better than sketches."

"You mean to photograph Indians?"

"Apaches, young man. Apaches."

"Live ones, sir?"

He guffawed, aimed an elbow at Jean, who skipped nimbly out of the way, but smiled.

"By George, Major, we are going to get along. Jean will photograph the dead or disabled and I will sketch the live ones."

"Colonel," Sullivan said, "could we not take a picture of the company? I would contribute and buy a print for myself."

"Do we have any money in the company fund?" Whigam asked me.

"We used six dollars of it," I said guiltily, "while you were away, for target practice."

"Six dollars!" Whigam exclaimed.

"The men voted for it, mostly. All of the men who had fought Apaches voted to practice."

"Six dollars is a lot of money," Sullivan said.

"All of the combat men can hit a target at a hundred yards," I said, stretching the truth, but then most of them had scored at least one hit. "They might have done much better if they could have had more than a single tube of cartridges."

"The army does not provide ammunition for its soldiers?" Ballard was amazed.

"Yes, sir," I answered. "But not for practice."

He shook his head ruefully. "Shoot some myself. For the table, you know. But a shooter must either shoot often, like a hunter or a soldier in combat, but, if not, then, by George, he must *practice!"* He bellowed the last word, and banged a large fist on the bar so hard, the bottles bounced. Sullivan caught one, neatly, before it rolled off.

"Oliver wants you to show him some Apaches, William," Whigam said.

Whigam had called me William!

"I cannot just *show* you some Apaches, sir. They are experts at appearing precisely when you do not want to see them."

"Let us try. I will get a story out of it. Something I can illustrate."

I frowned.

"It will reflect favorably on your regiment," Ballard added hastily. "Or will it not?" Ballard had a way of looking at me that was disconcerting. In some peculiar way, he reminded me of Whigam.

"Of course, we will. My men are better soldiers than most, and as good as any."

"Excellent." He peered at me, then nodded. "You have a good face. Strong, determined and militarily moral."

I winced inside.

"I believe," Ballard continued, "that I have the title for my first article." He waited a few seconds, looking at Whigam first and then at me. " 'On the trail with Major Billy Northey.' "

"Sir, I have always detested the name Billy. It sounds like a stage name for a two-dollar whore."

Both Whigam and Sullivan suddenly looked shocked. Ballard merely laughed. Jean smiled and shrugged. Perhaps he was more French than Indian.

"What is your second name?" Ballard asked.

"The same as yours, sir, Randolph."

"Randolph? Not mine, sir. My middle name is Richard, although I seldom use it."

I caught the sly grin on Whigam's face and spoke to him. "Did you not tell me that the *R* stood for Randolph?"

"No, William." Whigam was so delighted, he whinnied. Everyone except myself laughed politely, looking puzzled.

"And so it does. Were we not discussing *your* middle name?"

"Yes," I said. "So we were, Colonel." I turned back to Ballard. "I do not care much for Randolph either."

" 'On the Apache Trail with Major Randolph Northey'?" Ballard said, musingly, then shook his head. "No. It might work if you were a general, or even a colonel."

"How about 'Chasing Apaches with Bill Northey and his Buffalo Cavalrymen'?" Jean said.

" 'Buffalo Bill and his Black Troopers,' " Ballard ventured and then shook his head. "No. It does not ring out the way a title should. It will come to me. Out on the trail. It always does."

"Yes, sir. On the trail. You are mounted?"

"Yes, indeed." He must have sensed my skepticism, for he immediately added, "Yes, I have a horse a hand larger than any army mount, weighs close to twelve-hundred pounds. Jean has an Indian pony we picked for its looks. It is a picturesque little horse, but sturdy and it seems to live on air and a bit of grass."

"You do carry special equipment?"

"Oh, yes. You are worried about the photography gear. It is heavy and cumbersome. But then, if we must cut and run, why, cut and run we will."

"It is my own personal field photography equipment and it cost me dearly." Jean's voice raised an octave and his eyes flashed. He shook a finger at Ballard.

Ballard backed down. "Of course, Jean. It is yours. The mule too." He said plaintively to me, "The pack mule is Jean's too. It is a very good mule."

"Cut and run!" Jean turned his back to Ballard and stared out over the parade ground.

"We are well-armed," Ballard appealed to me. "I have two

of the newest repeating rifles. Metal cartridges, you know. Friend of mine gave them to me. Named Oliver too."

"That would be Winchester," Sullivan said. "Oliver Winchester?"

"Neighbor of mine." Ballard looked at me hopefully. "We have our own gear and food. I have traveled with the cavalry before."

"With Custer," Whigam said. "He did a story on General Custer fighting the Cheyenne Nation. Custer!"

Luckily, Ballard took Whigam's exclamation as one of admiration.

"With your leave, Colonel," I said, "I might scout to the northeast. It is unfamiliar territory."

Whigam nodded. "Excellent choice. Peter will be here within the hour. Mr. Ballard is anxious to leave. I ordered the first sergeant to prepare your platoon to move out at that time."

Whigam knew, of course, that the more traveled area between Las Cruces and El Paso would be the least likely for an encounter with Apaches. Nothing might be worse for the Ninth Cavalry Regiment than bringing home a dead, or even wounded, public figure such as Oliver R. Ballard.

Within the hour. Peter would be here before we left. Likely I would meet and smile at Peter Barragan before he rushed home to the arms of his wife. But would she receive him? No, she could not! But then, she must. She was his wife. But she did not love her husband. She loved me. She loved William Northey.

"William?"

"Yes, Raquel," I said.

"What? William, lad, wake up!" Sullivan smiled at me through a worried expression. "Would you take a stirrup cup with us?"

"Of course," Whigam said. "If you have the time?"

"Sorry," I said, knowing that Whigam's question was an order. "I must see to my men." I turned to Ballard and Jean, now facing me, and said, "It has been a pleasure. We shall ter." I turned back to Whigam, and said, "With your permission, Colonel?" I saluted and left, walking briskly past headquarters, and turned right, past the guardhouse. Out of sight of the porch and the colonel, I walked slowly, limping slightly, toward the stables.

The colonel put on a small show for our visiting dignitary and reviewed the squadron. When we paraded, we were always a squadron. Otherwise and usually we called ourselves Company E or Whigam's company. We were a sorry company, only two understrength platoons. Mine, the first, had just two files of troopers—seventeen active troopers. Eighteen, if I counted Joshua Clay. He had pleaded with Johnson to allow him to rejoin the platoon and I, taking into account the light nature of our patrol, had agreed, but he was still marked for light duty. Replacements for our company, long overdue, were supposed to be at Fort Stockton or Fort Davis.

Whigam sat Custer easily, as another man might slouch back in a chair and, moving his left hand ever so slightly, reined the horse exactly within his allotted space and received my report. We had formed in line, just before the third platoon— we had no second—and rode in smartly. They had spent at least half an hour just outside the post to clean and brush their uniforms and horses. Barragan's platoon, which had been out almost a week, looked at least as smart as mine.

When they rode in, we wheeled and formed by fours. They did the same on our right. The dark blue standard was brought forward by Private Dewey, escorted by Sergeant Johnson. Colonel Whigam drew his saber and saluted the flag. I drew mine and saluted. I heard a saber being drawn from my right. Only the officers carried sabers to the ceremony. Whigam had wanted sabers for everyone, but to my astonishment he had allowed me to persuade him that the time involved to ready and attach sabers and then restore them to their storage places for both platoons would delay our departure.

Dewey, escorted by Johnson, drew his gelding, Joe, in

short measured steps back to his place. Johnson would wait until Peter made his report, then accompany Dewey to return the special cavalry flag we called a standard to its shelf in the headquarters office. He would retain the staff and attach the company guidon. We still used the old-fashioned swallowtail banner with a cluster of thirty-six stars and seven red and six white bars.

On this patrol, we would ride out in style, our squadron guidon leading the way. We had no band to play a lively march for us, but two of our troopers could get more music out of their mouth organs than could some army bands equipped with horns and drums.

Whigam gave the order to dismiss the squadron, which was relayed to the sergeants. The second platoon rode to the stables to see to their mounts. My platoon reformed and walked the horses to the eastern exit from Fort Rivas's grounds to wait for Ballard.

Peter Barragan, slim and handsome in one of the uniforms that I envied, rode up to extend his hand, but my horse, Othello, shied and our hands did not meet.

Ballard, sitting a horse big enough to have pulled a plow, rode alongside Peter and just behind him, Jean, mounted on a white mustang with a splotch of red on one flank, lead a heavily packed mule.

Peter eased his horse alongside Ballard and shook his hand and then turned to salute Jean.

"You really should wait until morning. We will make a party, a real fiesta. It will be a very hot afternoon." He turned to me. "Major Northey. Can we not persuade the colonel to order them to stay until morning?"

"I am afraid not, Lieutenant," I said, willing myself to be natural. "These two gentlemen are determined to leave at once."

"Yes," Ballard said.

"No!" Jean said. "I say stay." Then, almost coquettishly, he tilted his head and asked, "Are all of you Mexicans redheaded with blue eyes?"

Peter raised his eyebrows but answered with a smile. "Thank you for the gallant remark. Some of us are red haired and some black. But we are all Americans. We were Spaniards for almost two hundred years, Mexicans for not more than twenty, and now we are Americans. Like you."

Jean smiled at him while he talked and then laughed musically. "Like me?"

"Jean, we are going, now," Ballard said angrily.

"We?" Jean said defiantly. I wondered who was working for whom.

"Yes. Oliver R. Ballard, renowned and wealthy journalist and artist, will definitely leave now, with or without the neophyte and unknown photographer, Jean Lajeunesse."

"Maybe," Jean said to Peter, "I will see you when we get back."

"Of course." Peter looked up at me. "Where is Raquel?"

"I have not seen Mrs. Barragan this morning," I said stiffly, and touched Othello into a walk. I did not look back, but I suspected that a perplexed Peter Barragan was watching us leave.

As we cleared the last building and just before I would have changed the gait, Maria, the Indian woman who worked for Raquel, called to me in Spanish. I reined up and she handed me a small cotton pouch that fit easily in one hand. It was so light it might have been a small down pillow.

"It is special, for the trip," she said, and disappeared amid the cactus and brush.

"I hope it is food," Jean said.

"You speak Spanish?" I was not surprised.

"A little. She is your maid?"

"No. She works at the post."

Before Jean could ask another question, I set Othello to a trot. The saber clanked and Othello shied. I sighed, then, touching Othello with a spur and rein, brought him back into a trot.

I opened the pouch by inserting one hand and spreading my fingers opened the mouth of the bag. My fingers touched the smooth sensual silk inside and I brought out a yellow scarf. My cotton bandanna came off easily. I tucked it into the bag and stuffed it in one end of my bedroll. Then I knotted the scarf, redolent with my love's perfume, around my neck. I divested myself of the useless saber and tied it to the cantle alongside my bedroll.

Within minutes, we had caught up to the column. When our two guests had found a place up front, relatively dust free, I rode ahead to where the scouts, Johnson and Redwood, led the way. Johnson saluted and Redwood grunted. I saluted and grunted in turn. Redwood would not look at me. I looked a question at Johnson, who shook his head in reply.

"Redwood, you do not like the patrol?"

"The patrol is good."

"The river?"

"The river is good." Before I could proceed, he added, "But the river has fish?"

"Yes." I waited for him to ask the questions.

"And Corporal Green, he has a plan to catch those fish?" His tone was accusatory.

"Yes, he has a net."

"And he said"—his voice ringing with indignation—"you will cook *and* eat those fish!"

"Yes," I said, feeling both foolish and guilty.

"The Apaches do not eat fish," Redwood said, "because they are a silly, superstitious people. However, fish are a disgusting thing and I will have nothing to do with them. I would rather eat a snake."

"What kind of snakes do you eat?"

He drew himself up and said with loathing, "I do not eat snakes. I do not even eat turkeys because they sometimes eat snakes." He glared at me and then added, "I will scout the trail further ahead," and left us.

Although I was not familiar with this "unknown" territory, both Johnson and Green had ridden through it earlier.

I sent Corporal Green, in charge of a detail consisting of the two cooks, and Jefferson, none of whom were at all averse to eating fish, ahead to the river. Before sundown we would be comfortably camped by a stream, its racing water still ice cold from the mountains and filled with cutthroat trout. This patrol would be unique. The food would be wonderfully different, the water abundant, pure and cold, firewood, plentiful and, best of all, no hostile Indians.

We had only a four-hour ride ahead of us, but the early afternoon sun was strong. I felt the heat through my wool coat and shirt and knew that sweat would be running from all of us in rivulets. However, we had full canteens, and the horses had been fed and watered at the post.

Wondering how Ballard was taking the heat, I rode forward. We had placed the civilians just behind the guidon to protect them from the worst of the dust. He was suffering. His naturally ruddy complexion was almost crimson. He had removed his coat and wiped the sweat from his head and cheeks with a bandanna.

"Mr. Ballard," I exclaimed, "we are only a few hours from water. Drink as much from your canteen as you wish."

He tried to smile, but failed and when Jean laughed, he turned in the saddle to snap, "You nasty little guttersnipe. You laugh at misery!"

"What is the matter?" I asked, puzzled.

"He has a full canteen and will he give me a swallow? No, sir, he will not!"

"Hold on. You have drunk all your water?"

"Correction, Major," Jean said. "He has drunk all his wine."

"But you had a full canteen, did you not?"

"Yes," Jean answered for him. "But what was it full of?"

"Oh," I said. "I see."

I unhooked my own canteen and gave it to Ballard. No hound could have shown more love in his brown eyes than did those of Ballard. He snatched the canteen and drank greed-ily, water dripping over his chin onto his shirt.

Reluctantly, he handed it back. It weighed very little. He must have drunk a quart. I gave it back. "You keep it. We will be at the river soon."

"You are a true gentleman." He accepted the canteen and then glaring at Jean, said, but this time without the venom in his voice, "And you, Jean, are not!"

Jean laughed again, a light musical laugh, and said some-thing in French that I could not understand, and Ballard guf-fawed. When I let Othello fall back into the column, they were chattering animatedly in that language.

Now that I had no canteen, I could think of nothing but water. I had said *soon*. *Soon* was two and a half hours. I turned my thoughts away and Raquel rushed into my mind. I could see and feel every lovely part of her body and smell her scent mixed with the perfume she wore, and then Peter smiled at me and I quickly thought of a river of icy water. I counted seconds and minutes, tried holding my breath for two minutes, and then deciding to check on the time, took my watch out, clicked the cover off and saw that fifteen minutes had tran-spired since I had given away my water. What a fool. Why had I not taken the canteen back? Why had I not at least taken one long swallow of that sweet cool water?

"Sir," Johnson said, a canteen in his hand. "Short Straw gave me his canteen on account of him and Long Straw riding up ahead to get supper going. One canteen was enough for them two."

I knew Johnson was lying. That was surely his canteen. But I wanted the water and almost extended my hand, but held back. What kind of a man was I? Could I not deny myself anything? Hedonist! My father had called me that once.

"Go ahead, sir. Ain't nobody drunk from this canteen."

"It is your canteen, Johnson, is it not?"

"Yes, sir, but my lips ain't touched it."

I knew now that he thought I would not drink from the

same canteen his lips had touched and it should be the other way around. I was the defiler.

"Take a drink now," I said.

"But, sir—"

"That was an order, Sergeant."

"Yes, sir," he said doubtfully, but he unscrewed the cap and drank.

"I believe I will have a swallow, at that, Sergeant." I held out my hand and he passed the canteen to me. I swallowed once, then capped and returned the canteen. "Thank you, Sergeant. That will do me to the river."

In a few hours, I would remember and regret not swallowing twice.

The column halted suddenly, and I rode up ahead at the gallop to find out why. Three riders galloped up, Corporal Green, Redwood, the scout, and an odd-looking trooper from another post. He was not even in our regiment. But then, how did I know that? How many men did I know outside of our own squadron? Of course, he was not in our regiment. And of course he looked odd. The cavalry sergeant was white.

"Sergeant Harry Lowell, sir." He saluted. "I am a messenger. There is a group of Mescalero Apaches on their way south to Mexico. Messengers are on their way to the forts along the border." He looked at Green and added, "Including Fort Davis."

Fort Davis was our regimental headquarters and not far from the Mexican border.

"You have cavalry following them?"

"Yes, sir. After the fight, we followed them until they took to the hills, but we cut their trail heading south."

"This is a war party. No women or children?"

"We didn't see anything much at all. They kind of snuck up on us, sir."

"How do you know it is a large party?"

"The agent told us that all his Indians just up and pulled out."

"That would mean whole families, would it not, Sergeant?"

"I guess so, sir."

He had ridden hard and looked tired. His eyes were red and his face white with dust. He was young for a sergeant, perhaps not yet thirty years old. He must have been in the War. His horse was black, with just a touch of white on his left forefoot. And the horse looked fresh.

"Jim!" I exclaimed. I looked directly at him and added, "You are riding Jim, Private Sam Long's horse."

"Yes, sir. I commandeered him. My horse was pretty near played out. I would have taken the Indian's horse, but he don't savvy English and he wouldn't give him up. Corporal Green brought me here. I'll send your horse back when I can, sir."

"Yes," I said. "Let me talk to my scout first."

I waved a hand at Redwood and he moved closer. Using my hands and as much Spanish as I could recall, I explained what the white sergeant had told me.

Redwood shook his head. "They will go south all right, but not by El Paso or near Fort Davis. No. Those Mescaleros they will go in the Blue Mountains. Not Chihuahua, but Sonora. Yes." He nodded as if he had explained the matter to himself and was satisfied.

"But then," I said, "they will cut through the country where we recovered the horse herd."

"Yes, they will," Redwood agreed.

"But this is a large group. The water we found was even then low when we left."

He nodded and then said, "But there is plenty of water at the cantina."

Of course. The Water Hole Cantina. It must have been their usual stop on their way to raid in Mexico before the Americans moved into the country and began to fence them out.

"There is no other water," Redwood said.

"No," I said, thinking that we must seize the opportunity. I turned to the trooper, excitedly, still speaking Spanish.

"Lieutenant, sir," he said, "I don't speak Injun."

"You should," I snapped, wishing that I did. Then I told him what Redwood had said, told him that we would attempt to reach the water hole before the Apaches and hold them there until the troops following overtook them.

We dismounted so that we could draw lines in the dirt. Sergeant Lowell showed us where the soldiers had begun their pursuit and the direction they assumed the Apaches had taken. I showed him where the water hole was, where we were and how by cutting across at an angle, we might reach the water hole first.

Redwood said that the Apaches did not like to travel at night and would do so only in extreme circumstances. But even if they did, if we hurried, we could keep them from the water. When I asked what we would do if they got there first, he shrugged and said we would be very thirsty.

"You understand, Sergeant?" I asked after I had explained Redwood's opinion.

"Yes, sir."

"Carry on then, Sergeant."

"Good luck, sir." He saluted, mounted the cook's horse and galloped away.

Ballard, refreshed now by time and my water, cried out, "Apaches, sir. You have found us some Apaches!"

"Perhaps," I said, "you might rather take Jean and the two cooks as an escort back to the post. They will be along in a couple of hours. We will be riding the rest of the day and likely all night to reach the Water Hole Cantina."

"Cantina. There is a bar at the water hole?"

"Yes," I admitted reluctantly, wondering if I had mentioned only the water hole, Ballard might have accepted my advice. But, as I found out later, it made no difference. The man craved danger as well as drink.

"You can wait here," I told Jean, "and ride back to the post with the cooks." I knew that they would likely be riding double, leading the sergeant's horse and the packhorse as well.

"All right," Jean said.

"What about the photographs?" Ballard objected. "I would like to have photographs."

"We will gallop the horses while there is light and then walk them at night. There will be little chance to rest, for us or the animals."

"I will go back," Jean said, grinning, "reluctantly."

"No," Ballard said, "reluctantly, you will go with me."

Jean shrugged.

I wrote a brief note to Whigam. Johnson built a small cairn of stones in the middle of the trail back to Fort Rivas and topped it with another rock to pin the note down. The cooks should find it and deliver it to Whigam.

Then, with Redwood leading, followed by Dewey, who held the guidon fluttering gaily in the wind, we rode south and west.

# Twenty-two

Although Redwood detested Apaches, he held many of the same beliefs. Even as we rode, or walked leading our horses through defiles, he refused to lead and fell back behind Johnson, convinced that black soldiers could see in the dark as well as the light.

"You fear the dark," I said, "just like the Apaches."

"It is not the dark," he said. "It is the snakes. They hunt at night and maybe you step on one." There was a shudder in his voice.

"But still you are walking in the night."

"I would rather make dry camp out under the moon."

"So would I," I said, "but maybe the Apaches, afraid like you, are also crossing the open places at night."

"Yes, they may, because of the women and children."

"I think that if we do not move quickly, they may reach the water hole first."

"When the moon is higher, we can ride at the trot and then maybe we will beat them," Redwood said.

"They will carry water?"

"Yes. In gourds or intestines, but not enough."

"Like us," I said, suddenly thirsty.

"Yes," he said. "Just like us."

When we emerged from the deep shadows of the abrupt rocky cliffs, it was almost like riding into daylight. The moon had risen. I gave the order to mount and Johnson with Redwood led the way, at a walk. Then, as we reached level country, Johnson called out the change and we moved forward at the trot. I held Othello back until an oversized horse and rider passed. I called out to Ballard, but he merely shook his head and rode. For all of his weight, he rode easily, standing up in the stirrups, keeping his large buttocks clear of the saddle.

Jean passed, riding lightly, also posting, the lead rope in his hand, the pack mule trotting behind. Jean was an excellent packer and obviously had transported the heavy glass plates and cumbersome photographic camera before.

When the last man, Corporal Green, rode up, I waved him on and then ate dust for the next hour until Johnson changed the gait to a walk and then ordered a halt to rest the horses.

We loosened the cinches and then the designated holders gathered reins through the bridle rings. I looked at my watch. Then I looked up at the Big Dipper and laughed.

Ballard, picking his way through rock and prickly pear cactus, followed closely by Jean, heard me.

"Major Northey, I would dearly like to laugh, but I am not in humor. Enlighten me."

I pointed up at the Dipper and said, "I just looked at my watch and the Dipper is fast."

Ballard not only laughed, but he guffawed and his laughter triggered Jean's falsetto, which caused me to laugh again and then it seemed that the whole platoon, with the possible exception of Redwood, preoccupied with snakes, and Stevens, who never even smiled, was laughing crazily.

"I don't suppose those Apaches can hear us?" Ballard said when the laughter died away.

"No. We are like two ships sailing toward an island that lies at 190 degrees from one and about 160 from the other. The Apache ship sailing from the northeast and ours from a bit west of north. If they have traveled by night too, we might converge at dawn."

"Would they send a group ahead to attack at dawn?"

"Yes," I said. "In their place I would attack at first light, secure the water, feed their people, take whatever they find useful and, by pushing on quickly, be safe in the Mexican mountains."

"Or," Jean said, "they might just wait quietly, guns ready, for the buffalo soldiers and their gallant major to ride in and furnish them with many rifles, ammunition, horses, and all of my photographic equipment."

Although I laughed, the thought was disquieting. I set the puzzle in my mind and would return to it when we rode out.

"What is the time?" Jean asked. "And when will we get there?"

"It is now midnight," I said. "And we shall arrive before dawn." I looked at my watch again, turning the face to catch the moonlight and said, "By five o'clock."

I was wrong. But then so were the Apaches. I never learned what their logistical problems were, outside of moving nearly a hundred women and children a hundred miles through mountains and desert with little water and not much food, but ours were simple.

Later on, Jean's surefooted little mustang stumbled and Jean, about to lose his seat, dropped the lead rope to clutch the saddle horn. The mule decided that it had had enough, turned and trotted off back toward the last water it had known. I sent Green and Jefferson—both fancied themselves as cowboys after herding the recovered Sawyer horses—to bring the mule back. They overtook the mule easily, but he would not lead. He set his heels and they could not budge him.

I knew about mules and called out, "Leave the mule. Resume the march."

"No!" Jean called out hysterically. "No. That is my mule, Pierre. He cannot be left behind."

He rode back. Ballard followed, yelling obscenities at the mule. I drew my revolver and rode back to the mule. Jean was out of the saddle, his arm around the mule's head, murmuring to the animal in a language I believe to have been French.

"We cannot wait on the mule, Jean," I said. "Stand aside."

"But, no! If you shoot Pierre, then shoot us both!" Jean, face wet with tears, looked up at me and with latin bravado, placed a hand at each shirt corner and ripped the fabric away, presumably, to reveal the bare flesh to a hail of deadly bullets.

Bare flesh was revealed, as were two small but perfectly formed breasts.

"Jeanne, for Christ's sake. Have you no shame?" Ballard called out, dismounting.

"My God," I said. "I had no idea."

"Well," Ballard said sorrowfully, "we didn't think you would take her. You know, a woman and all. So we decided that Jeanne would be 'Jean.'"

Ballard pulled her away from the mule. He sat her back on the Indian pony as if he were sitting a child on a rocking horse and then, grunting with effort, remounted his own horse, still holding the reins of the pinto. He called back over his shoulder as he led girl and horse away, "Do what you have to, Major. We will ride along."

"Move out," I ordered. "Green, make sure that there are no stragglers. Not one!" I emphasized, looking at Jean who had now become Jeanne. I leaned over, caught the lead rope, rolled it and tied it to the mule's pack. At least he would not trip over the rope in his wanderings.

"Pierre," I said, "you are on your own."

I think he understood me for he bared his teeth and lifted a foot. I reined Othello away quickly, for an angry mule can kick with any foot in any direction and this was one mean mule.

I returned my Colt to its holster, unfired and indeed, uncocked. I would never have fired it. We were too near the water hole and, perhaps, the Apaches as well. It was too dark now to see my watch, but I could feel the dawn near. I nudged Othello into a lope, then reined him into a trot at the head of the column.

"We are close," I said.

"Yes, sir," Johnson answered. "I make it fifteen minutes past that rise."

I said, "What rise?" before I remembered. The man had phenomenal eyesight, day or night.

"I will take your word for it," I said, but checked with Redwood to be sure. Redwood said that it was too dark to tell and besides, he had heard and smelled a snake just a minute ago.

"Smelled?" I asked, but he was still moody about the fish and would not answer.

Suddenly a cold light moved the shadow across the land, slowly washing the dark from mountains and foothills and then the floor of the desert. Then we could see the white rocks and lighter brush and cactus and finally the land in all of its color. We also saw a dust trail not more than a mile to our left.

"It must be them," Johnson said. "Shall we run for the water hole, sir?"

"Yes," I called out loudly. "At the run!"

And run we did. It was quite a horse race, but we had the advantage. We knew where they were and that they were running from cavalry. They did not know about us.

We had a couple of minutes before they saw our dust trail. We knew, because suddenly a new cloud of dust burst loose from their slow one and raced ahead toward the water.

While our horses were suffering from thirst, they had been fed a ration of oats and were bigger and faster than the Indian horses. Even so, it was a race until the last mile, when we could see the Apache riders falling back. I called out to Corporal Crawford to blow the call "To Horse."

He heard me, but held the bugle in one hand and yelled, "Charge, sir. Shall I blow the 'Charge'?"

"No," I yelled back. "I said, 'To Horse.' "

He looked at me as incredulously as I sometimes looked at Colonel Whigam, but he blew the call for the troopers to mount. I did not have time to explain that the boy soldier, Juan Jose, would be up to care for the stock and he would recognize that call and know that it would be soldiers riding in.

It would not take long for the Apaches to realize that we were not the large pursuing force of blue coats, but just sixteen soldiers and two civilians. We might have only a few minutes to prepare for an assault.

Juan Jose was waiting at the open corral gate, his musket at trail. I returned his salute as I rode up. I dismounted, slapped Othello on the rump and called out to the boy, "Keep the horses inside. When the last one is in, close the gate and report for duty."

He nodded, unable to speak, eyes big with pride, then leaned his musket against a rail and watched the horses come in.

"Green," I called out. "Do you remember where the pickets were stationed when we had the trouble here?"

"Yes, I do, sir."

"Good. Sergeant Johnson, set lines between those points to protect the corrals. You can have Green and five privates. I will want Brown in the cantina, Jefferson in the cookhouse and Crawford with me at the south end. Have your men dig in. Detail someone to fill the canteens. Load full tubes and do not set any of the rifles for single-shot fire. However," I added sternly, "I will want to know how many cartridges have been used and why."

"Yes, sir," Johnson answered. Every man, as a matter of course, rode with his rifle strapped over his shoulder and, I noted with pride, that during the night they had strapped on the Blakeslee boxes filled with loaded cartridge tubes. As they dismounted, they threw empty canteens into one pile and snatched blanket rolls from the saddles.

Green ran with five men to the rise beyond the corral and placed them about fifty paces apart. Johnson filled the gaps with the remaining men. Johnson placed Green at the top of the crescent line and himself at the lower end, nearer the cantina. When he assigned Redwood the center, the Indian drew himself up and saluted. He was that proud. Each man scooped out a shallow trench the length of his body. His blanket roll served as a rest for his carbine pointed to the east.

I had mapped out the ground on and off all night and knew exactly where I would place the men. To the east, the corralled horses would be protected from the advancing Apaches by the line of entrenched troopers.

The cantina itself would form the northern front and riflemen would be positioned at the two windows and door.

The cookhouse, a few steps to the west of the cantina, faced west. It had a dogtrot in the middle to let the breeze through. A barrel of beans and a sack of flour at the west end of the open dogtrot would protect two riflemen. Blondie's room opened to the dogtrot and had a window to the west. Another rifleman, Williams, would be at that window.

Washington Riley was not a marksman, but he had been on the patrol that recovered the Sawyer horse herd from the Apaches. I would take him with me to the south line.

The bodega, a squat windowless structure, kept under lock and key, held all of the bulk necessities of the cantina. If we had time we could knock holes in its south wall for several riflemen. But for the present we could only use the trunks of the two big cottonwood trees—a man could dig in on either side of each tree to anchor a line between the two. I counted rapidly. Sixteen. I would need Jeanne's rifle.

I turned and, as I trotted back past the cantina, met Bagley, canteens hung all over his body, on his way to the men at the corral. I plucked a canteen from him and drank deeply.

Within five minutes and just before the first attack, we had a very thin line of riflemen protecting the water hole. However, each man was armed with a repeating rifle. Mine, requisitioned from Jeanne, was the new 1866 model Winchester and, if I lived through the engagement, I meant to purloin enough of the .44 rim-fire cartridges to keep me in ammunition for my revolver for a year. I would never regret the six dollars I had spent converting my old dragoon revolver to take brass self-contained cartridges.

Although I had counted on Ballard's rifle, I had placed him in the most protected of the outbuildings, the cantina, under the command of Corporal Brown, now almost fully recovered, and Stevens, who had not even loaded his rifle until ordered to by Corporal Brown.

To my surprise, Jeanne relinquished her rifle gladly. When I told her that she would be staying with the lady who ran the establishment, she was delighted. Ballard opened his mouth, but when she raised her eyebrows, daring him to speak, he took a deep breath instead. He pushed a table up to a window, found a low chair, sat, and using the chair as a rest for his rifle barrel, swung the barrel to cover one half of the northern sector.

Out of the remaining nine men, only Crawford was a non-commissioned officer, but I needed him and his bugle, which is why he had the rating, to stay with me. I came to a decision.

"Jefferson!"

"Yes, sir."

"You will escort Jean, I mean Jeanne . . . that is Mrs.—"

"You will escort Mademoiselle Jeanne Lajeunesse to the room of"—she stopped, rolled her eyes at me, and exclaimed, with a theatrical wave of her hand—"the madam!"

"Corporal Jefferson, you and Private Clay will barricade the area between the cookhouse and the bedroom and hold the western sector. Place Private Williams at the window in the bedroom, but set his rifle for single fire."

"Yes, sir." Jefferson saluted, and said, "Joshua—" Then, looking like a grown-up Juan Jose, turned to me and said, "Corporal?"

"Acting Corporal Jefferson."

"Yes, sir." He tried not to grin and succeeded, but he could not keep the elation from his voice when he gave his first order.

"Private Clay, bring your rifle and ammunition."

Clay grinned openly. His rifle was slung over his shoulder as was the ammunition box. He said, "Yes, Corporal Jefferson."

Thinking that Williams, at the bedroom window, might need

a backup, I gave Jeanne my revolver. She said that she could shoot it and well, but would do so only to save her life, which is what usually prompts soldiers to shoot in the first place. I kept that thought to myself. She laughed gaily, stuck the large revolver through her belt, and would have taken Jefferson's arm, I believe, except for my frown and my new corporal's agility. Jeanne had to trot to keep up.

I slung a bag of loose .44 cartridges over my shoulder, and took the last two men with me to defend the vulnerable south side.

We hurried past the cookhouse where Clay stood guard, rifle at the ready, peering out the western end of the covered passageway between the cookhouse and the owner's bedroom, while Jefferson, and an anxious cook and her two frightened daughters, built a hasty rampart of a tilted table, backed up by sacks of beans. Williams looked at me uneasily, not wanting to go into that room with the two women.

"Leave the door open," I said.

"Come on in, honey," Blondie said, as I was leaving. "Today it don't cost nothing."

Twenty steps to the south, past the windowless bodega attached to the kitchen, there were two enormous cottonwood trees. They shaded all of the buildings from the summer sun, including a row of windowless but airy, well-ventilated cells where the girls took their clients and where they slept when not working.

I sent Riley to the eastern tree, which would put him no more than forty yards from Green's position at the southern end of the eastern crescent around the corral.

"Major," Crawford said happily, "they is a pretty hole right next to the trunk of this thick old tree. Plenty of room for two."

He was right. We had no sooner settled in, cartridges at hand, rifles pointing south, when we discovered that there was room for three as well. Juan Jose popped into the hole and aimed his musket purposefully toward the south. I saw that it was not capped and said that I would keep it for him while he alerted the civilians to take cover. He liked the idea and started to leave, remembered, and saluted. When I returned his salute, he grinned and ran toward the rooms where the girls worked and slept.

Thus it was that the first screams came, not from wild charging Apaches, but from girls scurrying under beds or tables.

When the attack did come, it was silent and deadly. And it came, unexpectedly, from the south. Crawford heard the click of a rifle being cocked and lifted his head to follow the sound. A second later an arrow slashed into his throat severing the jugular vein. He gushed blood, gurgled, clutched his throat and, eyes bulging, died. I held back for the count of five and avoided the bullet that followed the arrow. I glimpsed a white cotton shirt perhaps a hundred yards away, fired too quickly and missed.

To my left, protected by the trunk of the second cottonwood, Riley called out, "Major, they is sneaking up that little dry wash to your right."

He fired a single shot to mark the target, I thought. I saw dust rise. Then about ten yards to the west, I glimpsed another white shirt—or a rock. The sights were set for a hundred yards. I steadied the rifle against the tree trunk, set the front sight just at the center of the target and squeezed the trigger. I heard the bullet ricochet from the rock.

I had killed no Apache, but at least I knew that the rifle was sighted in properly.

At about three hundred yards an Apache, bare chest like a brown beer keg, wearing a cotton loincloth and knee-high deerskin moccasins, stood alone in a clearing. He brandished a rifle, one-handed, above his head, shouting insults at us in Spanish and, I assumed, his own language.

"Out of range!" I yelled. I was disappointed when a prohibited shot rang out, but elated when the Indian stumbled, fell and then crawled spasmodically back into cover.

"No, he waren't. Not by a long shot!"

"Charley Dirty Knife!" I recognized the gleeful voice of the old mountain man. "What are you doing here?"

"Not by a long shot, by God!" he repeated, then laughed again, delighted. He rolled and pushed himself up, back against the other cottonwood next to Riley, to the east about forty feet to my left.

"That tad, Juan Jose, he told me there was some red niggers about to put out your lights. I figured I had better look after you. Me and old Meatmaster, here."

He patted the butt of his Hawkin's rifle. He reloaded quickly, thumbing a measure from his brass powder case into the barrel, pushed a ball, patched to take the rifling after the powder, and then seated the ball with a quick measured stroke of his ramrod. He flicked off the old cap from the nipple with a thumbnail as thick as a knife blade, thumbed a new shiny copper cap in its place and, in the time he had taken to turn about and stand, his back to the tree, shielding him from arrows or gunfire, talking all the time, his rifle was ready to fire.

I stood up, like him, leaning my back against the tree as I and yelled, "Major Northey, here. We have a casualty. However, his replacement, the trapper, Charley Dirty Knife, just hit an Apache at three hundred yards. But don't you try it. Charley is an experienced marksman with a special long-range rifle. Our effective range is still one hundred yards or less."

There were a few scattered cheers, but no comment, so I called out, "All posts report."

"Sergeant Johnson, here at the east line, sir. I see much movement, three hundred yards or more. Shall I make the round of the posts, sir?"

"No, Sergeant. Stay put. We will all stay under cover as long as possible. North post, report!"

"Corporal Brown, sir. All quiet here."

"West post, report."

"Acting Corporal Jefferson, sir. Nothing to see from the west post."

"Private Berry, can you hear me?"

"Yes, sir." Berry had a small, squeaky voice. He himself was small, even for a cavalryman, but he was wiry strong and one I had marked for promotion.

"Bring your medicine bag and a blanket. Stay under cover all the way. There is at least one Apache within fifty yards of our position."

"Yes, sir. I be there soon." Berry spoke slowly with no more emotion in his voice than if I had asked him to doctor a lame horse.

Keeping low, Washington Riley, who had been forted up and fired on by angry white men not twenty feet from where he lay now, looked up at me from the natural depression on the near side of the tree trunk.

"Is Bugler Crawford bad hurt, Major?"

"Yes, he is."

"That black nigger lying there," Charley said. "He don't want no doctoring. Not even a Lakota medicine man could bring him back."

"God have mercy," Riley said and turned his face to hide his tears. He had been foremost in ribald comments about Crawford's interpretation of the bugle calls, which meant, that he was particularly fond of the bugler.

"I know the man is dead, Charley," I said. "But the rest of the men do not. Not yet." I let my words hang there until he nodded agreement.

"If that's the way your stick floats, it's good enough for me," he said, turning slowly, and then, nearly melting into the tree as he lowered himself to face south again.

"You want that arrow shooter?" Charley asked.

"I do."

"A bottle of the good mescal?"

"Two bottles," I said.

"See that cholla yonder to your right?"

I nodded.

"Next to it is a *nopal* big enough to hide a man with a short bow. When he pops out, you shoot."

"When he pops out?" I wondered if he were playing some kind of a game.

"Get ready to step out and shoot. But wait till I yell *go.*"

"How will I see him?"

"You will. He has got to step out to shoot true. Now he has a man with a rifle back there, so you just might shoot more than once. If you don't get that arrow shooter first shot, you might see if that nigger medicine man can bring me back to life."

"You stay put, Riley," I said, "but if you get a clear shot, fire." Stifling his sobs, he nodded, then pointed his rifle in the general direction of the *nopal.* "Once," I added, remembering that he was one of the three men who in our one and only time on the firing range had not hit the target once in seven tries. "Just shoot once."

"Yes, Major." He twisted his head around to look at Charley. "I don't hold with no Indian doctors. No, I don't," he added angrily.

"Don't pay any attention to the way he talks," I said. "He has been in the mountains too long."

"Oh," Riley said quickly. "Charley, he don't mean no harm. We get along with old Charley Barleycorn, all right. Sure we do. He tried to help us that night, Major."

"Barleycorn! Who you calling Barleycorn? If I wasn't busy shooting red niggers, I sure would show you the kind of medicine I can make!"

Riley snorted, but said nothing.

"Well?" Charley said, looking at me.

When I had fired the Winchester at the rock, I had instantly levered in another round which, superior to the Spencer, not only ejected the spent cartridge, but cocked the firing hammer as well. The rifle was ready. Was I? Breathing deeply, I visualized the Apache near the *nopal.* I turned and held the rifle out of sight, muzzle high.

"Ready," I said.

I waited for what seemed to be ten very long seconds until

Charley said softly, "Go." Out of the corner of my eye, I saw movement from the tree. Then I heard Charley yell obscenities in his crude border Spanish. I knew that he was out in the open, taunting the Apaches, who were sexually the equivalent of most of the prudish New Englanders I had met—excepting, of course, Oliver Ballard.

"You red men who live in the forest, send your women out to whore!"

I stepped out from the cover of the tree, the rifle to my shoulder, dreamlike. I might have been a young boy in front of the church congregation, caught naked, armed with a wooden gun, playing pioneers and Indians.

The Indian was there, out in the open, but the bow was bent, the arrow almost to his ear, aimed, ready to release and destroy the taunting, obscene creature, his white, whiskered enemy.

I shot a heartbeat too late. I heard the bowstring twang and the arrow strike just before my own bullet took the Apache through his left shoulder. I levered another cartridge in the chamber and shot again as he turned to run. The second shot took him lower and he would have fallen if he had been an ordinary mortal.

The unseen rifleman snapped a shot at me, or more likely, the smoke from my rifle. In any case, I flinched. An instant passed before I levered another cartridge into the chamber. I heard a shot and saw an explosion of dust at the feet of the rifleman, who came out of hiding to slip an arm under the bowman. The two of them staggered away, past the cactus, like two men bound together in a three-legged race.

"Get down, Major, or you be a dead nigger too."

I slid down behind the tree and turned to see Charley lying on his back, protected now by the trunk of the tree, a feathered shaft protruding from his chest.

"He's got a arrow sticking close to his right nipple."

Riley was up on one knee, staring down at Charley. Just as I called out a warning, I heard the bullet thunk into Riley's flesh. And now we are even, I thought. But even is not good enough. At least fifty of the best warriors in the world, their women and children with them, all desperate for water, would trade life for life, if they had to. And we were only fifteen soldiers now. And one well-armed journalist, who might, or might not, fight.

# Twenty-three

The new attack, not just a probe to check our defenses, came when the sun was high enough to shine directly into the eyes of our riflemen lying along the eastern crescent, outside the horse corral.

Again, just before the main attack, warriors armed with bows had attempted to get within fifty yards, a silent killing range which would save precious ammunition. Both Redwood and Johnson saw the first men and fired almost simultaneously, but at different targets. Both scored hits. We would not know until the engagement was over how many of the enemy hit were dead or wounded. We knew that Apaches would never, if it be in their power, abandon one of their own, dead or alive.

The element of surprise lost, their riflemen, firing only when there was a probable target, never just to simulate an attack or to keep their enemies' faces in the dirt, moved forward, the sun ever brighter at their backs and into our eyes. There was a flurry of shots and I could no longer hear well enough to communicate with Johnson.

A sudden clanking of metal behind me spun me around, my heart pounding and my cocked rifle pointing at the diminutive Juan Jose. He held my sheathed saber defensively in front of him.

"Don't shoot, Major!" I turned the barrel away, pulling the trigger, but holding the hammer back with my thumb, then releasing it gently to prevent it from striking the explosive rim of the metal cartridge.

Juan Jose pushed the saber at me hastily, explaining, "That big, fat white man, he said you should have your sword to kill the Apaches with." He turned to go, stopped and faced me to add, "I am also the messenger. The sergeant needs more soldiers. Many Apaches come from the east. There are many, many Apaches. And I am the first messenger of the first platoon."

"Juan Jose," I said. "Tell the sergeant that I will bring him three more men." He looked longingly at his old musket lying still uncapped beside the tree.

"No," I said as he took a tentative step toward his musket. "Run, Corporal Messenger. Now!"

He turned, ran two steps, then stopped and turned again. "Corporal?"

"Corporal," I affirmed.

He saluted and ran.

Berry and I had dragged and carried Charley Dirty Knife, barely conscious, into the shaded dogtrot. I attempted to pull out the arrow, but it would not come out. Berry thought that the metal tip of the arrowhead had curled around a rib like a fish hook. Charley lay there on his back, the feathered shaft moving as he breathed.

I had fired two warning shots to keep any Apaches away while Berry pulled the body of our bugler back away from the tree, close to the girls' rooms and covered him with his blanket.

Berry, now prone in the shelter of the tree where one man had been killed and the other likely mortally wounded, asked, hopefully, "Major, you want me to go fight with the sergeant?"

"No. Berry. I need an experienced man to hold this post. You are steady and you shot a good score on the range." He had hit the target twice, which in our platoon made him a marksman. I picked up Crawford's bugle. "Can you blow this?"

"I know I can make a loud noise with it, but—"

"Never mind. If the hostiles attack in force, make as loud a noise on that horn as you can and I'll send reinforcements right away."

Berry, an old soldier now with almost three years in the army, knew enough not to ask from what magician's hat I was going to pull even one extra soldier.

I moved back carefully, in line with the tree, then called Jefferson from the dogtrot, leaving the recuperating trooper, Clay, forted up in the open-air passage. Williams called from the window to say that he had four full tubes of ammunition. He asked and received permission to take his Spencer off single fire.

"I still have your loaded revolver, Major," Jeanne called to me, a tremor in her voice belying her bravado. "I decided to shoot anybody that tries to get in here without permission."

"Good!" Blondie yelled for my benefit. "Honey, you learn pronto. No *dinero,* no *permiso.* If they got money, they got the permission and—"

She screamed as a bullet struck somewhere inside the room. I jumped to the entrance. Blood streamed down Williams's cheek. A splinter of wood was imbedded just under his cheekbone. He levered, cocked and fired his carbine before he yanked the splinter out. Blondie, crouched low, below the window, handed him a square of cloth. He levered another cartridge into the chamber and cocked the carbine before he accepted the bandage and held it against his face while he kept watch.

"Good man, Williams," I yelled. "Keep firing."

Jeanne sat on the floor, the big revolver cocked and held steadily in both hands. Blondie had moved back to crouch behind her.

"Do not shoot my trooper," I yelled at Jeanne, turning to wave my rifle at Jefferson, and sprinting for the cantina. I paused at the porch to call out for Stevens, then ran to the end of the building, crouching low, the northern side to my left not yet under attack.

Our north side was covered by the men in the cantina. Corporal Brown, almost fully recovered now, an experienced soldier who had scored three hits on the target range, was in the cantina, backed up now only by the untried Winchester rifle of the famous Oliver R. Ballard.

"Major Northey," I yelled, "with Jefferson and Stevens ready to enter the line."

Johnson called out, "Major, there is a hole scooped out for you this side of Wilson, just down from Redwood. Jefferson, dive into the one on the other side of Redwood. Stevens, you flatten out on top, next to Corporal Green."

There was a moment of complete silence. I heard Juan Jose whisper from behind me, glanced back, and saw nothing. But then following the sound, I looked forward past the corner and saw a gun barrel protruding from the east wall of the cantina.

Someone had punched a hole there. From my angle I could see just the tip of the barrel. But I could hear the murmur of voices. I had suspected that the boy messenger had been well protected or Johnson would not have sent him. Juan Jose must have raced back to seize his musket to bolster our defense.

"We will give you a three-shot cover, Major. Will you give the order?"

"Yes, I will yell fire *and* we will run for our places."

"Yes, sir."

We knelt in the shade of that corner, safe for the moment. "Ready, men?" I asked.

"Yes," Jefferson said hoarsely.

When there was no answer from Stevens, I swiveled my head back. My eyes must have widened in surprise, for Jefferson turned, quickly, carbine ready to fire.

"Thaddeus ain't with us." He let the carbine hammer back down as he turned to say, "Major, I testify he came out the cantina door."

We had run out of time. No time to look for Stevens or summon another man. We would have to dare the deadly, empty unprotected space. Run. Be quick and dodge death. I cleared my mind like erasing the letters from a slate in our classroom, and then chalked onto the slate the positions of the men holding the line around the corral, from Johnson on the bottom to Green at the top.

"Get ready," I whispered. Then I yelled in my loudest parade-ground voice, "Fire!"

Johnson repeated the command. I straightened up and sprinted. I carried an ammunition bag with a full canteen inside, as well as over fifty brass cartridges, slung over one shoulder, the new rifle in my left hand and my old saber, scabbard and all, in my right.

The run was no more than a dozen steps and two or three seconds, but they were long seconds. I saw and heard the riflemen firing spaced shots. I had time to notice that one man, through excitement or fear, had not fired at all. There were no empty cartridges by his rifle. I landed, sprawled on my chest and face in a shallow depression in the dirt a few feet to the left of Redwood. I saw that he was wearing both his black issue cavalry hat and light blue coat. I snaked out from under the cumbersome cartridge bag, threw the sheathed sword to one side and looked for a target.

And the targets came running, darting through the *cholla* and *nopal* cactus, powerful brown thighs churning through the sandy soil. A few shots rang out at two hundred yards and then everyone was shooting. Shooting too fast and at too long a range.

Still, when the first warriors raced past a hundred yards, our steadier men and better shots stopped the rush. Not one man got past fifty yards. But when they raced back, they left two men, broken brown clay dolls, painted red with blood, less than fifty yards from our line. I called out for an ammunition count.

Green reported five full tubes. Thirty-five rounds. He had fired one full tube, seven rounds in the first surprise attack—three in the covering fire for Jefferson and me, and four against hostile targets. He was sure of one hit and possibly another.

When Bagley did not report, Jefferson, who was pushing up dirt around his blanket roll, cried out, "Ben Bagley is dead, Corporal. Ben is dead!"

"Quickly," I called out, "Corporal Green, before the Apaches return, pull Benjamin Bagley away—do not expose yourselves. Move him back and away. Jefferson, take his place, add your blanket roll to his. Green, you take his ammunition."

Redwood had expended only two shots. He had not understood the order, and told me with a straight face that he had not seen the bullets strike, but was perfectly satisfied that he had mortally wounded two Apaches. He had five full tubes, less the two cartridges fired, for a total of thirty-three.

When I reported fifty-four rounds, counting a full magazine and one in the chamber, Benson, on my right called out happily, "Major Northey got him a new rifle holds thirteen bullets and a big saber. He don't need us. We might as well retire to the cantina for a ration of cold beer."

We all laughed. Jefferson, his bunkmate, Bagley, lying dead, a few feet from him, laughed as loudly as anyone over the small joke that ordinarily might have raised no more than a smile. But we had all dodged Old Man Death and the relief was too much to bear silently.

"You shot well and not too quickly," I said, speaking to all the men. "But you are still shooting at targets that are too difficult. Wait until they are at a hundred yards before you chance a shot."

"I got four tubes and three left in my rifle," Benson said. Then he added querulously, "We going to have to pay for them cartridges we don't return back to the quartermaster, Major?"

"Why, certainly." I went along with him. "However, you might take into account that those Apache soldiers out there, they don't get bullets on credit like you do. So count your blessings."

We all laughed again.

"I got the same as Benson," Dewey said. "Less three, but,"

he added proudly, "I got a full tube in the rifle *and* one in the chamber."

"So do I," Robeson, who had been acting corporal in Brown's place for a few weeks, said, hastily changing tubes.

"Benson," Johnson asked, "if these fifty-caliber cartridges cost a nickel apiece, how many would you shoot to save your own skin?"

Another laugh and then a wait for Benson's sally.

"I guess a dollar's worth, but I'm a private. I doubt a sergeant would be worth more than two bits."

Another laugh and then Johnson said seriously, "I have four full tubes and three loose cartridges."

"How many hits today, all told, Sergeant?"

"Four, for sure and maybe seven. None, I think, will be running back here."

There might have been another laugh, but the Apaches came at us again, this time, at a dead run, without firing. Again, at two hundred yards, I saw puffs of dust twenty and thirty yards in front of the fastest of the runners. I called out for them to hold their fire and they did for a couple of seconds and then fired again. Once more we beat off the attack, but Robeson and Dewey were both wounded. Dewey, his right arm furrowed by a bullet, wrapped his bandanna around it and pronounced himself ready to fight. Robeson, a ball through his left leg, was infuriated. However the ball had passed through cleanly. No broken bones. He reloaded his rifle before he, following Dewey's example, tightened his bandanna around the leg until the blood stopped flowing.

While the men reported, I drank greedily from my canteen. The tepid water was a blessing. I wondered how long the Apaches could wait for water. I heard Juan Jose laugh from inside the cantina and wondered if the Indian children were crying.

Before a new cartridge count was made, they came again. The attack was so sudden that several rifles fired too fast and too soon. Some were emptied before the first runners were within a hundred yards. I heard and glimpsed men on either side of me fumbling anxiously with new tubes from the Blakeslee boxes. I never emptied my magazine, but then I had only to thumb in new cartridges directly into the tubular magazine built inside the Winchester.

We sustained no casualties and had wounded two, who were assisted from the battlefield and likely killed two. One was carried away and the other, the only one who had carried his bow to killing range, lay dead not fifty yards away. They had not fired a single shot.

I was worried. The sun was halfway to high noon, already hot. They must be frantic for water. If they must lose their warriors to our bullets, then that is what they would do. If they must trade lives for water, then that is what they would do.

When they made their final rush, maybe the next one, would we have enough ammunition to stop them? They would lose twenty, even thirty warriors if by so doing they could wipe us out and get to the water. I reached for my canteen and drank the warm water gratefully. At the same time I felt guilty, wondering how badly the others, the old people, women and children, were suffering from the agonies of thirst.

When we took the ammunition count, Johnson, Redwood and Green had three full tubes. They had a few loose cartridges lying in rows like small armless soldiers, waiting to be inserted in an empty tube or fired singly. Dewey, who was weakening, had fired all but one tube. Benson had loaded a full tube, but had in reserve only three bullets. Robeson had to be reminded to load a full tube, his last. Jefferson had one full tube and five in a reserve tube.

Counting a fully loaded magazine and my loose shells, I now had thirty. Ballard likely had fifty or more Winchester cartridges, but he might as well have been in El Paso to supply me with more ammunition.

"Mr. Ballard," I called. "Can you see through that hole in the wall at this end?"

"Yes, I can." He called out joyously, "I seem to be shooting mostly between you and the man who took the place to your left."

"You have been shooting!"

"Certainly," he said indignantly, then added proudly, "I have a pile of empty brass casings in here."

"How many unfired rounds do you have?"

"Fifty or sixty, I guess."

*Hallelujah!* We just might survive the next attack.

"Mr. Ballard, I am going to run ninety steps out toward the enemy, turn about and run back. I want you to shoot as fast as you can—do not worry about the ammunition—just aim exactly where you did before."

"Major," Johnson said, "I can run faster than any man in the regiment. Nobody can beat me at one hundred yards."

Judgment overruled pride.

"Do you know what I mean to do?" I asked.

"You mean to mark that hundred yards."

"Pass this to the sergeant," I said, tossing the scabbard and saber to Dewey. His right arm had stiffened, but Dewey, a left-hander, caught the scabbard in his good hand and flipped it deftly on to Robeson. The scabbard caught on a clump of prickly pear and stopped just short of Robeson's reach. His leg kept him from rolling over to reach the saber. He held his carbine by the muzzle, used the big cocking hammer of the Spencer as a grapnel to hook the belt buckle and pulled the scabbard to him.

"Lucky that lock spring is so thick," Johnson said, when Robeson laid the rifle aside and, using both hands, threw the saber to Johnson.

"Why, I ain't loaded this rifle, Sergeant," Robeson said angrily. "You said we was not to load until you put up the target."

"That is right, Jededia," Johnson said soothingly, as if he were talking to a nervous horse. "Don't you shoot until you see the target. Don't you fire one round until the major tells you to shoot."

"Sure," Robeson said. "Don't mind if I do." He laid his head on one arm.

"Listen, everyone," I called out. "You too, Ballard. Johnson will race out, stick the saber in the ground and run back to my rifle pit. When he leaves, I will run to his vacated position and give him fire support to his left. Ballard will fire to his right. Ready?"

"Yes, sir," Johnson said, gathering himself up onto one knee.

"Ready!" Ballard yelled.

"Run, man," I yelled, "run for your life!"

I snatched rifle and ammunition and trotted to Johnson's vacated position and threw myself down, prone, following his figure with my rifle, then swinging it a foot to the left, fired twice before he stopped suddenly and plunged the saber into the ground. Although Ballard had fired at least six shots to his right, and I three to his left, the Apaches did not react. We learned later that they thought the big black runner, a naked sword in his hand, was launching an insane attack on them all. When he turned and raced back, the religious fear that had seized them was dispelled. They now thought that they had been taunted, insulted and several of their best marksmen fired at him, sending up dust bombs at his heels. Any one of those bullets might have killed a slower runner. Someone like me.

I sent his carbine, uncocked, and ammunition, flying back, bypassing the delirious Robeson, but kept the canteen. It was no heavier with water than mine, so I felt justified with the exchange.

The charge of the single black warrior was the last straw. Goaded by the insult, desperate with thirst and fear for the lives of their women and children, the warriors threw themselves at us in one last charge.

"Not one shot!" I cried out hoarsely. "Until they cross that saber. Not one shot."

Of course, Redwood, who could not understand three words in English, shot one warrior, armed with a repeating rifle, fifty yards before he reached the saber, but no other trooper fired.

Another Apache picked up the dropped rifle and ran almost as fast as had Johnson. Left elbow on the ground, I lifted my rifle to follow the runner, who then spun sharply to his right and sprinted straight for me. When he was about five steps from the saber, I counted to five and squeezed the trigger. Three shots were fired from our line, almost simultaneously, mine one of them. He fell and did not move.

Then there were at least a dozen Apaches, all armed with rifles, running past the saber, pausing only to shoot once and then run again. I picked out a target, fired and missed. Then I swung the rifle back to my left to cover a warrior who had picked up a lever-action rifle from a dead warrior. I fired too late, for the warrior snatched the rifle and ran, slim, bare-legged, not at our line, but to my left, then cut back and was within a hundred yards, hidden in a tangle of brush, rock and cactus.

I swung around, aimed my rifle at the protective patch of green just in time to see gunsmoke rising. I saw the flash of another shot, but did not hear the report until the ball sang past my head. I turned my head to the right and saw dust rising from the slight rise where Green was lying, firing steadily, coolly.

I yelled as loudly as I could, "Corporal Brown, there is a rifleman enfilading our line."

I fired again at the hidden rifleman before I yelled again, "Brown. We are taking enfilading rifle fire from the north. Get that rifleman before others join him!"

Brown shouted an answer. I turned to see him and Ballard taking a prone position out beyond the veranda of the cantina, rifle barrels wavering uncertainly to the north, searching for the target.

To direct their fire, I fired at the clump where the rifleman was hidden. The hidden rifle answered immediately and smoke rose, pinpointing the sniper.

I heard glass break. There were only two small glass windows at the water hole, both in the west front of the cantina.

I looked back, briefly, and saw that Ballard was now sitting on the ground, left elbow on his knee, sighting carefully toward the cover concealing the Apache rifleman. He then shot in rapid succession three times and waited, as I did, to see movement. There was none.

Other men, armed only with bows, ran forward. But seeing the dead and wounded, paused, then ran back, away from the murderous rifle fire, dragging their dead and wounded with them. We held our fire, not to spare them, for our blood was up, and we would have killed them all, but to conserve what little ammunition remained. Jefferson darted over to the inert Robeson, flung himself down alongside the unconscious man and took up Robeson's loaded carbine.

Breathing deeply, my heart pounding, I saw the slim rifleman emerge from his hiding place, shake the rifle defiantly, and would have fired, but I heard a series of loud squawks from our trumpet. Berry was right. He could make a very loud noise with it. I turned and ran past Ballard, who had fired, and obviously missed the sniper, for he was scowling as he searched for his elusive target. Brown, who seemed unhurt, held his at the ready, as if awaiting orders. I yelled as I passed, "Watch out for a counterattack."

Rounding the corner, I shouted, "Reinforcements!"

Just before I reached the cottonwood where Berry had taken over from me, no more than twenty yards ahead, an Apache with bow drawn, ready to release, heard me and whirled. I shot as he turned. The arrow released, but it was from a dead hand and thudded into the adobe wall to my left where the girls slept, just above the body of the bugler.

"Is you all the reinforcements?" Berry called, peeking cautiously backward over his shoulder.

I did not answer. It was obvious that had I not been, he would have been dead.

"Yes," Ballard's voice boomed behind me. "We are here."

He moved up to the tree and, twisting his right hand expertly, levered in and fired round after round until the magazine was empty. When I moved cautiously up beside him, there were no Apaches in sight.

"That did it," he said exultantly, reaching into his pocket for more cartridges.

"I need ammunition, William." He held his hand out.

I shook my bag. It was empty. "I believe that I have five rounds left in this rifle," I said. "Berry, how many do you have?"

"Just the one tube in there. I lost count. Three left, I think. They been playing with me, Major, rushing in and out of them cactuses and then one comes in close enough to arrow me, but I Spencer him first and then—"

"Good. You held this point all by yourself. Now if we can just hold on until—"

I stopped, bent over and picked up the bugle, dried blood lying like rust on its yellow tubes. Tears welled up in my eyes. Ballard looked at me strangely.

"What is it, man?"

"Listen," I said. "Listen to the heavenly music."

From far off, we could hear the faint call. The pursuing cavalry had finally caught up. The Apaches would have to give up now. Forget about the Blue Mountains of Sonora and go back to the reservation that they likely hated.

I heard cheering and turned to hurry back to the front line of the corral, but as we passed the cantina, a warrior, mounted now, but that same graceful runner armed with a lever-action rifle—a Henry, its brass case shining in the sun—galloped up to me so close that I could see that the warrior was a young girl. Guiding her horse with her knees, she aimed the rifle directly at me. I threw myself to one side just in time to avoid the bullet that broke the other window in the Water Hole Cantina.

Although Ballard wrote about the Apache warrior princess, no one on the frontier believed him. But years later, the girl, a kind of sacred warrior called Lozano, would be famous among the Mescalero Apaches.

There were a few scattered shots and then no more. Up
ahead, the Apaches were clustering, mostly women and children around a piece of white cotton fastened to a long wooden
shaft that must recently have been a spear.

The quiet was so pronounced that we could hear the murmuring of the Apaches and the jubilant but angry voices of
the white soldiers.

"Johnson," I called, "find the commanding officer and tell
him that the water troughs are all full and the water is clean.
There will be plenty for all."

"Yes, sir."

He ran to the corral, slipped inside and whistled his mount
to him. The horse came quickly, eagerly, but had to settle for
a taste of salty finger instead of the hard candy he expected.
Johnson vaulted lightly onto the horse's back, guided him by
knee pressure to the rail. When Jefferson came running over
to open the gate, Johnson galloped off, without saddle or bridle, toward the white flag.

Ballard was at my side.

"Major, I would not give this day up for anything. No, sir.
Not for a harem of nubile Nubians, sensual Swedes or—"

"Nor would I," I agreed, cutting him off as Blondie and
Jeanne, chatting like old friends, strolled up.

"Hello, *mí Generale*. You want to go see what them Apache
*cabrones* did to my *cama?*"

I smiled, but Ballard absolutely fawned over her. Jeanne still
had my revolver in her belt and, swaggering, laid her hand on
it. I was ready to take it back when there was a cry of recognition followed by laughter and cheers. Trotting toward us from
the north was a mule.

A mule is not only obstinate, but intelligent. More so than
horses or men. It will not pull a cannon gun into battle nor
carry a rider anywhere near where someone might be shooting
at mules. But now that the fighting had died down and there
were no ominous noises, Pierre, his pack still intact, trotted
directly toward the water troughs. There was no need to inter-

fere. A mule, unlike a horse, will stop drinking before it kills itself.

*"Mon Dieu!"* Jeanne said. She smiled at me and said, "You did not kill my Pierre after all. I think maybe you are soft-hearted. I like that. I hope you are not soft elsewhere."

"Jeanne. What you say?" The Guera said. "Don't you be a *grosera!"*

A *grosera* is a foul-mouthed woman. The pot was calling the kettle black.

I was tired, very tired, but I was elated as well.

"Guera," I said, "open the bar. I owe my friend Charley Dirty Knife two bottles of your best mescal. If he does not live to drink them, then they shall be buried with him. And for those of my men who are able to drink, the bar is open. I will personally guarantee the bill."

"So will Oliver R. Ballard." He put an arm around my shoulder, and repeated, "So will I, William. Charley," Ballard repeated in a puzzled tone. "Charley. Not Charley Barley, the trapper?"

"He does trap wolves for a living," I said.

"That man posed for me. He is the original Rocky Mountain Trapper. Met him in St. Louis. Cost me two bottles, too. Whiskey, it was, or what passed for it there."

"Come along with me." I led the way back to the dogtrot. Clay had leaned his rifle against the wall and was peering down at Charley. Before he could straighten up and salute, I called out, "As you were. I am going to commend you for sticking to your post in spite of all the noise and celebrations."

"I was not thinking, sir, of my post as much as I was of this old man. He's the one saved me, ain't he?"

"It is old Barleycorn himself!" Ballard said.

"And I'll piss up a tree if it ain't that horny old painter Ballard."

The voice was weak, but clear. The shaft wobbled; its feathers blew motes of dust through the air, now lit by the sun slanting in from the west.

"Can't you pull that arrow out or cut it off, like at Brown's Hill?" Clay asked.

"No, boy, he can't, 'cause its tip is rapped around a rib. That's what that black medicine man of yours said."

I suddenly wanted to lie down beside Charley and sleep. But there was something I had to do first. Of course.

"There will surely be a surgeon with the cavalry," I said. "I will send a rider for him now."

" 'Druther have the nigger doctor," Charley said and closed his eyes.

"Berry," I called. "You out there?"

"Yes, sir."

I called him in, but he just shook his head sadly when I asked him if he could pull out the arrow.

There was a clatter of horses' hooves outside. I stepped to the opening and saw that it was Johnson. A white man, in uniform, a captain, but carrying what I recognized as a surgeon's case, stepped down from his saddle. He wasted no time, but nodding to me, bent over Charley.

"Why is the shaft still in this man?"

"I tried to pull it, sir, but could not."

He nodded. "I have an extractor that will turn that arrow point. He might live, if he is in good health. He has lost a great deal of blood."

"He is an extremely tough old man," I said.

"Good. Help me move him into the light." I did. Charley did not murmur.

The surgeon asked for another bag fastened to his saddle. Berry jumped to get it and brought it to him. He opened it, brought out an apron and shrugged into it.

"Who might assist me?" He was a man in his early fifties, I guessed. He had a round face with blue, slightly slanted eyes. I wondered if he might be a Finnish Buddha.

"You may have your pick, sir," I said, "but Private Berry here treats us for our small ailments."

"Berry will do fine." He took out a scalpel, and a rod and

wire-loop affair that made me gag when he began to explain to Berry what he must do to slip the wire over the shaft and then the arrowhead while he slit the wound farther open.

When Johnson asked if he might talk to me privately, I hurried away from the blood and pain. We stood in the shade of the cottonwood trees with our backs to the bodies of Crawford, Bagley, and Riley, now lying side by side.

"Those Indians don't know what is going on, Major," Johnson said. "They got no one to talk to them and I think some are about to die of thirst."

"Round up the able men to assist, saddle up quickly and tie as many canteens as you can onto the saddles. My horse, too. Lead them back and take Redwood with you."

"He would just as soon let them drink dirt, but if you tell him to go, I think he will."

"I'll tell him," I said.

"Hey," Ballard called, "where are you going?"

"To see the Apaches," I said and walked quickly to the corral. The cook's daughters were helping Jeanne unload the mule. Her tent was up and she had a camera on a tripod ready to take photographs. When she found out where we were going, she strapped the camera to Pierre, now a well-behaved, good-mannered pack animal, and leading the mule, followed us to the corral. A couple of hundred yards farther was the group of Apaches, huddled together, looking fearfully at the white soldiers ringing them. When they saw the black ones, some of them moaned and covered their faces. The black ones were their killers.

I reported to the white squadron commander, Captain McClellan, no relation, he told me immediately, to the famous Civil War general, George "Little Mac" McClellan.

He shook his head and said, "Not one of these savages speak English. We told them where the water is and we showed them our empty canteens, but they just don't savvy."

"Did you try Spanish?"

He cocked an eyebrow at me and spoke to me in simple language that he thought I might understand.

"No, Lieutenant, these are Apache Indians. They are named Apaches because that is the language they speak."

"Yes," I agreed. "However, my scout there, can talk to them."

"You have an Apache scout?" he said, obviously surprised.

"No, he is Navajo, but speaks the language."

"I can see where he might be useful."

I spoke in Spanish, telling the captives that our men had the extra canteens for the weaker ones, but that there was plenty of water not three hundred steps away and they could have all they could drink, as well as fill their water gourds.

Before Redwood spoke, there were women who held their hands up reaching for the canteens, but they were restrained by the old men and boys. It was obvious that some of them understood Spanish. I waved to Redwood to interpret.

He stood up in the stirrups, a primitive king, his crown, a black cavalry hat set squarely on his head. In spite of the heat, he wore his blue army coat with brass buttons and he carried his scepter, a Spencer carbine in one hand.

He spoke to them, searching out the faces of the men, mostly old men and young boys. He talked for at least five minutes to say what had taken me one. I assumed that he had added several phrases of his own. He had a feel for theater and I was not surprised, years later, to see his name on a circus poster advertising him as one of the most ferocious of the Apache warriors.

When he finished, he turned his horse and walked it back, followed by almost all of the captive Indians. Canteens were handed down from horses lead by my men to anxious mothers and older women.

McClellan stared at me in awe. "Where did you learn to talk Apache?"

"On the train out to Denver," I said. "I learned it from an Apache primer. Of course, I don't speak fluently."

"No," he said, "I could tell you were using little words."

I nodded, saluted, for he was the captain of the company, and walked my horse back. I would look in on Charley and check on Benson and Dewey and run down Stevens, and then I would find out just how good the good mescal was.

# Twenty-four

Within three days, Jeanne, now Jean, once again in her male role, convinced Ballard to ask for Peter Barragan to escort them south to El Paso. They might call it a patrol, she said, and do another article. Ballard suggested they ask Whigam instead, but she laughed and said, "I already have a pony."

Although Ballard grumbled and even threatened to stay at the post, when she mentioned taking more photographs of the Water Hole Cantina, he agreed readily.

Peter was eager to go, and I in my misguided, guilty puritanical mood, confided to him about Jean and his strange intimacy with the cantina owner, Blondie. I even suggested that the Frenchman was strangely feminine. I could not state what several of us had already witnessed, the obviousness of the sex of the photographer. Still, I thought Peter might be reluctant to accompany them, but he surprised me. He smiled and called me an old prude. I shrugged and wished him well.

While they readied for the journey, I observed Jeanne, now seeing clearly the feminine form under the male clothing and wondered if the ladies had known all along. When they had packed up, Jeanne gave me two photographic prints, one taken of the patrol before and one after the battle at the Water Hole Cantina. She promised to send me more prints, but she never did.

However, I eventually saw prints taken of the Apache women and children and the dead warriors published in various periodicals. Once they had surrendered, the warriors, even the wounded, mingled with the women and children and then just drifted away. Jeanne did not get one picture of a live male Apache between the age of thirteen and fifty. Neither did the nonrelation of General McClellan find a firearm that had been manufactured after the Revolutionary War.

"These savages live in the stone age. Bows and arrows. That is their preferred weapon, sir!" he told me, explaining this phenomena.

However, Ballard was a living camera. His quick sketches, at times done between firing his own rifle at the Indians, had more real detail and life than any of Jeanne's posed photographic pictures. He had sketched the indomitable Apache warrior brandishing the rifle over his head, defying me, my platoon, my army, my world, the total non-Apache universe.

Ballard gave me one of several such pencil drawings he had done of Johnson driving the sword down into the dirt. He had titled it, *Sergeant Johnson Sets the Range*. He had also signed and dated the sketch. Years later, I could have sold it for a small fortune. It belongs to the Ninth Cavalry now and hangs in their company room somewhere out beyond the western sea in the Philippine islands.

Ballard gave me a big hug, and said, "William, I don't think you know how big this story will be. It is going to be very big. Newspapers all over the country will print my story with my sketches and photographs. There can be no doubt that the Ninth Regiment personified by your platoon can and did fight and defeat the most fierce and implacable of the great savage warriors."

"Yes," I said. "I thank you, Oliver R. Ballard, author and artist. However, I have a certificate here that you just might value almost as much as your story. It declares that you are an honorary member of the First Platoon of the E or Whigam Company of the Ninth Cavalry Regiment of the Army of the United States of America."

I handed it to him, saluted and said, "It is signed by every surviving member of the battle."

His eyes grew moist. He read the paper text quickly, then glanced at the signatures.

"I do not see Sergeant Johnson's name," he said.

"It is there at the top. It is the first and only *X*. Raquel, Mrs. Barragan—she works with me teaching the men writing—aided some of them to write their names, but not Johnson. He insisted on the *X*. He is as proud as he is stubborn."

"Johnson is as intelligent a man as I have met anywhere. He should learn easily."

"I hope so," I said. "Or I will have to buy a case of champagne for the colonel."

Ballard had heard about the wager, of course, and smiled. Then he frowned and asked, "Did Stevens sign? The one that ran. I don't see his name here."

"He was there, but he was also not there. Brown tried to protect him, but you know better than I, that he left his post. Deserted it. Whigam has your deposition written in your own hand."

"I could easily forget that piece of paper. Repudiate it?"

"You cannot and, I am afraid, that the army will not."

He sighed. "Might he be executed?"

"A firing squad is likely."

"Would he be shot if he were a white trooper?"

"Yes," I said. "Save a presidential pardon. I am trying to save the man's life, but I doubt that President Grant will be as lenient as was Lincoln."

"You will try?"

"Yes. His execution would reflect badly on our whole regiment. You might leave the incident out of your story." I did not tell him that I meant to stop it before it got past Whigam's desk, let alone, arrived at Grant's.

He shook his head sadly, negatively.

For the first time since I had been assigned to the post we

had a prisoner in the guardhouse. I did not look forward to my interview with Thaddeus Stevens, but it was my duty. I shook the thought from my mind. I would cross that bridge when I came to it. I smiled at Ballard, and changed the subject.

"Will you take Jeanne with you when you leave the territory?"

"Yes," he said. "El Paso is in Texas. But, I believe I shall leave her where I found her, in New Orleans. She has an idea about photographing beautiful nude girls and selling the prints to men like me. Should make a fortune."

He laughed and so did I. He mounted his oversized horse and rode up to where Jeanne, mounted on her Indian pony, leading Pierre, once again packed with her photographic paraphernalia, was talking animatedly to Peter.

When they rode out on the expedition, Ballard turned to wave good-bye. Jeanne did not. I would never see Ballard again, but his effect on my life, indeed on the lives of us all at Fort Leper, as Whigam called the post, was as dramatic as it was unexpected.

Officially, Stevens was charged only with abandoning his post. I might not have had him confined to the guardhouse were it not for the deadly hostility displayed by the survivors, and shared by the entire garrison, with the exception of Sergeant Johnson, myself and possibly Whigam.

Oddly enough, only Johnson, the veteran military man, the disciplinarian, would even talk to the coward who had not only deserted his comrades in battle, but was a traitor to his race.

Stevens, under arrest, had ridden to the post, seated alongside the driver of our ambulance, the assistant cook, Long Straw.

The cooks had straggled into the post the morning after the battle, leading the packhorse, with the exhausted horse of the white cavalryman, trailing after them. They had taken turns riding the first cook's horse. Whigam sent Long Straw, who had been a special friend of Bagley, with our old ambulance to bring back the wounded.

He had been with us on our second encounter with the Apaches, but had yet to fire a shot at an enemy. When he learned of Steven's dereliction of duty, he was angrier than any of the veterans of the fight. He despised Stevens, blaming him for the death of his close friend.

Our guardhouse was only a few steps across the parade ground from headquarters, but I walked slower and slower until I reached the squat building. The guard presented arms and reported automatically that there were no prisoners, caught himself and said, "Private Thaddeus Stevens is a prisoner awaiting charges."

I nodded, dismissed him with a salute and then had no alternative but to go inside. An opened padlock hung on a nail alongside the door to the single improvised cell, now provided with a cot and a tin pitcher of water.

Stevens sat on the cot, an open book, a Bible, I supposed, on his lap. He looked up at me as if awakening, and then, slowly stood up. Before he could salute, I motioned him back and said, "As you were, Private Stevens."

He sank back to the bed, the Bible still in his left hand.

"Would you like me to read a passage from the Bible to you?"

"No, sir," he said dully. "I was reading the commandments."

"Reading?"

"Yes, sir. Sergeant Johnson said I could be a corporal and do all the writing, but I wanted to be a real soldier, with a gun. But the Holy Bible says 'Thou shall not kill.' "

"You can read and write?"

"Yes, sir." His face twisted into a small sneer and his voice took on the edge that had so annoyed the other troopers.

"I was a house nigger. The white boy I grew up with—I belonged to him—made his pa let me sit in on his classes with the tutor. I read a lot. More than Master Edward did. He let me read what I wanted. Books and periodicals. We played together and went hunting and fishing together, but then he went off to school and grew up. He came back for the War, already in a uniform. He took me with him. He called me his nigger. One day one of his officer friends came back and found me in Master Edward's tent, writing in my journal—it was *my* book—and beat me.

"My master knew I was keeping a journal." His voice softened and he grimaced as if in pain. "It was his idea. He didn't like to write. Never had. He read the journal. It was supposed to be his own account of his heroic actions.

"My master, Lieutenant Edward Lee Ralleigh, was so enraged when he came back, that he found his friend and called him out.

" 'Johnny,' he said. 'You beat my nigger and I don't doubt that he needed it. But, by God, if he does, I'm the one that will do the beating!'

"He was shaking with rage, tossing his long blond hair back and forth and waving his whip in one hand.

" 'How would you like it if I did that to you?' he asked his friend, waving that whip at him.

"Well, Johnny, he cringed and put up a hand to protect his face, but Master Edward stepped right past him to where his own nigger had just brushed out his pretty roan horse and he whipped that horse bloody before it could break free. They both went for their pistols. Master Edward, he got his first and shot Johnny while he was pulling his revolver from the saddle holster just inside his tent. Johnny turned and stumbled out, shot through the back, his shirtfront red with his blood. He sat down and cocked the revolver—it looked just like yours, Major—and he shot Lieutenant Edward Lee Ralleigh through the chest. After Edward fell, he kept on shooting him. When I ran out into the woods, on my way north, I counted three more shots.

"I came upon a flock of slaves like me following Yankee troops north to freedom."

He bobbed his head as he talked, like a Hebrew at worship, his eyes open, but not seeing. He closed his mouth and ground his teeth as if in pain.

"Did you know Johnson from before?"

"He recruited me. He figured that a man who could read and write might even be an officer one day. In those days we still had funny ideas.

"He asked me my name and I didn't have one—except for Joe. I was called 'Boy', or 'Little Joe.' I guessed that my pappy might have been called 'Big Joe,' but I never knew him. I can remember my mammy, I guess, but not after I got to be a house nigger. I knew how most niggers took the names of their owners when they became free, but I was not going to use the name of Charles Lee Ralleigh, ever. I had read about a government man who was dead set against slavery from before the war and I took his name. I did not think he would care."

"So you took the name of Senator Stevens," I said. Then I added, "No, he would not care. He might have been proud."

"Proud of a coward! A man who betrayed his own people?" He shook his head sadly and then looked into my eyes and asked, "Will I be shot for cowardice in the face of the enemy?"

"I hope not," I said. "Not for your sake, but for the Ninth Regiment and all the other Negro regiments. I know that the records show that the white soldiers are no better and in some cases, much worse, than the colored soldiers, but there are too many whites ready to jump on any mistake that we make."

"If I were dead, there would be no one to criticize, would there, Major?"

"My God, no! The worst thing you could do would be to kill yourself. We will work this out. You can redeem yourself. You can be the teacher instead of me. You can be useful. Promise me you will not commit suicide, Stevens?"

"Yes, I am much too cowardly to take my own life." He smiled then, but the smile was worse than tears.

"Why did you attend our school?"

"George—Sergeant Johnson asked me to. He thought that maybe my literacy would rub off on him."

"Maybe it will," I said, and left before he could rise and salute.

Raquel was waiting outside the guardhouse. She looked up at me and smiled. "Good morning, Major Northey, sir."

She held her hand out to me to be kissed, but I could not tear my eyes away from hers.

"What is it, William?" she said softly so that the sentry might not hear. "Why, you are crying!"

I wrenched my eyes from hers, bent, kissed her hand, and said in a normal voice, I thought, "Might I walk you home?"

"To the store please, Major," She glanced at the sentry and said, "I heard about you, Private Jefferson. You are all heroes."

"Thank you, Mrs. Barragan," Jefferson said.

"You are welcome, Thomas. Tell all the others what I said."

"Yes, ma'am."

"Private Jefferson," I said. "Has Sergeant Johnson been in to see the prisoner?"

"Not to stay, sir. Not yet."

"Ask him to speak to me first."

"Yes, sir." A present arms and a return salute and Raquel and I were walking slowly toward the trading post.

"You should not take things so hard," she said.

"But it is sad, very sad."

"Yes, it is, William, but on the other hand, Peter will be away for a week, maybe more."

"What are you talking about?" I asked, confused, still thinking about Stevens.

"What do you think I am talking about?" she said. "Peter will be off with Ballard and his boy-girl."

"Jean, Ballard's boy-girl?" I said. "Ballard's lover?"

"The very one."

"Jean. But Jean is not a . . . girl-boy. Her name is really Jeanne and she really is a girl."

"Jean is a girl!" Her eyes grew round as did her mouth and then she shook with laughter.

I laughed uncertainly. I did not understand, then she said, "Wait until Peter finds out!"

She was still laughing when we reached the trader's store.

"Hey," Sullivan called from inside, past the porch, "is that Mrs. Barragan laughing like a bird?"

"It is," Raquel said, then squawked softly in my ear. But I could not laugh.

"Do not torture yourself, William," she whispered huskily. "I love you, not Peter. And the back door will be open at midnight."

She melted my bones with her smile, cocked her head at me and held the pose for a second and then, laughing again, ran up the steps.

Realizing that she had never understood the reason for the tears in my eyes and puzzled about her seeming lack of concern for her husband's possible romantic liaison, I came to a firm decision that while I would love Raquel forever, there would be no carnal love in our ethereal relationship. I resolved that I would not see her alone, ever.

Just before midnight and the changing of the guard, I slipped by the small shack where the two servants slept, and opened the back door of the Barragan house.

# Twenty-five

"But, sir," I said reasonably, "you sent me out with Ballard. That lost me three full days."

"But then I did not order you to the Water Hole Cantina, did I?" Whigam said generously.

"You had promised me three full weeks."

"Life is not reasonable," he said, reading my mind.

"I have been talking to Stevens," I said, seeking a way out. "He is as literate as either of us."

"He is? Marvelous. In three months you have given him the equivalent of a university education. But your first sergeant remains blissfully ignorant of the alphabet."

"Stevens has been literate since he was a child," I said, determined to stick to a point, if I had one. "It is part of his problem. Johnson's too."

"Johnson is also a university man?"

"No," I said, knowing that Whigam had drawn me into one of his word games. "He was beaten because he opened a book when a child. Stevens was beaten because he was writing one as a young man."

"Are you telling me that you cannot teach Johnson to read so you want to promote, instead of court-martial, Stevens?"

"No. I mean, yes. That is, I need more time with Johnson and if we can save Stevens from a firing squad, he might very well be a sergeant some day."

"William," Whigam said kindly. "You really must try to be more direct in your thoughts and not flit about from one thing to another." He leaned back in his chair. I shifted my weight from my right leg to my left.

"Well, then," he mused, "Peter should be back soon. He asked permission to stop over at that border brothel you young officers favor."

"Where is that?" I wondered why I had not heard of the brothel. "Maybe it would be safer than the Water Hole Cantina."

"That is the very one. You should ride over there one day."

"Yes," I answered wearily. "I suspect I should."

"Soon, William, soon." There was no hint of laughter in his wild blue eyes, nor a smile flickering at the corner of his mouth. I wondered if he knew about Raquel.

"Did you know about Jean, the one with all that photographic equipment?" Whigam asked.

"Know what?"

"He is a girl."

"Yes," I said. Whigam knew because I had told him.

"That old lecherous artist. They said that tent they slept in was light-proof so that Jean could develop images on glass plates. Do you think they did any of that?"

"I know they did," I said. "I showed you a print taken from one of the plates."

"So you did."

"About Stevens, sir?"

"You can take him with you to El Paso."

"El Paso? Why?"

"He was at the cantina twice, right?"

"Twice? Oh, yes. That first time, when Clay was wounded."

"Well, you might as well take him along with you. The sheriff has a friend in very high places."

"The sheriff? Pace, Sawyer's flunky from El Paso?"

"The very one. He sent his deputy with the papers."

"Rex Miles. He is tied in with Sawyer too."

"Good. You can explain that to the judge."

"What judge?"

"His name is there someplace. It is a preliminary hearing. Pace sent me a note. Very pleasant note. He admires me. He congratulates you too, for recovering Sawyer's horse herd, but he thinks we should find out what our troopers did with the rest of the horses. He reminds me that Yankees are not familiar with the colored race. They are a wonderful race, he writes, with many admirable traits, but they *will* steal."

"Colonel Whigam, I wish to state officially that I oppose vigorously complying with any order issued by Pace and his group of politicians. A federal court run by a corrupt judge has no jurisdiction—"

"First Lieutenant William R. Northey!" Whigam cut me off, his voice easily heard from the headquarters building to the guardhouse at the far end of the compound. "You have no jurisdiction! I, Captain Horace P. Whigam, commanding officer of Company E of which you serve, have jurisdiction. Am I correct?"

"Yes, sir, but—"

"You obey the commands of your superior officer?"

"Yes, sir. Which men of my platoon are named?"

"All of them. They want every trooper who was there the night of the incident."

"Including the ones who rode to the rescue?"

"Yes."

There was a bugle call in the distance. A mile away, but the notes floated clearly throughout the post. It would be Peter Barragan, returning from El Paso. He would have seen to the brushing of uniforms and animals and, resplendent in his own immaculate, perfectly tailored uniform, would soon be riding into Fort Rivas. "When Lieutenant Barragan rides in, you will ready those men who were present at the cantina that night to travel to El Paso."

"But, sir, I cannot leave the seriously wounded. Perhaps in a week—"

"Yes, indeed, the wounded. Of course you all had wounds, some more visible than others. Your friend, Dr. Smith, has left us an abundance of bandages. The men must be bandaged."

We heard the riders, and stepped outside to watch Peter dismiss his five-man escort. I wondered if he could look at me and know that I had lain with his wife in his house.

"El Paso del Norte is a lively border town." Whigam looked at me speculatively. "You will be on detached duty for the trial. I suppose you might take a few days off. Send the troopers back with Johnson."

What did he mean by that?

"If they come back," I said.

Peter stopped before the steps and saluted. We both returned his salute. Peter cocked an eyebrow at me and shook his head ruefully.

"That Jeanne," he said. Then, following Whigam into the office, he added, "Ballard met the mayor and the sheriff. He charmed the editor of the 'Greatest Newspaper West of the Pecos,' the *Eagle,* and then decamped with his lively young aide. I allowed the men to cross the river to learn some Spanish and absorb a bit of Mexican culture. And here we are."

He turned to me, and said, "The sheriff is running for reelection against a candidate who hates vice and corruption and has almost as much vote money as Pace. Almost as much, because Sawyer is backing Pace and, according to the newspaper publisher, Sawyer has his own private mint."

"Did you see the deputy, Rex Miles?" I asked.

"Yes, but he rode out the same day we arrived. He did not greet me."

"You know him?"

"We have met. He knows me. He recognized me but we did not speak."

"They want to try my troopers—all those that were at the cantina when Clay was cut," I said. "They want them there. Negro soldiers charged with a crime in a southern border town!"

"There is a very bad element in El Paso," Peter agreed. "Wild armed men with no respect for law, unreconstructed Confederates, deserters from both the North and South, men wanted for crimes, ready to slip across the river into Mexico, or living in El Paso to avoid being shot for crimes committed in Mexico.

And, of course, there are people there who hate Negroes, who have never seen anyone darker than an Indian."

"Or a Mexican," I said.

"Or a Mexican," he agreed, "but the whites who control the city are color-blind when the voters cast their ballots. The Negroes do not vote. The Mexicans do."

"And you, Colonel," I said bitterly, "want to send my men as prisoners there."

"No," Whigam said, gently for him, "I do not want to, but I shall. You will arrange your itinerary to accommodate the rate of travel of the ambulance."

Whigam then held up a hand to ward off my protest. "You will take the men unable to ride in the ambulance. You must arrange your calendar so that you arrive in El Paso at midday. You will lead your platoon into the city, with guidon flying, brass gleaming, uniforms impeccable, horses' coats brushed to perfection, heads up, men and mounts, proudly!"

I could see his vision as he saw it and I was stirred. My chest expanded with pride. But then I saw the crowd grow ugly and knew that someone would cast the first stone. There was always some miserable being who would throw the first rock, fire the first shot. Would we be dragged to the nearest tree to be hanged?

"Then, what I must do," I said, "is deliver to the jurisdiction of the federal court in El Paso, those men, myself included— even the wounded—who were present at the incident at the Water Hole Cantina."

"Yes," Whigam said, still enthralled with his vision, "You will wear your sword. You will all wear sabers."

"We prisoners will be armed with sabers?"

"Of course. And rifles."

"Loaded rifles?"

"No," Whigam said reluctantly, "but you will carry ammunition in the Blakeslee boxes. As will your escort."

"Our escort, sir?"

"Yes, Major. Every man of your platoon, not present at the cantina incident, shall form an armed escort for the men charged with criminal acts. You shall all ride in as if on parade, with sabers, rifles and ammunition boxes strapped to your shoulders."

"Could I be in charge of the escort?" Peter said eagerly.

*No!* I wanted to scream, but said nothing.

"They will need to leave soon," Whigam said. "You have not even seen Mrs. Barragan yet."

"No matter," he said, grinning at me. "We have never made a patrol together, have we, William?"

"No!" I said, too loudly.

Peter eyed me curiously and said, "Something is wrong?"

Before I could answer—I know not what I might have said—Whigam saved me.

"Peter. You have been away from your wife too long." Whigam turned to me and said, formally, "I have written orders for you in case they be necessary for the legal people. I would like to see you leave the post within the hour. The surgeon told me that while the trip might be uncomfortable for the two badly wounded men, their recovery will not be endangered."

I accepted the paper, saluted and left. Peter called out to me as I walked away, but then Whigam asked him for his full report and I was free. I sent the messenger at the double to alert Johnson, then increased my stride. I stopped suddenly, in agony. My treacherous right leg shot pain all the way up into my hip. I shifted my weight until the pain subsided, then limped toward my quarters.

We rode out, as ordered, within the hour that afternoon. Private Dewey, his arm immobile in a rigid sling, and Private Robeson, his bandaged leg propped up on a bag of oats, lay comfortably on blanket rolls in the back of the ambulance.

This time there was no Indian woman with a message from Raquel waiting just outside the post. I wondered what she was doing right now and then what she would be doing later that night. The thought burned my brain. I took refuge in my war-learned therapy. I blanked out my mind and asked that the two men with mouth organs play what had become our platoon song.

As we rode toward El Paso and a federal judge, the troopers

all sang, up and down the scale their own melodious version of the alphabet. At the end, as a surprise to me, Dewey called out in his clear tenor, "Who can spell 'sir'?"

Benson in a deep basso counterpoint sang the answer, "I can," and drew each letter in the air as he sang them.

Jefferson, a higher tenor than even Dewey sang the next question and was answered by Long Straw, a baritone.

Even Johnson answered one, spelling correctly the word "major," but he did not write the name in the air as the others had done. Then, Benson, the clown, sang out, "Who can spell 'mescal'?" mispronouncing the word for the rhyme.

When no one answered, I knew that it was meant for me and that it was a great compliment. The invitation to sing was doubly gratifying, for I had no musical ability and the men all knew it. So I sang the answer, trying to sing the letters to the scale. I failed miserably, but then I was supposed to and we all laughed together.

That night, with two sentries posted as a formality, we had our coffee sitting by the campfire. Stevens sat across from me, huddled in the protective shadow of Johnson. They all knew, now, that he could read and write better than their teacher, but he took no pride in it. He had not answered one of the musical questions, nor sung the alphabet. But now, as the harmonicas played a spiritual, he joined in, a good clear tenor, and we all sang the last lines.

*Don't you hear the trumpet sound?*
*If I had died when I was young*
*I never would had the race to run.*
*Don't you hear the trumpet sound?*

# Twenty-six

Whigam had asked me to ride into El Paso at high noon, proudly, as if on parade. I meant to do just that. When we saw the thin green treeline a handsbreadth on the horizon, swinging left to follow the Rio Grande, I knew that we were close to El Paso del Norte, once Spanish, then Mexican and Texan, but now, for more than twenty years, just plain El Paso, a frontier town bordering Mexico in the state of Texas, U.S.A. It would be straight ahead, huddled in the elbow of the Rio Grande, where it turned from almost due south to east by southeast to empty into the Gulf of Mexico.

The men opened saddlebags, pulled out currycombs, brushes and polish and, as always, cared for their horses before themselves. An hour later, we were assembled for inspection. Dewey, his right arm in its cumbersome sling and Robeson, balanced on one leg, supported by a crooked crutch roughed out from a mesquite branch, took their place in line.

Robeson, teetering on his good leg, presented his rifle for inspection. I touched it and gave it back quickly before he fell. Dewey, who could neither salute nor present his rifle, compensated by standing at rigid attention.

A buckboard, driven by a well-dressed man, who could have been a rancher, with his wife on their way to town, pulled up and stopped.

He waited until I dismissed the men, before he asked, "You the ones that were in that fight at the Water Hole. The one with the"—he glanced at his wife and thought briefly before he added—"cantina?"

"Why, yes," I said, surprised. Ballard must have talked about us. "How far to town?"

"Your wagon will take about twenty minutes," he said, tipped his hat, and drove off at a trot. His wife, wide-eyed, turned her head to look at us until the horse and buggy faded from view.

At twenty to twelve by my watch we rode in. I led, followed by those men who would be interrogated and the ambulance. Johnson, who had not been present at the incident, was in charge of the escort which rode behind the ambulance. The canvas sides had been rolled up, hiding the green cross, but with Robeson on his crutch, clutching the front corner post to the roof, leg in splints, bandaged from thigh to ankle, and Dewey, crouched in the opposite corner, arm in his large white sling, the vehicle was obviously an ambulance.

Corporal Green was at my side where, normally, Johnson would have been. The first indications of violence came as we rode into the outskirts. Small groups of men, passing bottles back and forth, hooted and shouted at us. They were still at a jovial stage. I relaxed—momentarily—for up ahead, there was a roar and shots were fired.

"Escort," I called out, "ready your carbines." I had not known what my decision would be, but there it was. If there was no other way, we would fight.

Ominous sounds of metal against metal sounded from behind me as the twelve-man escort unslung rifles, inserted loaded tubes into the Spencer carbines and then levered cartridges into firing chambers. If I gave the order to fire, the troopers would need only to thumb back the stiff-springed hammers and pull the triggers.

As we drew nearer, I saw the mob rolling toward us. Men, and even a few women, screamed at us.

"Prisoners," I ordered, "unsling and load your carbines."

"Major," Green said urgently. "They is cheering us."

"What?"

"Listen, sir."

He was right. They were yelling a welcome to us. What I had taken for epithets were praises. I was dumbfounded. White and brown people were cheering my black troopers. I wondered where the Negroes lived, but then, as I craned my neck to look over and around the crowd, I saw black faces, with big white grins shining in the sun, standing back, apart.

I countermanded my order, then took off my hat and waved it to the crowd. There was an even wilder ovation. We were almost at the town square when I called for a halt to read a message on a white banner spread from one side of the street to the other. It had been painted and hung hastily, for some of the red letters had dripped. But they were large and easy to read. I stood up in the stirrups, yelled for the column to halt and for the escort to sling rifles.

I read the sign in as loud a voice as I could: WELCOME TO EL PASO, SOLDIERS OF THE NINTH CAVALRY REGIMENT, HEROES OF THE BATTLE OF THE WATER HOLE CANTINA, AND SAVIOURS OF WEST TEXAS FROM THE SAVAGE APACHES. LEELAND P. LUTHER. REFORM CANDIDATE FOR SHERIFF. The candidate's name had been lettered in black.

Cheer followed cheer, but changed to jeers and catcalls when several men on foot, wearing badges and revolvers, cleared the street in front of us.

Behind them, on horseback, Rex Miles shouted over the rude noise of the crowd, "Major Northey, the sheriff is waiting for you at the courthouse."

"Very well." I waved the platoon forward past a street intersection to what appeared to be the town square. There were two platforms, one facing the other. They looked identical, but one, flaunting a banner asking the voters to reelect Honest John Pace, crime fighter, was filled with men. I recognized both Pace and Sawyer.

There were only half a dozen on the other, which bore a large sign that declared that Reform Candidate Leeland P.

Luther would kick all of the crooks out of El Paso, starting with the entire staff of the present sheriff's office.

"Major Northey, sir," Pace yelled. The noise abated. The crowd wanted to hear what Pace had to say. Would they listen to me?

"Yes, Sheriff."

"You are prepared to deliver the prisoners?"

"All of the men whom you have requested to be delivered to a federal court, are here or accounted for. Sergeant Johnson," I said, "who was not present at the first incident at the Water Hole Cantina, will report to me as I read the names of those soldiers who were."

"First incident?" Pace did not fall into my trap, he jumped in headfirst. "What was the second?"

"The Battle for the Water Hole Cantina," I said in my normal voice which carried easily through two seconds of quiet. Then the crowd erupted again and there could be no conversation. Pace shouted until his face turned red and then gave up and waited until, little by little, they stopped cheering and yelled for Pace to continue.

"We congratulate the army on its victory, but, Major Northey, we are both public servants and we have our duty to do. Proceed, Major. Call your roll."

I let Othello move a few steps toward the other platform. A tall, thin man with side whiskers that would have shamed General Burnside, seemed to be in charge. Although I addressed myself to Pace, I was also talking to candidate Luther and I felt sure he knew.

"My rank, Sheriff Pace, is first lieutenant and this is my platoon." It was a small barb, but I wanted him off balance for another minute. "I will dismount my men, sir, and as the names are called, I will ask them to ascend the platform to my right—there are only a few men there—with your permission?"

Pace did not have an opportunity to agree or refuse. The crowd yelled approval and I took the sheriff's inability to speak over the crowd for assent. I mouthed the order. Green and Johnson dismounted and the men followed an order that they could not have heard. The horse holders ran reins through the bridle rings and moved the clusters of horses down the street away from the rest of the platoon.

When the crowd quieted, I called out, "Sergeant Johnson, run up on that platform and report."

Johnson, every inch a first sergeant, trotted to the stage, paused for permission, received it from both Luther and the crowd, then turned to face me, ramrod stiff, at attention.

The crowd was quiet now, waiting to hear the names.

"Are all of the men accused or suspected of committing a crime at the Water Hole Cantina present and accounted for?" I asked.

"Yes, sir!" Johnson spoke in his loud but melodious parade-ground voice which, I thought, could be heard several blocks away.

"Private Benjamin Bagley." I raised my voice slightly.

"Killed in the fight at the Water Hole Cantina," Johnson said.

A few of the drunks cheered, but they were silenced by others.

"Private Daniel Berry."

Berry walked briskly to the platform and up the steps and stood at attention to Johnson's far right, leaving space for the rest of the men to align themselves with him.

"Private Joshua Clay."

Clay, a slim young man, had not regained the weight lost while in the hospital and, although he attempted to emulate Berry, he had to pause at the first step to rest. Luther reached down to offer him a hand. Clay glanced up at Johnson and received a nod of approval. He smiled up at Luther and took his hand. Clay was as handsome a young man as I had ever seen, and when he smiled his thanks, even as he grimaced in pain upon taking the first step, there was a collective sigh from the women and a few of the men. He took his place alongside Brown.

"Corporal Victor Crawford," I called the name.

"Killed in the fight at the Water Hole Cantina." Johnson intoned the phrase again in the dead quiet.

There were no cheers. A few of the men muttered and glared at Pace.

"Private Leroy Dewey."

There was a sharp intake of breath as heads turned to focus on the two men who helped Dewey down from the ambulance. He marched to the stand, up the steps and took his place in line.

"Corporal Lester Green."

Green turned to me, asked permission to leave the platoon, saluted, executed a perfect about-face, and marched as if in time to a piece of martial music to his place next to Dewey.

"Private Washington Riley."

"Killed in the fight at the Water Hole Cantina."

This time there were more than mutterings. A tall angry man raised a clenched fist and shouted, "What are you trying to do with these brave men, Pace?"

The crowd erupted again, this time against Pace. Insults rained upon him.

When the crowd was quiet, I called out the name of Thaddeus Stevens. He looked and walked like a man condemned to death and the crowd commiserated with him, wondering, I supposed, what tragedy had occurred in the battle to so affect him. He stood next to Green.

"Jebedia Robeson," I called the next-to-last name. Two men helped Robeson to the ground, much as they had helped Dewey, except the splinted leg made it almost impossible for him to walk except by taking one short step, advancing his rude crutch a foot, bearing his weight on the good leg, swinging his splinted right leg again forward and again moving the crutch a foot forward. The crowd watched in stunned silence and then a voice called out each step with the word "Pace!"

The crowd took up the chant. Every step Robeson took was marked by the name "Pace," an epithet, marking each painful step like a drumbeat. Pace struggled free from one of his followers—I saw that it was Sawyer, face contorted with rage, waving his arms in negation. No one could have heard him over that funereal chant.

Just before Robeson reached the steps to the stand, Luther stepped to the edge of the platform, held both hands up, mutely pleading for silence. The crowd stopped the chant to listen.

Luther turned to face Pace, his arms still held high, like a preacher at a revival meeting, his voice filled with religious fervor.

"Why must this man, wounded fighting for us, take this stand? Why must any of them? Why?"

The chant turned from "Pace" to "Why?" A few bottles and rocks were thrown at Pace's group. Men put their hands to the butts of revolvers.

I held up my hands and the crowd quieted, but when Pace tried to speak, he was hooted and threatened. He gestured toward me and the crowd cheered.

I waited while everyone yelled at everyone else to be quiet. When I could speak, I said, "The facts are that two of my men were beaten half to death and Private Clay, there, on the stand, had his stomach ripped open with a sickle. One white man was shot, accidentally, by the revolver of that man on the stage behind Sheriff Pace, Howard Sawyer!"

Pace stepped away from Sawyer, then taking advantage of the silence called out, "All of these boys, they are all good boys and soldiers. There will not be charges against most of them."

I had seen a tall cowboy wave up at the stand. Joshua Clay grinned and nodded. Then I saw a shock of hair, sticking out like red straw from the large felt hat and knew that it was Clay's friend, Sandy.

Not far from the group of Sawyer hired hands, taking advantage of the chance to advertise and see the spectacle, Blondie and a few of her girls were bunched together, twirling parasols and waving fans.

"What are the charges and who are the witnesses?" I asked.

"Why some cowboys and a white lady who defended herself against one of the soldiers," Pace answered.

"That would be Private Joshua Clay." I turned to point. "Put up your hand, Joshua. Did you molest any woman at the cantina?"

"No, sir."

"Your witness?" I asked Pace.

"She will be in court," Pace said uneasily.

"Is her name Beth Anderson?"

"Why, yes, it is," he said, surprised.

"I see her standing right over there. Could we ask her if she will testify in federal court?"

The crowd roared out its assent, drowning out whatever Pace might have said. Beth Anderson, obviously frightened, was escorted to the stand. Apparently most of the men knew Blondie's girls.

Luther had taken a black hand in his and helped the man up the steps. But he would not touch that of Beth Anderson. He stepped back and away from her when she mounted the platform.

"Did Joshua Clay attack you?" I asked.

"Sheriff," she wailed, looking toward Pace. "You said I wouldn't have to go to court."

"Maybe you won't," I answered before Pace could. "Just tell us the truth."

"You Goddamn well better tell the truth, you whore!" Sawyer had shoved Pace aside.

"Watch your language, Sawyer!" Luther shouted.

"Just tell the truth, Beth," I said. "No one will hurt you."

She looked fearfully at Sawyer, then looked straight at me, and said, "No. He didn't hurt me."

She closed her eyes as if to shut out the world. Then, speaking softly, her little-girl voice heard clearly in the absolute silence, continued. "He paid me like the others. Then they came back and saved us girls. We'd all be dead, wasn't for them Buffalo Soldiers."

"Well," Pace said quickly and loudly, "that is settled. I personally would like to shake hands with every soldier on that stand."

"Wait a minute. Is there not a miscegenation law in this state? That woman bedded a nigger and that is against the law!" Sawyer's words might have been the screams of a person in agony.

Beth Anderson opened her eyes and turned to face Sawyer. No soldier who had received a medal for acting in the face of danger with valor above and beyond the call of duty, could have shown more real courage than did that frightened girl.

"No, it ain't, Mr. Sawyer. Not if I'm part nigger myself."

There was a complete stunned silence. Then Sawyer went for his gun. He likely would have shot someone. The girl or perhaps me. We would never know, for Miles cracked him across the nape of the neck with a sap, caught him neatly before he fell and sat him on a chair in a corner of the stage. Only a few people even saw it happen.

Pace took advantage of the silence to call out, "These men are exonerated and what's more, we got free beer and tamales right here in the park. Hooray for the Ninth Colored Cavalry! Three cheers for the heroes of the Battle for the Water Hole Cantina!"

After the cheers, which might have been heard as far south as the city of Chihuahua, I held up my hands for quiet.

"I thank you," I said, "but I have one last name to call. First Lieutenant William Northey."

I dismounted, took one step, and felt the agony of that traitorous leg and, to my embarrassment, as I limped, heard people refer, with great sympathy, to my "battle wound." Which it was, even if the battle had been fought five years earlier.

Acting Corporal Jefferson caught me to whisper a request to which I agreed. When I reached Robeson, I slipped my shoulder under his arm in place of the crutch, and we climbed the steps together, slowly and painfully.

When we were both in the line and standing at attention, Johnson turned to face me and sang out, "Lieutenant Northey, sir. All soldiers of the first platoon of Company E, Ninth Colored Cavalry Regiment, who were present at the incident at the Water Hole Cantina are present or accounted for."

Our dead comrade, Crawford was an indifferent bugler, but he had mastered "Taps," the haunting notes of the good night call for a soldier to sleep. The call came from one end of the park. The thin reedy but clear and high notes of "Taps" were played on a mouth organ. I took one step forward and saluted for us all. Then the echo of "Taps" was played by a trooper concealed at the other end. Tears came to my eyes.

I was not alone. Even our iron man, Sergeant George Johnson, lost his voice momentarily and had to repeat his request to dismiss the formation.

There was no segregation that day in the town square. There were not enough soldiers to go around. Both candidates pleaded with our troopers to drink their beer and eat their tacos or tamales. Even our horses were stabled nearby, watered and fed by the city.

Except for Johnson, no one spoke to Stevens. He was like Banquo's Ghost at the banquet and only Sergeant Macbeth could see him. I accepted an invitation to sit at the Luther table, shook hands with that gentleman and others, and found myself alongside a gaunt man with burning black eyes, lank black hair, wearing a black frock coat and black trousers. His shirt was as white as a cloud and so was his skin. I thought he might be the town undertaker. He was not.

"I know you, Major William R-for-Randolph Northey," he said. "I know your Sergeant Johnson and Corporals Crawford, Brown and Jefferson. And most of the privates. I even know the Indian, Redwood, but he is not here."

"And you, sir, are a friend or collaborator—perhaps both— of one Oliver R. for Richard Ballard."

"I have that honor. When my press has not been recently smashed or my type pied by fun-loving friends of Sheriff Pace, I set the type and print the advertisements for the merchants. If there is any news, I print that too."

I drank a beer and took a tentative bite from a tamale.

"You also write for the periodical for which you set type."

"Yes, if there is any need to. The last *Eagle* carried the signature of Oliver R. Ballard. His story and his illustrations."

I had suspected that Ballard had publicized our encounter with the Apaches with more than conversation.

"You do not have a copy of the *Eagle?*"

"Certainly." He reached down into a black bag and withdrew a folded paper. He presented it to me with a flourish and then said, "That will be three cents."

"Yes. If I read it all, I will pay you the full price."

He smiled then and said, "I am Norman Goldman. I publish and edit the *Eagle,* but I am happiest when setting type and printing. Have a drink."

He looked away from me to his right and then furtively took a thin bottle from his pocket, passed it to me, waited anxiously for me to swallow, then retrieving the bottle, swallowed twice and replaced it as quickly as a magician on stage.

"This is the good mescal?" I asked, wondering if old Charley Dirty Knife still lived. When I last spoke to the surgeon, he had merely shrugged and said, "He is, as you said, a tough old man. He might surprise me."

"The best," Goldman explained, "Aged two weeks."

I unfolded the paper. The headline was predictable. NINTH CAVALRY DEFEATS APACHE NATION IN BLOODY FIGHT AT WATER HOLE CANTINA.

The story was romanticized, but mostly true. Ballard could write. And draw. The sketches, done hurriedly and in line only so that they could be reproduced by the *Eagle* were superb.

There was one showing the girls, fainting and weeping, protected by a white soldier with a saber. I laughed. Goldman whose penetrating eyes followed mine as I read, said, "I had that done on my own. Paid for it. Not bad, eh?"

"No," I said. "Neither was that mescal."

His hand swooped like an ethereal seagull into the black sea of cloth and came up with the bottle in its beak. I knew the drill now. I swallowed twice, quickly, then snapped the bottle back.

"But the white officer is not correct," I said. "The white soldiers came later, behind the Indians. They were not in the fight. Not for the water hole."

"Well, sir, you are wrong. That brave white officer defending the honor of the fair young ladies is none other than Major William R-for-Randolph Northey."

"That is not fair," I said. "I don't count. I am the platoon leader."

We had a heated discussion, another quick drink and, when I admitted that his mescal was indeed the good kind, he took the paper from me and turned it over. There on the back was a sketch done by inking the paper with black ink and then scraping away the black to leave lines that delineated the scene. This one was superb. It showed a black sergeant who had just plunged a saber into the ground. He was looking fearfully back toward the enemy.

The printed line identified the picture as *Marking the Range*.

I worried a five-cent piece out of my trouser pocket, gave it to him and said, "Keep the change."

He did.

The barn at the stable was turned over to us. Some of the men had been shyly asked to stay with Negro families in the town and had accepted. A few had thought of crossing to the other side to see the girls. They would have to wear civilian coats and no army insignia. I left it up to Johnson, who had crossed before. He took Green, Jefferson, Stevens and our camp cook, Long Straw, who despised Stevens. Johnson asked to borrow my copy of the *Eagle* to show to a certain lady who lived in Mexico.

I decided to sleep in the barn with the men. I warned everyone that they must be back for the roll call at reveille. I sent Brown and Green and the two wounded men in the ambulance with the arms to the barn. Then I agreed to have a nightcap with Goldman and Luther at a bar so old, Goldman told me, that Oñate himself had dropped in for a drink of mescal two hundred years earlier on his way to settle Santa Fe in New Mexico.

We stood at the bar, long enough to hold a file of soldiers, saw ourselves reflected in a mirror the size of a door, and eyed an array of oddly shaped and colored bottles on a long shelf just under the mirror.

The bartender served us small glasses of the good mescal, along with quartered limes and salt. Goldman sucked lime, drank mescal and tongued salt. Luther did just the opposite. I decided an editor would know more than a preacher—Luther really was a preacher—and emulated him.

After agreeing that Luther should be sheriff, later mayor and finally, at least governor of the state, I made the mistake of criticizing the sketch of me protecting the girls at the cantina.

"You know not of what you speak, sir."

Goldman stepped up onto the bar rail to intimidate me, I suppose, but Luther thought it was part of the mescal-drinking rite and perched upon the rail also. He was at least two feet taller than Goldman, who was my size. I sighed and joined them on the rail.

"I do not illustrate nor write without the best of documentation, Major. The best!" He took out a print from an inside breast pocket and laid it on the bar. Luther looked down and gasped. The bartender craned his neck, and said, "Oh, my God." He turned red, and said, "Pardon, Reverend," and moved to the other end of the bar. It was an excellent photograph and could only have been set up by Jeanne and triggered by Ballard. She would have placed the camera outside the dogtrot, the sun coming in from behind the camera lighting the three girls perfectly.

The large photographic plates showed all of the gradations of light that gave the illusion of color. Jeanne, wearing nothing but an impudent smile, stood in the middle. She was as dark as Stevens and as light as Clay. Her breasts were the size and color of dark pears. Her pubic hair was dark and wooly. She had her hands over the shoulders of Blondie and the white girl, Beth Anderson. She held the dark nipple of Blondie's melon sized dark, but not black breast pinched in her left hand. She held the long, light—its real color would have been pink— nipple of Beth Anderson between thumb and forefinger of her right hand.

Blondie's narrow waist accented large, shapely thighs. Her pubic hair should have been brown and was gently curling while that of Beth Anderson who had claimed to be a Negro when accused of miscegenation, was so white as to defy further definition.

# Twenty-seven

We had no bugler to announce our arrival, as had Peter Barragan, just a week ago, so we rode in singing the alphabet. Everyone not on duty and a few who were, was waiting to greet us. I saw Raquel standing next to Mary Sullivan and doffed my hat to them. Across the way Peter Barragan counted the troopers and then held up his hands and flashed fingers. He waved his hat back at me and smiled. Not one trooper was missing. It was in its way a bigger victory than that of the Water Hole.

Whigam was standing on the veranda in front of the headquarters building, so I drew the platoon up there, guidon flying and sabers rattling. We, too, like Peter had paused to tidy up and strap on sabers.

I saluted Whigam with my saber. He waved one of his "away with you" salutes but I could tell that he was pleased.

"You brought them all back?" Whigam said.

"Yes, sir. Every man that left is present," I reported.

"Did you shoot any civilians?"

"No, sir, although I did have a duel of sorts with a newspaperman friend of Ballard's."

"Have you had the time to write a report?"

"No, sir. But I did dictate as we rode and Private Stevens made notes while riding in the ambulance. At camp last night he wrote the report which I signed and dated." I brought out a sheath of papers from my saddlebag and flourished them.

"One of our colored troopers wrote a report!" Whigam said. I took the exclamation as a cry of joy rather than a question. "May I dismiss the platoon?"

"You may. Then report inside."

I gave the order to Johnson, who passed it on. The men dismounted and led the horses off to the stables. They were weary but in good spirits. There was no bugler to blow the stable call, but as they trudged off leading their mounts, and mine, my saber slung from my saddle, they sang the words troopers had put to the call:

> Oh go to the stable
> All you who are able
> And give your poor horses
> Some hay and some corn.
> For if you don't do it . . .

I closed the door behind me, shutting off the last lines of the call, saluted, handed the report to Whigam and waited. He motioned me to a chair and read the report. Whigam was a rapid reader. He put the paper aside.

"This report is essentially a good military report. All the unembellished facts presented in an orderly manner. Much better than the reports you write."

Knowing that it was useless to point out that I had dictated the report, even if I had not actually written it, I agreed.

"Now," he said, opening the drawer that was his office liquor cabinet, "let me have your oral report with the embellished facts."

I did, pausing only to scowl or laugh and occasionally drink with Whigam. When I was through, he glowed with what I took to be paternal pride.

"William, I shall write a report that, should it reach our erstwhile commanding general and presently our President, will cause him to jump you to colonel of the Ninth Cavalry, Colored Regiment."

We drank to that. Then he surprised me again. He put away the bottle. He sighed and said, obviously embarrassed, "You must not pay so much attention to Mrs. Barragan. Adele O'Donahue has been making pointed comments and even her sister, that sweet soul of charity, Mary Sullivan, said something to Mrs. Barragan privately that caused her to stamp out of the trader's store."

"What can I do?" I wrenched the words out.

"Chase Adele for a bit. She is too skinny for my taste, but she does have good breasts." Now that he had warned me, he was again in good spirits. "But," he mused, "not as good as Rosa Maria's, eh?"

Rosa Maria? Blondie. I had told him about the photograph, but not in detail. I said, "It's a matter of color. I think I like brown better."

"Yes, that's it. Brown is better. We must ride over to the cantina one day. Go over the ground. Show me where Johnson marked the range with your saber!"

"Whenever you like, sir."

"And speaking of Johnson, George Sullivan and I will be at the school this Friday for his graduation."

"Graduation?"

"Yes. Dean Sullivan will either give him a diploma or you will give me a case of champagne. Sullivan has had it a long time now and must turn it over for a profit. That's his business, you know."

Yes, I did know. I wondered if George would trust me for the champagne.

Whigam had arranged a party for all of the men. He spoke briefly, congratulating them on their conduct in El Paso. The two wounded men would not be returned to duty until Smith declared them fit, but they would sleep in their own cots and eat with their comrades. The third platoon's bugler—we had no second platoon, the replacements had not yet arrived—who now played all of the daily calls was instructed to play "Taps" a bit later. Around midnight. There was a good bit of raillery between the platoons, but the third had prepared and paid for the food and drink. Of course, a trooper's first loyalty might be to his own file, but certainly to his own platoon and then to his company and, finally, to the regiment. Or, I shrugged mentally, eventually to the Army of the Unites States of America.

We ate a plate of pork spiced with hot New Mexican chiles, black beans, pungent with *epazote* and thanks to Maria, the Barragan maid, fresh, hot, wheat tortillas. We made pork tacos, sopped up the juice from the beans with fresh soft bread and drank cold beer. We then stood up, the colonel and I, and asked to be excused. Peter Barragan had been there briefly, but as officer of the day, left early.

Following protocol, Sergeant Johnson protested, but we politely insisted. As soon as we were out the door, the singing began. Whigam and I paused, briefly, to listen, and then walked to the Sullivans' where another party awaited us. Whigam stopped short of the steps and looked at me quizzically, I thought, although it was too dark to be sure.

"Did you hurt your leg?"

"No," I said reflexively, defensively as I had done ever since the long stay in the hospital.

"Then why are you limping?"

I could think of no reason, but I did not have to answer, for he bounded up the steps, calling over his shoulder, "Come along, William. It is time for wine."

The scene might have been from a recurring dream in which you have an impossible task to do and you know that it is impossible, but you must try, over and over, for all eternity—or until you wake up. I suppose that not waking up would be hell. Although we were at the trader's home, otherwise it was my first night all over again at Camp Leper. Even Bell, waxed black mustache and perfect white teeth, just as handsome as I remembered was there. He gestured as he talked, touching Peter's arm and then Raquel's wrist. The three of them giggled constantly. I decided that my first impression of him as an arrogant ladies' man had been correct.

Adele was alone, the chair beside her vacant. I waved a hello to the room, called out a good evening, then went to the bar and plucked two glasses of red wine from a tray and approached Adele.

"You are lovely tonight, Miss O'Donahue." I bowed. "Might I offer you a glass of wine?"

"Why yes, Major. That is Dr. Smith's chair, but he will be gone for a while. Do sit down."

She turned toward me, twisting her leg far enough to touch mine, locked my eyes with hers and smiled, with what I would have taken for open invitation had we been at the Water Hole Cantina.

"I read the newspaper about the battle and all, Major, but what I liked the best was how you used your saber to save those poor little girls from those awful Apaches. And Mr. Ballard caught your spirit, a picture of a brave and handsome man."

I glowed and smiled foolishly, and at the same time felt embarrassed. I looked away across the room straight into the burning eyes of Raquel. She averted her eyes instantly and fondled the immaculate sleeve of the toy soldier, Bell.

"Would the doctor be looking in at our wounded?"

"He said he must go to the infirmary."

"The school," I corrected her, then explained. "When there are no wounded there, we call it the school. The men have been given leave to stay in the barracks. I thought the surgeon would know. Has he been gone long?"

"No. He went to fetch his instruments from the ambulance."

"I will find him for you," I said.

"It is stuffy in here," Adele said, breathing deeply to illustrate her point as well as the size and shape of her breasts.

Whigam had suggested that I chase after Adele, I remembered. Then, as lust mixed with anger, I decided that I would indeed heed Whigam's advice.

Setting my wineglass on a side table, I stood, held my hand to her, and asked, "Would you accompany me to search for our missing surgeon?"

"Why, thank you, Major. You are so gallant."

"And you," I said, loudly enough for Raquel Barragan to hear, "are so beautiful."

"You are such a flatterer, Major." She took my hand and rose, flashed a smile at Raquel, and then took my arm as we walked out of the room.

After the first few steps, she turned to me and said, "I think the ambulance is the other way, Major."

"Please call me William," I said, pausing and looking into her eyes as she had mine. I added, "The ambulance *is* the other way."

"Do we have time to look at your rooms? I have never been inside a bachelor officer's quarters."

"If we hurry," I said. And hurry we did.

Even so, an impatient and angry Smith awaited us. We had, he announced to the room, been gone for half an hour. He was right. I had timed our frantic encounter at twenty-five minutes. We did not undress. It was more a matter of unbuttoning and shifting material, of groping and thrusting. Then an urgent climax was followed by a hasty reversal of the opening process. The walk to and from my rooms had taken another five minutes.

"It was my fault," I said. "We went looking for you and I turned the wrong way."

"You certainly did. And who," he snapped, "gave you permission to remove the wounded men from my hospital?"

Whigam came to my rescue.

"Inasmuch as you released those two men from the hospital to make a three-day trip in an ambulance"—Whigam enunciated each word clearly as if talking to someone not proficient in English—"I decided that you just might allow them to leave *your* hospital and sleep in their own beds."

Whigam's logic was irrefutable. Which was unfortunate. So

Smith turned from the unanswerable to the despicable, which was, of course, William Northey.

"You, sir, venture to sully the reputation of my betrothed!"

*Judas Priest,* I thought. He is going to challenge me to a duel.

I was saved again. This time by Adele O'Donahue.

"Betrothed! And who, may I ask, Dr. Smith, informed you that we were"—she spit the word out—"betrothed?"

Smith was stunned. His eyes bulged. "But, Ideal, my dear, it was understood."

"Understood by who?"

I thought for a second that he meant to correct her grammar and almost felt sorry for the fiery little man with the frog voice. But he closed his mouth, then his eyes. When a minute of utter silence had passed, he withdrew a small pouch of chamois from a vest pocket. He opened it and extracted a ring with a brilliant big enough to sparkle brightly in the lamplight.

"I had thought to propose tonight," he said, his tone now completely conciliatory.

"Why you darling," Adele said, eyeing the ring. "You are proposing to me then?"

"Of course," Smith said, then added in a rueful voice, "I guess I just have. Will you marry me, Miss O'Donahue?"

"Of course, I will." She held her hand out for the ring.

The surgeon placed it on her finger and Adele, radiantly happy, smiled victoriously at the room. I was included in her smile, but not dwelled upon.

However, when the happy couple retired to the parlor with sister Mary as a chaperon, Smith, now the amiable fiancé, turned to me and said, "Did you and Adele just take that moonlight walk to make me pop the question?"

"Well," I said wistfully, "not entirely. But she is a clever girl."

"That she is," he agreed, but paused to add, "but now she belongs to me. Understood?"

"Yes," I said. "Understood."

Across the room, Whigam, a squat brandy goblet in his hand now, caught my eyes and called me over. He was standing next to Sullivan. They would be the same height to the inch, I thought. But a Sullivan sliced down the middle would have provided enough material for two Whigams.

"William," Sullivan said softly, "congratulations. The colonel thinks he will be buying you a case of champagne."

"George, I wish that it were true, but I really need another few weeks."

"Friday," Whigam said. "Matriculate or evacuate."

"Yes, sir."

"Good evening, Major." Bell extended his hand. I would rather have shaken the pad of a prickly pear cactus. It was a hearty handshake, but Bell did all the shaking.

"At regiment we have a dozen copies of Ballard's story, "The Battle for the Water Hole" printed in the El Paso *Eagle*. The story was reprinted in most of the cities in Texas. I was told by a new officer that he had read the story in a Denver newspaper."

Raquel turned to smile at me then. But there was no smile in her eyes and little in her voice.

"Major Northey has become a celebrity, at least as famous as Oliver Ballard and his young photographer. I feared he might leave without greeting the less-known Barragans."

Bell released my hand. "I am sorry, Mrs. Barragan, but first Adele took the major away and then I did. I am sorry."

"Please forgive me," I said, not knowing what I should say. "I think that I might have been involved in an attack on Dr. Smith's flank."

"I suspect," Raquel said, "that it was not the doctor's flank that was endangered."

Bell was an excellent soldier. I never saw him in combat, but he must have been cool under fire. He smiled at Raquel and then said, seriously, "You might not have heard, Major, but I have been assigned here again to await the recruits to bring the Whigam Company up to strength, including another platoon. When it arrives, I will be the leader of the second platoon."

"Yes, Max," Raquel said, "I am so pleased. I know how you wanted the post. But there is little to do here. Of course, it is different for you men. You ride off to the Water Hole Cantina and save the dancing girls from the savages."

I could have strangled Ballard had he been there.

"That drawing," I said earnestly, "was solely Ballard's invention. It was fiction. Sheer fiction."

Now they were all laughing at me.

"Methinks," Peter Barragan, who had been grinning at my discomfiture, waiting to speak, said, "thou dost protest too much."

Raquel laughed again and, to my great relief, when she spoke to me I could see no anger in her lovely turquoise eyes.

"Did Peter tell you about the photographer?"

"No."

"You should have warned him." Raquel was teasing, it seemed, but I was not the victim.

"But I did," I replied.

"What?" Both Bell and Raquel replied, but strangely enough, Bell seemed more surprised than Raquel.

"Warning?" Bell asked.

"The lad turned out to be a lady," Whigam said.

"And Peter, out of uniform of course," Raquel said, "escorted the photographer across the border to photograph the Mexicans."

"The girl or the boy?" Bell asked so seriously that we all laughed. But not until Peter answered did Bell join in the laughter.

"I don't know, Max." Peter grinned. "The photographer, while in Mexico, wore no clothes at all."

"Men should always wear clothes," Whigam said. "Can you imagine taking orders from a naked, old, pot-bellied man? How could you tell the generals from the sergeant majors?"

After a long silence, I decided to steer the conversation

along more conventional lines and asked Bell, "Where will you be billeted?"

"We brought a tent and planks for a floor on the supply wagon. It should be ready to move in soon. In the meanwhile, I have been invited by the Barragans to sleep in their guest room."

"Peter has a trooper they call Chips who is a first-class carpenter," Sullivan said.

The doctor strutted out the door, said good night to Adele, kissed her on the cheek, nodded pleasantly to all and hurried outside. He would sleep in *his* hospital. Peter, who had the duty, would sleep at headquarters and, I suddenly realized, that Bell, not yet assigned any duty at all, would sleep under the same roof as Raquel Barragan.

"Perhaps Lieutenant Bell would like to share my quarters tonight," I said.

"What?" Bell was startled.

"But you have only one bed," Peter said, eyeing me strangely.

"We could borrow a bed from the infirmary," I said.

"What are you talking about, William?" Peter asked. "We have offered a room to Max and he has accepted."

"Maybe," Bell said, "it might be better if I did sleep elsewhere this first night."

"Are you inferring," Peter said, for the first time showing the temperament attributed to redheads, "that there is something improper? With servants in the house!"

I knew where the servants slept at night, but I said, "Of course not."

Adele and Mary were at the door, whispering and laughing together. It was time to go. I nodded to them. Then, remembering Whigam's ultimatum, spoke to Peter.

"Would you allow Mrs. Barragan to assist at the school for a few days? The colonel has decided that this Friday, Sergeant Johnson must pass his literacy test or I will be out a case of champagne."

"Now that you have a company clerk," Raquel said, looking at Peter, "I seem to have lost my job. Let me pedagog some more."

"Yes," Peter agreed and then added thoughtfully, "but I think that will be your graduation day too."

"Good night then." Raquel extended her hand. I barely brushed my lips over it, suddenly worried and ashamed that I might transfer the strong, lusty scent of Dr. Smith's betrothed.

# Twenty-eight

"You tutor him when you can, Stevens," I said. "Whenever you can slip out of headquarters. The class will be conducted, as always, after Retreat. Mrs. Barragan will work with us. You remember how Sergeant Johnson responded to the sketches she drew."

"Yes, sir, I do. But I think you can teach him if anyone can. He will learn if you talk to him right."

"What is right?"

"Just tell him that it is a good thing for a colored man to learn to read and to write, even if he once was a slave."

"I know he can learn!" I said bitterly, frustrated.

"So do I, sir, but that does not mean that he will."

"Why will that man not learn? Do you have any idea at all?"

Stevens pursed his lips and then shook his head. "Have you ever seen the sergeant with his coat off, when it's hot and he leaves his shirt off?"

"No," I said. "Why should I?"

"I may lose the only real friend I have in the company," he said sadly. "He will not like me telling you."

"Stevens, think of the man's future. He could easily be sergeant major at regiment. Maybe even an officer."

"Johnson is a Negro, blacker than most. An officer?"

"We have to start somewhere. Maybe not soon. Someday."

"Someday? In this century, Major?"

"Of course. Look back just ten years. You and Johnson were slaves."

"And we are free. I am free to be a soldier who cannot fight and Johnson a sergeant who cannot write." He smiled. "I have been around Colonel Whigam too long."

"He grows on you," I said. "Will you help me?"

"I would not be alive to answer had it not been for you and the colonel."

"We did it for the regiment, mainly," I said reluctantly. "And you can still prove yourself. You might be a sergeant."

"I know, Major." He sighed. "I shall miss my chess games."

"Chess! You play chess?"

"I suppose it must be my white blood." He looked at me slyly and then added, "But then, I taught Sergeant Johnson and he is all black. He also wins more often than I." He corrected himself. "Did win. No more chess until school is out."

"Will you tell me about Johnson?"

"He has bad scars—I am familiar with scars—that must be over twenty years old."

"He would have been just a boy then."

"Yes, sir. I think he might have been ten years old."

"But what has that got to do with reading and writing?"

"Remember what I was beaten for, sir."

"Yes. But that was because you could read and write better than—" I stopped, suddenly enlightened. In several of the Southern states it had been a felony to allow a Negro to become literate. The owner could be fined and the slave whipped.

"You think that a small black boy was caught looking through a book and someone beat him for it. Whipped him badly enough to leave scars?"

"He will not talk about it. But when I told him about Master Edward and my beating, when I was in the guardhouse, waiting to be shot, he understood. He told me that a lot of us slaves had problems to overcome, but that we had to forget and move on."

"You think he might talk to me? Like you have?"

"Man to nigger?" Stevens and Whigam did have a similar cutting wit and a need to demonstrate it.

"Man to officer," I said.

"Yes," he said seriously. "If he will talk to anyone, it would be you."

"All right, I shall try, tonight, after school." I stood and Stevens popped up. He had been seated at his desk where he kept the company records.

"Help me, Corporal Stevens," I said. "If you can."

He said, "Yes, sir," and saluted. I returned his salute and left.

At the guardhouse the muster was forming for roll call. I hurried across the square into the school and shut the door just before Bugler Montgomery from the third platoon sounded retreat.

Our school had progressed. We had a blackboard that Bell had brought from Fort Stockton and our occasional carpenter, Private Young, had fashioned an eight-foot-long bench, along with a similar bench two feet higher for a desk.

I groped for and found a box of school supplies stored in the same closet as our emergency medical supplies. I turned, set it on the waist-high operating table, found a match case and shook loose a phosphorus match. I lit it with my thumbnail, reached up to tip the lantern wick toward the match, then turned as I heard the door open and slam shut. The draft blew my match out, but not before I saw the smiling face of Raquel Barragan.

She was already in my arms when I dropped the burnt match. "Raquel," I cried out, "not now," but she closed my mouth with hers and I was lost.

She said throatily, "We have half an hour, dear William."

I swept the box off the table, sent chalk and slate crashing to the floor, and lifted her up onto the table. Suddenly I could hear Adele simpering, and then Whigam's warning and I paused. But then a bared breast touched my lips and I cared for nothing else in the world except my lovely Raquel. In my frenzy, I cared not that her last name was not Northey, but Barragan.

I had moved from the table, leaning against it, heart still pounding, and breathing heavily, when I heard the footsteps and whispered hoarsely, "Raquel, hurry! It must be Too Soon Dewey."

I fumbled frenziedly for a match, but Raquel said soothingly as if speaking to a child, "It is all right, love. Just wait a bit."

There was a rap on the door, a pause, then three more in rapid succession and then the sound of the outer screen door banging shut. I raced to the door, opened it a sliver, but could see nothing except a tall man that might have been Johnson walking rapidly across the deserted quadrangle.

I found the match case underfoot, along with loose matches. I picked up one, stood up, groped for the lamp, banged it with my hand and it rang like a bell. I grasped it with my left hand, scraped the match into flame and lit the wick. The light blinded me. When I could see again, Raquel, looking as if she had just left her dressing room, was writing the day's lesson on the board.

I tugged and wrenched and buttoned and ran my fingers through my hair, then asked, "Do I look all right?"

"Yes," she said, laughing. "But we had better erase that scarlet letter from your forehead."

She was an amazing woman. I had been terrified. Likely as much or more for myself than fear for her. I smiled too, but it was more a reaction of relief than humor.

The steps squeaked again. "This time it will be Dewey," I said. I called out, "Come on in, Private Dewey."

The door opened and Peter Barragan greeted me with a smile and a salute.

"Max has knocked me down to fourth-ranking officer, but you go too far, Major."

I laughed too loudly and long, but Peter did not notice. He looked at the lesson on the board, approved it casually, and when the first man—it *was* the private nicknamed Too Soon

Dewey—arrived, he said that he must get back to Bell, who was officer of the day, to join him in a glass of cognac.

He turned to leave, then stooped and lifted a small bundle from the floor, near the door. He turned and set it on the long desk. "You must have dropped your books on the way in, Raquel," he said, nodded amiably and was gone.

Jefferson and Green, who were competing for first place in the class, came in together, followed by Brown and Clay. Johnson came in last, but on time and took his place, standing by the door.

Raquel joined me at the lectern, untied the bundle and took out half a dozen thin primers, the ones called "readers," printed for children learning to read.

"Once you have mastered these," she explained, "I will bring others from our own library for you to read. But"—she waved a warning finger at Jefferson and Green, seated next to each other—"the first one to pass the test with a perfect score gets the best book."

"What do the books say?" Dewey waved his left arm for attention.

"Simple sentences. The kind we have been learning. And you will not have to write with your left hand, Dewey. Until your right arm is mended, we will stick to reading."

Everyone laughed. We all knew Dewey was left-handed.

"Maybe I would be better at reading than writing," Johnson, who seldom spoke unless answering a direct question, said.

"Maybe," Raquel said cheerfully. "They are called 'readers' and are all the same, so we can study them together, but each with his own book. Be sure to write your name in your book."

She distributed the little books, each with a freshly sharpened pencil. We waited patiently until they had laboriously but proudly written their names. I watched Johnson sign his and knew by the two abrupt strokes that he had written an *X*.

I asked Raquel if she might allow the two of us to slip just outside while I tutored Johnson personally. She nodded and said, "You must try."

While the men inside chanted sentences like, "The cat ate a rat," or, "The lazy brown dog sleeps on the floor," we talked.

"You signed that book with an *X*," I said.

"Yes, sir. I made my mark."

"Stevens signs his own name."

"He is smart and educated." He looked into my eyes and said, "He was a—an officer."

"An officer. Of what? Where?"

"Louisiana Native Guards. Third. It was changed to the 75th Colored Infantry. He was commissioned a second lieutenant."

"But why is he not at least sergeant major of the regiment?"

"He would not shoot. He let a white boy that looked like his master walk up to him and take his revolver away. He been trying to learn to shoot people like I been trying to read books."

"He can't shoot Master Edward? He is a soldier who can't kill anybody."

"He told you?" Johnson asked, incredulous.

"Yes, he did. Well," I clarified, "he told me how he was beaten for writing." I waited for Johnson to talk to me as Stevens had. But it was not to be.

"Stevens is the most intelligent man I ever had for a friend," he said.

"You beat him at chess."

"He told you that, sir?"

"Yes, he did."

"I win sometimes. But it is a game. Not like writing."

"I also play chess. I have not played with Stevens. I did not even know he played chess until today. But chess is not just a game. Anyone who can beat Stevens at chess has to be intelligent. Intelligent enough to learn to write."

"Major Northey, if I could, I most certainly would. My head hurts and my brain shrinks when I want to draw a letter."

"How about your back?" I said quietly. "Does that hurt when you try to write?"

His eyes changed color. How, I do not know for they were

as bright and black as obsidian. Perhaps it was an increase in the luminosity brought about by tears. I could sense the tremendous amount of energy he must have used to bring himself back under control. He straightened to a posture of formal attention before he spoke.

"Lieutenant Northey, I have neglected my duty. I must return to the stables. May I be excused, sir?"

"Yes, Sergeant," I said wearily. "You may be excused. As you know, the writing class is for volunteers."

We exchanged salutes. He did a precise about-face and disappeared into the darkness. I sat down on the top step and listened to the voices, near and yet so far, reading in unison the simple sentences from a child's primer.

I let my mind roam, floating through space and time, seeking a solution. I found none, but then a noisy sound—a cheer, and then applause—brought me back. I stood up and opened the door.

Dewey looked up at me, grinning, and announced, "Major, Mrs. Barragan told us about the diplomas. Everybody, even those what got wounded in their right hand, gets one!"

Raquel beamed at me. She was as delighted as the soldiers.

I managed a smile, but I remembered that the reason for the school had been to teach an unteachable man to write.

"I have them at home," Raquel said. "One for each student. We will give them out on Friday."

"Three days," I said. "I have but three days."

"For what?" Raquel asked.

"To change the world," I said and then dismissed the class.

They left excitedly, laughing, the way young people do who have enjoyed a party. And, for them, it had been a party. They had so little to do outside their routine that even a dangerous patrol could be attractive to a bored trooper.

Corporal Green lingered at the door.

"I will close up, sir," he said. And then he added, "Did the sergeant know about the diplomas?"

"No. He had to return to the stables. He had forgotten something."

"Yes, sir. I'll tell him, sir," Green said. What he had left unsaid was that he knew that Johnson would not, could not, receive a diploma unless it would be for the ability to sign his name by crossing one line over another to form an *X*.

Raquel and I strolled back, talking, but not touching, to her quarters. I told her about Johnson.

"He plays chess. Peter and Max play chess. Sometimes until midnight, they say," she told me.

"Max?" I stopped walking. "You call Lieutenant Maxwell Bell, Max!"

"William," she said soothingly. "Not so loud. He is a dear friend."

"Of course. He is a dear friend and I, William, am a passing acquaintance."

"Come along," she said, looking about nervously. "You know how I feel about you, William."

We resumed walking, slowly.

"But you are jealous of Max!" This time it was Raquel who stopped to whisper and laugh.

"But of course," I snapped.

"Come along then, Major," she said, laughter still in her voice.

"What is so dammed funny?" I asked angrily.

She waited to answer until we were in the faint light from a curtained window at the Barragan house. Looking around quickly, she kissed me, and said, "Bill Northey, my love, it was Max who came to warn me. It was he who rapped on the door."

She turned, laughing still, and ran into the house, leaving me openmouthed, wondering, remembering Whigam's welcome speech about the people, volunteers all, who were the white inhabitants of Camp Leper.

# Twenty-nine

Until I was promoted over two other boys and one girl to the sixth grade which was a desk next to that occupied by the only member of the eighth and graduating class, Johnny Wright, star pupil and youngest son of the teacher, I was a bright but naive boy who believed almost anything he was told.

Of course, my father, intelligent, self-educated, and well read, saved me from being engulfed by the narrow religious beliefs of our small Mormon community. He guided my reading through suggestion, but allowed me to read freely from his library, which I later learned, contained more literature than did the Wright School.

So it was that I overheard Mr. Wright say to his son, "Then, if that is so, Johnny, define infinity."

"You just go and go and go," Johnny said.

"To where. A stone wall?"

Johnny shrugged and said, "All right, a stone wall."

"But then," his father said softly, "what is on the other side?"

I do not remember what Johnny said, but his father's words struck me like a thunderbolt. I could hardly sleep and that undefinable word haunted my waking hours. Finally, I went to my father. I told him what my teacher had said to his son.

"It is a most disquieting thought and the inability of our

minds to understand the concept has troubled many philosophers."

"What does it mean?"

"You have read the Bible, the New Testament and the Book of Mormon."

"But they don't explain about infinity."

"No. Not really, but the religious teachers, the Christian ones, usually connect infinity with God and our inability to understand either one. For some, merely to discuss the idea, is heresy."

Then the really terrible and obviously heretical thought struck me. "But if we do not understand infinity or God, what about heaven? What about my mother? Is she in heaven . . . or just dead?"

My father seldom showed emotion. But his eyes teared and he wrenched the words out as if each one were an infected tooth. "I do not know."

And that Friday evening, on my way to fetch the colonel to a useless ceremony, I was thrust into a similar and just as painful experience, when I was intercepted by a clearly nervous Peter Barragan.

He saluted perfunctorily and then took me by an arm and, speaking softly, almost in a whisper, although there was no one near, said, "We are friends, are we not?"

"Of course," I said, my heart beating rapidly. Had he found out?

"Might we use first names?"

"Of course, Peter," I said, puzzled.

"You think I am a good soldier?"

"Excellent and a better rider than I."

He smiled then and asked, "Would you trust me to ride the river with?"

I had not heard that expression for the kind of trust a man has who places his life in the hands of a comrade, but I knew what he meant and said sincerely, "Of course."

"I knew you did not do it to hurt me," he whispered. I

wondered what he meant, and said nothing, waiting for him to continue.

"Max begged me not to. He said, 'Do not shake the boat. Leave Raquel and Northey a secret.' "

"Raquel and Northey?" I blurted out.

Then Barragan straightened up and struck me hard with the palm of his hand and cried out, "Adulterer!"

I put my hand to my face and backed away.

Barragan then said quite loudly, "Let us say that you have insulted me, called me a coward. Leave everyone else out of this. We will meet tomorrow at dawn."

"Meet at dawn. What for?"

I was not yet aware that I had been challenged to a duel.

"You, there! Lieutenant Barragan, you have struck a superior officer!"

I had no idea how long Whigam had observed us from the porch of the building that we called headquarters, but I emerged from the deep fog of confusion that had enveloped me and answered before Barragan could speak.

"No. He did not strike me."

"That is true, Colonel," Barragan said. "It was a symbolic slap. Major Northey insulted me. Called me a coward! I demand satisfaction."

"Good God," Whigam said. "Is it a duel you mean to provoke?"

"It is an insult I cannot bear," Peter said, trembling with rage.

"Peter," I said, offering him my hand, "I spoke hastily. I apologize."

He struck my hand and my own temper flared. "All right, Lieutenant Barragan," I said. "What will it be? Pistols or sabers?"

"You two will report to my office, now, on the double, or you will both shortly face a court-martial."

Whigam glared at us for a second, then spun around and was back inside. Both the messenger and clerk scurried out.

I glanced at Peter, but saw only rage and tears in his eyes. I turned and marched the few paces up and into the office. I heard steps behind me as I entered, saluted and, at attention, waited. I felt Peter take his place alongside me.

"Dueling is, besides being a pastime of idiots, a court-martial offense. For an officer to kill another officer in a duel deprives the army of two trained men: the victor—assuming the asses do not kill each other—will be executed."

Whigam turned his head to speak directly to me. "Lieutenant Northey. You were struck by a junior officer. Will you prefer charges?"

"No, sir."

"You wish to charge Lieutenant Northey with insulting behavior, Lieutenant Barragan?"

Peter hesitated and then said, "He called me a coward."

"Major?"

"I never meant to insult Lieutenant Barragan," I said.

"But you called him a coward?"

"I retract what I said." Few times have I lied. I detest liars and if forced to lie, feel guilty, and as a result if I do lie, I am usually found out.

"Just what did you say?" Whigam did not quite believe me or perhaps realized that I was shaping the truth to fit my own needs.

"I asked him," Peter said, "if I would do to ride the river with, and he said no."

"And that is all?"

"Yes, sir."

"Would you ride the river with Lieutenant Barragan in hostile territory, Major Northey, if your life depended on him?"

"Yes, I would."

"Good, because that is almost exactly what you are going to do. I am going to send you both out with the best men of the combined platoons to terminate once and for all the stealing of stock from the Sawyer ranch."

"Help Sawyer!" I protested. "I want to send him to jail."

"Maybe," Whigam said, "we can do both. Sit down, gentlemen."

He showed us a note addressed to "The Fort Rivas Kernel." It was barely literate, but suggested that soon the raiders would strike the Sawyer ranch and was signed, "a friend."

"Who would that *friend* be?" Whigam asked.

"Sandy," I said immediately. "The cowboy who was in our hospital. I taught him to write."

"You did? Have you thought of adding spelling to your curriculum?"

"Sandy Morey," I repeated, ignoring Whigam's comment. "He still works for Sawyer. I saw him in El Paso with Sawyer's hired hands."

"You think him truthful?"

"Yes," I said. "How did you get the letter?"

"He left it with Rosa Maria."

"La Guera," Peter said.

"Blondie," I said.

"Who brought it here, Colonel?" Peter asked.

"I did. The cantina is a short ride if you have a fast horse. You young officers should visit it more often. Take your mind off the dull routine, petty quarrels and such."

"When will we go, sir?" I asked.

"The morning after your graduation ceremony. However, I warn you right now: If Johnson fails, your new sergeant will be Stevens. We will not have noncommissioned officers who are not literate."

"But, sir, I need Johnson. He is one of the best soldiers I have ever known."

"He is," Whigam said. "One day there will be Negro officers and that stubborn devil could be the first. But he damned well better be literate or Private Johnson will be taking orders from Sergeant Stevens. And that is an order."

"Colonel," I said. "I came to escort you to the graduation. It is to take place in a few minutes. But even if he should not be quite literate, our company needs Sergeant Johnson."

"Then we had better attend the ceremony and find out what grade Johnson will hold tomorrow."

I opened my mouth to object, but Whigam turned those crazy blue eyes on me. I breathed deeply for a few seconds and then turned to Peter and said, "We will take a small group, no more than a dozen men, not counting Stevens, the acting first sergeant, or Redwood the scout. I want Johnson, Green, Berry, Jefferson, Wilson and Dewey. Pick six men from your platoon. Draw the supplies for," I paused, looked at Whigam and said tentatively, "a week?"

"A week it is," Whigam agreed, then stood up and added, "Shall we pick up Sullivan?" Then, as if reading my mind, he said. "He will extend you credit, William."

"You will see Raquel at the school." Peter finally looked at me as he spoke. "Please tell her about the patrol."

"You will have the night at home, Peter," Whigam said.

"Thank you, Colonel." Peter saluted and left.

"Two officers with a dozen men," I said. "Why?"

"Because," Whigam said, in a good humor again, "the officers are white."

I took his words for one of his epigrams that made no sense at all unless you could follow some intricate turn of his mind. However he had foreseen events that I had not.

"Yes," I said. "Shall we lepers attend the ceremony, Colonel?"

"Yes," Whigam said, delighted. "We ghostly ones shall mix with the real people." Then he added wistfully, "Maybe they will notice us?"

The ceremony was a great success. Unfortunately, Johnson did not receive a diploma. However, he had even less chance than I had given him. He did not attend. Stevens came in his place and spoke privately to me while Whigam met with Raquel and Sullivan inside the crowded schoolroom.

"He will not be here, Major," Stevens said.

"I will see about that," I said angrily.

"He cannot come. Not now. Not for maybe six hours."

"He is drunk?"

"Yes, sir. Dead drunk. He tried, sir," Stevens said. "He really tried. We was in the school this morning before reveille. Chalk broke in his hand. It was like that chalk burned him."

I had failed Johnson. I had failed Raquel, Peter and, most of all, myself. My face must have reflected anguish, for Stevens saw something that prompted him to speak.

"It is not his fault, sir. Nor yours. Maybe we could blame slavery, but it does no good now."

"No," I said. "It does not. Cut the stripes off his coat and sew them on your own. You will be acting first sergeant on a patrol that will leave at dawn. Make sure that Private Johnson will be at roll call."

I listed the other men I wanted, and slowly went into the school. Raquel led the applause when I entered. I nodded, limped to my place behind the operating table, now covered with a bright serape, removed my hat and made my little speech.

"Ladies"—I nodded to Raquel, who smiled through an expression of worry or doubt—"Colonel Whigam and our civilian guest whom you might know." There was laughter at this point. They all knew and liked Sullivan. "And students."

I turned to Raquel. "Our headmistress, Mrs. Barragan will call out the name and status of the student."

"Yes, sir, Dean Northey," she replied, smiling still, while I was closer to tears than laughter. "In alphabetical order: Benson, William.

"William Benson will pass to the blackboard and write a sentence from the book. Mr. Sullivan, please pick a reading card."

The room had to rearrange itself while Benson made his way to the new blackboard and picked up a piece of chalk.

Sullivan, enjoying himself immensely, covered his eyes with one hand and reached into a box where wooden slats taken from a crate had been laboriously painted in letters an inch high with sentences taken from the primer. There were seven slats, one for each student.

Sullivan held the slat in front of Benson. "Read the sentence, William," Sullivan said.

" 'The cat . . .' " Benson paused, moving his lips to shape the next word silently, and then said happily, " 'drank.' "

"But what did the cat *drank?*" Sullivan asked.

" 'The cat drank,' " Benson began again, paused and then said triumphantly, " 'the milk!' "

"The student will now write the sentence." Sullivan flipped the sign over so that Benson could no longer see it to copy the letters.

"Yes, sir." Benson held the chalk firmly between thumb and forefinger and made slow, but sure strokes until he had printed every letter.

"Well," Sullivan mused, "the sentence should start with a capital letter, but then they are all capitals, so that is all right. But you must add a period, William. A sentence must end with a period."

"A what, sir?"

"A dot at the end."

"A bullet hole to stop the sentence dead, Benson," I said. "Remember?"

"Yes, sir, I do. That was Mrs. Barragan drew that bullet hole. Here. It goes right here and that sentence is dead."

He twisted the end of the chalk, and made the period. Sullivan proclaimed him literate. I handed him a document, also written and illustrated by Raquel.

"Hooray for Bottom Benson!" Dewey yelled and everyone clapped. Benson, with a sly look at me, reached around and pretended to yank out the arrow that had given him his nickname, sighed in imaginary relief, and went back to his place.

Brown and Clay, with the dubious advantage of convalescing in the middle of our schoolroom, both passed easily and were roundly cheered.

Dewey, a natural left-hander, complained about his handicap, his right arm was still tender, but passed anyway, writing rapidly with his left hand.

"You finished too soon, Too Soon," Benson said. More laughter and cheers for the little man who was always early.

Raquel called out the name. "Lester Green."

He walked quickly to Sullivan, took his test card and hurried to the board. He wrote surely, confidently, *I am a soldier of the Ninth Colored Cavalry Regiment of the United States of America."*

He was cheered, but seemed not to notice and left the room immediately, diploma in hand.

Jefferson merely glanced at the sentence held up by Sullivan, wrote quickly, *John built the house,* then signed his name, Thomas Jefferson, beneath the sentence.

"Thomas," Dewey said quickly, before Benson could, "my, my. And to think that I knowed him when his name was Tomato."

There was more laughter and applause and then a silence as they waited for Raquel to call the next and, alphabetically, last name on the list.

"Johnson, George."

I broke the absolute silence.

"Johnson, George," I said, "is indisposed."

"Would that mean," Whigam asked, "that you owe me a case of bubbly?"

"George," I said, speaking to Sullivan, "would you deliver a case of unopened champagne to the colonel's quarters?"

"Unopened! Bill Northey!" George pretended indignation and I pretended amusement.

"I have contributed beer for the students," Sullivan said. "How about a glass of wine for the teachers?"

"I imagine that the faculty will accept, but Dean Northey will now put on his military hat and see to his men."

"Stevens?" Whigam asked.

"You mean Sergeant Stevens?"

"Yes," Whigam said. "Put him to work on Johnson."

"Yes, sir." I saluted. Raquel looked longingly or perhaps just curiously at me and then took Whigam's arm and the three of them left.

Corporal Green was waiting for me outside. He saluted and asked, "Major, is the sergeant all right?"

"No. He is not. Not all right and not a sergeant either. Where would a drunken trooper be?"

"The sergeant—that is Johnson—would be in his room at the end of the barracks."

"Come along then, Corporal, and we will look in on him." As we walked, I told him about our new patrol, that Johnson would be a private, Stevens a sergeant, but that he, Green, would be for all practical purposes, the acting sergeant and that I was counting on him as if he were Sergeant Johnson.

It was a sobering thought for a man not yet twenty-five years old who had been in the army less than three years. Just before we reached the barracks, he paused at the door and said, "I ain't no Johnson, sir, but you can count on me to do like he would do, if I can."

I nodded. I had my man. Even if I managed to rescue Johnson, Green would be a sergeant one day, even if I had to transfer him to another platoon.

We found Johnson, facedown, one arm dangling over the cot like a dead snake. Green set the lantern on a small table. A brown bottle rolled off and fell with a thud to the floor.

Green put a hand on his shoulder and called out, "Sarge. Wake up!"

He shook the shoulder and called out again, then looked at me, shaking his head slightly.

"Pull his boots off and roll him into his blankets," I said.

Green straddled each leg and yanked the black boots free. Then lifted Johnson, who was no taller than I, but weighed at least twenty pounds more, by the legs and then the torso while I pulled his blankets from under him.

"Not yet," I said, as Green fluffed out a blanket to cover Johnson with. "Pull up his coat."

"His shirt, sir?"

"It has been a hot day. Do you have a shirt on, Corporal? No. Don't answer. Just roll up his coat so I can see his back." Who would be wearing an unseen flannel shirt under a heavy wool coat even if it was regulation?

Green pulled the coat up until we could see his suspenders and most of his back. I picked up the lantern and held it closer.

"Dear God almighty!" Green said. "That is the worst I ever seen."

The scars ran across his back like miniature weathered iron cables binding his body together. The scars must have continued under him to his abdomen, for they were visible down to the waistband of his trousers.

"The men do not know about his back?"

"I don't think so. He washes like us all, once a week, all over, but he don't mix much."

"All right," I said. "Do not mention this to anyone else."

Green pulled the shirt back down, then covered him.

"He will be all right, Major," Green said. "He always is."

"Yes," I agreed. "But tell Stevens—Sergeant Stevens—to look after him anyway."

"Yes, sir."

Back at my quarters, sitting in the fine chair on loan from Peter Barragan, I drank the last swallow of brandy in the glass and set it on the table. I reached for the bottle, and like that on Johnson's bed table, it was empty. Tilted by my clumsy fingers, it rolled and fell to the floor. However, my bottle, being of a different quality, broke into long sharp shards.

# Thirty

Each morning a lookout, my field glasses slung around his neck, would scale a rocky boulder, already named "Lookout Peak," thrusting up from the seasonable water hole where we had camped before when we had recovered the stolen Sawyer horse herd.

Redwood had scouted ahead, found that the water had been replenished by an abundant rainfall, and told me that there could be no better place to observe the raiding trails leading to and from the Sawyer ranch.

When we had been camped a week and observed nothing larger than a jackrabbit, I sent Dewey, his arm sling thrown away, riding at night, with a report. I received a laconic instruction from Whigam, to stay put until we ran out of food.

I did receive a private letter, a note scrawled on a scrap of paper that read:

> *Dear William, If only one of my officers returns from your patrol, he had better bring the cadaver of the other well-pierced by Apache arrows, or I will have the survivor shot. Cordially, Colonel Horace Whigam.*

Cordially! He would have one of us shot cordially.

I laughed aloud when I read it and reflexively called for Peter to share the humor with me. I had forgotten momentarily that we were speaking only officially, but it did not matter. He and his platoon sergeant had ridden out just before dawn to another vantage point some ten miles away.

I took my plate of bacon, beans, hard bread and coffee up into the sun. In an hour it would be hot, but the high desert cools quickly at night. Last night the men had doubled up to share blankets and warmth. I might have done that with Peter before, but it was out of the question now.

Later, when the sun had brought the heat to our hidden vale, I found Stevens setting up the chessboard in the shade of a wind-carved swirl of sandstone. The uniform of the day was gray shirts and suspenders, without jackets. Stevens stood up, but I called out a quick, "As you were," and he did not salute.

I removed my blue wool jacket, folded it and laid it atop his near the flat rock that held the chessboard. He had arranged two flat knee-high rocks for chairs. When I sat down, he sat opposite me, then held out both hands, closed. I tapped his left hand and he opened it to disclose a white pawn. He spun the board around. It would be my first move. I moved my king's pawn to his king's pawn two, as I always did, preparing to follow the Ruy Lopez opening, if he so allowed. Stevens did not play automatically, as we both usually did, for the first seven or eight moves, but spoke instead.

"You think that if we, Private Johnson and Sergeant Stevens, were white, we might be officers?"

"You most certainly could be. Johnson, if he could read and write, would be."

"But not for a while yet."

"No," I answered, wondering where he was leading me.

"You ever see colored troops during the War?"

"No," I admitted, "but I heard about colored troops at the Crater and some Massachusetts infantry under Colonel Shaw. They fought well at Fort Wagner."

"No Negro officers?"

"No." I knew of one, but I thought it would be better for ex-Lieutenant Stevens to tell me his story when he was ready.

"There was more colored troops in that action, sir. From

Louisiana, raised by General Butler." He smiled and added, "He called them *Le Corps d'Afrique*."

I had not heard of the African Corps and said so.

"Butler was one of the political generals," Stevens said. "He formed that corps, named it, and gave it Negro officers."

"What happened later? After the War?"

"I don't know," he said thoughtfully. "Maybe you could find out for me. For all of us."

Why not? I thought. We might even add a few volumes of pertinent history to our library in the company barracks.

"But," I said aloud, "we have no library."

"Sir?"

"I was thinking," I said, "that we should start a library. You must write an account of our company. A journal of our experiences in the Ninth Cavalry. If we had good colored officers then, why not now?"

"Major Northey, sir. You know what happened to me the last time I wrote a journal for a white officer."

"I promise you," I said, smiling, "I will never, willingly, fight a duel."

"Maybe you can count on me too, Major. I wonder why one man is born a coward and another a hero?"

"Some men break and run when the first shot is fired, but later they learn to overcome fear."

"How do you do it, Major? An intelligent man, not a dull farm boy who has no concept of human death or a man who would just as soon die quickly to step right into another sweeter world. How do you do it?"

"I don't know. I can tell you that I have been and will be terribly frightened before the fighting begins. When it does start, I seem to blank out my mind and everything gets very slow and as clear as the brightest day, even if it happens at night."

"And how do you blank out your mind?"

"I don't know. I guess everyone finds his own technique. I think that a soldier must think first of his own survival, but depend as well on the survival of his file, platoon and company for if he is to win—and live—ultimately, the men who make up the file, platoon and company must all be brave and skill-ful."

He nodded, not in agreement necessarily, but as if accepting my premise and played his king's pawn to meet mine. A few plays later, well into the Ruy Lopez opening, Stevens had opted for the Sicilian defense. Johnson and Redwood approached and waited quietly until I turned and answered Johnson's salute. Redwood might have saluted or merely shrugged. He was not much for military protocol.

"Major, we thinks we had better make a long scout tomorrow," Johnson said. "Leave at dawn and go way south, along the border."

"We?"

"Redwood and me."

"How do you know what Redwood thinks?"

"He told me."

"In what language?"

"Navajo, Spanish and some signs."

"You are learning Navajo?"

"Yes, sir. Some. It is like Apache, but better."

I had to believe him. Redwood had told me the same thing in Spanish. I had meant to learn the Apache language, but had learned nothing. Johnson was picking up Spanish and Apache. Yet the man would not read nor write. I could feel a vein in my forehead pulsate.

"You are an exasperating man, Sergeant— Private Johnson!"

"Yes, sir," he said, nodding.

"Make your scout. Stick together. If you meet hostiles, out-run them and return. Come in before dark.

"Redwood," I said, speaking Spanish, "make the scout and be back before dark. I do not want to have another Indian scout shot—" I almost said *by mistake,* but caught myself and said instead, "Do what the sergeant says."

"He is not a sergeant, not now."

"On the scout tomorrow, he will be your sergeant."

He nodded, turned and melted into the sand and rock. Johnson stared down at the board for a bit. Then, in a very low voice, said, "Major. I am sorry as I can be."

I looked up at him then and managed a thin smile before I replied.

"I too am sorry, but then, we are not through, yet. We have to recover the cost of a case of champagne that you cannot afford to lose. Not on a private's pay."

He smiled at me for the first time since his demotion. Relieved, I smiled back. At least we could talk informally.

He glanced down at the board and said, "He's going into that crossed-horse defense, Major. Better take the pawn now."

Johnson saluted and left. I glanced at the board, raised a rueful eyebrow at Stevens and took the black pawn.

We played three games. I won the first, eventually advancing a pawn through the opening left by his sacrificed pawn, and in the havoc of exchanged pieces during the bitterly contested endgame, converted the pawn to a queen. He resigned.

Playing the whites he won, leveling out the match, but then, when I, playing the whites, was certain of victory, he lured me into a stalemate. And a tie is a victory for the man playing the blacks.

"Good game, Sergeant. I expect we should make the rounds."

"Yes, sir." He swept the small chessmen into a separate drawer of the box that not only housed the chessmen, but opened up into a foot-square, black-and-white chessboard.

At Redwood's insistence, we slept well away from the water so that the other animals, the four-legged ones, could come in at night and drink.

We walked by the sleeping quarters ranging from soft sand mattresses to a two-room, rock-walled mansion shared by Jefferson and Dewey. We saw the pickets changed and the lookout relieved and I noticed how the currycombs moved faster as we neared the corral.

"Major," Dewey said, after saluting. "Why don't we leave these here ropes here so as when we come back we don't have to disturb all these rocks again?"

"Dewey," Stevens said uncertainly, "I do not think the major is interested in a permanent corral."

"No, I guess not." Dewey glanced at me out of the corner of his eye, but pretended to be speaking to Stevens. "But I sure am."

There was no malice in Dewey's voice, not yet. But he was testing to see how far he could push Stevens. Johnson would have squashed him by now. But then Stevens was not Johnson.

"Sergeant Stevens. Make a note to be delivered to the quartermaster." I walked along the ropes, like lines spun by a spider, attached here and there to large rocks or knobs of rocks and an occasional scrub cedar, nodding to myself as if calculating.

"Private Dewey will be charged with twelve thirty-foot cavalry issue ropes."

"Major!" Dewey was aghast. "I can't pay for no dozen ropes."

"How many can you pay for?"

"Maybe one or two but—"

When the men grooming the horses laughed, Dewey stopped in midsentence, and noting my smile, he joined the laughter.

"Major Northey," he said, enjoying himself again. "I reckon I'd just as soon put these old ropes up again as new ones. These old ones are rubbed nice and smooth. Them new ones are as prickly as cactus."

We moved on up to the first rise leading out of the tiny valley. I measured the time by my watch and the sun. We would have an hour before sunset. I sent Stevens to accompany Green as the new watch was set. The men not on duty would be making fresh coffee and reheating beans from yesterday's pot.

Our lookout, aided by two ropes tied together, slid down Mount Sawyer just before the sun touched the western rim and was in camp just as Peter Barragan and his sergeant rode into the already darkening vale we called "Camp Hideaway."

With my blanket roll, with my great coat rolled inside, over my shoulder, a cup of coffee in one hand and a small candle lantern in the other, I walked cautiously up above the water, past the rope-and-rock horse corral to a shelf where Peter and the men from his platoon had eaten together. Our whole group would not have made up a full platoon and yet, here they were, except for two men on watch, together. Soldiers are a clannish lot.

"As you were," I called. "I want a word with Lieutenant Barragan."

"Here, sir."

I followed the voice and my candle lit Peter sitting on his blankets, a cup of coffee in his left hand.

"May I join you?"

"Of course, Major." He made room for me, but I dropped my roll from my shoulder and then, careful not to spill the coffee, lowered myself to a seat alongside Peter, but sitting on my own blankets.

He waited for me to speak. Earlier, he had reported an uneventful and boring day of scanning an empty horizon.

"I heard from Whigam," I said.

"Yes. We stay and starve."

"No. I mean I got a personal note." I fumbled through my mind, found nothing more to say, and thrust the note at him, clumsily. Then, as if to make amends, I held the lantern so that he could see to read.

"What?" he said. Then, repeated, "What? Cordially!" He shook with laughter. I laughed too, nervously at first and then freely as we took turns between fits of laughter, imitating Whigam's nasal Maine accent as we brayed the word, *cordially.*

Slowly from wild laughter to guffaws and chuckles we finally ceased and then laughed a little more, but softly now, as we listened to the men laughing too, not knowing why—or perhaps they laughed in relief, sensing that something wrong had been righted.

"You plan to sleep here?" Peter asked, indicating my blankets.

"With your permission?"

"Of course."

"It will be cold tonight. I almost froze last night," I said.

"Yes, me too," Peter said.

"I thought we might share blankets," I said.

"Of course," Peter said quickly.

We laid an oil cloth on a stretch of the sandy soil that had been smoothed and cleared of rocks, to insulate us against the cold ground, doubled it with mine and then laid a blanket over both ground cloths to further block the cold. Then, alternately tucking one blanket over and then under the next, we made an envelope. I rolled up my coat for a pillow. Fully dressed, except for boots, removed with the aid of Peter's patented boot-jack, we squirmed down between the layers, grateful for the warmth.

"Good night, Peter," I said and blew out the candle.

# Thirty-one

Suddenly I was awake. A horse neighed nearby. I reached for my revolver. However, although I was clothed, my gun belt was not strapped to my waist. Of course it would not be. I pushed the blanket covering my face away and looked skyward. The stars were dim. The night was black, but morning was near. Johnson and Redwood would be preparing to ride out.

I fumbled for the lamp, found it and the match safe inside. I fingered a match free from the safe, lit it with my thumbnail, saw the wick by the flare and lit that too. Then, by candlelight, I eased myself from under the blankets. I patted Peter's shoulder.

"Half an hour to dawn," I said.

"No, *papá*," he said in Spanish. "I do not want to go."

Well then, I thought, do not go.

I unrolled my great coat, saw my gun belt like a large black pit in its core, strapped it on, then shrugged into the coat, pulled my boots on, picked up my candle lamp and carefully made my way through the rocks and cactus, down to the corral. I smelled the coffee before I could see the small cooking fire.

Johnson and Redwood, squatting, were already eating hard bread fried with bacon and drinking coffee.

"Major Northey, approaching," I said. "Do not get up."

Johnson set his plate down by his coffee cup and called out, "Wilson, the major is here."

"Yes, sir, Sergeant. Coming."

"I am not a *sir,*" Johnson said sadly. "I am not even a sergeant. Major, I wonder where it is they find these recruits."

"Lee," I said. "The night I came to Fort Rivas. You assigned John Lee as my orderly. He called you sir too and you were not a *sir* then either, nor a sergeant."

"Yes, sir. Johnny Lee might have been a good soldier."

True, I thought. He might have been, had he not died horribly in a violent convulsion brought on by an arrowhead somehow poisoned with rattlesnake venom.

"Where is Stevens?" I asked.

"Sergeants Stevens, Logan, and Corporal Green are about to send out lookouts. The new pickets have eaten and are on their way to relieve the last watch."

"Good." I found a rock that I could sit on without doing a deep knee bend, accepted a plate from Wilson, who was acting as cook for the officers and the troopers on duty who were unable to come down to the fire. Wilson set a cup of coffee alongside me, but stood in front of me, waiting for something.

"Yes?" He had done well for a recruit on the previous raid as well as at the fight at the water hole. He needed time to learn the little military courtesies, but he was already a combat trooper, which is why I had chosen him.

He rolled his eyes to Johnson, who caught the glance, picked up his coffee and moved away from the fire into the dark.

"Major, I got to tell you that I ain't never been so scared as at the fight at the water hole."

"You held your place and you shot when you had a target."

"That's just it, sir. I was too scared to run."

I did not laugh or even smile, but said, "You did not run and that is what counts."

"Yes, sir. But what I mean is I called Stevens a coward and said he should be shot."

"And what do you think now?"

"You did right. A man deserves another chance. Don't he?" he asked anxiously.

"Yes," I said. "Tell Sergeant Stevens that."

"Yes, sir, Major, sir." He saluted, did an about-face and marched the two steps back to the fire.

I ate quickly, dropped tin plate and cup into a bucket and made my way to the corral. Two riders were in the saddle. Green and Logan were together by the riders.

"Lieutenant Northey," Logan greeted me, saluted and said, "the lookouts is leaving."

"Canteens topped up?" I spoke to the riders, but Logan, Peter's acting sergeant, answered for them.

"Of course, suh. That's the way we do it in the third platoon. Go on, boys."

He waved them on, but I said, "Not quite yet, Sergeant."

"Suh?"

"Throw me your canteen," I spoke to the nearer rider. I could scarcely see the horses, let alone the riders, but I lifted my lantern and caught the canteen. It was too light. I tossed it to Logan who dropped it, cursed and picked it up. I could not see his face clearly, but there was a scowl in his voice.

"You call that a full canteen, Sergeant Logan?"

My voice was not overloud, but would carry throughout our small camp.

He did not answer, but threw the canteen back at the horseman. The horse shied and only good riding saved the rider from a fall.

"Get down off that horse and go fill that canteen all the way up, like the major says." He turned to me, his round baby face, visible in the candlelight jogged my memory and I smiled. His nickname was Tadpole.

"No. The first lieutenant says that the sergeant who said the canteen was full will take it and the other one and fill them now, before the sun comes up."

"But the other one is full," Logan said.

"Would you care to bet your stripes on that?"

"No, suh." He would have liked to have opened the second canteen, but he was not much of a gambler. He slung the canteens around his neck and walked slowly into the dark.

I heard the sound of a shoe striking a rock, smelled leather and horse and turned to see Johnson and Redwood leading their mounts. Okay, the only buckskin in the company and perhaps in the whole U.S. Cavalry, followed Redwood. Johnson led his prize black gelding Baldy, named for a small white patch on his crown.

Logan reappeared from the shadows. The blackness was evaporating. He trotted by and delivered the canteens, turned and saluted smartly. "Canteens full, Major."

I nodded, returned his salute and turned back to Stevens.

"Is our scouting party ready?"

"Yes, sir. The scouts have two canteens and a packet of hard bread and bacon. Oats, shoes and nails for the horses. Full Blakeslee boxes." Stevens, ticking off the items as he talked, paused and Johnson spoke.

"Sergeant Stevens, I got two canteens," Johnson boomed out for the camp to hear. "Both filled to the top of the top."

"All right," I said. "Remember what I said last night. You see Apaches, even one small one, you race back here. Understood?"

I repeated my orders in Spanish. Redwood got huffy about the reference to the Apaches and rode off in a sulk. Johnson stepped close to me, his horse standing still, and said softly, "Major, one way or the other, we going to get that champagne back."

He saluted, turned, floated up into the saddle and walked Baldy carefully up out of the tiny valley. I followed, walking easily, not far behind. Up on the rim, I looked down onto the desert floor, whitened by the first light. I watched Baldy change from walk to canter and then to a trot as Johnson overtook Redwood. I took my hat off to wave, just as Johnson turned in the saddle to do the same. I do not believe in Gypsy fortune tellers, or wild-eyed ladies that speak to the dead, nor, I suppose, premonitions. But why did I wave to Johnson?

When I went back to pick up my blankets, Peter was up, whistling cheerfully and preparing to shave. He invited me to

share his hot water and soap. I agreed, but went to fetch my
own razor and mirror.

We walked up the slope until the sun warmed us, then hung
small mirrors wherever we could and either stooped or
stretched to apply a hot cloth, let it burn for three or four
minutes, and then applied lather over the stubble.

"You know why Grant and Lee were the top generals in the
War?" I asked.

"No," Peter said, stropping his razor while he listened.

"Because," I said looking at my mustache in reflection,
"they didn't waste time shaving."

"That is why you had time to get up early; you don't need
to shave under your nose."

I laughed, tested the edge of my razor, then refused the loan
of Peter's leather strop. I had spent five minutes the afternoon
before putting a fine edge on my old razor. I stroked away
lather and whiskers on one side of my face, flicked the lather
from the blade and did the same on the other.

"My father has a beard," Peter said. "I think he always had
a beard."

"He must have been a handsome baby."

"He is a handsome man," Peter said. "A barber comes in
every day just to trim his beard and any other hair presump-
tuous enough to stray from its fellows."

I would have finished first, but my mustache needed trim-
ming. I had left my scissors in my valise, but Peter loaned me
his.

"I saw your men off," I said. "Johnson and Redwood are
off on the scout."

"You should have wakened me," he said.

"I did and you said, in Spanish, 'Papa, I don't want to go.' "

"No!"

"Yes, so I thought that this morning you would not have to
go."

"That is what I said when my father sent me to the military
academy," he said sadly. "I did not want to go."

"But you did. And to the academy at West Point too."

"Yes, but that was ten years later. *Papá* decided that a Barragan should be an American soldier. So I joined the army." He smiled. "And, strangely enough, there is nothing else that I would rather do."

"All right, Lieutenant. This morning we shall amuse ourselves in different fashions. You will oversee the education of the horsemen and I the riflemen."

Peter took four of the available troopers and their horses, keeping below the edge of the rim. He discovered quickly that Dewey and Jefferson were far ahead of the other riders, and sent them to me for rifle practice.

Dry firing with a Spencer carbine is not quite as exciting as waiting for water to boil. All you need is an empty shell case, a rifle and a trooper who has no other recourse except to follow orders. A target was set up at thirty feet, which I decided would be at one hundred yards. They dutifully set the sights for that distance, fired ten rounds from prone, sitting and offhand positions.

The soft copper rim of the empty cartridge protected the firing pin from damaging its point when striking against the edge of the steel receiver.

I left them clicking away and walked up to the rim. I thought I saw a dust trail far away to the north and west. My binoculars as well as those of Peter were in use by the lookouts.

I called Peter and envied the ease with which he ran up the hill, not even breathing hard, to report. I pointed out toward the mountains, blue in the distance, and asked, "Do you see a dust trail?"

"No. Yes." He peered silently and then exclaimed, "Oh yes. I would guess on one or two riders. No more."

"Send your best runner up to the lookout. Hurry."

"Yes, sir."

It appeared that Peter was, or thought he was, the best runner, because he turned, sprinted to the rocky base, and, as agile as a mountain goat, scaled the crag, reached the rope and walked up the sheer cliff, hand over hand on the fixed lines. Then he was erect on top, peering through the binoculars toward the faint dust trail.

He came back down like a sailor from the mainmast of a clipper ship. sliding down the ropes, skipping from rock to rock, until he hit the slope and by that time I was there to meet him.

"Redwood," he gasped. "It's Redwood, riding at a gallop."

I turned and called loudly, "Bugler, sound 'To Horse.' "

The camp erupted. The lookouts came down quickly. We would have to pick up the two who had left that morning to another vantage point half an hour away. Everyone except the two sentinels were busily leading their mounts from the corral to where each man had placed his own saddle, blanket and bridle.

Horses already saddled were picketed and the pickets replaced by men ready to ride. Others, their blankets rolled and tied behind their saddles, cleaned up the campground.

I stood up high, in the direct rays of the sun, and waved my hat at Redwood. We had no guidon on this patrol to wave from the rim, so he paused prudently, out of the effective range of our rifles. He did not want to be shot as an Apache warrior. We could not signal him, although he had learned some of the bugle calls.

I was about to order the bugler to play the mess call when Redwood spotted me. His eyesight was equal to that of Johnson's and he recognized me easily. He galloped up to the trail, then walked his buckskin up and then down into the camp.

Jefferson came running up to tend to the horse while Redwood reported.

He lifted a hand in what might have been his idea of a salute. I returned it, caught Peter grinning and held the salute until he shrugged and returned the scout's salute.

"We found tracks. Many tracks."

"But how," Peter said, speaking Spanish, "could they have taken a herd of horses to Mexico and not passed us?"

"Yes, how?" I searched my memory for some flaw in our plan.

"They did not pass here."

"But how will they get to Mexico?"

"They will not. The trail goes there." He pointed to the north and west."

"Apaches?"

"I think not. They travel slow. No hurry."

"Sergeant Johnson," I said automatically.

"He is following the herd. He wanted to see the riders. There are seven riders. All of the horses are shod."

"How long since you left Johnson?"

He pointed at the sky and said, "The sun was there."

One hour away. The herd was moving slowly. They must have been sure that they would not be followed. Were we after boy warriors again?

Johnson, who could see like an eagle, would not have to get close to follow them, identify them and estimate their numbers and arms, and then, safe, wait for us. We could ride quickly to the point where Redwood had left the trail, rejoin Johnson, then close in on the herd and most important of all, the raiders.

We should move out quickly, but how could we pick up our lookouts and what about Redwood's horse? I put the question to Peter.

"Diablo will ride double and the buckskin can trail along. We will likely pass close enough to the lookout to signal them to join us."

The idea was sound, but when we were ready to give the command to mount, Redwood shook his head.

"Redwood, the lieutenant's horse will ride double."

"That may be, but I will not."

And he would not. He did consent to hold the stirrup of Othello and run while we loped for half an hour. He was breathing easily when we called a halt a couple of hundred feet below the mesa top where our lookouts were posted.

Sergeant Logan rode up ahead and circled counterclockwise, the *rejoin* signal. Our alert lookouts came down, leading their mounts. We turned, at the trot, and resumed our route to the northwest.

Within half an hour, Redwood called for a halt, remounted Okay, and rode ahead at a trot. He found the trail, easy to follow now, and galloped where the terrain permitted. Even I could see that the horses were walking, stopping occasionally to nibble at some desert grass.

After a few minutes I pulled up alongside Redwood and asked, "Should we not find Johnson soon?"

"Yes. I think so," he said, but he was as puzzled as I.

We rode at a gallop for another ten minutes and then I raised my hand for a halt. Something was wrong. Redwood thought so too. So did Peter when he rode in from a flank to confer.

"I have been near here, once, I think," Peter said. "Sawyer had a line cabin somewhere up in these foothills."

We rode warily, up higher, into piñon tree country, still following a clear trail made by some twenty horses. And as we turned into more open country, my stomach contracted. A black spiral of buzzards was settling down on something dead or dying.

"I want one man to reconnoiter," I said, but even as voices called to volunteer, Stevens spurred his horse to a run, screaming at the vultures. The two or three that were on the ground took off awkwardly as he reined his horse back on its haunches, dropped the reins, looked around quickly and then waved his hat at us to approach. He bent down to look at the object on the ground and then lurched away. To vomit, I suspected.

When we rode up I saw why. The trooper lay facedown, an arrow stuck into his back and his scalp roughly removed. There were moccasin prints near the body. "Apaches," I said.

"No," Redwood said. "Apaches do not take scalps. Neither

do we." He yanked the arrow out easily. Too easily. "It is an old arrow. A play arrow for children," he added.

I checked the terrain and saw the weathered rock and log cabin built alongside a small spring. Its door swung on leather hinges, open. I sent a man to look inside before I dismounted. I dropped my reins to hold Othello in place and bent over the body. Even as I rolled him over, I knew that it would be Johnson's eyes, open but just as clouded now as they were when he could not see to read. And now he never would.

Stevens was back. His face, never very dark, was whiter than mine. He pointed down, where Johnson's right hand had been when I turned him over, and said as if in great pain, "Look. Look what George Johnson has written."

There, on the hard dry surface, First Sergeant George Johnson, had written, in blood, the name *Sawyer.*

# Thirty-two

Stevens, so strongly affected by death or violence, insisted on wrapping Johnson in his own oilcloth and blankets. His horse took the funereal burden without shying, surprising me. Perhaps the inert bundle was somehow still imposing his will on the horse. They had all been trained under Johnson's supervision. Stevens would have walked, leading his horse, all the way back to the post, if necessary, but it was not.

Redwood walked slowly around the scene in ever widening circles until, like a hound testing the wind, he found prints from Johnson's horse. He trotted away toward a clump of trees, then stopped and raised a hand in discovery.

Peter was in the saddle and with Redwood before I could bring myself to accept that Sergeant George Johnson was dead and I must say good-bye to one of the finest soldiers I had ever known. I did so and then anger followed sorrow.

First, we found the horse, bridle reins still looped around a broken branch, dead from a bullet fired close enough to have left flash burns alongside the head shot.

"I'll get the hull and bridle off," Dewey volunteered. "Blankets and gear too. His rifle's gone, but they left the saddlebags and the canteen. Bedroll too."

"They rode out too quick, running the horses north," Redwood told me.

"How close might they be?" I asked.

"Close. Very close."

We caught up with the herd, driven up a blind canyon and abandoned. Dewey cut out a good-looking sorrel with Sawyer's brand on its flank, saddled it with Johnson's hull and rode it around in a circle. He nodded approval, dismounted and handed the reins to Stevens, who attached a picket rope as a lead for his own horse, then mounted the sorrel and led his horse.

Seven sets of tracks, deep enough to indicate the horses were all ridden, cut off from the herd, broke into a run, and then split into seven different trails, all heading south and east, toward the Sawyer Ranch.

Redwood pointed to one set of tracks, and said, "I know these. I have seen these tracks not too long ago. At the cantina, before the fight."

"Follow them, then. If you lose the trail"—Redwood snorted disdainfully, but I continued—"we will ride directly to the Sawyer Ranch."

We did not lose him. The rider was either unafraid, oblivious to pursuit, or highly agitated, for we followed him, Redwood leading, at a gallop, straight through the empty Sawyer horse pasture, past the windmills and a strangely empty horse corral to the ranch house. The ranch seemed deserted. There were no saddled horses awaiting riders. Not one hired hand intent on his chores.

I formed the men into line, and called out, "Sawyer. You had better come out. If not, we will come in after you."

There was no sound at all until a door snapped open and Rex Miles stepped out onto the porch. He was wearing his Colt, like mine converted to take metal cartridges, but unlike mine, pearl handled. He placed his right hand on his hip, just above the handle and said, "Mr. Sawyer is taking a nap. You got any business with him, talk to me."

"You want to take his place on the scaffold when they hang him?"

"Whoa, there, Northey. You watch how you speak about the owner of this ranch."

"I say he is a murdering coward."

"And I say you are a liar. Boys, you had better come on out. Bring your long guns, those that have them."

Eight men filed out of the house, only three of them armed with rifles. Miles put a finger in his mouth and whistled shrilly. A dozen more men came running out of the bunkhouse, all armed with revolvers.

The men on the porch moved down the steps to face us and the other hands lined up with them. I saw Sandy, looking uncertainly at us and at Miles. Morrison, with Sandy, was still sweaty from the sun and I could see a fresh scratch across one cheek.

"You want to tell me what this is all about?" Miles said.

"We found the body of Sergeant Johnson not far from your 'stolen' horse herd. Did you report the loss before the raid?"

Miles put a hand on his revolver.

I called out the order to unsling rifles. The men facing us drew in breaths and several of them lifted hands away from their weapons.

"Listen to me, Northey. Some of the boys was hot on the trail of that stolen herd. But there was only three of them and when they saw that dead trooper, scalped and with arrows sticking in him, they cut and run for home."

"You learn about Apaches in a saloon, Miles? Apaches don't scalp, and that arrow was a toy. My sergeant was shot at close range with a large caliber bullet. It might have been a .44 from a revolver such as you carry."

I waited for a denial, but when he did not answer, I continued. "There were seven riders with that herd. They split off, but every one of them rode this way. We followed one straight to your ranch. He rode right up this roadway."

I looked directly at Morrison and said, "That's right, isn't it, Tommy?"

"Yes, sir. I mean no, sir. I mean I was there, but I didn't shoot nobody."

"Was Rex Miles the shooter?"

"No, sir."

Miles smiled at the young cowboy. "Sure, Tommy was there. Good man. Maybe there were a few more. But none of them shot your sergeant. It must have been the Apaches."

I looked at Redwood and he shook his head in that gesture of complete disagreement that was as final as eternity.

"I plan to deliver those seven riders to the new sheriff in El Paso," I said.

"He is not yet in office," Miles said, for the first time angrily. He glanced quickly behind him at a shaded window, then said decisively, "The only thing you will take away from here, will be some dead nigger soldiers."

"Cock your rifles," I called out. The clicks were sharp and clear, menacing. Several more ranch hands stepped back and pointedly moved their hands away from their weapons. The ones with rifles lowered the barrels.

"Hey, Mr. Miles," Sandy called out, "I don't want no part of fighting the army."

"Me neither." Another man stepped away. The two of them moved off, forming a neutral group.

Two others followed and one man from the porch said, "Sorry, Mr. Miles, I ain't no hired shooter," and keeping a worried eye on Miles, sidled down the steps and walked away toward the bunkhouse.

"Look, boys," Miles said urgently. "Niggers won't fight. Not unless a white man tells him to. If the white officers here do not take their nigger soldier boys and ride away, I will shoot the two whites and the rest will hightail it."

Most of the men frowned, but a couple shrugged and even smiled. They all knew Miles was a fast, deadly shot. He could draw and shoot Peter and myself before we could get our revolvers out of their holsters, even with the flaps open, as they now were.

"These troopers will shoot," I said loudly so that all, in and out of buildings would hear. "These are the same men who fought and beat Apache warriors at the Water Hole Cantina."

Some of the men murmured and I saw another man edge away, but Miles sang out, "You there. Stay put. You all stay put."

"Me too, Deputy Miles?" Peter said, dancing Diablo out from the line at my side, then sidestepping the gelding delicately to extreme right flank. Twenty feet now separated Peter and myself, the two white men Miles meant to kill.

"I warn you, Barragan," Miles said. "Your father cannot help you here. You ride out now or die right here."

Peter nodded politely and then said, "That may be true, but if you men find yourself in a federal court in El Paso, my father will carry much more weight than Sawyer and his hired killer."

"Now, now, Lieutenant Barragan," Miles said genially, but I kept my hand on the butt of my revolver. And it was a subterfuge. He had decided to act. His Colt was miraculously in his hand. He was still talking when his first shot took a piece of Peter Barragan's heart out through his beautifully tailored dark blue jacket.

Othello, trained to ignore loud noises such as gunshots could not ignore the hurried shot that Miles snapped at me. The bullet before it burned into the upper thigh of my much damaged leg, cut a piece of his ear and stung the unusually calm horse into a lunge forward. I reined him in just before the steps leading up onto the veranda. My pistol out now, arm straight, I sighted between Othello's ears, my revolver barrel level with the ground and pointed directly at Miles's chest. I squeezed the trigger just before Othello jumped again. My shot took Miles in the breastbone between the lungs. He dropped suddenly to his knees, then toppled forward onto his face.

"Hold your fire," I called out.

The door opened. Sawyer, wild-eyed, glared at his men, then at mine and finally at me. He looked away, staring at Miles, facedown, blood dripping down the steps.

Then, his forehead wrinkled as if puzzled, he looked up at Peter's body, still in the saddle, supported by a trooper on each side. He held his hands behind his back as if he were about to make a speech. And to my surprise, he did.

"I do not like you coming here and shooting my men, Northey. I do not. However, I suppose you had a reason. Likely a good reason. Besides, Miles was not all that good after all, was he?

"We will have to work this out, Major. I know you are a reasonable man and you know I am. Now that I no longer have Miles to manage my affairs, I could certainly use a man of your ability. And I would not be niggardly—" He stopped to giggle, then frowned as if he were trying to remember an important point, then brightened and continued. "No, not a bit. I am a generous man. Ask my boys."

"I would rather ask you, Mr. Sawyer, about the murder of Sergeant George Johnson," I said.

"No. You Goddamn well cannot!" The glare was back. "There is no connection, nothing to link my name to the death of the nigger sergeant. No matter who did the killing, Apaches or border ruffians." He changed from angry to amiable and said, "Right, Major?"

"No," I said, replacing my revolver. "I am the wrong major. Sergeant Johnson, his finger dipped in his own blood, wrote as he lay dying, a name in the sand. The name of his murderer, *Sawyer.* And I will so testify in federal court and so will all of my men who were with me so testify."

"You traitorous nigger-loving white scum, you will testify in no living court." He brought his hands out from behind his back and leveled a Spencer carbine at me. In the eternity before he pulled the trigger and I saw the hammer descend to strike the firing pin, I knew that the maniac had kept the rifle issued to Johnson by the United States of America. Strangely I heard three reports, the last one louder than the first two. But then the lead that killed me burned into my mind and I cried out in terror, "No, no, no!"

# Thirty-three

To: Captain Horace Whigam, Commanding Officer Company E. Ninth (Colored) Cavalry, Rivas Post, New Mexico Terr.

From: First Sergeant Thaddeus Stevens, Sergeant Samuel Logan and acting Sergeant Lester Green.

Subject: The happenings at the Sawyer line camp and at or near the Sawyer ranch house last September 3, 1870.

A scouting party made up of Sergeant George Johnson and the Navajo scout, Redwood, found tracks of a horse herd headed northwest, away from the Mexican border. Johnson kept on the trail but sent Redwood to report to Lieutenant Northey. We gathered in our lookouts and rode in pursuit. Redwood had reported that they were moving the horses carefully, slowly, not hurried as Apaches or border bandits might.

1. When we reached the vicinity of the line camp, we found the body of Johnson, scalped and an arrow jammed in his back. But when Lieutenant Northey turned the body over, we first noted that Sergeant Johnson had been shot through the chest and while dying had written, with his finger dipped in his own blood, on the dry crust of the sandy soil alongside his body, the word *Sawyer.*

2. We found the horse herd shortly, saw where the raiders had left the herd and raced back to the Sawyer Ranch. Redwood knew the track of the horse ridden by Thomas Morrison. When the riders split up, we followed his tracks right into the road in front of the ranch house.

3. Deputy Sheriff Rex Miles responded to a call by First Lieutenant Northey by appearing on the veranda of the ranch house. Shortly thereafter, he called armed men from the ranch house and the bunkhouse. They were armed with rifles and revolvers.

4. When questioned by Lieutenant Northey, Miles denied everything, but then admitted that a few of his riders had followed the herd in pursuit of raiders. He claimed that when these men found the body of Johnson, fearful for their own lives, they had fled back to the ranch.

5. Lieutenant William Northey pointed out the errors in his story:

A. Redwood, whose people speak practically the same language and, although bitter enemies, share many cultural traits, stated that the Apaches do not scalp and that the arrow that had been jammed, not shot, into Johnson's back was one used by Apache boys.

B. Johnson's horse, an excellent mount, as good as any in the supposedly stolen horse herd, had been killed with a revolver shot to the head.

C. There were no other tracks of any other riders, no unshod tracks leading in any other direction. The only horse tracks found were those of the herd, and those followed by Redwood and Johnson and later by the special unit of Company E commanded by Lieutenant Northey and aided by Second Lieutenant Peter Barragan.

(1) The riders escorting the horse herd, shortly after Johnson's murder, abandoned the herd. The seven riders split up, but all tracks led toward the Sawyer

Ranch. Redwood, who keeps in his memory hundreds of tracks of horses he has noted, recognized the track followed as that of a horse ridden by the Sawyer employee, Thomas Morrison.

D. There were no horses in the corral nor saddled that had just been ridden or waiting to be ridden. Several of the men, including Morrison, were dirty and scratched as if they had lately made a hard ride. Morrison was agitated and did not support Miles.

6. Unable to refute Lieutenant Northey's accusation, Miles became abusive. He stated that if the white officers were not there, the niggers would not fight. He said that if he shot both the white officers, the soldiers would run away.

7. Lieutenant Northey refuted this statement and called his attention to the fight at the Water Hole Cantina against the Apaches. He ordered his men to unsling rifles. Some of Miles's men moved away from him. They did not want to fight the army. When Miles became even more threatening, Lieutenant Northey gave the order to cock rifles, but not to shoot until the order to fire was given. A few more hired hands then abandoned Miles.

8. When Miles repeated his threat to shoot the two white officers, Lieutenant Barragan, a superb rider, moved his mount from his position next to Lieutenant Northey to the extreme right so that the professional gunfighter could not shoot them both easily.

9. Miles pretended to continue the discussion, but instead, drew his revolver, shot and killed Lieutenant Barragan and attempted to shoot Lieutenant Northey, but missed with two shots. Lieutenant Northey shot him dead.

10. The ranch owner, Harold Sawyer, came out of the house onto the veranda, apparently unarmed, his hands held behind his back. He was extremely agitated and abusive. He acted insane. When Lieutenant Northey refused what seemed to have been an offer to run his ranch and

said that he would testify against Sawyer in a federal court, Sawyer brought out a cocked Spencer carbine that he had been concealing behind his back, and fired. He meant to kill Lieutenant Northey, but two soldiers, Sergeant Stevens and Corporal Green had fired instantly, killing Sawyer. Lieutenant Northey, apparently shot in the head, fell from his horse.

11. A wagon was commandeered, and Lieutenant Northey, badly wounded, was sent to the post.

12. The Spencer carbine used by Sawyer to shoot Lieutenant Northey, the same one issued to then Sergeant Johnson, was confiscated.

13. Thomas Morrison made a statement, written down by Sergeant Stevens, and attested to by several troopers as well as the cowboy called Sandy Morey and one other Sawyer employee, Robert Burns, a literate man.

14. That statement, attached to this report, is here summarized.

My name is Thomas Morrison. I been a Sawyer hand since I was fourteen, four years, now. I knew about them Apaches, the ones that stole the horses. But they didn't steal them. We would leave them in the horse pasture, and they would take them away to Mexico.

We never chased them, but we would ride out and make tracks over theirs like we was. Sometimes we even fired a few shots in the air. We thought it was fun and nobody got hurt.

Sawyer always gave us an extra month's pay when the herd was delivered. I don't know how much he got, but it was in gold—American money—and Miles brought it. I know because he paid our regular wages in silver Mexican pesos, but when Miles came up, after the horse herd was gone, he paid us with gold eagles.

They was seven of us, but Mr. Sawyer knew a Mexican that traded with the Apaches and he took care of their end of the trade.

But when you found that herd and killed some of them Apaches, we was some scared and Mr. Sawyer went out of his mind. We forted up for a while and when they came down as far as the Water Hole, I thought we was goners. I don't take to niggers, but Mr. Sawyer, and Miles too, was dead wrong. They sure can fight.

I didn't want to go on that last trip and I was thinking of quitting. That's when I told Sandy to write that note to the colonel.

We didn't have no more dealings with Apaches, but Mr. Sawyer said it would be easy. We would take the horses up to the line shack, leave them there by the water and some *vaqueros* would ride up from Mexico to get them. Mr. Sawyer was mad at the nigger soldiers and the Apaches the same. He figured on blaming the Apaches for the stealing so as to collect what he called damages from the government.

He meant to give the Mexicans some worn-out moccasins and a busted arrow to leave along the trail somewhere near the border for the soldiers to find if they ever got that far.

But we didn't know we was being followed. Not until we reached the line camp. We built a fire and was having coffee, when the nigger soldier rode up. Mr. Sawyer, he got right up, treated him like a white man. Sent me to tie his horse in a clump of trees. I did. I was almost back to the fire when Mr. Sawyer handed the soldier a cup of coffee. He told him to drink it in Hell and shot him. The nigger fell on his face, twitching and groaning something awful. Mr. Sawyer slipped that Spencer rifle off his shoulder and was trying to pull that big old hammer back—he meant to shoot him again—but one of our boys, Willy Brown, it was, he was up on the ridge watching the herd, yelled at us that there was some bluecoats galloping along the trail, heading right for us. Well, we mounted up, but Mr. Sawyer, he howled like a wild Indian and took them moccasins out of his saddlebag. The arrow was in there too. I was the one with the smallest feet, so he made me get down and pull my boots off so I could run around making tracks. If you could have seen his face, you would have done what he said too. He was ready to shoot someone else. Anyway, I ran. He shoved that arrow in the nigger's back and then he took out his folding knife and he scalped that man. It made me sick. It looked like somebody didn't know how, had skinned a black lamb.

He said he threw it away, along with the rifle. But he lied about the rifle, so I guess maybe the scalp is somewhere around the ranch.

I never killed nobody and neither did any of us seven. I guess the only bad thing we did was stand up for our boss. But if you don't stand up for your boss, what kind of an outfit would you have? What kind of a man would you be?

*X* (his mark) Thomas Morrison

# Thirty-four

Everyone has awakened from a nightmare and experienced the intense relief when realization finally dissipates the horror. When I regained consciousness, I felt that blessed relief, but only briefly, for a short second later, the nightmare suddenly, once again, became dreadful reality. The tremendous guilt that I felt could not be borne. I screamed, or thought I did.

"Major Northey? Is you awake?"

I turned my head to follow the sound. It was Berry speaking, but I could not see the man. My eyelids were stuck tightly together. I willed them open. I had known that I was in bed, but had thought it mine. I was lying in a cot.

Berry, his head dividing into two and then rejoining, looked down at me anxiously.

"You is awake. Can you talk, Major?"

"Of course," I said. "Why would he think I could not?" I had not meant to ask the question aloud. I even wondered if I had, for the voice might have belonged to another.

" 'Cause you been asleep now for more than a week."

"What about Sergeant Johnson and Lieutenant Barragan?" I tested reality.

"They took the lieutenant to Santa Fe to bury, but Sergeant Johnson is in our own graveyard."

"How about Northey? Did they bury him here?"

The unofficial doctor the men used to call Pappy, but lately had taken to calling Doc, looked at me, his eyes soft with pity.

He had looked like that at that poor young boy, John Lee, when he was out of his mind, dying out in the desert.

"I better get Dr. Smith," he said. "I be right back."

I lifted myself up on an elbow. The pain in my leg was so intense that I cried out.

Berry stopped at the door and turned to look at me.

"Morphine," I said. "Tell him to bring morphine."

"Yes, sir."

The door slammed shut. The pain was as intense as my guilt and I wondered where they had put my revolver. That, I thought, would be the best morphia. For mind and body. I counted the steps and wished that little Berry might run as fast as Johnson. I counted out loud, reached a hundred and twenty, and cried out in pain. One hundred and twenty steps? He should be back. But that little frog Smith would be slowly hopping along, meandering.

Boots sounded on the steps. Smith was inside by my cot. He peered at me, using a pocket mirror to deflect bright sunlight from outside and send it through my eyes to sear my brain.

"Stop that!" I said. "Keep out!"

"You asked for morphine," Smith said. "What hurts?"

"My mind, you fool. Get that mirror out of my mind."

"There is no morphia for the mind," Smith said smugly. "Only for the body."

"It is my leg," I pleaded. "My leg is killing me."

"Of course, it is. I shall give you enough morphine, not only to deaden the pain, but enough so that you will feel nothing when we cut off that malignant leg. It will never trouble you again."

"Never?"

"Never!"

He was a surgeon. He must know. It was the leg. I should have allowed the surgeon back in Washington to amputate.

"Well, Northey. Yes or no? I have all my instruments here. My assistant can be here in a minute. Shall we do it?"

"If you say so." I was tired. But the pain had ebbed away, and my old doubt returned. "Maybe I had better wait."

"Nonsense." He opened the door and called out, "Goebell, bring my case and the green carpetbag in here."

"He will bring the morphine?" I asked. Then I heard boots striking the outside steps, and I called out, "Goebell, have you got the morphine?"

"No." It was Whigam, looking taller and thinner than ever, who peered down at me. "You have had a concussion. I never heard of giving morphine to a man with a concussion."

"It is for his leg," Smith explained. "He is suffering extreme pain in that same useless leg again. I will amputate within the hour."

"Would there not be some foreign body in the leg causing the pain?" Whigam suggested. "Why not remove that?"

"If you were a surgeon, my dear sir, I could explain to you why the leg must come off."

"William," Whigam said, "do you wish to have your leg amputated?"

"Yes, I guess I do."

"Which one?"

I started to say the right one, but then it was the left that I needed to get a boot into a stirrup so it might be that one.

"I think it is the left one," I said.

"It is the right one," Smith said.

"The right one is the right one?" Whigam said skeptically,

"Maybe it is the right one," I said weakly. "But it doesn't hurt now."

"It will," Smith stated with such certainty that he convinced me.

"All right," I said, exasperated. "Cut the damned thing off."

"Good. We will have it off before you know it."

"You most certainly will not," Whigam said coldly. "There will be no surgery performed on this man until he has recovered from the concussion."

"Colonel Whigam, I protest—"

"Good. Protest. But do it elsewhere, Dr. Smith."

Smith glared at Whigam and at me and then, meeting the elusive Goebell on the steps, took him to task for being too slow.

"Do you see me clearly, William?"

"Yes. But I think I saw two Private Berrys when I woke up. What gave me a concussion? I thought I was dead. It was Sawyer. He shot me with John's Spencer rifle!"

"I suppose you mean Johnson's Spencer carbine. In any case, according to the witnesses, several events saved you. Both Green and Stevens shot and hit Sawyer just as he fired, likely affecting his aim. And your mount flinched and moved at the sounds of the firing." He shook his finger at me and said sternly, "You simply must see to that horse's training."

It seemed to me that Othello had flinched very well indeed, but I did not intend to contradict the colonel.

He bent over to look at something alongside my head.

I reached upward to feel for a wound, but he intercepted my hand and said, "Wait, William. Here, have a look." He tilted the mirror backing of the lamp so that I could see my face. Whiskers covered my high cheekbones. My mouth was barely visible between mustache and chin whiskers.

"I look like a general," I said.

"Of course, you do. One with a furrow in his skull plowed by a .50-caliber bullet. Thank your druid gods for . . ." He paused, found the phrase, whinnied with delight and intoned, "That thick Welsh head or you would be dead."

"Will Raquel Barragan come to see me?"

"She went to Santa Fe for the funeral. She sent two wagons for their personal belongings. Not from your quarters. Those are to be yours, I believe."

"Gone? Not here?"

"That is right, William. She is gone and being gone is not here. Now you rest. When you wake again, we shall feed you, shave you"—his long nose twitched—"bathe you and then you may have visitors. I myself will have some news for you."

"Tell me the news now," I said and went to sleep.

True to his promise, Whigam not only had me fed and bathed—I refused the shave and instead scissored whiskers and all into a General Grant beard—but allowed me to walk, assisted by Privates Jefferson and Berry, to my quarters and my own bed.

Sullivan, his wife, Mary, the eager bridegroom, Smith and a radiant Adele, were admitted by my self-appointed nurse, Doc Berry. Adele inspected my room again, but this time with a bride's predatory eye. Smith examined my wound, now scabbed over, and pronounced it satisfactory. He seemed disappointed when I claimed to be better, then led Adele away before she could do more than stroke my head and call me her "poor sick darling."

George Sullivan gave me a bottle of brandy, not as fine as the French cognac that Peter gave me, but good enough to toast my health with. Then he looked warily at his wife, Mary, before he turned to speak to me.

"Bill Northey," he said earnestly, "I want you to go with me to the silver mine. We will make ourselves wealthy men."

"But George, I have no money to buy a share."

"Raquel Barragan wants nothing to do with the mine. It was Peter, poor lad, that wanted a go at it. Not for money, but the adventure. She wants you to have it."

"Peter's share? But why would she leave here?"

"William," Mary said gently, "Peter is dead. She has no reason to stay here."

Yes. Of course. Whigam had said something to me about her furniture, but I was barely out of a coma and remembered only the high points of that morning.

"She has taken up residence in Santa Fe?"

"Yes, in the Barragan mansion. It is the largest house in Santa Fe."

"I have never been to Santa Fe," I said.

"It is not a long journey for a well man," George said, "but not for you. Not yet."

"She will live in the grand style there," Mary said. "She will have a part of the big house for herself and her servants. She will have her own carriage."

"We will be as rich as Don Pedro Barragan within the year, Bill. There will be gold as well as the silver, but," he added hastily, "we will keep that part secret as long as we can. I do not want the Apaches going out of their way to find us."

"I will leave you two to talk business then." Mary shook her head as I made a motion to rise. "Next week, when you are better, we shall have a dinner for you. And do not fret so. Who are we to understand why God moves in such a mysterious fashion?"

George refilled his glass, but I covered mine with my hand.

"How about the money to hire guards and exploit the mine?" I asked.

George grinned hugely, and said, "Oliver R. Ballard. He gave me a draft on a bank in El Paso. All I have to do to get the money is for you to countersign the draft."

"Me. But why?"

"He wants you to be in charge of organizing the expedition. You choose the guards: maybe ex-soldiers, and an Indian fighter, like your friend, that old mountain man, Charley."

"Charley Dirty Knife. Then he lived."

"He did. I spoke to him. He is available if you are."

"I don't know, George," I said honestly. "The army has been my life, but . . ."

"I know the but." George lowered his voice. "Raquel Barragan would never go against the wishes of old Don Pedro. And Don Pedro Barragan respects nothing but the power of money."

"What kind of money might I hope for?"

"We would share, between five and a half stockholders, countless tons of silver, each ounce a silver dollar and the gold would likely pay all of our operating costs plus a good salary for you and me."

"Salary?" I asked.

"What about three hundred a month and living expenses?"

"Three hundred in gold?"

"U.S. dollars."

"That would allow a lady to live comfortably with a servant or two, and even a buggy and a driver," I said.

"Sure it would, lad. Why it's more than Mary and me have ever had. But the silver is there, farther west in the Arizona Department."

"I must see the lady first," I said.

"When you are better. It is a long jolting journey on the stage."

I leaned back and closed my eyes and brought her face into my mind. I looked at the beautiful Raquel Barragan. No, now she would be Señora Raquel Genovés, *viuda* de Barragán. Until she remarried she would be identified to all as Raquel Genovés, the Widow of Barragan.

"I see you are tired," George said. "I will be leaving now, but you think about our venture. Make plans. Lists of supplies. We will not go on the cheap."

I opened my eyes. He pressed my hand firmly, smiled and was gone. A big exuberant man with a silver dream.

Half an hour later I awakened to a persistent rapping on my door. When I called out in irritation that the door was not locked, Whigam entered. He carried a sheath of papers; one, doubled, its edges sealed with a turquoise-colored wax, looked familiar.

"Sullivan made his offer?"

"Yes," I said, surprised.

"It's all right," Whigam said. "I am a stockholder myself."

I told him what Sullivan had told me.

"Now, let me speak for the army," Whigam said.

"Of course, Colonel."

"No, I am no longer a colonel. I have been promoted."

"Promoted?"

"Yes, to major." He smiled and added, "I will be transferred to Fort Stockton with the rank in the regular army of major."

"Congratulations. I think the army made a wise choice." I was sincere, and he knew so.

"However, this company has received and is receiving more men. We are almost up to full complement. Two more lieutenants are arriving, one a first lieutenant. However, we will need a captain to command Company E. I have recommended you, but will not go on record, until you accept the command."

Too much had happened to me too soon. In the postwar army I should have had another two years, or even more, in rank, to be promoted to captain.

"You have a task while you recuperate, but it will require nothing more than a leisurely trip, a vacation really, to El Paso. Better, it will be paid for by the army. All you must do is deliver the Stevens and Green report, as well as your own testimony to the sheriff concerning the events leading up to the shooting at the Sawyer Ranch."

"Stevens and Green will accompany me?"

"Stevens will have to stay at headquarters until the company is reorganized."

"Then it will be Green and me."

"Yes. Here are the reports. Oh!" He looked at the folded paper, sealed with a wax that might have been melted turquoise, as if he had never seen it before. "I suppose this is for you too. From Peter Barragan's widow, you know."

Yes, I did know. I took it with trembling fingers, aching to rip it open, but not in front of Whigam. He stood up, looked longingly at the bottle and said, "When do you think you can travel?"

"The day after tomorrow," I said. "Take the brandy with you. The surgeon says I should not drink spirits for a few days." He had not, but I was afraid to immerse myself in that bottle.

"Thank you," Whigam said, picking up the bottle by its neck. "You might give me a glass of bubbly later. You did win the case of champagne after all. I knew that you could teach Johnson to write."

"He did learn. He would have been literate. The day before he was killed, he said we, Johnson and I, would pay for that case of champagne."

"And he did. Or," Whigam said sadly, "I guess that I did. Anyway, it is on my bar bill."

He sauntered out. The moment the door closed, I picked up the folded paper and immediately a fragrance filled my nostrils. I did not have to read my name printed in the beautiful script written by Raquel to know she had written to me. She had not abandoned me.

# Thirty-five

*Letter to Major William Northey*
*From Sra. Raquel Genovés, Viuda de Barragán*

Dear Friend William,

Words cannot express my joy that you were spared death while others, including my dear husband, Peter, were killed. I meant to stay until you were out of danger, but I could not. However, Colonel Whigam has promised to give you this letter once you recover, and I have prayed with all my heart for that recovery.

Although my family emigrated to Mexico just after the conquest and once held huge tracts of land complete with Indians to work it, the land, little by little, a hundred thousand acres here and another hundred thousand there, was sold or confiscated. By the time I was a young girl, we had only one small hacienda, fifty thousand acres, and it was deeply mortgaged to the church.

Don Pedro Barragan came to Mexico to interview suitable ladies to marry his son, in deference to the new politics in New Mexico, named Peter. The qualifications included the usual ones of beauty, domestic abilities, musical skills and language. It even included intelligence, listed last. However, as my father was overjoyed to learn, money was not one of them. No dowry. Just the opposite.

After an interview with my father, Don Pedro sent him away and we talked, at first guardedly, then more and more openly. He showed me a miniature done by an American portrait painter of Peter and assured me that it was a good likeness. I was eighteen, conscious of the difference money made in my status, and eager to better myself.

He told me frankly that Peter had not met a girl that attracted him. But I knew that I was beautiful and desirable, even if poor, and I was confident that I could win Peter's love.

Don Pedro himself declared that were he younger and not married, he would take me with him back to New Mexico, even if he had to abduct me.

Don Pedro again warned me that Peter might be difficult. He was sensitive, brooded a great deal, and then would be overflowing with good humor. He did not, he said regretfully, join the other young men of society in the constant chase after women of low reputation. At the time I thought it odd that he would not boast of such a virtue.

Again, I repeated, we would love each other, and I, such a child, was already in love with a wealthy blue-eyed young American who would in turn love me.

We made a contract then, Don Pedro Barragan and I, Raquel Maria Mendoza Genovés, and shook hands. Then we called my father in.

While my father loved all of his six children—he had five daughters—he doted on his son and heir, who was old enough to help his father spend what little cash came into the family coffers. My father was dumbfounded when he heard the offer.

Don Pedro would employ and pay a manager for the hacienda. He would buy back the onerous mortgages and pay off all outstanding debts. The manager would be in complete financial control of the hacienda, but should it not produce the equivalent of fifty thousand silver pesos a year, Don Pedro would make up the difference.

There was a condition that Don Pedro did not gloss over, but pointed out. Upon the death of my father, the property would be left, not to his son, my brother, Agustin Fernando Genovés Mendoza, but to his daughter Raquel.

My father shook off the condition as unimportant, called for his carriage, and they set off to see the civil and ecclesiastical powers, to ensure that the contract would be an enforceable document.

There was a month of balls and dinners and theater parties. My father absolutely glowed. Toward the end of an evening, when he had drunk enough, he would boast of his business acumen and how Don Pedro, his intimate friend and he were combining family fortunes.

My mother, whom, of course, had never been consulted, but caught up in the mystic rituals of the church and its many outlets for a sickly, frustrated woman, seemed vaguely pleased at the family's good fortune and asked that our contribution to the convent of her choice be increased as soon as possible.

Then, one bright morning in the cool clear air of Mexico, I gazed from the terrace of our town house, waiting for my new trunk, a gift from Don Pedro, to be carried downstairs.

I was hypnotized by the two volcanos, one like a crumpled white sheet along the eastern rim, the other, not far away to the south, a triangle of white paper pasted against a cloudless blue sky. With no idea why, I began to cry. Tears were streaming down my face when my Aunt Lilia, who would accompany me to America in place of my mother who was too ill—and too busy—to travel, found me. She held me in her arms until I ceased sobbing.

Later, when the rest of the family assembled to kiss me good-bye, there were no more tears from me, although everyone else, including my father, cried a great deal.

My sickly mother is still alive and contributing her time and money to the church. My father died within a year of my marriage to Peter, likely from an excess of rich food and strong drink. My brother, incensed when he discovered that my father had left the property to me, attempted to fire the manager, then change the will. He could not, and in his anger, joined the French forces supporting the monarchy, and was killed by Mexicans fighting for Benito Juarez and a democratic government.

Although I could never win Peter's love, I did win his affection. Peter left to me a considerable sum of money, including a share of stock in the Sullivan Silver Properties, which I have signed over to you. George Sullivan will have given it to you when you are well enough to read this letter.

Now, my dear friend, I must say that I do not expect to see you again. I will never forget that you and I did share, briefly, a strong bond of love.

I have sent a letter with the supply wagon to be sent on from El Paso to New Orleans to book passage to Vera Cruz. I shall shortly be living part of the year in the beautiful valley of Mexico, where the most beautiful city in this hemisphere sparkles in the sun like a jewel. But this time, I shall be among the grandest of the grand. I plan to keep a chateau for occasional stays in Paris, while I buy a trunkload of the latest styles for myself and my four sisters—they were all married shortly after I recouped the family fortunes.

In any case, I shall leave for New Orleans within a week after the funeral. I cannot bear Santa Fe without Peter and I must not remain too close to you.

I can write no more. Remember, *Raquel Barragan*

I was stunned. What good would a silver mine do me if she was already rich? Was it that she did not love me? I could not believe that. She must think that I would never recover, or that slimy surgeon Smith had told her that he was cutting off my leg. I had been unconscious only a few days. She would not have left yet. There was still time.

I somehow managed to dress myself, boots and spurs as

well. They tell me that I even had my sash and sword on when Corporal Green found me in the stable trying to saddle my horse.

He promised to put me on the stage to Santa Fe if I would just go with him to the stage office to buy tickets. On the way we picked up Doc Berry and Stevens and between them, they put me back into bed. It was another week before I was able to read the letter again and then I added a few teardrops to what I hoped were those of Raquel to the bottom of the letter where she had signed her name. I filed her letter with my other precious documents from my father and the army, then banished her face from my waking hours.

# Thirty-six

My wedding gift to Dr. and Mrs. Smith was the loan of my quarters for a week-long honeymoon while I was away with Corporal Green in El Paso. The surgeon, overflowing with good will and a bottle of Whigam's champagne, and coerced by wife, Adele, reluctantly loaned me his new buggy and fine Morgan mare.

I also borrowed a buffalo robe and a miner's tent from George Sullivan. We would spend just two nights on the road, but a norther was blowing and although it was only the middle of September, it was bitterly cold.

The first night we set up the tent, made coffee and then decided to shiver inside the tent, under the buffalo robe, rather than freeze outside, trying to cook in a gale that would have been blowing snow had there been any moisture in that arid land.

The next morning, the bottom of the coffeepot had a six-inch layer of rock-hard brown ice. We bundled up against the cold, fed Dolly, shivering under her heavy wool blanket, packed the pot to be thawed out later, and set off at a trot.

When the sky lightened enough to make out a faint image of a sun reluctant to shine, but hinting at warmth, we stopped by a clump of dead gray mesquite. While Green strapped the feed bag on Dolly, I fished out the fire-starter wood from under the buggy seat, took off my gloves long enough to light candle and tinder, and then, gloves on again, fed small broken pieces of the hard wood to the hungry fire.

"Major," Green said as he set the coffeepot next to the fire, "them steaks we brought might freeze, but they ain't about to spoil."

"Corporal Green," I said. "Men have been jumped from private to captain for no better reason than the idea you have suggested. We shall eat steak for breakfast."

At the other stops, we ate hard bread soaked in coffee at night and steaks, or thick slabs of bacon, and beans for our midday breakfast. Only Dolly, our borrowed little mare, had three meals a day.

"I don't expect we'll get a parade this time," Green said, when we finally reached El Paso.

"High noon," I said. "That was quite a day. But then, it was a hot day. A terribly hot day. At least it is not hot today."

I was right. It was not hot. We rode down the deserted main street, wearing greatcoats and gloves. We had even wrapped gray woolen scarves under our black cavalry hats to cover our ears. And the heavy brown buffalo robe was tucked around our legs.

Then it snowed. It snowed until the icy wind from the north blew almost all of the fine grains into our buggy.

Green drove right up to the stable, handed me the reins and jumped out. He banged on the door, but there was no answer. The door was not barred. Green pulled it open wide enough for the buggy. Before I could speak or even flip the reins, Dolly pulled the buggy inside and then turned her head to look back at me as if to say, "Close the door. Were you born in a barn?"

Green unhitched the buggy, unharnessed Dolly and after folding the harness into the buggy, lifted the singletree and pushed the two-wheeler out of the way in a corner. I retrieved his rifle and ammunition, as well as my revolver and, too hot now, peeled off my greatcoat. Then, feeling a source of heat, I followed it until I saw light emanating from a closed door.

My arms, full now with coat and weapons, I rapped on the door with the barrel of the rifle. The door swung open and a skinny man wearing glasses and holding a paperback book dropped the book and raised his hands.

"Don't shoot," he said.

"Shoot what?" I answered automatically and then, realizing that he was fearful for his life, added, "I am Lieutenant Northey. We are just looking for a place to leave our equipment and some hay and grain for our mare."

"It's Major Northey. You *are* Major Northey." He dropped his right hand to point at me, accusingly.

"I did have a brevet commission of major," I said defensively.

"Major?" Green appeared. "Can I help?"

"No, Corporal Green, I startled the stableman and—"

"You are Green, the corporal?" He turned his head like an old white leghorn rooster eyeing a grain of corn.

"Yes," Green said, edging back from the old man. "That is my name and I am a corporal."

"Well I'll be blowed to heck and back. It is you all."

"Yes," I said soothingly. "We would like to keep our horse and buggy here for a few days." He shook his head in what I took to be negation, so I added, "We will pay in advance."

"I will be durned if you will. Not in no stable run and owned by Samuel B. Jones." He glared at me, then swooped to pick up the book. He shook it at me angrily, I thought, then said, "Do you think that I would take money from them as rode and fought with Oliver R. Ballard his own self?"

"The government will pay our expenses," I said weakly, then added, "of course, Corporal Green and I would be personally grateful for your hospitality."

He stuck his hand, with the book in it, straight out at me, then switched it to his other hand and shook hands vigorously with me. While he shook hands with Green, I gently took the book from his left hand and looked at the cover. I saw a line drawing of myself, a revolver in each hand, flanked by Johnson and Green, looking defiantly at the reader. The title, printed over the lower half of our bodies, read *Oliver R. Ballard Rides with the Negro Cavalry or the Fight for the Water Hole Cantina*.

There was a small box printed below the title. I gave it to Green, who read it slowly, following the letters with his finger. He then flashed a wide smile and said aloud, "Fighting Bill Northey, Major, flanked by Sergeant Johnson, who marked the line with his saber, and Corporal Green, who held the crescent. They defeated the fiercest warriors ever seen, the invincible Apaches.

"Major, what does 'invincible' mean?" Green asked.

"Unbeatable."

"But, sir, didn't we beat them Apaches?"

"Yes, we did, but now that you can read, you are going to discover that a lot of literate people do not write as well as they should."

"You can't mean that Oliver R. Ballard didn't put down the best word for whatever?" Jones asked testily.

"No," I said hastily. "I know that the people who manufacture the books write the words on the covers."

That satisfied him, but after he had put Dolly into a stall, tossed a forkful of hay for her to munch on, he said plaintively, "No one is going to believe you two soldiers was right here in the Jones Stable."

"Do you have a pencil?" I asked.

"Why, I got both pen and pencil. I make my bills out in ink."

"Let me borrow the pen and ink?" I asked.

I followed him into the office, picked up the book, dipped the pen in black ink and wrote my name across the face of the indomitable Major Northey, and then handed the pen to Green.

"That won't work for me," Green said solemnly, holding the pen just above the inkwell. "Less you got some white ink."

"Why, no. I ain't got white ink. I never even hear of—"

Green smiled, his fine white teeth dazzling against his black face.

I laughed. Jones was puzzled. Green, laboriously, signed his name under the illustration of the scowling Corporal Green.

Jones suddenly got the joke and cackled delightedly. Before Green could hand the book back, I took it from him, and under Johnson's portrait, I made an *X* and signed his name, George Johnson.

"Why didn't the sergeant come with you?" Jones eyed the new signature dubiously.

"He was killed just a couple of weeks ago."

"Apaches?"

"No. A horse thief shot him without warning."

"Oh," he said. "Maybe Mr. Oliver R. Ballard will do a book about him."

"Maybe," I said. "Where is the *Eagle* located?"

"The newspaper?"

"Yes."

He gave me detailed instructions, which boiled down to a two-block walk down the street, and a cross to the opposite side. We rearranged our coats and scarves and pulled on gloves. I picked up my oilcloth case full of documents for the sheriff and we walked out a small side door into a bright sunny day. The temperature must have gone from freezing to balmy in half an hour. We went back inside.

Jones was sitting on the buggy seat, fondling the Spencer carbine. Green started for him, but I whispered, "Let him dream awhile."

We left our cold-weather gear inside his office. On impulse, I strapped on my revolver. We went back outside quietly. Jones never noticed.

Smoke was still rising from the chimney of the unpainted adobe building housing the newspaper. The only color about the building was a large wooden sign hung from the eaves in front of a large window facing the street. Green read it aloud. *The El Paso Eagle.* Black on yellow with a red eagle, head and wings extended to cover the sign from one end to the other.

The sound of metal crashing against metal grew louder as we neared. When we crossed the street, I did not bother knocking. A bell rang as we opened the door, but if I had not seen it swinging above my head, I would not have known.

We stood watching for several minutes as Norman Goldman floated a white sheet of paper onto a flat metal bed filled with type and several metal squares. He then leaned his weight onto a lever, the upper plate swung down onto the paper, lifted when he reversed the lever and then he lifted the sheet, printed side down, flipped it over and hung it on what appeared to be a drying rack.

As he turned, he saw us and beamed.

"Major Northey. I was hoping to see you soon." We shook hands. He peered curiously at Green, who was just as deeply black as Goldman was snowy white. "I know you. Corporal Black?"

"Close, Mr. Goldman, but I am Green."

He tried to keep his face impassive, but Goldman saw his lip twitch and said, "The hell you are," and burst into laughter.

Green and I laughed with him.

"If you gentlemen will wait upon a poor printer," Goldman said, "the publisher will buy you a drink of the good stuff."

"You might want to look at a couple of reports I am about to deliver to the sheriff."

"Pace?"

"He is still sheriff, is he not?"

"One more long month," Goldman groaned.

"Read the documents," I said.

"You mean about the mixup where some bandits shot your Sergeant Johnson. Killed Miles and Sawyer too."

"Yes." I smiled. My instinct had been right. Pace was still protecting his own posterior. "Although I saw it a bit differently. As did Corporal Green."

"Amen!" said Green.

"I will scan them, but I really have to get this edition out in another hour."

He began with the report written by Stevens and Green, reading it while standing, ready to continue printing. After a few minutes, he looked up at me, twitched his nose, which looked like a peeled white radish and sat down. He read all of the papers, then began again, reading more slowly. He stopped, shook his head in disbelief and said, "The publisher and editor has just stopped the presses."

He separated the papers, picked up a long and narrow metal box and, standing in front of what seemed to be a big box divided into many small ones, began to pick type up with his right hand and place it into the receptacle in his left.

"Should we wait?" I asked, wondering if he was fast enough to set all of the type necessary for his story in less than an hour.

"I can fill a stick faster than most," he said, "but you had best wait for me at the Texas Saloon. Tell Johnny that it is to be on my cuff."

"Where is the saloon?" I asked.

"You were there with Luther and me. Big mirror. Nosy bartender. He is Johnny."

I waited, wondering how to pose the question, but Green solved the problem by asking, "Where could I wait, Mr. Goldman?"

"Where? Why right there. Don't worry, Corporal. You can drink there no matter if you are Green."

We laughed, but I could tell that Green was worried. I did not wish to have a confrontation with an abusive bartender either, but I did have a great deal of confidence in Goldman's judgment.

We left, striding down the street when suddenly my leg betrayed me. I cried out in pain. I would have fallen, but Green stepped in close to me and I put an arm over his shoulder and waited, unmoving, until the pain subsided.

Green was surprised, shocked, I thought. Johnson had

known, but had never spoken about my bad leg. Not even to Brown, whom he had picked for promotion. After several long minutes, the pain subsided enough so that I could walk, slowly.

I limped down the street until we found the Texas Bar. We walked in together.

As it turned out, we had no reason to worry. The bartender remembered me and smiled and shook hands with both of us. We sat at the bar and drank the good stuff. Green knew the ritual better than I and followed Goldman's technique: lime, mescal, salt.

There were no more than half a dozen customers sitting at a table playing a game of good-natured poker.

"Major," Green said tentatively, "have you told the surgeon about your leg?"

"He knows," I said. "He wants to cut it off."

"It must hurt bad, sir, if Dr. Smith wants to saw it off."

"It does," I said, wincing. "But what could a one-legged man do? The trader, George Sullivan, wants me to join an expedition to work a silver mine. He wants me to keep the Apaches away from the mine while he digs the silver out. He won't want a one-legged man."

"Yes, sir, I know. But he might. Me and Benson and Dewey been paying into that mine ever since we knowed Mr. Sullivan. He is a good man, Major."

"The three of you each have a share in the mine?"

"No, sir. The three of us are still paying for half a share to split three ways."

"That is George Sullivan," I said, laughing.

Johnny brought another round of drinks I had not ordered. I had money enough for our food and a night's lodging, but not enough to buy drinks.

"We have had a round of drinks on Mr. Goldman," I said. "I do not want to run his bill up any more than that."

"Major Northey, sir," he said smiling. "The first round was on the house. The second comes from the gentlemen over there playing poker. You cannot spend any money in this town. Not today."

I turned and waved at the table and we both called out thanks.

"If you was to leave the army, what would we all do?" Green asked.

"Why you will get a first lieutenant just as capable as I. That is the reason the army is run the way it is: to make sure that the officers, commissioned and noncommissioned, are all qualified for command."

He said, "Yes, sir," and for a second I could see Johnson there, using that tone when he disagreed with me. I turned away, afraid that my eyes might be tearing, but Green misunderstood me.

"I only mean, sir, that we all think you are the best officer we have had—even if the colonel is a real good company commander."

The beaming bartender brought us another round, but when I protested, he smiled, shrugged helplessly and pointed to the other end of the bar where three men wearing belted revolvers and high-heeled boots were drinking.

They evidently knew us, but I did not recognize them. One of them threw me a professional salute. I returned it and said, "Thank you."

"If they did cut off your leg," Green said, "could you still be a major?"

"First lieutenant," I corrected him. But my liquor-loosened tongue said, "Actually, I could be a captain. In the regular army. I could be company commander of E, if I stay in the army."

"We would call it the Northey Company," Green said.

"But if the good surgeon amputates . . ." My leg twinged painfully. Suddenly I wondered if I had better sit down.

"I heard of a one-armed general," Green said.

Another round of mescal, limes and salt arrived. Johnny just smiled and pointed behind me. When we turned to acknowledge the drinks, the room had filled. I lifted my glass as did Green, but they all yelled and clapped. We would never know who was buying the drinks now.

"About that one-armed general," Green persisted. "Wouldn't a one-legged officer be just as good as a one-armed one?"

I felt that I was losing an argument, but I was not quite sure what it was.

"Sure," I said suddenly. "I guess he would."

We had another drink and I became nostalgic, remembering the long rides, singing the alphabet song, the jokes the troopers told, often ribald, to each other. I remembered the songs sung softly by the dying campfire. I put the bad times out of my mind.

"Major," Green said defiantly, "I don't care if the army finds a captain what is wearing a halo. I would rather have a one-legged Major Northey as company commander than any other officer, even if he had as many legs as a centipede." He nodded emphatically.

More mescal arrived and the cheering was even louder. Two other men in aprons were helping Johnny at the bar.

I looked into the mirror and all I could see staring at me were white faces. A sea of them.

"Look in that mirror," I said. "Did you ever see so many white faces?"

"No, sir. The only black face in this saloon is mine," Green said.

*"Judas Priest!"* I said. "I thought it was mine."

# The Wingman Series
# By Mack Maloney